KRISTINE KATHRYN
RUSCH

CITY OF **RUINS**

an imprint of **Prometheus Books**
Amherst, NY

Published 2011 by Pyr®, an imprint of Prometheus Books

Parts of "Sector Base V" first appeared in different form in *Asimov's Science Fiction* magazine, October/November 2010, as the novella "Becoming One with the Ghosts."

Cover illustration © Dave Seeley

Inquiries should be addressed to
Pyr
59 John Glenn Drive
Amherst, New York 14228–2119
VOICE: 716–691–0133
FAX: 716–691–0137
WWW.PYRSF.COM

15 14 13 12 11   5 4 3 2 1

Library of Congress Cataloging-in-Publication Data

Rusch, Kristine Kathryn.
City of ruins / by Kristine Kathryn Rusch.
p. cm.
ISBN 978–1–61614–369–5 (paperback : alk. paper)
ISBN 978–1–61614–370–1 (e-book : alk. paper)
I. Title.

PS3568.U7C58 2011
813'.54—dc22

2010053103

Printed in the United States of America on acid-free paper

For Dean

acknowLEDGMENTS

*T*hanks on this one go to the readers of *Asimov's Science Fiction* magazine who have consistently supported this series. I also need to thank Sheila Williams, the editor of *Asimov's*, who always has something excellent to contribute. Thanks also go to my husband, Dean Wesley Smith, without whom this book would not exist.

THE BEGINNING

ONE

*T*he *Ivoire* dipped, then rose, then flipped and doubled back. Inside the bridge, the crew could feel no difference despite the rapid movements. The only way anyone could tell if something had changed was the flow of data coming through all the monitors.

The six-person bridge crew had fallen into their various roles, speaking rarely. They all knew what to do. They had to evade the ships, which were coming at them fast and furious from Ukhanda.

The ships were small and feather-shaped. They looked harmless, but already two of them had seared the *Ivoire*'s exterior with some kind of blast weapon.

The *Ivoire*'s captain, Jonathon "Coop" Cooper, had been in tight situations before. He knew how to maintain focus—his own and the crew's. He had just ordered the wall screens on the bridge darkened. Normally he could see through the screens to whatever was happening on the ship's exterior.

But seeing things just outside the wall as if he was looking out a window didn't help him now. He had the navigational images front and center. Along the sides, a smaller image of the ship herself, and the enemy vessels pursuing her.

By rights, those ships shouldn't be anywhere near the *Ivoire*. The *Ivoire* had left Ukhanda's orbit nearly a day ago to rendezvous with the Fleet and figure out what had gone wrong.

No ship the Fleet had ever encountered had the speed to cover that distance in such a short time.

And this wasn't just one ship. It was a damn armada.

"Whose ships are these?" he snapped at the bridge crew.

The question was legitimate. Sixteen different cultures called Ukhanda home, although the Fleet had had contact with only two of them.

Anita Tren answered. She was tiny—so small, in fact, she didn't fit regulations for bridge crew. But she exceeded all expectations, outperforming every other officer in her class, and Coop couldn't see any reason to deny her the post she'd earned.

Even if she did have to kneel in her chair half the time to see what was happening on her console.

"Quurzod," she said.

That surprised him. He knew the Quurzod were advanced enough to have space travel—they had taken their war with the Xenth into space more than once—but he hadn't expected such sophisticated ships from them.

He had expected something big, with more weapons than power. He should have known that expectation would be wrong. The Quurzod were the most violent human culture he had ever encountered, but the violence was ritualized, damn near beloved. Their approach to violence was sophisticated, so why wouldn't they have sophisticated violence delivery systems?

"I suppose good information on the ships is scarce," he said dryly.

"The Xenth captured only one," Anita said. "The Quurzod had already destroyed the command center. But those things have a lot of weaponry."

As if to prove the point, six ships fired at the *Ivoire*. Coop could see the bursts of light on the navigational screens. Nothing showed up on the screens that depicted the ship's exterior. Of course not. The Quurzod had made the blast weapons difficult to see.

Coop's first officer, Dix Pompiono, moved the *Ivoire* laterally, and the shots went under one of the gull-shaped wings on the left side of the ship.

"Captain, those things have greater maneuverability than we do." Dix was hunched over his console, but then, Dix always hunched over his console. He was tall and thin. Yet he could bend himself as if he were made of string and fit into the smallest of places. "They're tiny and they're fast, and in large numbers they're a real threat."

Coop nodded. The ships were like insects. One or two were annoyances. But a swarm could overwhelm a larger and more powerful foe. And the *Ivoire* was alone. The Fleet was at least a half day away.

"I can maneuver around them maybe twice more," Dix said, "and then they'll have us all figured out."

"Another wave of those things just left Ukhanda," said Kjersti Perkins, the junior officer on the bridge crew. This was her first space battle. She clutched her console a bit too tightly, her short blonde hair mussed. But to her credit, her voice didn't shake and she seemed as calm as the rest of the team.

"How many?" Coop asked.

"Twenty-five. No. Thirty. Make that thirty-five." She looked over at him, her blue eyes wide. "An entire other wave. Did we know they had this many ships?"

"I don't think anyone knew," he said. "Yash, figure out if they're single-shot ships or if we have a bigger problem on our hands."

Yash Zarlengo, his on-site engineer, nodded. He trusted her more than anyone else. A former athlete, raised planetside, she had her family's knack for anything technological.

"Those things are built to fight," she said. "If I had to guess—and that's all I'd be doing, since they're still too far away to scan—I'd say they're stocked with weaponry."

"Given what we know about the Quurzod," Dix said, "I'd expect the fight to be vicious, bloody, and to the death."

Coop flashed on the images of Mae he'd seen when they brought her on board the ship: blood-covered, too thin, eyes wild. The Quurzod had killed twenty-four members of her linguistic team. Only three survived, and two of those had fled before the massacre. Mae had somehow managed to escape during or after the bloodbath.

"I think you're right, Dix. We're in for a real fight." Coop cursed silently. He hadn't wanted this. He didn't have the weaponry for this—not if the Quurzod swarmed.

"Send a message to the Fleet," Coop said. "Let them know the situation. We're going to engage the *anacapa*. Twenty-hour window."

"Yes, sir," Dix said.

Coop hated using the *anacapa* drive, but he saw no other choice. The *anacapa* created a fold in space. If the ship was in trouble, it activated its *anacapa*, moving into foldspace and then returning to the same point in regular moments or hours later. Sometimes moments were all it took to confuse the enemy ships.

The *Ivoire* had the firepower, but not the maneuverability. Staying would subject the ship to too much damage, damage he could avoid with a simple sideways movement into foldspace.

"Fifty more ships, sir," Perkins said. "Maybe fifty-five. They just keep coming."

Coop nodded. That was what worried him. Too many small ships, too many small weapons.

"Activate the *anacapa*," he said to Yash.

"I hate this thing," she muttered, but hit the codes, then slammed her palm against the console.

As she did, half a dozen shots hit the *Ivoire*.

The *anacapa*, going through its cycle, froze. Dix's gaze met Coop's. Coop held his breath—

—and then the *anacapa* reactivated.

The *Ivoire* slipped into foldspace for just a moment while it waited for the Quurzod to give up.

VAYCEHN

TWO

I travel to Vaycehn reluctantly. I don't like cities. I never have. Cities are as opposite from the things I love as anything can get.

First, they exist planetside, and I try never to go planetside.

Second, they are filled with people, and I prefer to spend most of my time alone.

Third, cities have little to explore, and what small amount of unknown territory there is has something built on top of it or beside it.

The history of a city is known, and there is no danger.

But I'm going to Vaycehn on the advice of one of my managers. She has a hunch, and I am funding it, although the closer we get to the city, the more I regret that decision.

I made the decision because I'm learning that a single woman cannot manage an entire corporation on her own. I used to run my own wreck-diving company, but I hired people when I needed them and let them go when the dive was over.

Now I oversee hundreds of employees, with dozens of tasks before them. I need to learn to trust.

Even in the area of exploration.

Especially in the area of exploration.

And I find that to be the hardest of all.

Vaycehn sprawls along a great basin on the eighth and most centrally located continent on the planet Wyr. Wyr is tiny and warm as far as planets go. It exists in the habitable zone near its star but is a little too close for the bulk of the human population.

The planet does have plenty of air and edible indigenous plants. A lot of farming communities have sprouted in its arable sixth and seventh continents. But the planet's only major city—as cities are defined in this part of the universe—is Vaycehn.

I'd heard of Vaycehn decades ago. Everyone who works in antiquities, history, and collectibles has. Vaycehn boasts the earliest settlement in this part of the galaxy. Its history has continued, uninterrupted, for at least five thousand years.

The city has moved several times, but its footprint remains in what the people of Wyr call the Great Basin, a dip in the planet's surface so deep that it's visible from space. That dip provides shelter for the storms that buffet Wyr, and it also has temperatures twenty degrees lower than surface temperatures anywhere else on the planet.

The perfect location for both an ancient and a modern city.

A place I never thought I'd go.

Until now.

My team and I fly in on six orbit-to-ground skips, and land them in the spaceport at the edge of the Basin. We're in the City of Vaycehn, but it doesn't look like a city here. There are buildings, and a lot of dry brown ground. We're only on the ground long enough to disembark from our skips and sign them into their ports. Then we get into the six government-owned hovercarts that were, Ilona discovered, one of the only ways to travel in Vaycehn.

We left my ship, *Nobody's Business*, docked on Wyr's orbital business station. The *Business* has a cloned identity, one we adopted when I became a fugitive inside the Empire, and that's how the *Business* is registered with Wyr. Fortunately no one seems to care who we are, so long as we spend money planetside.

We're spending a lot of money to come here. I look at this visit as an experiment; I'm not sure our search for stealth technology should even include land. All of the stealth technology we've discovered so far has been in space.

But Ilona thinks differently. She has hired the ground team—with my supervision—and she believes in this project.

I do not.

In fact, part of me wants this project to fail spectacularly. Then I never have to think about land-based operations again.

The hired pilots fly us into the Basin. I sit behind the copilot, separated by a clear wall. I almost wish the cockpit was blocked off so that I can't see what these people are doing.

These pilots aren't one-tenth as good as I am. They make tiny mistakes that would kill them in the tight situations I've flown through.

But they know the Basin, and they're cocky. They come in too fast, going deep at the beginning of the crevice that marks the Basin, and get too close to the stone walls for my comfort. I grip the armrests so hard I'm probably leaving indentations.

I hate cocky pilots, particularly ones whose skills clearly aren't up to an emergency. Should the wings of the hovercart nick one of the stone walls, the craft will spin out of control. From my vantage, I can't see any automatic overrides that will prevent such an accident.

And I don't have time to break through that clear wall ahead of me, hit a few buttons, and stop the craft from spinning before it crashes.

If something happens, I'd go down with the craft, just like everyone else.

The bumpy ride makes it hard to enjoy the scenery. Behind me, the main team—Ilona, Gregory, Lentz, and Bridge—talk about the mission ahead.

They are all scientists and researchers. Never before have I brought them to a site without examining it first. They're excited, thinking that maybe they'll be able to be actual explorers.

Maybe by their definitions, they will.

But I've also brought a full dive team as well as some archeologists and a few historians. And I've brought the Six. They're scattered throughout the other craft because if one of these things goes down, I don't want to lose all of our most valuable people.

We land on a wide patch of empty ground. Other hovercarts are parked in the distance, and large buildings outline the empty middle.

I'm glad we have a lot of room for the landing. We still bounce on the ground's surface—something I would never allow one of my pilots to do—and it takes several seconds for the rocking motion caused by the bouncing to cease.

The doors open, and I sneeze as planetside air filters in. Planetside air has unfamiliar scents—in this case, both sweet and dry.

Most of the air I breathe is recycled. It has a faint metallic edge, and sometimes a warning staleness. I'm used to that. I'm not used to air that has a taste, air that tickles my nose and makes me feel a little light-headed.

This air is also warm. I'd been warned that Wyr was a hot place, but I'd also been told that Vaycehn was one of the coolest locations.

If this is cool, then I don't want to visit any other site on the planet. I'm already sweating as I step off the craft. The metal railing of the makeshift stair is warm beneath my touch, even though it's only been in the light from Wyr's sun for a few minutes.

Heat shimmers across the pavement in little waves that look like turbulence before a planetside storm. I've already decided I don't like it here, and this is only the first of thirty days.

Ilona is already talking with our guides. Ilona is slight, with black hair that looks almost blue in this light. She wears it tied back, but some strands have come loose in the wind. She brushes at them as she speaks.

The guides—all male—watch her hands. The guides' uniforms make them easy to identify. The uniforms are brown with red piping. Sleeveless, with shorts instead of pants. The men wear sandals on their feet. They also have their hair cropped so short that their scalps are visible.

"Well, this is going to be interesting," says a voice beside me. I turn to see Mikk, one of my best divers. He's not built like a man who space-dives. He has too many muscles because he does a lot of weight work to maintain his bone structure. He's also large.

Most divers are small people with such delicate bones that being on a planet with normal gravity will hurt them. I've left some of my best divers behind because I don't want them subject to the planet's g-forces. Unlike me and several others, those divers grew up in space. I'm landborn and can handle gravity. I just don't like it.

Two divers and one of our pilots are getting off the second craft. So is Julian DeVries, one of the Six. He's tall and broad shouldered. Out of all of my team who have landed so far, he looks the most out of place. He's wearing a blue silk suit that has to be too warm. But aside from removing the coat and slinging it over his shoulder, he doesn't seem affected by the heat at all.

"You think those people know what they're doing?" Mikk asks me. He's still looking at the guides.

"I think they know how to take us to the caves," I say. "I suspect they'll get us to our accommodations with a minimum of fuss, and I hope that they don't have too many regulations to follow."

"What about canned speeches?" Julian says as he joins us. "I loathe canned speeches."

Mikk frowns at him. "Meaning what?"

"Guides," I say. "They usually have a small spiel about the history of a place."

"Which we theoretically know," Julian says.

"Emphasis on 'theoretically,'" I say. "It's always good to listen to the stories and the myths and the legends. You can learn a lot from them."

Mikk gives me a nervous glance. He used to pooh-pooh the idea of the importance of myths and legends until he dove the Room of Lost Souls with me. Then he learned how oddly accurate legends could be.

"You don't think we've tapped everything," he says.

"I don't think we've even started." I watch as the third hovercart eases down. If only we'd had that pilot. He, at least, is cautious, using the craft to hover before landing, just like it was designed to do.

This machine lands close enough to swirl dust and dirt around us. Mikk covers his eyes, but Julian merely adjusts his suit coat so that it blocks the worst of it.

When the engines shut down, Julian continues as if the conversation hadn't been interrupted at all.

"That ride in was bumpy."

I nod.

"I have a hunch things are more dangerous here than we planned."

He sounds like he's been involved from the beginning. But he hasn't been. He has no idea how dangerous we think this is.

Five years ago, the city suffered a groundquake, and an entire section of old buildings fell into the caverns below, revealing caves no one had ever seen before. Like many ancient cities, Vaycehn has an underground component—old transportation routes, basements, and quarries where the original buildings were dug out of the rock. Supposedly, these new caves are different, structured with walls. They look like someone had built them purposely and then forgotten them.

When Ilona requested the visas to travel and work in Vaycehn, she was warned that the underground caverns were unsafe. The Vaycehn government denied her requests several times—and not because we were using false identities. Our identities, while fictitious, are impenetrable.

Any time we enter the Empire, we run the danger of being arrested. But we've been in and out so many times that we know no one is tracking these identities. We know we're safe, so long as we don't attract any notice.

As for Vaycehn, the problem was the city government itself. It didn't want us in the caves. We finally had to sign waivers protecting Vaycehn from liability should any of us die. We also had to sign confidentiality agreements; we couldn't run to any form of press—whether it was Vaycehnese, Wyrian, or systemwide—and tell the story of our explorations beneath the city.

What little off-planet income Vaycehn made came from tourism, and the government was afraid that negative publicity would destroy that tiny trade. Our guarantee that we would not do anything to harm their tourism industry got us into Vaycehn. I hope that we do not stay long.

The fourth, fifth, and sixth hovercarts land in a perfect row, as if they've practiced the maneuver. The engines shut off in unison, and before long, my entire team has gathered around me.

I have never brought so many people on a single exploratory mission. Thirty, plus equipment. Keeping track of all of them will be difficult, particularly when I have duties of my own.

The team knows the risks.

But I've learned over the years that knowing the risks and living with their consequences are two very different things.

THREE

I used to work for myself. I ran my own wreck-diving business out of my ship, *Nobody's Business*. I specialized in historical wrecks. I'd dive them, but I wouldn't salvage, believing that history should remain intact.

My first encounter with a Dignity Vessel taught me the dangers of intact history. That encounter also changed my life.

Now I run an organization so big that I don't know the name of everyone who works for me. We operate out of a space station that orbits one of the planets in the Nine Planets Alliance.

The Alliance sounds more official than it is. In reality, the Nine Planets Alliance is a kind of no-man's land, ignored—at the moment—by the Enterran Empire. Right now, any imperial ship that ventures too deep into Nine Planets territory gets destroyed.

Someday, the Empire will think it important to fight back.

Fortunately, that day hasn't come.

Although I might be the one to provoke it.

The Empire and I are both searching for the secret to something called stealth tech. It's a lost ancient technology, something no one entirely understands. The Empire has learned how to re-create it, but in order to do so, they need bits of actual ancient equipment, and so far, they can only take that equipment from Dignity Vessels.

Our mission, at least at the moment, is to find any Dignity Vessels in this sector and keep them out of imperial hands. Right now, we have four Dignity Vessels in various states of decay docked to the ring on our space station. We have parts of two more on a nearby ship—a decommissioned imperial military science ship that we bought through a proxy at auction.

I let my own team of scientists work on stealth tech. I'm in charge of finding more. Stealth tech doesn't just exist on Dignity Vessels. We've also found it in a place called the Room of Lost Souls that we believe to be an ancient abandoned space station, though we don't know that for certain.

We don't know much for certain.

What we do know about stealth tech, though, is that it is deadly. It has killed three of my friends.

It also killed my mother.

It didn't kill me, because I have a genetic marker that allows me to work inside stealth tech with no ill effects. The Empire has discovered thirteen of us with that marker.

Six have chosen to work with me.

We find, learn about, and will ultimately re-create ancient stealth tech. Then we will sell it to governments other than the Enterran Empire, in the interest of keeping the balance of power within the sector the same.

If there's ever any serious deviation from that mission, I will shut us down and disband. I see no other way.

Vaycehn has sixty-five hotels, the best of which are in a ring around the city's center. We've booked two floors in the Basin, one of the oldest and grandest of the hotels.

I saw to this part of the trip personally because I knew what I wanted. I wanted a hotel that wouldn't mind thirty guests who arrived nightly covered in dirt and mud; a hotel that would cater to our every whim at any hour of the day; a hotel that would be able to provide secure communications off-planet since we would be so far from our ship; and a hotel that would guarantee our privacy from any inquiries not just during our visit but for years afterward.

I have the penthouse suite in the west corner of the top floor: six rooms, including a conference area, a kitchen, a bedroom suite, a "guest" bedroom, and a private sitting area. I'm going to need all of it.

We will have our meetings here. Some of my staff will set up the replay equipment in the conference area. I've already ordered the hotel staff to remove the furniture from the guest bedroom so that I can put some dedicated computer equipment inside.

I set up that equipment alone. I am the only one who knows how it works, and I want to remain that way. Usually I set up equipment like that in my own bedroom, but this is a hotel, not a ship. I can take advantage of the room.

From the conference room, I have a view of the city below. It sprawls. Buildings crawl up from the ground as far as the eye can see. Humans live and work in each of those buildings. Hundreds of buildings, maybe thousands. And if I think about that too much, I get claustrophobic.

I think the staff of thirty that I've brought with me is twenty-nine people too many; if I think about the millions who've settled here in Vaycehn, I will drive myself crazy.

Still, it's a pretty place. The basin walls rise up around the city itself like the walls of a space station. Sunlight falls on ruins in the distance—one of the many abandoned sections of the city.

Those sections have been explored by historians and archeologists through the ages. Vaycehn is one of the most studied areas in this sector of the galaxy.

As I stand in these windows and look at the orangish light settling on the rooftops below me, I realize that layers are visible before me. If I squint, I can see the Great Ages of the city just in its architecture, and that makes my heart pound.

This is not one of the Great Ages of Vaycehn. Now it is merely the largest settlement on Wyr. The city itself has several million inhabitants. But in some of the more populous sections of the galaxy, there are permanent space bases that boast a similar population—and those are sprawled over a greater area. Attached by warrens and cubbies and gangways, those large stations were once small stations that joined with others for the sake of power or wealth or sheer greed.

Vaycehn became a city because of its location. It remains one because it has done several things: it has preserved its history; it serves as the center of trade for this small region of space; and it has the longest-existing continuous government in the known universe.

Ilona thinks Vaycehn is a major source of stealth tech.

I don't think stealth tech can exist on land. I think the technology is too unstable, and too dangerous.

And even if it did somehow manage to exist on a planet, there is no way that the stealth tech could have remained hidden for thousands of years, only to reveal itself in a dramatic and frightening way just a few years ago.

Ilona argues differently. She says that since stealth tech originated on Earth, it was probably invented on land, and there were safeguards for working and living with it.

Maybe so, I have said in response, but in no way would those safeguards exist so many light-years away from the home planet, in a place those ancient Earthers could not imagine.

I feel safe in my argument; I have had several direct experiences with stealth tech. Ilona has not.

But she does have one small point in her favor.

The Six.

They all—and me, so really, we all—are built-in safeguards because we can work with stealth tech and survive.

The Six are in my conference room, along with the rest of the team. We are mapping the morning strategy session. The Six are Orlando Rea, a quiet, bookish man with a surprising amount of gumption; Fahd Al-Nasir, black-haired, dark-eyed, timid; Elaine Seager, a fit middle-age woman who hangs to the back of any group; Nyssa Quinte, skinny and tough, who should be my best diver, and is not; Rollo Kersting, a charming man, very fond of his comforts; and of course, Julian DeVries.

Our guides—who are not here—already know that we are not average tourists. Ilona spent an hour after our arrival explaining that we will not follow the same path as the other archeologists.

One guide has already threatened to quit. I'm sure others will as well.

The key point is whether or not we can legally work on Vaycehn without the guides.

I assign Ilona to discover that piece of information. She makes a note, while I continue directing the staff.

We will have six teams, composed of a diver, an archeologist or historian, a scientist, a pilot, and one of the Six. I will head a seventh team, and what I don't tell them—but which becomes clear as I make the assignments—is that my team will have the best people from each division. I'm going to work the site just like everyone else, and if there's a discovery, I want it to be mine.

Only two teams will go down with the guides each day. The other teams will explore the city, interview residents and experts about the city's past as well as its legends, and investigate the fourteen deaths that preceded us. So far the Vaycehnese government does not want us to discuss those deaths with the locals. But I have promised Ilona that on my days off, I will fight that prohibition in the name of safety; I will say that unless we know what happened, we cannot know what went wrong.

I don't know if that will work—I'm a diver, not a diplomat—but it's the only argument I can come up with that the local government might back. From all the work we've done off-planet, the only conclusion we can come to is that no one knows what's been happening here since the ground collapsed.

The collapsed section is visible from the conference room window. The section is a black smudge near the convergence of the basin's two steep walls. I glance at it as I speak, pausing occasionally to wonder at the darkness below the surface.

When I finish laying out my plans, I open the discussion to the team.

Lucretia Stone, one of the archeologists, says, "I don't understand why we need pilots on each team. The guides will drive the hovercarts."

She's squarely built, with muscular arms and legs. She's worked all over the galaxy, on some of the most famous digs in recent years. That she signed on with us is surprising until you get to know her history; she's lost five digs in the past ten years to imperial interference. She likes the fact that we're not part of the Empire.

Signing on with us was as much a political statement for her as it was a personal one.

But this is her first off-site, on-planet work for us, and I can already sense how much she dislikes not being in charge.

"I'm not going to run this like a dig," I say. "I'm running it like a dive."

"A space dive?" She frowns at me. The other two archeologists look to her for guidance. In the past few months, they've all gone diving with me because I insisted. But it was tourist diving on established wrecks.

Even then, the archeologists were terrified. To them, space suits are something you wear in an emergency, when the ship you're riding in loses its environmental controls, not something you don voluntarily to go into abandoned ships in the emptiness of space.

These people are, perhaps, the exact opposite of those of us who have spent our lives diving. The archeologists love the firmness of the ground beneath their feet. They understand gravity and they love to sift through dirt.

We prefer to float, and dirt is something dangerous, something that can clog our oxygen supply and damage our suits.

Not for the first time do I feel a slight hesitation. Maybe I am configuring these teams wrong. Maybe I should dump the historians and the archeologists and the geologists for people who understand dangerous free-floating situations.

Because if I'm wrong and Ilona is right, we will be in a dangerous space-type situation underneath the city of Vaycehn. We will need every bit of diver's creativity that we have.

"You're running this like a dive." Lucretia repeats my words with a touch of incredulousness. "We're going to suit up and everything?"

I nod. "We're bringing our suits. That's why I want an experienced pilot on the hovercart. It's too bad the Vaycehnese don't allow other vehicles inside the site. I would prefer something with more maneuverability and power. But they're afraid that something with that kind of thrust might cause more collapse."

"They have a good argument," says McAllister Bridge, one of the scientists. He's a slender man with long fingers and the glittering eyes of someone who has had expensive reconstructive eye surgery. "If you're not sure what's down there, you don't want to do anything that could potentially shake it up."

"The walls have held for five millennia," says Roderick. Roderick has been with me since our mission to the Room of Lost Souls. In the intervening years, Roderick has piloted us out of some very tight situations. When I met him, I didn't like his style, but now I trust him almost more than I trust myself. "They'll probably hold for five more."

"Except in the area that collapsed," says Bridge.

"That's something we need to find out," I say. "How many other collapses have there been in Vaycehn's history? And were any of them followed by deaths, just like those of the archeologists?"

Fourteen archeologists have died in Vaycehn in the past few years. All of the archeologists were working in the oldest parts of the city. And none of their bodies have ever been recovered.

That alone intrigued Ilona. But the fact that some claim the bodies vanished intrigues her more.

"You'd think information on collapses and deaths would be in the databases," Julian says. He's not a scientist or an archeologist. Until the Empire found him, Julian was an accountant in a small firm on Zonze, one of the most populous cities in the entire sector.

"Not if Vaycehn has always been as secretive about its problems as it has been about the fourteen dead," I say.

"I don't think they're being secretive." Ilona sits close to me, her fingertips tapping lightly on the tabletop. "After all, I was about to find out about the deaths."

"Because most of those people were well known in their field," Stone says. "If they came here and disappeared, it would be more suspicious than if they died."

One of the other archeologists, Bernadette Ivy, nods. "We all know the risks of working underground. We don't think twice when someone dies at a dig off-planet."

Then she stops because we're all staring at her. We all don't know the risks of working underground. Most of us only know the risks of working in space.

"What risks?" Tamaz asks. Tamaz has also been with me for years. He sounds tentative, which is unusual.

"Ground collapse is one," Ivy says.

"Probably the biggest one if you're in a cave," Stone says.

"Then there's cultural issues," Ivy says. "Sometimes the local population hates it when you touch something sacred—and you had no idea it was sacred."

"Local laws prevail in some of those cases," Stone says.

"Except in digs that are sanctioned by the Empire," Ivy says, and then she bites her lower lip.

"Okay, so be honest," Tamaz says. "The work you archeologists do is mostly safe, right? You don't die if you make a mistake."

He stated it like a sentence, but it was really a question. A nervous question.

"That's right," Stone says. "Mostly we don't die when we make mistakes."

"I mean," Tamaz says, "if your clothes rip, you're fine. You don't usually need extra oxygen or some kind of gravity boot to keep you on a path or—"

"Enough," I say.

Ivy's cheeks are flushed, and Stone actually looks angry. I don't want my people comparing their specialties. It does no good.

Tamaz bites his lower lip, as if he wants to say more. But he doesn't.

I continue. "I think we get the archeologists' point. Because those fourteen deaths occurred over time instead of all at once, they didn't look that suspicious."

"Exactly," Stone said with a glare at Tamaz. "It just looked like that particular dig in Vaycehn was a treacherous one."

"It took Ilona to put some of the facts together," I say. "Like the fact that the dig itself didn't collapse. These people died in a perfectly clear area."

"And some of them," Ilona says softly, "mummified in the short hours they were inside that area."

Mikk shudders so violently I can see it across the table. A few of us have seen this before. Mikk saw it at the Room of Lost Souls. I've seen it more than once. First with my mother, then with one of my divers on the first Dignity Vessel I found, and finally, at the Room of Lost Souls.

"If you work this like a dive," Stone says, going back to the original topic, "then we could lose a lot of archeological data. We need to spend time with each patch of ground, examining the layers of soil for evidence of—"

"You've only gone on tourist dives," Tamaz says. "A wreck dive forces you to spend time in each section. You have to, or you really will die."

An edge in his voice makes me hold up a hand. "I'm sorry to say that the in-depth archeological information is less important than the stealth tech. But you knew that when you signed on."

Stone leans back in her chair.

"If we don't find any tech," I say, "then you and the other archeologists can stay if you want, and do some real fieldwork. The rest of us will return to base."

"But there won't be any more funding, will there?" Stone asks.

I'm paying for everything. Or rather, the company is. As a result, any discoveries we make will be the company's, as is any information on how those discoveries were found.

"Whether or not the funding will continue depends on what we find." I think, but don't add, that it will also depend on how easy Stone is to work with now that she's on-site.

"It seems strange to go into a dig with a preconceived notion of what we'll find," Stone says.

"Oh, spare me," Bridge says. "You always have a notion of the area's history before you go in. You know that the early colonists stopped somewhere nearby or that someone settled the area before the Colonnade Wars. You have a hunch or you wouldn't dig in that area in the first place."

Stone glances at him sideways but doesn't answer. She's finally realized that her comments haven't made her popular with the group.

If she's like me, she really won't care about that.

But I'm slowly learning, as I'm managing more and more staff, that people actually care what others think. Sometimes that's even a motivation for misbehavior.

I take a deep breath and let it out slowly. I will have to remind myself repeatedly that the very structure of this excursion is an experiment. And that will require some flexibility on my part.

"My team goes first tomorrow," I say. "I want to know exactly what we're facing."

And whether there's any hope that Ilona is right.

FOUR

*T*he first morning dawned clear and hot. I almost regret my order to bring our suits. The very idea of pulling mine over my sweaty skin makes me shudder, even though the suit's environmental controls will probably give me a more comfortable day than the natural environment of Wyr.

We meet our guides just outside the collapse zone. The Vaycehnese have not rebuilt this section of the city. Instead, they put reinforcing walls around the hole and have removed the debris from below.

Signs plaster the few remaining nearby buildings, warning of danger and proceeding at your own risk in almost every language used in the sector. The roads are all blocked off, and floating signs higher up warn that the drivers of any unauthorized flying vehicles will be subject to search, arrest, and crippling fines.

Five guides sit beneath the first set of warning signs. All five are men of about thirty, wearing uniforms and the same expression—a reluctant wariness to take even more researchers to the grounds below.

But Ilona's work yesterday has paid off. We have permits to work the site for the next six months if need be. And as part of the agreement, the months are measured in Earth Standard, not Vaycehn Normal, which is nearly ten percent shorter.

Still, we don't need five guides for six people. I'm about to tell them that a few can go home when their leader walks over to me. He's a big man tending to fat, which surprises me. Most of the people I see can't have extra weight, either because of their constant space travel or because they dive. He has a mustache that somehow narrows his face.

"Before we take you below," he says, "we will tell you our regulations."

He speaks with an accent. He brings a music to Imperial Standard, as well as a precision that I rarely hear in speech. He pronounces each word carefully, as if he's afraid he'll be misunderstood.

"First," he says, "regulations require five guides, no matter how small the tour group is."

I want to correct him. We are not a tour group. But he holds up a pudgy hand, silently instructing me to hold my questions until he is done.

"The five guides have different skills. We are required by law to have two pilots, two trained medical personnel, and one area specialist. I am the specialist. The medics have badges on their arms. . . ."

In spite of myself, I glance at them and see that the two men in the middle—the only two in any kind of good physical shape—do have small round insignias on the biceps of both arms.

". . . The pilots are the only ones licensed to fly the hovercarts. In case the pilots are disabled, we will send for another licensed cart operator to remove the team. Under no circumstances may anyone not licensed fly the carts below."

I do not nod at this. I can think of a dozen circumstances that would require one of our pilots to fly. On this team, there are two of us who could handle the flight—me and Roderick.

Right now, Roderick is standing very close to one of the carts, inspecting its tiny pilot array, his body almost vanishing in the brightness of the light.

The guide continues. "You may not touch anything without official permission. You may not—"

I wave the documentation at the guide, which startles him into silence. Now I feel the need to correct him. "We're not a tour group. We're scientists. We're here to study. We will touch."

He takes the documents from me. The Vaycehnese government prefers everything in triplicate: computer files, like the rest of the sector; hardcopy files, which is just plain odd; and a video agreement, in which both parties verbally acknowledge they've entered into a contract.

The hardcopy files—the actual documents—must accompany us everywhere.

He studies them, then hands them back to me. "I do not think 'study' is advisable. You will look only."

"We will look, touch, dig, or do whatever we need to," I say.

His cheeks are flushed, which makes his eyes seem extra bright. "The last study group did not do well below. I am opposed to this action."

I shrug. "It's your laws that state we need guides. Either find us someone who is not opposed or take us below."

His flush is even deeper. He hands the documents back to me. He's about to speak when Bridge comes up beside me.

Bridge looks at the guide but says to me in a loud voice, "Maybe you should tip him."

The guide straightens his shoulders. His face is so red now that it looks painful. "We are not allowed to take gratuities."

He makes the word "gratuity" sound like it's obscene.

"Then I think Boss here is right," Bridge says. "You do your job or find someone who can. Because you're wasting valuable time, my man."

The guide nods once, then walks back to his group. He talks to them softly, waving his hands as he does so.

I turn toward Bridge. "I can fight my own battles."

"Oh, believe me, I know that," he says.

We've had a few run-ins of our own. I realize after he speaks that he's never taken control from me before, unlike Stone, who dislikes anyone else being in charge.

"But," Bridge says, "this is a male-dominated culture. I figured it might be better to go with the cultural norms rather than lose the morning fighting against them."

It's my turn to flush. I knew that the culture was male-oriented. I'd actually warned my female staff about it, telling them to let a lot of gender issues slide because of our cultural differences.

The guide pilots head toward the carts. The medics grab their gear.

"You want to act as liaison between me and the so-called specialist?" I ask.

Bridge grins. "Not really. But I'll do it for the sake of getting this operation under way."

"Good." I sigh. "Tell him that we're in charge of how fast we move, what we examine, and what we touch. We set the pace, not him. If we have questions, he answers. If he doesn't like it, he can—"

"Find someone who does." Bridge's grin grows. "I got that."

He walks over to the leader and speaks to him just as carefully as the man spoke to me. They clasp elbows—a sign of agreement among the Vaycehnese—and suddenly all the problems evaporate.

The guide directs us to the carts. He frowns when he realizes how close Roderick stands to one of them, but says nothing.

The carts are strange contraptions. They hover and fly just like the large enclosed hovercrafts that brought us into Vaycehn do, but they have a more limited range. Theoretically, they have more maneuverability, but they don't look like it to me.

The tops are down, revealing one pilot seat up front and three bench seats behind. The top is crumpled behind the bench seats, ready to go up if the pilot needs it.

The carts might be maneuverable, but I wouldn't pilot one without the top up all the time. A quick dodging motion might cause a passenger to get clipped or worse.

I wonder if I should mention the tops when the guide leader presses a button on the back of the nearest cart. A hinged trunk opens, revealing more storage space than I would have imagined.

"For your gear," he says to Bridge.

The other team members—Mikk, Ivy, and Dana Carmak the historian—dump their gear into one of the carts. Dana is a strawberry blonde whose skin is already turning bright red in the heat.

I make sure I'm in one cart and Roderick is in the other one. We both sit in the first row behind the pilot's area so that we can jump into the pilot seat if necessary.

The morning has grown even hotter. Sweat runs down the side of my face and gathers in drops on my chin. The guides have brought bottles of water and salt tablets; apparently the heat is a problem for many of the groups they ferry below.

My cart has the local pilot, me, Mikk, the guide leader, a medic, and Bridge. The rest of the team has found its seats in the other cart.

"Before we go below," the guide leader says from behind me, his voice amplified by some kind of system I can't see, "let me tell you how this place was discovered. A cave-in . . ."

I tune him out. I know this part of the history. The others watch him as he waves his arms toward the remains of destroyed buildings below us.

The entrance to the caves is black. The opening is wide and arched. The structure itself is curious. What little I've seen of Vaycehn architecture shows an affinity for layered construction, bricks placed on top of bricks, sections placed on top of sections.

But the arch seems to be one smooth piece of blackness, shiny in the headlamps of the carts waiting to go in.

"We've known for centuries that some of the earliest settlers lived in this part of the Basin," the guide was saying, "but we never knew exactly where. Not until this latest cave-in showed us an astonishing set of ruins."

The word "latest" catches my attention. Both Ivy and Bridge glance at me. They caught it too. But we seem to decide as a group not to interrupt the guide—or perhaps they are waiting for me to interrupt him.

The guide has a spiel. I'm going to let him run through it. If I have other questions, I will have Bridge ask them later.

When the guide finishes, the carts rise simultaneously. Our pilot nods at the other pilot, who then goes into the archway first. We follow at a reasonably safe distance, although I do notice that the air—which had smelled faintly of some kind of flower—now smells harsh with a chemical afterburn.

I ask our pilot about raising the cart's top, but he doesn't even turn around.

"We're not going far enough," he says.

The lights from the other cart reflect against the black wall ahead. That darkness I saw was part of the construction, not a darkness of an unlit area. The cart hovers for a moment, then eases downward as if it's going into a shaft.

It disappears. The light on the far wall is diminished by half, and I can almost see the materials.

Our pilot eases our cart into the archway, and immediately the air cools. The afterburn smell is gone; here the air is tangy, almost salty, as if there is an ocean nearby.

I don't have time to reflect on that. I barely have a chance to look at the walls around me before we descend.

The descent is slow. We are going down a shaft. The pilot holds the cart at a steady speed. If it weren't for the reflections of light on the smooth walls, undulating in a strange wave, I would think we aren't moving at all.

There's almost a feeling of weightlessness to this slow descent. I feel a pang. I understand weightlessness. Even though I'm landborn, I've spent most of my life in space. The idea of going down a shaft into the dark ground, the weight of an entire city above me, makes my stomach clench.

Finally, we reach the bottom of the shaft. The shaft opens onto a large chamber with the same smooth black walls. Only here there is lighting, and it looks like nothing I've ever seen. It's bluish, recessed into the smooth black wall, and seems to coat everything.

My skin seems paler than it ever has. Paler, with a touch of blue. The light seems almost cool—the opposite of that harsh sun above. I blink and realize that my eyes don't hurt for the first time since we landed on Wyr.

The carts hover next to each other.

"Normally," the lead guide says, "we continue forward down various passages, giving the history of this place, but you are in charge here."

Then he looks at me with such contempt that I start. He waits for a moment, studying me.

Finally he says with a bit of annoyance, as if I haven't answered a question, "What would you like to do?"

There is nothing in this chamber except the lights, the walls, the ceiling, and the floor—all made of that black material.

"I think we should disembark," I say.

The guide's lips thin.

The carts lower and my team climbs out. The pilots remain, letting the carts hover. The other guides get out slowly.

Ivy immediately heads to the walls, slips on a pair of gloves, and touches the surface. I'm busy trying to keep my balance on the slick floor. This material is as smooth as it looks—maybe even smoother.

The other team members gather around me, awaiting orders.

I'm watching Ivy.

"You didn't build these, did you?" she asks the lead guide.

"No," he says. "We think they grew."

Mikk starts beside me, but I'm not quite as surprised. I knew that some of the caves had walls that were "grown," but I thought they were made of a recognizable stone. I figured the caves would be natural caves, with natural caverns created by water, time, or more cave-ins.

"Grew," Ivy repeats. "This doesn't look like a natural material to me. Is it native to Wyr?"

Bridge tries to walk to her. He slides and nearly falls. One of the guides crosses his arms, looking satisfied.

They don't like us, and they resent our presence. I'm not sure if that's the typical attitude Vaycehnese who work with tourists have—I know I had it when I ran tourist dives—or if their resentment is directed at us for altering the format of the tour.

"We don't know if it's native," the guide says.

Bridge puts on his gloves as well. He pulls a small device from his pocket. I haven't seen it before. He holds it close to the wall.

"You don't know," he says conversationally. "Does that mean you've seen this before?"

"There are other places below the city that have black walls," the guide says, then hastily adds, "and they're not open to the public."

We're not public, but I'm not going to remind him of that.

"What makes you think it grows?" Bridge asks.

The guide licks his lips. Two of the others look at him and shrug. He tilts his head just a little.

"This chamber wasn't here before the collapse," he says.

We are all looking at him now.

He flushes under the scrutiny and looks from one of his men to the other. But they say nothing. They let him tell us.

"The collapse revealed stone walls, like the Basin walls," he says.

I get the sense that he's choosing his words carefully, possibly revealing more than he should. That flush of his is telling; if nothing else, it shows us all how uncomfortable he finds this topic.

"After the first day, the black threaded through. No one noticed it right away, but the images taken of the site showed it. We went back after . . ."

He let his voice trail off. He gives the other guides a helpless look. They look away from him.

Curious. Has no one asked about the black walls before?

Bridge has his hands behind his back. He's watching the lead guide as if he were a test subject. Ivy has taken her hand from the wall and is surreptitiously glancing at her fingertips, as if they make her nervous.

"After what?" Bridge prompts. "You went back after what?"

The guide swallows. "After the room formed. We examined each day's images. It grew over the stone. All this black. It just grew."

"Into this chamber."

He nods.

"And the shaft we came down?" Bridge asks.

The guide thins his lips but nods again.

"But it didn't continue along the surface?" Bridge had noticed that. I hadn't.

"It stops about a centimeter from the lip of the shaft," the guide says.

No one says anything for a moment. I'm feeling a little dizzy, which could be the unexpected information or it could be the unusual climate. I make myself drink some water and take several deep breaths.

Bridge is frowning. It's a look of concentration, as if he's trying to absorb everything the guide is telling us.

Ivy has started to rub the tips of her fingers. Dana Carmak walks over to her and, after putting on some gloves of her own, removes Ivy's, placing them in a specimen bag. Then she hands Ivy some extra-strong cleaner.

The guide doesn't seem to notice. He's watching Bridge for some kind of reaction.

"I take it your scientists have studied this," Bridge says.

The guide nods.

"What do they think happened?"

He shrugs.

One of the medics steps forward. He has been watching Ivy. "Our scientists say it's not harmful. We've brought hundreds of people down here. No one has gotten ill. No one has had black grow on them. It doesn't seem to leave the cavern."

"And it goes all the way back?" Bridge asks him.

"All of the caves have it," the medic says.

"All of the caves on this side of the city," Bridge says.

"No," the medic says. "All of the caves in the Basin."

I feel my breath catch. Mikk glances at me, apparently trying to see if I'm following the discussion. He doesn't seem real sure about it.

But Mikk knows more about relics and history and shipwrecks and diving. He has never professed to know much about science.

"But you said there was no black when there was a cave-in." Roderick has joined the discussion. He's looking at the leader. "Have you seen it grow before?"

The guide looks trapped. "I haven't, no."

"But there have always been stories," says the medic. "Quarantined houses because they accidentally punch through the subbasement wall, and then the entire lower level is subsumed."

"What do you mean lower level?" Bridge asks.

"The subbasement. The basement. Anything below ground."

"But the black stops when it gets above ground?" Bridge asks.

The medic nods.

"Even if that above ground area is protected by a roof or shade?" Bridge asks.

The medic nods again.

"Is this simply rumor or do you know this as a fact?" Bridge asks.

The medic rubs his hands together. It's his turn to give his colleagues an uneasy glance. "Fact," he says. "My grandparents lost their home to a quarantine when I was a boy."

"So you've seen the growth before," Bridge says.

The medic nods.

"How come you don't study it?" Bridge asks. "You needed to study science to have medical training. Why didn't you branch into a study of the cave walls?"

"That's not a course of study," the medic says.

I frown. I'm not quite sure what Bridge is getting at, but I'm finding the path there interesting.

"The walls aren't a course of study," Bridge says.

"That's right."

"But don't the local geologists want to know about this? Or do you think it belongs in the biological sciences? Maybe bio-chem?"

The medic seems confused. The lead guide steps in again.

"We are a small city," he says. "We don't have the scientific resources available to people from other places."

"Surely you could have brought them in," Bridge says.

"It's a natural phenomenon," the guide says. "Nothing more."

And with that, he has clearly closed off his part of the conversation.

I'm trying to review the data I've studied about the Vaycehn ruins. I remember mention of growth on the walls, but not this. And I seem to recall that the implication was that the growth preexisted the discovery, that it didn't grow afterward.

"Is the material removable?" I ask Ivy. After all, she's the one who has been studying the tips of her gloves, where she touched the blackness.

"I don't know," she says.

"We'll take a sample," Bridge says. "Not just here, but at the top. We're at a disadvantage, though. We're to look for a certain kind of tech, which is a higher form of physics than we're familiar with. I don't think this is."

I appreciate Bridge's discretion. He doesn't mention stealth tech in front of the guards.

"Because this stuff grows?" Roderick asks. "Or because it stops near the surface."

"Certain fungi won't grow above a certain level. The different environment on the surface doesn't allow the growth." Ivy is still rubbing her fingertips together, as if she's afraid of what she touched.

"Yeah, but to grow that fast . . ." Mikk lets his voice trail off when several of the others stare at him. "Right? Nothing grows that fast."

"Bacteria does," Ivy says. "So do a lot of other natural organisms. You just don't encounter most of them in a vacuum."

Meaning that those of us who work primarily in space are ignorant of what we're facing here. Which is probably true. Although I knew that many things grow quickly. Just because we work in space, doesn't mean we haven't encountered deadly bacteria or viruses that run through a space station in a matter of hours.

But I'm staying silent through this discussion. That's one of the many management tricks I've learned. I hire the best I can find. I have to trust them to do their work, which is what this speculation is.

Bridge turns back to the lead guide. "Was this room shaped like this, then, when the blackness came?"

The guide shakes his head. "This was a—" He pauses, as if he had been about to say something forbidden. "A certain kind of cave-in. The blackness covered it and created the shaft. That's why no one came down here for years. They were afraid they'd get trapped inside."

"But the growth stopped," Bridge says.

The guide nods.

"After the chamber was formed."

The guide nods again.

"Fascinating." Bridge glances at me. His eyes seem brighter than usual. He's excited about this.

"We're spending our day here?" I ask him.

"I think this is important," he says. "We need a lot of samples."

I try not to sigh. I want to go deeper, to see what's ahead. I just want a sense.

Then I realize that he doesn't need all of us for the samples. "You and Ivy and Roderick stay here. I want Dana and Mikk to accompany me farther into the tunnels. I want to know what's ahead so that we can plan."

This is not how a dive would work. On a dive, we would all stay together and let the person whose work takes precedence take charge of that part of the mission.

But my archeologist, scientist, and historian don't know that. Only Roderick and Mikk do. They're looking at me in surprise, but they say nothing. They know this is a different kind of exploration.

"You," I say, pointing to the lead guide. "You'll join us, along with you—" I point to the medic who told us about the blackness "—and whatever pilot you feel is necessary."

"It's not accepted protocol to break up the group," says the lead guide.

"But it's not accepted protocol to stop here, either, is it?" I say.

He nods once, reluctantly.

"We're trained for dangerous situations, just like you are. We'll take every precaution we can. And we won't be gone long." I say that last for the three I'm leaving behind.

The guide looks at the other two members of his team helplessly. They say nothing. He goes to the cart I rode in on and climbs aboard. After a moment, the medic joins him.

Then I get in, followed by Mikk and Dana.

"Where are we going?" the guide asks with that bitterness he seems to reserve only for me.

I give him my most level look. "We're going to the edge of the section where the fourteen archeologists died."

FIVE

The group stirs around me. Apparently they think I've just contradicted myself. I say we're going to be safe, and then I suggest something reckless.

But I'm not going to justify anything. I need to see that site to know what we're facing. I won't get close. I doubt the lead guide will let me very close anyway. He seems a lot more cautious than I am.

I'm paying so much attention to the negative reaction from my team, I almost miss what the lead guide is saying.

"They didn't die in one place."

We all turn toward him.

He looks pleadingly at Bridge. "We do not always know where there is danger."

Bridge raises his eyebrows as he looks at me. He's asking if I want to change my mind.

"If we're looking at the same stuff we've seen before," I say, unwilling to use the words "stealth tech," "then we need to know where it begins and ends. We have to map it."

Mapping is a big part of diving. The more we know, the more detail it's in, the better off we are. I realize as I say that we need to map that I'm moving myself back to a more comfortable, familiar position.

Apparently, I'm more on edge than I realize.

"Surely you have maps of the places you know are dangerous," Bridge says to the guide.

"Of course," he says. "We all carry them. We do not want to accidentally go down the wrong corridor."

"Good," I say. "Then we'll be safe."

"Don't get close," Bridge says, but it's more for the guide than for me.

Still, I nod.

Roderick lets out the breath he's been holding. He comes closer to our cart. "Maybe I should go with you," he says.

I understand the implication. I'm the only one of this group who has the marker and can work in stealth tech. I'm also the only pilot on the mini-mission. If I'm somehow disabled, then the entire group has to rely on the Vaycehnese pilot, who clearly doesn't have the skills Roderick and I do.

"I'd rather have you close to the exit," I say.

He nods. He understands. He has to be here and be ready should we need to get someone out quickly. He knows I'll contact him if I can.

We all wear small communicators around our ears. A single tap, and we can speak to each other. I've already tested to see if mine works down here. It does, although I'm not sure I can contact the others back at the hotel.

"You cannot talk her out of this?" the lead guide says to Bridge.

Bridge laughs. "Me? She's the one in charge."

"And that," the guide mumbles loud enough for all of us to hear, "is why no one should ever listen to a woman."

We all ignore his protest. Instead, I tap the top of the pilot's seat ahead of me.

"Let's go," I say.

As I do, Mikk says to me, "Should we suit up?"

The guide hears. He turns toward us. "In your space suits?"

Mikk isn't looking at him. Mikk is watching me.

"We have air here. We have cool air here. Drink your water and you will be fine," the guide says.

But Mikk is waiting for my answer. They all are.

"We're not going inside the area where they died," I say. "We're just going to figure out where that area is."

"Those areas," the guide says again. "There is more than one."

"Still," I say to Mikk. "We'll just look. We won't go deep."

He sighs, but nods, then settles back in his seat. The pilot still hasn't moved.

"I guess we should go, then," Mikk says.

The guide hasn't said anything. He's still looking at me. "We cannot see all the death sites."

"Why not?" I ask.

"They overlap," he says.

I frown. I think I know what he means, but I'm not sure. The measurements of the station that houses the Room of Lost Souls have changed in the intervening years, as if the station is growing. Squishy, my stealth-tech expert, theorizes that the station is slipping out of one dimension into another.

If we are looking at stealth tech and not some localized phenomenon, then it would be logical to have the areas where the dead were found encroach on other areas.

"Show us what you can," I say.

"From a safe distance," Bridge adds.

That surge of resentment is back. But he hasn't said that because the guide will listen to him instead of me. He's said that because he wants me to be as careful as possible.

"I do not go close to those places," the guide says. "I have warned my tours against them."

And he's trying to warn me.

"Let's go," I say, and this time the guide gives the order. The cart moves forward, deep into the chamber, the strange blue lights reflecting off the cart's surface like sunlight on the edge of a shuttlecraft.

We pass four corridors before turning down one. Mikk is using his wrist guide to record all of this. I'm doing the same. Carmak is watching everything as if she's never done anything like it before.

I guess, if you don't count the tourist dives I've taken her on, she never has.

"Do you have a spiel for this part of the tunnels?" I ask the lead guide.

He swallows hard, and then nods. After a moment, he leans forward. "We do not know how to date these," he says. "The blackness looks the same throughout, but the lighting is different."

He sweeps his hand upward. For the first time, I notice that the lights have changed from that cool blue to a frosty white. The air is even cooler here, to my relief.

I'm almost beginning to feel at home.

"Our own history says that the first settlers found these caves. They used them as a base while building the first city of Vaycehn."

"Which means that someone was here before them," Carmak says.

The guide looks at her. "We believe these tunnels have grown," he says. "We believe they are natural."

He says that with the conviction of a devout man who has just heard something potentially damaging about his own religion.

"Even the lights?" Mikk asks.

The guide shrugs. "We think some early settlers may have put them in."

"Like you put in the blue lights in the chamber," I say in my most agreeable tone.

The guide looks down. I feel a surge of excitement. They didn't put in the lights. The lights formed when the black smoothness formed.

"What kind of records are there of that first settlement?" Carmak asks. "Did you find actual evidence of their existence?"

She can barely contain the eagerness in her voice. The guide hears it and smiles for the first time.

"We found a lot of evidence," he says. "You can find it all re-created in the City Museum of Vaycehn. The section on the first settlement takes up an entire floor."

"What did you find?" I ask. "Furniture? Clothing? Equipment?"

"Yes to all," he says. "We found so much that the museum staff is still cataloguing."

"I'm sure there are items that can't be catalogued," Mikk says. He's gone with me on many dives since the Room of Lost Souls. On the Dignity Vessels we've found, we've recovered all kinds of things, from spoons to devices that make music with the touch of a button.

He's always been fascinated with those things, and he seems fascinated now.

"Yes," the guide says, only now he's leaned back, reluctant again. Does he think we're going to loot their museum? Or does he simply not want to talk about things he does not know for certain? "There are hundreds of items we can't identify. The City Museum has hired experts to evaluate these things."

Experts. He says that as if we're amateurs. I suppose, on some level, we are. We don't care about Vaycehn or even Wyr history. We care only about the possibility of stealth tech in this place.

The guide suddenly sweeps his arm toward yet another corridor. "Down there," he says. "The first two archeologists died down there."

We are hovering in the corridor we've come down, several meters from the entrance to the other corridor.

"How close can we get?" I ask.

"This is close enough," the guide says.

The pilot's hands are gripped tightly on the controls. His knuckles have turned white.

"How far away did they die?" I ask.

"What do you mean?" the guide says, frowning at me.

"A meter? A kilometer? How deep were they in that other corridor?"

"Seven meters," the medic says.

The guide glares at him.

"My father was on the recovery team."

"They got the archeologists out?" I ask. We've had to abandon a corpse to stealth tech before we knew that I could brave it and survive.

"No," the medic says. "But it was clear they were dead."

"They were mummified, right?" I ask.

The medic nods. "He says he's never seen anything like it."

"Have you?" Mikk asks.

The medic closes his eyes. "Four times," he says softly.

I put my hands on the side of the cart and ease out. The floor is slippery here too. I have to hold onto the hovering cart to get my balance.

I hate that part of gravity. I want to float to my destination, not walk toward it on unsafe surfaces.

The guide grabs my wrist. "I can't let you do this."

"I'm only going to the entrance," I say.

His grip remains tight. "No," he says. There's real fear in his voice. "I told you, the areas change. If we're wrong about where it begins, it will kill you."

"That's the beauty of it," Mikk says. "It can't kill her."

The guide stares at him for a moment, then looks back at me. "It kills everyone."

"I'll be careful," I say.

He shakes his head. "I cannot be responsible for your death. If something happens, I will blame your recklessness. I will say you were warned and you ran away from us and we couldn't catch you."

"Cover your ass as best you can," I say. "I have nothing against that. And if I'm dead, my reputation won't matter at all."

Mikk grins. The medic has gone pale. The guide looks ill, but he lets go of my wrist. His fingers have left red marks on my skin.

I resist the urge to rub it as I walk cautiously down the slick corridor. It feels even colder closer to the ground. The lights come on as I move—thin, white things that somehow manage to cover every centimeter of the place.

I am listening as much as observing. The active stealth tech that I have been near makes a series of sounds that my brain interprets as music—usually choral voices singing in harmony. The weaker stealth tech sounds like humming, and the tiny stealth tech I've encountered—my father had a working bottle experiment—had a sound so faint that I had to strain to hear it.

But I did hear it.

At the moment, I hear nothing except my own ragged breathing.

It takes longer than I thought it would to reach the branching corridor. I stop at the opening. There are no lights, and it is so dark down there that the hair rises on the back of my neck.

At least in space there is an ambient light. Nothing is ever completely black. Not like this. If I walk into that darkness, I will effectively disappear.

I try to remember. Did the lights come on as the cart approached an area or when the cart was already inside? I have a hunch the cart's lights covered a lot. Maybe it was a motion sensor that made the lights come on.

I take a deep breath of that wonderfully cool air, then stick my hand into that corridor.

Behind me, I can hear the guide shouting. He doesn't want me to do that much.

I wave my arm around, and after a moment, rows and rows of lights flicker on. When one is triggered, the others get triggered as well. I wager they get triggered at some set distance.

These lights have a rose tint to them. The area looks less black than a deep red, thanks to the lighting. That redness is oddly welcoming. I have a hunch we're getting closer to the heart of these caves.

I keep my arm in the corridor and make a point of moving it so that I can continue to see. Deep in the corridor—maybe seven meters ahead, maybe farther—I can see shapes. I'm not sure what exactly. They might simply be reflections on the shiny walls, although my mind reassembles those shapes into furniture or boxes or tables. All seem plausible. But for what I know, those shapes could also be debris—

Or other bodies.

I pull my arm out before I have a chance to reflect on what I've done. The lights remain on for several seconds before they flicker off. The farthest away disappear first—a nifty design that won't leave anyone in darkness too long.

My heart is pounding. It takes me a moment to catch my breath. I feel like I sometimes do when I stumble on a very important wreck.

I wait until I make it back to the cart to say what I'm thinking.

"We're diving this."

Carmak nods. The guide looks scared. Mikk grins.

"You saw something," he says.

"Oh, yeah," I say. "I saw a lot of somethings—and I want to know what they are."

SIX

*T*he problem is that of the people with the markers, I'm the only experienced diver. The others have had training, of course, or they wouldn't have gone into the Room of Lost Souls when my father begged them to. But the Room is an empty place, without a lot of obvious dangers.

None of the Six have the ability to dive a dangerous area. None of them know how to do an excavation, and I wouldn't trust any of them—no matter how smart—to attempt one even in full gravity.

By the time we have our nightly meeting, my mind is full of half-completed plans. I don't tell the others what I'm thinking; it's too early. But I have a hunch we'll be here quite a while, excavating the areas where the archeologists died.

I also have to set up an emergency evacuation plan. The longer we're here, the more risk we run of getting discovered by the Empire. I talk to Ilona before we start the meeting. I have her lay out plans for a quick escape.

Essentially everyone must head for the ships in the spaceport as quickly as possible. We'll decide at the time (if there's time) which equipment to take and which we trash. And Ilona and I must drum it into everyone's brains that if an emergency evacuation gets called, we all leave immediately, no matter what we're doing.

"You think it's stealth tech now, don't you?" Ilona says as we finish moving chairs in the conference room.

The hotel staff has covered the table with specialty dishes as well as fresh fruit, vegetables, and crudités. We are going to eat a Vaycehnese feast, something the city is famous for. Glasses of sparkling water line the sideboard behind me.

I had the staff remove the wine the moment I arrived. I left all the beverages with caffeine and a single jug of local ale for the team members who cannot survive without their evening alcohol. But I make sure there isn't enough for anyone to get drunk on.

I wanted to limit the food, too—overeating is just as bad when you're trying to do something athletic—but I couldn't do that without ruining the feast. I have to trust my team to have some sense.

Ilona grabs one of the yellow-and-brown spotted apples that Vaycehn is known for, then sits on a chair near the head of the table.

"Well?" she says to me. "Are you convinced?"

"Let's say I'm more convinced than I was," I say. "There are a lot of strange things in those caves."

"Not all strange things in the universe come from stealth tech." Roderick has just come in the door. He stops when he sees the food spread as if he hasn't eaten in weeks.

"I know that," Ilona says with irritation. "But these are probably caused by it."

"Probably not," I say.

They both turn toward me.

I smile and grab one of the spotted apples for myself. "But we are going to wait for the others before I tell you what we found."

The remaining members of the team straggle in. To my surprise, my team arrives before all the other teams are complete. My team looks tired— Carmak in particular, even though she didn't do much physical work—and a few have wet hair from showers.

Ivy's hands are scrubbed raw. I didn't realize how upset she is from that simple touch. I would think that an archeologist, used to working in soil, would be used to touching strange and possibly dangerous things.

She sits across from Ilona. As the rest of the team filters in, they grab fruit or a slice of bread. A few pour themselves ale—although none of the ale drinkers are my divers or pilots. They're used to remaining clean during a mission.

The drinkers are primarily the Six, the historians, and a few of the scientists. I'm glad I've left only one jug of ale because it's gone quickly. Rollo Kersting, one of the Six, pours the last dregs into a coffee cup and turns to me.

"You should ask for more booze next time," he says.

Mikk stifles a laugh. Roderick turns his chair away so that his grin isn't apparent.

"I should," I say in mock agreement.

Kersting's name fits him. He is rounder than the others, although he manages to stay in shape. His chubby cheeks and tufts of brown hair accent the roundness. His love of beer is the reason for his extra weight. Much of what we do on missions with Kersting is designed to keep him from that extra glass with dinner.

Kersting doesn't notice. He slides into the nearest chair and eyes the covered dishes.

"We have a lot to report," I say. "The hotel has thoughtfully provided dinner. Let's serve ourselves, and then conduct the meeting over food."

I don't have to tell people twice to grab plates. Fortunately the hotel was wise enough to repeat the same courses on both ends of the sideboard. Everyone dishes up platefuls of food, then returns to their seats. I take a small bit of each dish. Nothing is recognizable.

I set my plate in front of the head of the table, but I don't eat. Everyone else tucks in.

I give the overall report of what's below, spending quite a bit of time on the black walls and the strange lighting.

"I wasn't able to see more than the first death area," I say, "but it looks like the Vaycehnese haven't let anyone back there. There's a lot to be excavated."

Tamaz lifts his head when he hears that. "We're going to dive," he says with a smile.

"We are," I say. "But we're going to run this like any other mission. Mapping first."

"I would think there's also a problem." Kersting has finished his ale and taken a glass of sparkling water. "If the guide is right, then that stuff is in a stealth-tech area."

"Possible," I say. "It's something we're going to have to work out."

Because if it all is truly in a stealth-tech area, then I'm the only trained diver. The Six will have to dive with me, and that will be like taking tourists on a dangerous deep-space dive.

"What I'm most interested in tonight are two things," I say. "I want to know what the rest of you discovered in your researches today. And I also want to know if the scientists have any early thoughts on the black stuff. First the black stuff."

Bridge glances at the other scientists. He's the one who spent the most time with it today, the only one who could really postulate anything.

Still, I like the way he included the others, even if it was only with just a look.

"It's really preliminary," he says. "We took a lot of samples, not just from the chamber they took us into, but from the area around the top, any edge that we could find. Then I went deeper into the chamber, away from the collapsed area, as far back as the cart pilot would let me go without your approval, and took some samples there."

"I'm assuming they're different," Stone says. A few of the others glare at her, but she ignores them. I may be in charge, but Stone is going to pretend she is.

"That's the surprising thing," Bridge says. "With a cursory analysis from the equipment we brought with us, they're not. It's the same material—and here's the curious thing—it's the same age."

"Meaning what?" Mikk asks. He's always the one who is the most impatient with science. He only wants to know how to use it, not what makes it work.

"I have no idea. I'm not even sure what we're dealing with," Bridge says. "The components are unbelievably small and not something we've seen before."

"Infectious?" Ivy asks, rubbing her fingertips together.

Bridge gives her such a look of annoyance that I wonder if she's been asking him that question all day. I don't know why she's so worried. She wore gloves.

"I don't know if they're infectious," Bridge says. "Certainly not in the sense that we understand it. But something that small and powerful might do some harm if it gets into the lungs. I think until we know what we're dealing with, we wear masks."

"Lovely," Stone mutters.

"Are the guides right?" I ask. "Is this a natural material?"

"Not on any world I've been to," says Bridge. "I'm guessing and we're going to have to do studies, but I'm pretty sure these are man-made."

"That magically appear when a wall collapses?" Carmak asks. She seems to have perked up now that she's eaten and had some coffee. She actually sounds intrigued now instead of overwhelmed like she had late this afternoon.

"Yes, possibly," Bridge says. "They formed quickly, reinforced the collapsed walls, and created the shaft where there was none. And then there's the matter of the lights."

That catches my attention. The lights fascinated me from the moment we went below.

"What about them?" Stone asks.

"They form too. And they seem to respond to some kind of stimuli. In other words, they turn off when they're not needed."

"I'm pretty sure that's a motion sensor of some kind," I say. I explain what happened in the corridor.

"Built into that black stuff?" Mikk asks. "This stuff is sounding more and more amazing all the time."

"Why shouldn't it be?" Ilona says. "If the same people who built this built stealth tech, then of course this is amazing. Stealth tech is."

"Amazing in how fast it kills," Roderick says.

Both Mikk and Roderick, who saw a member of our team die in the Room of Lost Souls, loathe stealth tech. They're here to conquer it, not learn everything they can about it.

"It's amazing how it works," Ilona says primly, as if she disapproves of their attitude.

I'm still not sure we're dealing with stealth tech here, but I am sure that whoever made that black stuff had more scientific knowledge than we could pretend to have.

Since our science is the best it has been in thousands of years and we don't understand this stuff, that means it's ancient science. The ancients knew so much more than we ever will. I constantly find myself in awe of them.

"We're here to find out whether or not those fourteen archeologists died in stealth-tech accidents," I say. "Aside from my discovery today, did anyone learn more about that?"

"It's hard to find information," says Gregory, one of the scientists. His narrow face is wan, and I wonder if he's getting much sleep. He doesn't like travel, although he'll do it when he has to. He's always the last to volunteer for an away mission and the first to volunteer to go home.

"None of the officials want to talk to us." He's playing with his fork as he speaks, turning it upside down, banging the end, and then repeating the procedure. "They wouldn't even point us to the scientific labs around here."

One of the other scientists, a slightly overweight man named Lentz, nods. "I finally gave up and went to the universities. Vaycehn has three, and they're all well known. I wasn't allowed to contact any of the science departments directly, although in the cafeteria, I ran into a scientist I knew from a few conferences. He says they'd love to meet with us, but Vaycehn has regulations about sharing potentially difficult information with outsiders, and so in order to have a formal discussion, we'd have to spend months going through channels."

"I hadn't heard that part about channels until today," Ilona says before I can ask her why we haven't gotten all our permissions lined up.

"What does 'potentially difficult' mean?" Bridge asks.

Lentz smiles. "I asked that, too, and he answered me. Anything that could interfere with the tourist trade. The caves are the primary example because many of them are in the oldest areas of the city. People love to visit the ruins."

"One-point-two million visitors a year," says Gregory, "and those are the official ones."

It seems he has gotten the tourist lecture too.

"We'd be considered unofficial, even though we have a guide. We're not here on vacation." Gregory sounds surprised at that, as if he doesn't understand the limiting of the word "tourist" to vacationer alone.

"Was your friend able to tell you anything unofficial?" Bridge asks.

Lentz's grin grew. "Well, two old friends, you know, we'll talk about anything."

My breath catches. Lentz got some information.

"And we did. We talked about our friends, our colleagues, our research."

Stone sighs, as if she wants him to hurry to the point.

He leans back in the chair and puts his hands behind his head. "My friend is researching the death holes."

Lentz has everyone's attention now, and he seems to be enjoying it.

"It seems that the Boss's guess was right. Others have died here, all through Vaycehn's history. In fact, one of the reasons the city center moved so much was to avoid the holes."

"There are that many?" Stone asks. "I thought there were only a few."

"All through the city's history," Lentz says, "areas just collapse. It's not the weight of buildings or the ground above that causes it—although sometimes that happens too. But there are entire death hole areas in the Basin. That's why some of the ruins are off-limits to tourists, and that's why some of the history of the city is vague."

Bridge has steepled his fingers. I'm wishing I knew more detail about the five-thousand-year history of Vaycehn, like how often the city center moved and where.

"He thinks there's a scientific reason for all of this?" Carmak asks. Her eyes are sparkling. She's not the same woman who was in the field this afternoon. "Besides a geologic one, I mean. Because the histories say that Vaycehn was initially built on unstable ground, and the oldest colonists had no way to know where the stable ground was. They searched until they found an area that could support their city."

"Sounds plausible, doesn't it?" Lentz says. "Until you remember that humans aren't native to this place. The colonists had enough scientific skill to travel through space, then colonize this area and begin to farm it. You'd think they could figure out rudimentary geology."

"Science doesn't always follow a linear path," says Ilona, but she's frowning. She's thinking about this.

Both Mikk and Stone are restless. But I'm fascinated. I have to force myself to eat some of the food on my plate. Not even the tastes are familiar, except on a basic level—bitter, sweet, salty, bitingly spicy. I pick at what's before me, then push the plate away.

"Well," Lentz says with a small shrug, "whether or not you agree with the premise for his research doesn't matter. He started the work because he didn't believe his own country's history."

I'm glad Lentz is the one describing this. Gregory doesn't have the people skills, and Ilona is too invested in Vaycehnese life.

"He dug through old records and found a lot of the basic stuff you're talking about, Lucretia. He found the measurements, as well as stuff on whether the ground is stable, whether or not there's bedrock, how deep the solid layer goes before they find ground water, all of that kind of thing."

"And?" Mikk isn't even trying to mask his irritation at the way the scientists present things.

"And," Lentz says, "the old studies confirm what he suspected."

"Which is?" Mikk asks.

"That these death holes appear in solid ground. The catacomb of caves here were created by the phenomenon that creates the death holes. And it's ongoing."

"Like volcanic activity?" Stone asks. Now she's intrigued.

"Not quite," Lentz says. "Because there's always a history of volcanic eruptions in the past."

"Maybe a groundquake, then," she says.

"On an unknown fault line, maybe?" Carmak asks.

I shake my head. Even I know this. We have the capability to map tectonic plates from space. There are no unknown fault lines on any settled planet.

I'm about to say that when Lentz shakes his head.

"It's more like an explosion from underground," he says. "With a directed charge, made to create a hole in the surface above."

"Have they gone down to check what causes the explosion?" Bridge asks.

"Initially," Lentz says. "Which is why they're called death holes."

"Because the investigators mummify," Mikk says.

Lentz shakes his head. "Because the investigators vanish."

"Vanish?" I frown at him. He's enjoying dragging this out. "What does that mean?"

"It means that they're never found," he says.

"Does anyone search for them?" I remember how reluctant the guide was to let me down the corridor.

"Not after the first one or two don't make it back," he says. "Then they use animals to test. Usually after a dozen years or so have passed, something survives, and then it's deemed safe. But until then, no one goes in the death holes."

"Sounds like they learned about these places the hard way," Ilona says.

Everyone turns toward her, as if her statement is obvious.

"I mean," she says, "they have a protocol and a name for the phenomenon. So that means that these holes repeated, and then after a while, they needed a way to deal with them."

"Ilona's right," Bridge says. "A culture doesn't name a phenomenon if it's extremely rare. And it doesn't create a protocol if the phenomenon happens once every hundred years or so. How many of these have there been?"

Lentz shrugs. "I didn't talk to him all day."

"But you found out a lot," I say, wanting him to continue. "Does he think it's odd that these places eventually become safe?"

"No," Lentz says. "He says it validates his theory, that some kind of gas or something builds up and then explodes. It then dissipates over time, and the hole becomes safe."

"If there was gas, it would be released into the atmosphere, contaminating the area around it," Gregory says. "Did he find that?"

"He's only had two death holes to study since this became his expertise. But the records don't show any areawide deaths."

"Because," Ilona says, "they clear the areas when a death hole appears. You told us that."

"History tells us that," Carmak says.

"I'd like to know what happened the first time a few death holes appeared," I say. Because it doesn't have to be a gas. It could be a field. An expansion of a stealth-tech field—a different kind than we experienced in the Room of Lost Souls, but an expansion nonetheless.

Still, I don't say that. I'm still not willing to admit this place is tied to ancient stealth. We haven't seen stealth tech act like that.

Or have we?

I turn to Gregory, whom I hired because he once specialized in stealth tech. He was one of the government scientists who tried to reverse-engineer stealth tech with Squishy.

"When you guys were trying to re-create stealth tech in the lab," I say to him, "did you get some localized expansion phenomena? Something that would resemble what's going on here?"

He sighs. He hates talking about that time. What Squishy told me in as little detail as possible was that in the two hundred years the Empire has been trying to re-create stealth tech, the program has lost ships, materiel, and people.

When he remains silent, I add, "Squishy told me that a lot of people died while she worked on the program. I assumed they got trapped in the stealth-tech field. Is that what happened? Or were there 'explosions' to use Lentz's word? Did the field expand unexpectedly?"

"C'mon, Boss," Roderick says, "we've already seen that. In the Room. The way the station just kept getting bigger."

"But that looked like it was falling out of the field," Mikk says. Even though he gets impatient with scientific theory, he does remember it. Sometimes I think he's too smart for the rest of us, which is why his patience with people who establish fundamentals before they get to the point is so short.

"Greg?" I ask. "Did it suddenly explode?"

"'Explode' is the wrong word," he says. "Sometimes it would expand. It would be concentrated in one area, like air going through a tube."

"Or a narrow field coming up through the earth," says Stone.

Even though we're not on the Earth, no one corrects her. We know what she meant.

I sigh. "This isn't evidence, you know."

"It's another piece," Ilona says.

It is that.

"Can you get more information from your friend?" I ask Lentz.

"I can try," Lentz says. "I can ask him to lunch or something. But we have to be really informal. He can lose his job."

"Hell, why don't you just hire him, Boss?" Mikk says. "That'll take care of the cloak-and-dagger stuff."

"I'd like to know if he has something to add before I do," I say.

"Besides, hiring him might cut off his access to these death holes," Ilona says. "It's becoming clearer and clearer that the Vaycehnese are protecting the reputation of their city, and they're doing it at great cost."

"Cities do that all the time," Carmak says. "Governments lie. They don't want the bad stuff to get out. That's normal."

"But sometimes it's just there." César Voris, one of the historians, speaks up for the first time. He's one of my new hires. Carmak recommended him because he's an expert in this region of space. He specializes in ancient history, but he loves modern as well, and he spends his off time studying. I've never had another employee work quite that hard.

"What do you mean, 'there'?" Carmak asks.

Voris shrugs. He's a big man with a shock of white hair that makes his brown skin seem even darker than it is. His eyes are very black and very alert.

He looks directly at me. "You said to find out what we can about the death toll in the caves, so I did."

"We couldn't find anything," Gregory says. "No one'll talk."

"That's right," Voris says. "But we're interested in information. History, when you come down to it. So I went to the City Museum."

"The director wouldn't talk to me," says Ilona.

Voris folds his hands together and waits until the others stop speaking.

"The City Museum of Vaycehn," he says like the teacher he used to be, "is an amazing place. It has a great library, and so many fascinating exhibits, I doubt anyone could see them all in the space of a month."

"Yeah, yeah," Mikk says. "Don't tease us with information and then not give it."

"The thing is," Voris says as if Mikk hasn't spoken, "the exhibits cover the history of Vaycehn as accurately as possible. There is a quick viewing area that the tourists usually go to, and indeed are directed to, being told that the rest of the place will take most of their trip to see."

Mikk sighs impatiently. I grab another spotted apple and turn it over in my hands.

"But if you go in with an agenda, you can see quite a bit. I decided my agenda was the caves. The longer I was there, the more I realized I needed to know about the way the city center changed location all the time." Voris raises his bushy white eyebrows and looks at all of us, individually, before going on.

Now Stone sighs.

But Voris doesn't seem to care. "So I wandered, found an old ruin actually brought into the museum intact—that was interesting—and then found that each display has an information button. You push it and a holographic guide tells you everything you want to know and a few things you don't. If you push it twice, you can get a hard copy of the transcript, and if you push it three times, you can download that transcript to your own personal system, so long as you sign a few waivers promising not to use it for profit in any way."

"What did you learn?" Mikk asks.

"That the fourteen archeologists were mentioned for precisely the reason that Dr. Stone said. Because they're famous throughout the sector and it would look bad for them to just disappear here."

Stone nods. She clearly feels vindicated.

"But," Voris says, "I also learned that hundreds of Vaycehnese have died over the centuries in those so-called death holes. And for generations, the caves were off-limits to the Vaycehnese because people would die in weird little pocket areas."

I take a bit of the spotted apple. It's sweet and sour at the same time. I could easily become addicted to these things.

"There's even some images of the first mummies—people they found in those pockets and then removed. There's an entire section of the museum dedicated to the mummies of Wyr."

Ilona lets out a breath of air.

"My God," Bridge says.

"You're kidding," Lentz says, but it's not because he believes Voris is lying, but because he's stunned that Voris has learned this.

"You think your colleague knows?" I ask.

"I have no idea," Lentz says. "I'll ask him tomorrow."

"He probably does, but doesn't associate it with the death holes," Voris says. "The reason the City Museum is there is for the schools. Children parade in and out of that place on assignments all the time. The mummies are one assignment, but they're considered a mystery. Are they the first humans who came to Wyr before the colonists, or are they native? People connect certain areas of the caves with the mummies, but not the death holes themselves."

"But you just said that the fields in these death holes recede," Mikk says to Lentz.

Lentz nods. "I think the people who get trapped inside move away from the area where they entered. They lose oxygen or something—I don't know—and they die. Then when the fields recede, someone goes in and finds a mummy—not where the person originally vanished, but farther inside."

"That's a theory," Stone says.

"But a good one," Ilona says, mostly because it reinforces her stealth-tech idea.

"Wouldn't the Vaycehnese figure out that these phenomena are related?" Mikk asked.

"Not necessarily," Voris said. "We're looking for something specific. They're all looking at the various peculiarities of their home."

"Some of those peculiarities are just accepted," Ilona says.

"Research blindness," Bridge says. "That's why we try not to have preconceptions."

I sigh. I am starting to hate that word.

"We have preconceptions," Ivy says. She is still rubbing her fingertips together. "Maybe they're clouding our vision, too."

"Maybe," I say, "but let's listen to César. I suspect he has more to tell us."

"Oh, yeah," Voris says. "Because there's a modern mystery to this place."

There are a lot of mysteries on Vaycehn, more than I want to solve, simply because I want to get away from this hot, gravity-filled planet.

"You mean besides the fourteen archeologists?" Stone asks.

"Sixteen," Voris says. "There were sixteen."

We're all staring at him now. He has a slight smile on his face, and his black eyes twinkle. He looks both impish and pleased with himself.

"Sixteen?" Stone says. "We would know if two others were missing. It would be big news."

"It wasn't big news because they were postdoctoral students," Voris says.

"They were working on some project of their own, hoping for recognition, when they just disappeared. The guides say they never came out. They hadn't followed instructions, had gone into an off-limit area, and disappeared."

"Like the guides were warning us about," Ivy says nervously.

Bridge glares at her again.

"Yes," Voris says. "Maybe that's why. I'm thinking we should talk to the guides, try to find out how many of their noncompliance tourists have died in those caves."

"Do that," I say.

"Before we start your dive?" Stone asks, as if I'm the one who has suggested something out of line.

"No," I say.

"But what if this isn't stealth tech?" Stone says. "What if you're right and this is something else?"

I shrug. "Then we might die."

Five of the Six gasp. But the divers nod. They know the risks. We face them every time we dive.

"You knew that when you signed on with us," I say to the five. "That's part of what we do. We take risks in dangerous places. You signed waivers."

Half the team looks at their empty plates. Gregory takes more food, as if eating it will protect him.

I half expect someone to say that waivers aren't the same as realizing the risks. I've had tourists tell me that when I take them wreck diving. Then I would keep those tourists in the ship, not allowing them to dive.

But to my team's credit, they don't complain. They know what they signed up for, and they're not going to back out just because the risk has become real to them.

"You think it's stealth tech now, don't you?" Ilona asks me.

I'm not willing to concede that, at least not yet. But I do give her this: "I think the chances have gone up. But this could be something else. Maybe the Vaycehnese are right. Maybe this is a localized phenomenon."

"That makes its own lights?" Bridge asks.

"There are stranger things in the universe," I say. But not many. Things that act man-made generally are.

"Should we track the deaths?" Ivy asks, clearly not wanting to go back into the caves.

I shake my head. "The historians need to find out about Vaycehn's earliest settlers. Take César's advice. Go to that museum. See what the prehistory stuff says. See if you can find evidence of what's been forgotten."

"If it's forgotten," Stone says, "then no one will find it."

I smile. My business has always been about handling forgotten things.

"Forgotten doesn't mean invisible, Lucretia," I say. "Forgotten sometimes means misunderstood."

"Or ignored," Ilona says.

"Or buried," Bridge says.

I nod. For the first time, I'm enjoying this project. I'm even looking forward to the work below ground.

Maybe that's because diving is my element, whether it's underground or in space. Or maybe it's because I finally believe we'll discover something.

Stealth tech or not, there's something here. Something old. Something interesting.

Something unexplained.

SEVEN

*T*he dives are both easier and more difficult than they are in space. We can walk through sections, but we have trouble reaching the ceiling, where those magical lights are. We don't float away from the area we're examining, but we can't pull ourselves forward, either. We have to walk, to view everything from a single perspective.

I am frustrated and fascinated. I hate the feeling of gravity, but I love mapping.

We take each section bit by bit. We examine each area for changes. The guides watch as if we're crazy.

I bring most of my good divers down—at least in the beginning—to train the Six how to do real wreck diving. The guides have precise maps of the areas in which the deaths occurred—not just the sixteen recent deaths, but all of the deaths since the Vaycehnese started exploring their own cave system.

The guides show us these things, not to help us, but to discourage us. They want us to know how dangerous this place is, just so that we'll give up and go home.

Which we don't.

The deaths intrigue me. There are a lot of them—so many deaths, in fact, that the Vaycehnese forbid actual exploration by anyone and only allow tourist visits of the extreme edges. It is a sign of the Vaycehnese prejudice against foreigners that they allow any of us down here at all. Our lives are less precious than the lives of locals.

If they lose a few of us, they seem to believe it doesn't matter—so long as there isn't a section-wide incident. It is known throughout the section that the caves are dangerous, and anyone who goes down into them is taking a risk.

The guides think we're foolish in our dive suits, standing in front of a smooth black wall, taking notes and talking to each other in jargon. I'm happy for the suits. Much as I hate pulling them over my sweaty skin, I love the suit's automatic environmental controls. If it isn't for the gravity, I can almost believe that I'm back in space, diving a particularly unusual wreck.

It takes us nearly two weeks to explore the "safe" areas of the caves. By then, the Six have learned the routine. They're still rookies, but they're better than they were.

On the first day of the third week, I dive with the Six. We're going to the area where the postdoc students died. It's farther away than the areas where the archeologists have died, and Ilona argues that we should explore those areas first.

But in the time between our meeting and this dive, the historians have learned what the postdocs were working on. The postdocs believed that some kind of force created the caves—some kind of field that is part of the planet's interior, a force that expands and just as quickly contracts. That force comes upward, like geysers on Earth or the spitting rocks of Fortuyuna.

Planets shift and change. They're living creatures, like we are, only older, larger, and slower-moving. They adjust their comfort levels, and that causes volcanic eruptions or groundquakes or an occasional eruption of steam. Those adjustments, no matter what they are, release a lot of pent-up energy.

These postdocs believed that Wyr had a unique way of adjusting its own comfort level, a way that released energy that could be farmed. My scientists are still examining the research, trying to understand why the postdocs made that assumption, trying to figure out the energy readings (if any) that the postdocs took before they died.

But the fact that they were trying to take energy readings is more than enough for me. If the postdocs were right, then there is some kind of natural field down here. If we're right, there's a man-made field.

And if Ilona is right, that field is stealth tech.

So only the Six can move forward from now on.

Because we're in an environment that's not as hostile as space, I load the Six up with extra equipment, things I wouldn't make them carry into a real wreck. Lots of holocameras, lots of flat vid, lots of scientific sampling equipment.

I assign Kersting the job of sampling the walls every meter or two. I make DeVries record everything. Orlando Rea is the only one of the Six who shows an aptitude for exploration, so he's at my side. The rest must map each square meter before moving forward.

Rea and I do something I would never do in space: we explore sections of the corridor without normal backup.

I call them cursory explorations. We walk ahead to see if we find anything interesting.

We finally find something interesting about one kilometer from the place where the postdocs died. The black walls here are pitted. For the first time, the shiny black material looks old.

We bring the entire team forward, and as three of them map, DeVries records, and Kersting removes core samples, Rea and I continue down the corridor. Only now we're going a meter at a time, using our own equipment to film each section.

I have a slight headache, which could be caused by the stress of the dive. But I pay attention, because sometimes the sound that accompanies stealth tech starts as a vibration—a throbbing, one that could, in the right circumstance, be registered as an irritation rather than a noise.

The lights here are gray. That irritates me. The other lights come from the spectrum—blue to red—but gray doesn't fit. Finally I grab an equipment box, climb it, and wipe at the lighted area with my glove.

Something flakes onto my suit, and that section of the light turns white.

The lights here are covered with flaked bits of wall. For the first time, I'm happy for the suit. I remember Bridge's comment from that first day: *Something that small and powerful might do some harm if it gets into the lungs.*

We all stop and take samples of everything—the air, the ground, the walls, and the lights. We haven't been able to remove the lights from the walls—the lights are truly grown in—but we scrape the surfaces. Just like we scrape the ceiling and the floor.

When we come out with our flaked treasure, we use hazardous-procedure techniques to remove our suits. We have no idea how dangerous that flaked stuff is—if it's dangerous at all.

The flaking worries everyone but me. I'm finally happy to see something new and different. I was becoming afraid that we'd explore hundreds of miles of caves and find nothing except lights and black walls.

I know now that such a worry is silly. We're going to find something. I know it as clearly as I know my name.

We're going to find something, and we're very, very close.

EIGHT

I t takes two days.

We map that flaked corridor centimeter by centimeter. We examine each part of it.

Our scientists determine that the flakes are nothing more than particles that have come off the walls, just like I thought. Only they're able to date those particles by comparing them to the samples taken from our very first day.

The particles are at least four thousand years older.

I say at least because Bridge says at least. He really can't predict. When he presented the data, he reminded me that the older sections of the wall—those that formed years ago—showed no more aging than the newer sections. So he has no idea—the scientists have no idea—how long the walls stand before they start showing evidence of age.

He makes his guess based on the historical record. He knows that we have found areas that are at least three thousand years old with no sign of aging at all.

The corridor here is murky—we've disturbed so many particles that the air is gray—and a day ago, we started to get readings that reminded me (and Roderick and Mikk) of readings we got near the Room of Lost Souls.

My headache remains, but now I know it comes from stealth tech because I hear a low humming, as if voices are harmonizing softly. Three of the Six hear it as well.

Something is here, something strong. I almost wish it wasn't so I can bring in a real dive team. It's clear that the Six are out of their element. DeVries, Quinte, Seager, and Kersting are tired. Rea and Al-Nasir wonder why we have to pay so much attention to detail.

They think the minuscule is unimportant, and their impatience infects me.

I take Rea down the corridor two meters farther than we should go. I take him because that part of the corridor remains dark.

"Maybe," he says as he turns on the lamps built into his suit, "the wall lights are completely covered in particulate."

"Maybe," I say, but I don't think so. I have already trained my headlamp at the top of the wall, where the lights usually bulge out. I see no bulge. I see nothing to indicate lights at all.

I stand in the center of the corridor and wave my arms, thinking maybe the motion sensors will pick up something, but they do not. All I manage to do is swirl the particles even more. It's as if we're in the middle of a dust storm.

Then the light from my headlamp catches something directly in front of me. A movement. My heart starts to pound.

"Did you see that?" I ask Rea.

He turns, training his headlamp in the same direction as mine. The movement repeats and I realize it's a reflection.

Something is blocking the corridor.

"Let's check it out," he says, and starts forward. I catch his arm.

Now more than ever procedure is important.

"We map," I say, and I can hear his sigh echo through our suit comms as well as through the air. We map, we go slowly, we figure out what's ahead.

It takes two more days before we understand that what's ahead is not the end of the corridor, as some of the team speculated, but a door.

A door.

An old, old door without warnings, markings, or lights.

Just a latch that no one has turned in at least four thousand years.

NINE

"I'm going in with you," Roderick says.

"Me, too," Mikk says.

They stand outside the hovercraft, their suits already on. The guides watch us like we're the science experiment. The Six stand in the corridor, holding their equipment like shields.

Roderick and Mikk have seen that. They know that the Six are frightened, and they know that frightened divers make mistakes.

They also know that I'm eager, and eager divers make mistakes as well. A different set of mistakes, but mistakes just the same.

"No," I say. "You can't go in. We're getting readings that remind me of the Room."

"We never really tied those readings to stealth tech," Roderick says.

"And these readings are significantly different," Mikk says. "The group has been studying them for more than a week."

"They're similar," I say.

"They're similar the way light and sound are similar. They're both waves, but they're not the same thing." Mikk's education is showing, and he doesn't even realize it.

I shake my head. "That's a specious analogy. These readings are similar in ways I don't like. It's as if this field is fresher than the one near the Room. Or more active."

"Or stronger," says DeVries. He's come closer to us, apparently wanting to hear the argument. "Whatever's down that corridor, it's powerful."

"And it might be behind that door. The source. Think of that," Roderick says.

"I do," I say. "Then I remember that through another door was a seemingly empty room where both my mother and my friend died. I don't want to risk both of you."

"What if this isn't stealth tech?" Mikk asks. "Then we're risking all of you."

"It's stealth tech," I say. "I can hear it."

They look at me. No one except the few of us who can hear stealth tech understands what I mean. Not all of the Six can hear it. I'm not sure what the difference is, but it's an important one.

And I think it's a good, nonscientific way to recognize stealth tech—at least for people like me.

Someone behind me drops an equipment box. We all jump. The sound echoes in the enclosed space.

"Risk is what we signed on for," Rea says. He has gained a lot of confidence in the past few weeks. "We're going in."

"Maybe we should tether," Mikk says to me. "So we can pull you all out if there's a problem."

I shake my head. "If there's a problem, then the tether might decay before you realize we're in trouble. I'm not sure how far the field extends. It might only be a few meters, but it might be more than that."

Mikk frowns at me. He's right. We need some kind of backup.

I say, "Here's what I'll do. I'll station two divers at the first junction. Two more near the door, and then three of us will go inside—provided we can open it, of course. If we can, one will remain near the door, recording, while two of us start mapping."

"I don't like it," Roderick says.

"I know," I say because I can't say what I'm thinking, which is, *I don't care what you like. This is what we're going to do.* "It's our best option."

"Your best option," one of the guide says loudly, "is to go home."

That would be true of most anyone else. But I have no real home. Just a mission.

I'm not sure how the others feel, and I'm not going to ask them. They did sign on, and they will do the work.

And I hope—no, I pray—that each one of us will come out alive.

TEN

*A*ge and time have warped the door shut. It takes all five of us to pry the edges away from the frame, but once we do, the door moves with surprising ease. I pull on the lever, and the door squeals open.

As it does, lights go on. Red lights at first, flaring like warning lamps, and then they turn green before they fade to white.

Lights turn on in the corridor as well—along the floor, though, where I hadn't thought to look. A quick check makes me realize that these lights are recessed. There was no way to locate them under the flaked particles until they revealed themselves.

The lights coming on scared the two at the junction. They use the comm to see if we're all right, and I reassure them. Only after we sign off do I realize they also want to know what has gotten loose. They're so untrained they think someone else has turned on the lights, not that the door triggered them.

I bite back irritation and peer inside.

What faces me is not a room, but a cavern. And it's not empty. It's filled with equipment. Old equipment that's slowly powering up. I can hear the whines as it restarts, see the lights on the consoles flicker on, watch as screens sparkle to life.

Rea curses.

DeVries makes a sound of awe.

I make no sound at all. I'm staring at the wording on the floor.

It's in Old Earth Standard, a language I've been learning because it's the language of the Dignity Vessels.

I flick the comm inside my suit, hailing Roderick and Mikk. I've never tried to communicate from this deep in the corridors before, and I'm not sure when the two men will get the message—if ever. But I have to send it.

"It's a gold mine," I say. "But you have to stay away. I'm pretty sure now that we're in a stealth-tech field."

And if we are, that message could be lost to time. Or it could be delivered in a blink of an eye.

"Ilona was right, then," Rea says.

I nod. And stare. And wonder how the hell I'm going to keep this secret from the Vaycehnese, and their tourist board, and their publicity machine.

Because the moment they announce a grand discovery, then it'll go out through the sector. Eventually the Empire will figure out what's here.

Eventually, they'll try to take it over.

And then we'll have the fight I've been expecting. The fight I've been preparing for. The fight I want to avoid as long as possible.

The interior of this chamber is huge—too big to be called a room. It goes on as far as the eye can see. The ceiling is domed. The walls, the floor, everything is covered with that black material, and here it hasn't flaked.

We continue to follow the rules, mostly because I'm scared of the traps that lie within. I think of the way the lights came on, and I wonder what else we can trigger—and if that trigger will be harmful, even to those of us with the marker.

I make Kersting take samples from the walls and the floors to see why this area is different than the exterior. I want as much information as possible.

To that end, we plan to map and record every centimeter. We won't make it in one dive—this place is bigger than some cities. We also won't touch the consoles—I'm afraid of triggering something—or the screens. We just look and wave our cameras over each section; then we describe.

For the first time, I miss the scientists. I want their on-scene analyses, something I won't get until we go above ground.

We're timing this dive, like we time all the others, even though I want to stay for the entire day. No one knows the effect of stealth tech on people with the marker, so we are limiting our exposure.

Ivy suggested this the night before we got in the door, and I agreed with her then. I knew I wouldn't once I was inside, and I was right. Even though the field readings—whatever they are—are stronger than anything we've ever seen, I don't feel any effects.

Neither do the Six.

But they're not experienced, and I tend toward the gids—something that happens when oxygen is low. There is no one to monitor us but ourselves, always a dangerous situation, and if we all get the gids, we will make bad choices.

The bad choice that looms is my own. I want to go deep into this chamber. I want to see how far it extends. I want to know everything about it *now*, not weeks from now. I want to know what it is, what it's used for, and why it was abandoned.

For now, I have to satisfy myself with what I can see from the area near the door. Two dozen consoles, linked screens along the walls, and chairs built into the floor.

There is nothing in the middle of the chamber except clear floor—no stains, no markings, nothing. Around the consoles, instructions written in Old Earth Standard in large letters. I recognize only one word.

Danger.

I would have expected nothing less.

The consoles seem uniform except for one about ten consoles down. That one I can't examine yet. From a distance, I note that it's bigger and has more buttons, but that's all I can see.

That the consoles have buttons surprises me. There are flat areas, like we have, areas that imply a touch command. But the buttons suggest that to make things work, someone must press them or move them or toggle them, which I think is terribly inefficient. Over time, the switch itself can decay and make errors.

Another reason not to let anyone touch the consoles. We do record as many as we can from top to bottom, examining the sides and the casing, lingering on the words so that the team outside this room can translate for us.

After we finish the first and second consoles, we're out of time. As I stand, the screen above me flickers to life, and I worry that we've somehow turned it on.

What I see is an image of space. At least, I believe it's space. I'm not sure where or when, for that matter. I don't recognize any of the stars. I have never seen the placement.

"What the hell is it?" Rea asks from behind me. I turn a little, about to explain, when I see what he's looking at.

He's looking at a different screen—the one over the big console. Numbers scroll across it.

"I can't record it," DeVries says. "Can I get closer?"

"No," I say, but the word is hard to utter. I understand his impulse. I want to record too.

Screens farther down the wall have activated as well. One shows the corridor we just left (at least, I think it's that corridor), and another shows blackness growing on some rock.

I curse softly.

"What's the matter, Boss?" DeVries asks.

"I just want to get closer," I lie. I don't want to tell him that I think we've done something here, something that might be irreversible.

My stomach is queasy and I'm feeling light-headed. I get that way when I'm nervous. I also get that way when I'm low on oxygen, before the gids start.

I still hear the humming, but it seems more focused—not singing, exactly, but concentrated, as if someone has compressed the sound.

"We have to go," I say.

"But it's just getting interesting." That from Kersting, who usually hates the long dives.

"It is," I say, "and it'll be interesting tomorrow. Maybe by then, we'll know what some of these readings say."

The entire team groans, but they obey. I make them leave the chamber single-file. I pull the door closed behind us, then press it to make certain that it shut tightly. If that door is a protection between the corridor and the chamber, I want it at full strength.

Then we walk down the corridor. The moment we get past the area where the postdocs died, I send all the information from my comm links back to Mikk, with instructions to have him leave immediately and get the downloads to the scientists.

The other downloads can come out with us. But we need the scientists working hard before our evening meeting. I need some sense of what's going on here.

I need to know if we've done something wrong.

ELEVEN

"**I** think this is where they built the Dignity Vessels," Ilona says. She's set up a holoreplay system in the large conference room, and she's actually using an old-fashioned pointer to tap an image of the center of that chamber.

The rest of the team is scattered around the table. As usual, the hotel has given us a fantastic spread of food. If I'm not careful, I might actually gain weight on this job.

"Dignity Vessels came from Earth," Ivy says. "Everyone knows that."

"But we've never been able to adequately explain how they got out here," Ilona says. "Maybe the specs were brought here, and the vessels were built here."

"Underground?" Bridge asks. "Not likely."

"Maybe there's another way out," Ilona says. "From what I can guess, that chamber is deep in the mountain. Maybe there was an opening like the one we went down, and maybe it closed."

"Or maybe this place has a different function," I say, "one we haven't yet figured out."

Ilona shakes her head. "The words 'vessel' and 'assemble' are everywhere."

"And so is the word 'repair,'" Gregory says. "Maybe this is just a maintenance hub."

"Have you found the phrase 'Dignity Vessel' yet?" I ask.

"No," Ilona says. "But it's only a matter of time."

I look away from her. "Anyone recognize that section of space that appeared on the screen above us?"

"We can't even pinpoint it," Bridge says. "It's not in our database or in the Vaycehnese's or in the sector's either. It's unknown."

"And the numbers?" I ask.

"You didn't get a good enough look for us to examine them," Ivy says.

I know that, but I had hopes.

"What about the console? Any idea what it does?"

"The words are shorthand," Ilona says, setting down her pointer and returning to the place at the table. "Like we would have on a child's console. 'On,' 'Off,' 'Start,' 'Stop,' that kind of thing. But nothing that suggests what comes on or what starts and what stops."

"The intriguing word is in the middle," says Gregory. "'Open.'"

"I didn't find that intriguing," Lentz says, speaking up for the first time since the meeting started. "What I found intriguing was the blinking light over the word 'automatic.' Isn't the entire place automated? What does that mean?"

I lean back in my chair. "I don't know. I was hoping you guys would know by the time we had the meeting."

"This isn't guesswork," Voris says. "We must be precise. You know that, Boss. You're the one who drilled that into us."

Once again, the soft-spoken man makes the best point. I sigh and get up. I can't sit long.

"We know that the team has suffered no ill effects from the dive," Roderick says.

"That have shown up yet," Ivy says. "We don't know what long-term exposure does."

I nod. I've had us checked by medics, our biologists, and several scanners, in addition to the *Business's* decontamination chamber. So far, we're fine.

I'm still not willing to risk a longer dive. But I'm going to violate space rules. I'm going to let all of us dive again tomorrow.

"We're going back in the morning," I say.

Roderick shakes his head. "Boss, you know that's risky."

"I think we activated something. If we wait the standard two days between dives, we might not know what got triggered," I say.

"Maybe saving yourselves," Ivy mutters.

I let that go. For the first time in one of these meetings, I look at Stone. I expect her to take command, but she doesn't. She's watching something on her handheld and taking notes. It's as if this meeting doesn't concern her.

And, at the moment, it doesn't. She can't go into the chamber. She's effectively shut out of everything.

"I'll keep tomorrow's dive short," I say. "But I'm planning to go in every day until we have an idea what's going on."

"You saw the word 'danger' on the floor, right?" Mikk asks.

I nod. "But we don't know what it refers to. And we know how old Earth systems work. If the Earthers believed the chamber was dangerous, that word would have been on the door."

The historians immediately concede the point. The others shrug, all except the Six, who watch me with something approaching fear.

"Come on," I say to them. "Enjoy this. This is probably the most important discovery any of us will ever make."

"And we can't even investigate it," Bridge says.

I look at him. He's sitting with the other scientists. They seem frustrated.

"You can't do good science with recordings," he says. "We need to be hands-on."

"I know," I say. "But I don't know how to get you there until we determine if that field reading we're getting is not stealth tech."

"It has to be," Ilona says.

"It doesn't have to be anything we already know," I say. "The sounds are different. And we're not sure about the technology. We have to be careful."

"I think we're being too careful," she says.

My cheeks heat. "I think it's bad policy to determine what something is in advance. We need to go slowly."

"I am not disputing that," Ilona says. "Just your interpretation of existing data."

I shrug. "Right now, we're all guessing. And I can hardly wait until the guessing ends."

"Me, too," says Ivy. "Because I keep looking at that word, 'danger,' and wonder what you're dragging the team into."

"The Boss always takes us to risky places," Roderick says. "If you don't like it, you can leave."

But Ivy remains seated. So does everyone else, including—to my relief—the Six.

"Okay," I say. "A short dive tomorrow. Maybe after that, we'll have some answers."

TWELVE

he chamber looks no different when we return. The lights are still on. The numbers run on that screen ten consoles down the wall. The screen above me shows that weird spacescape. The consoles glow.

I am more convinced than ever that we shouldn't touch anything. But now I'm willing to fan out just a little. I let Rea handle the middle of the room with DeVries beside him. I send Seager and Kersting to the space to the right of the door. They'll never make it to the far wall—not today—but at least we're moving.

After about an hour, I look up from my examination of the second console. Something has changed, although I don't know what it is.

Then I realize that the screen above the first console has gone dark. I stare at it, and realize that I'm wrong. The screen isn't dark. It's showing complete blackness.

The dark screens have a different look and texture. This one is showing a view of someplace completely without light.

In spite of myself, I shudder. Then I glance at the other screen—the numbers screen. I can't tell for sure, but it looks like they've changed too.

I turn toward the rest of the crew to tell them and see Rea a few meters from me in that broad expanse of floor.

He must catch something in my body language, because he says, "It's easy to map a floor and emptiness."

I nod. He's right, of course. But he's doing something besides mapping, something that he stopped doing as I turned.

"You were moving funny," I say. It's just a guess, but that's the sense that I had, that he was making odd movements.

"Flapping my arms." There's a smile in his voice. I wish I can see his face. "I figure if our movement triggers the lights, maybe my movement will trigger some lights buried in the floor."

"What's in that floor might be what the ancients called danger," I say.

"Or not," he says. "So far, I have had no results."

"Well, stop it," I say. "Just map."

He sighs, but lets his arms fall. He's going to listen.

I start to turn back toward the console when the air waves. Like heat mirages. The air is actually rippling.

My breath catches. I turn toward Rea and realize that the rippling is stronger near him. Has he created it? Or is something happening there?

"Rea!" I yell. "Run!"

He doesn't seem to understand.

"Get out of here!" I yell.

The others head for the door. I do too. Rea moves a little slower. The rippling gets worse. He looks like a video that's falling apart. Then he slides out of the area and gets to the doorway.

Something whooshes behind me.

I whirl and blink, unable to believe what I'm seeing.

A Dignity Vessel is parked in that broad expanse of floor. An intact, clean, vibrating Dignity Vessel.

I murmur something—a curse maybe, or just a sound of awe. I'm aware of making noise, but not of what kind of noise I'm making. Rea pushes up against me.

DeVries says, "Oh, my . . ."

No one else speaks.

"Was there something solid on that floor when you were there?" I ask Rea.

He shakes his head.

"I was standing there," he says. "I would've been crushed."

The ripples. That Dignity Vessel became visible. We just saw the transition between stealth mode and nonstealth mode. Or something like that.

I glance at the numbers screen. It has stopped on the last set. Nothing runs. Then I look at the other screens. The one that had gone black now shows a black room with little white figures in it. Human-shaped.

It takes me a moment to realize those figures are us. We're seeing ourselves in our suits staring at the screen.

Looking away from the camera. Which has to be on the Dignity Vessel.

It wasn't in stealth mode in this chamber. It had been somewhere else until a little while ago. Somewhere with that strange patch of space.

"We triggered it," I say.

"What?" DeVries asks.

"I think we summoned it back here." I make myself record everything— the screens, the changes in the console.

"What do you mean, we summoned it?" Rea asks.

I shouldn't say this, with all my lectures about theories and suppositions. But I do. "We entered the chamber and it came alive. When it did, it must have sent some kind of message—maybe that someone is here. Maybe that the chamber is functional again. It called the vessel here."

"Called it home," DeVries says softly. "Ilona *was* right. This is where they were built."

I shake my head. "She's right about the stealth, and she's right that Dignity Vessels are connected here. But look at this chamber. The vessel fills this part. There's no room to build. This is an arrival port or a maintenance unit."

"Or both," Rea says.

"That's why the danger," I say. "No one can stand where you were. There's not enough warning to get out of the way."

No klaxons, no bells. I glance up. The ceiling didn't open. Nothing changed except the vessel appeared here.

"I'll bet there's a death hole on the surface," I say.

"Above us?" Kersting asks.

I shake my head. "Maybe around us. Behind us. Horizontal. Taking some of the force of that extra stealth energy."

"That's what death holes are?" Rea asks.

"It's a guess," I say. It's all a guess. Until we can examine everything.

I walk forward. A functioning Dignity Vessel. Probably with some kind of homing program, some way to come back here to this base.

If our entry has called one vessel home, how many others will come?

Maybe not many. Of all the Dignity Vessels we've found, none have been functional.

This one is, by some miracle.

This one is.

SECTOR BASE V

THIRTEEN

They landed smoothly, which surprised the hell out of Coop. The *Ivoire* had suffered more damage than he ever could have imagined, and yet the venerable old craft had gotten them here, mostly in one piece.

For a brief moment, he bowed his head. He took a deep breath and let a shudder run through him—the only emotion he'd allowed himself in more than a week.

Then he raised his head and looked.

The walls had full screens, top to bottom, just like he'd ordered. It didn't matter much when the *Ivoire* transitioned, but now that the ship had arrived at Sector Base V, the walls told him a lot.

A lot that he didn't understand.

The *Ivoire* had landed inside the base, just like usual. The ship stood on the repair deck, just like it was supposed to.

The base was cavernous. It had to be. Like the other ships of her class, the *Ivoire* was large. She comfortably housed five hundred people, providing family quarters, school, and recreation in addition to being a working battleship. Two ships the size of the *Ivoire* could fit into this base, with another partially assembled along the way.

Not to mention the equipment, the specialized bays, the private working areas.

The sector base was huge and impossible to process all at once.

But what Coop could process looked wrong.

For one thing, no one manned the equipment. Much of it looked like it wasn't even turned on. The lights were dim or off completely. The workstations—the ones he could see in the half-light—looked like they'd suffered minor damage.

But he didn't know how they could have. Like all the sector bases, Sector Base V was over a mile underground in a heavily fortified area. No one could get in or out without the proper equipment.

To his knowledge, no sector base had ever been attacked, not even in areas under siege. Granted, his knowledge wasn't as vast as the history of the Fleet, but he knew how difficult it was to damage a sector base

Although it looked like someone had harmed this one. Because it had been fine a month ago.

Before the battles with the Quurzod, he'd brought the *Ivoire* in for its final systems check and repair. He had known that he wouldn't get another full-scale repair for a year, maybe more. Particularly if the Fleet conquered the Quurzod and moved on, like planned. Then the *Ivoire* and the other ships in the Fleet wouldn't get the full-scale treatment for five years. It would take that long to build Sector Base W, at the edges of the new sector of space.

He hadn't planned on ever returning here.

He certainly hadn't planned on returning here in defeat.

Or what felt like defeat.

And now the base looked wrong.

"You sure we're seeing Sector Base V?" he asked Dix Pompiono.

Dix stood at the station farthest from Coop, in case the bridge got hit. Dix figured that if as much distance as possible separated them, one of them would survive.

Coop had always figured if the bridge got hit, the entire vessel would disappear. The *anacapa* drive—small as it was—was located on the bridge itself. If the drive took a direct hit, then the drive's protections would fail. Half the ship would be in this dimension, half in another—if they were lucky. If they weren't, the entire thing might explode.

Maybe it was the half-and-half dimensions that made Dix want to stay separate from Coop. They'd never discussed it, and they weren't about to now.

"It sure as hell doesn't look like Sector Base V," Dix said. "But the readings say it is."

It looked like Sector Base V to Coop. He recognized some of the specialized equipment, built with parts of the indigenous rock.

"We're in the right point in space," said Anita Tren. She stood at her post, even though her built-in chair brushed against her backside.

"Have you confirmed that we're under Venice City?" Coop asked.

Venice City, the latest settlement. "Latest" was technically accurate, but the location, on the most remote planet in this sector, had been settled fifty years before Coop was born. At his first visit here, on his tenth birthday, he had thought the city old.

His father had laughed at that, telling Coop there were places in this sector that had been colonized for thousands of years. Human habitation, his father had said, although no one knew where those humans had originated.

The Fleet, everyone knew, originally came from Earth, but so long ago that no one alive had seen the home planet or even the home solar system. Earth felt like a myth, something rare and special and lost to time.

The base looked dimmer than usual. The equipment seemed smaller in the emptiness. Some lights were on, but not many. And the bulk of the base disappeared into the darkness.

"Is something wrong with the screens, then?" Coop asked Yash Zarlengo.

She had left her station. She had walked up to the nearest wall screen and was investigating it with her handheld, as well as with the fingertips of her left hand.

"I'm not reading any problems. These images are coming from the ship's exterior just like they should be," she said.

Coop frowned and wished, not for the first time, that the original Fleet engineers had thought it proper to build portals into the bridge. He would like to do a visual comparison of what he saw on the wall screens with what he saw out the portal.

But he would have to leave the bridge to do that.

So he snapped his finger at the most junior officer on deck, Kjersti Perkins. She didn't even have to be told what he wanted. She nodded and exited.

Perkins would have to walk three-tenths of a mile just to get to the nearest portal. The bridge was in the nose of the ship, completely protected by hull. The original engineers had thought the portals were for tourists, and didn't insert any until the ship widened into its residential and business wings.

But Coop couldn't just worry about what was outside the ship. He also had to worry about what was inside the ship.

"Give me updated damage reports," he said.

"Nothing new," Yash said, which was a relief. Coop had been expecting more damage all over the ship. Normal activation of the *anacapa* drive often revealed weak spots in the ship, and this activation had been anything but normal.

It had been desperate—more desperate than he ever wanted to admit.

Fifteen days of drift—full engine failure, at least on the standard engines. The *anacapa* had worked—it had gotten them there, after all, wherever there was, which none of them could exactly figure out. It seemed like they'd moved dimensions just like they were supposed to, but something had gone wrong with the navigation equipment, confirmed by scans.

An asteroid field where there shouldn't be one. A star in the proper position, but not at the proper intensity. A planet with two moons instead of the expected three.

Nothing was quite right, and yet a lot was. Coop hadn't even wanted to think about the possibilities.

He hadn't dared.

He'd set up the distress beacon, the one tied to the *anacapa*, so that it could reach any nearby bases, and prayed for an answer.

Which hadn't come.

So he'd increased the scans. The *Ivoire* hadn't been able to move yet—not with a regular drive, anyway, although repairs were coming along, as the engineers said—but everything else seemed to be working.

They should have gotten a response from two different bases: Sector Base V and Sector Base U, which was at the very edge of their range. Not to mention Starbase Kappa, which—according to the records—wasn't that far from here.

Nothing. He'd left the signal on, but had checked it and had asked the science whiz kids in the school wing to work the design for a new signal, something a little less formal, he said, and he'd told their teacher what he really wanted was for them to build a new signal from scratch.

Just in case the old one had been damaged in the fight with the Quurzod, and somehow that damage hadn't registered. He couldn't spare the engineers to do the work. He needed the students more than he ever had before.

He hadn't told the teacher that, but she clearly figured it out. She looked grimly determined and told him the kids would get on the project right away.

They were only half done when Dix caught the edge of a reply.

Automated from Sector Base V: *We have heard your distress signal. We are prepared to use our own drive to bring you to us. If that is what you need, turn on your* anacapa *drive now.*

Without a second thought, Coop turned on the drive, and the *Ivoire* whisked out of the drift, their drive piggybacking on Sector Base V's.

The *Ivoire*'s journey took half a minute, maybe less. They were drifting in an unknown part of space, and then they weren't.

Then they were here, in Sector Base V, beneath the mountains that towered over Venice City.

They were here and they should have been safe.

But they weren't.

Coop had a sense they were in more trouble than they'd ever been in before.

FOURTEEN

A Dignity Vessel.

An intact, functioning Dignity Vessel. My heart rate has increased and my breathing is shallow. My environmental suit issues warnings, thinking I'm in space, thinking I could die at any moment.

If I were wreck diving, my team on the skip would be talking to me via the comm. They'd tell me to leave the dive, return to the skip.

They'd accuse me of having the gids.

But the four in this room aren't experienced divers. I haven't even told them to turn on their monitors to monitor each other's suits. They should have thought of it themselves; after all, they've gone on practice dives.

Not that it matters.

We're not in space.

I make myself take a deep breath, will my heart rate to slow, will the gids to go away. Even though they're not the gids.

What I'm feeling is excitement.

I've seen a few intact Dignity Vessels, and they are pitted and scarred and ruined and empty.

This one—this one glimmers with newness.

Finally, my brain kicks in. "Check the environment," I tell the team. "Make sure nothing has changed."

Our readings so far have shown that we're in an oxygenated environment. We could survive without the suits, but we don't. I'm glad for that since flakes swirl around us.

The Dignity Vessel has disturbed the entire area. The ripples caused some kind of disturbance, which makes sense. One moment the area in front of me was empty; the next it was filled with a gigantic ship.

I feel tiny beside it.

Here, in this cavernous room, I get a true sense of how big a Dignity Vessel is. They look tiny in space because space is so vast.

Here, though, here the vessel is bigger than any building we've seen on Vaycehn, bigger than some active spaceports.

I have to force myself to take another breath. In fact, I have to use a trick Squishy taught me back when we dived together. I count my breaths—inhaling for five seconds, exhaling for five seconds—until my breathing evens.

I'm having trouble concentrating on the breathing. I'm having trouble concentrating at all.

I've never dreamed I'd be in this position.

All of my life, I've chased history. I've dived the oldest, most decayed wrecks I could find, not to loot them, but to study them, to learn about them.

The history of the sector is rich and vast, and we've forgotten ever so much more than we learned. I'm firmly convinced that no one person can know everything that has happened in this sector since humans started colonizing it. Every historian I know specializes, in a culture, in a war, in a planet or a technology.

None of them are generalists about the sector, although we all learn sector history—its broad sweep from early colonization to the beginnings of the Empire to the Colonnade Wars.

We study it. We imagine it.

We don't see it.

Not as it was.

And yet, here before me is a piece of history. Not decayed or damaged by time. Not ruined by some long-ago battle. Not abandoned centuries before I was born.

Glistening, shimmering ever so slightly. Making slight noises as its hull adjusts to the temperature inside the cavern—a temperature that has dropped precipitously because this vast ship in front of me has brought the coldness of space with it.

I swallow hard. My breathing is finally regular. I take another step toward the ship.

"It's colder in here than it was," Kersting says. "But otherwise, I get the same readings."

"Yeah," Rea says. "You'd think that there'd be something different in the air. Maybe less oxygen or some hint of a fuel or something. But I'm not getting anything either."

"Me, either," DeVries says.

"Is it really there?" Seager asks.

Good question. I suspect the ship is in front of me because of the temperature differential, but none of us has touched the ship. We haven't even gone near it.

For all we know, this is some kind of elaborate illusion, something designed to keep us away from the platform.

My stomach twists at the thought. I want the thing before me to be a Dignity Vessel—a real, functioning Dignity Vessel, not an illusion designed to chase people from the cavern.

"Let me find out," I say.

"Boss, one of us should deal with it." Rea takes a step toward me.

I turn slightly and shake my head. "I know what I'm doing." With wrecks, anyway, which this decidedly is not. "You stay there."

I walk to the ship's side. The external temperature recorded by my suit has lowered even more. Something is in front of me, or else the illusion is so grand that it includes temperature.

I wonder if it includes smell as well. I'm not willing to take off my helmet to find out.

I stop only centimeters from the ship. The side is smooth, black, and shiny, like the new walls at the exterior of the caves. I expected something more metallic. The Dignity Vessel we found all those years ago—the first Dignity Vessel, the one that started me on this path that led me to Vaycehn—had a metal hull and rivets holding plates together.

This has no rivets, no bolts, no old-fashioned parts. The side is so smooth that I can see my reflection in it.

Through the particles, that is. The particles are flaking off the walls, not the ship. The ship's side is as smooth as glass.

My suit pings me. I'm holding my breath again. I make myself breathe; then I extend a hand before I can talk myself out of it. I press my palm against the ship's side.

It's solid beneath my glove. The suit protests—the ship is so cold the glove adheres to it for just a moment, and then releases. I have the suit take readings from the surface.

"It's real," I say with more relief than I intended. "It's real."

FIFTEEN

*P*erkins returned quicker than Coop expected. She had to have scurried down those corridors.

"It's the same," she said, somewhat breathlessly. "The view's the same."

He had expected that, and yet had hoped for a different outcome. Dix bent over his console. So did Anita. They checked their readings again, probably for the fifteenth or sixteenth time.

Coop took a deep breath. He didn't need the repeated readings. The equipment said they were in Sector Base V, so they had to be in Sector Base V.

A different Sector Base V than the one he had left a month ago.

He ran a hand over his face. The *anacapa* created a fold in space. That was how the ships continued to travel through hundreds of years. They rarely got damaged in battle, and when they did, they could go elsewhere to repair. The Fleet had learned long ago how to do extensive repair in space, but they had also learned that sometimes parts simply wore out. Repair could only do so much, particularly when spread over hundreds of years, thousands of battles, and countless trips via the *anacapa* drive.

That was why the Fleet built settlements on hospitable planets, usually choosing a mountainous region, always picking a hard-to-reach (by ground) location far from the main civilizations (if there were any). The settlements were mostly underground and were never considered permanent.

Sector Base N, for example, had been abandoned for nearly four hundred years. No one from the Fleet went back to that sector, so they didn't need the base.

Although on every settlement, a handful of people chose to stay. Some married into the indigenous population. Some simply liked life planetside better than life in space, although Coop never understood why.

As a kid, he'd thought about all those lost bases like he thought about the nearly mythical Earth, and wondered what it would be like to return to them.

His father kidded him, saying Coop was the only child whose adventurous spirit turned backward instead of forward.

Coop let his hand drop away from his face. Then he looked at the wall screens again.

"It doesn't make sense," he muttered.

The others were watching him. He wasn't sure how many of them knew what he was thinking.

And he wasn't exactly sure what he was thinking. Had someone left the base's *anacapa* drive active, even though the base had been under attack? That didn't make sense, because every commander—on base and on ship—was instructed to shut off an *anacapa* drive before enemy capture.

Shut off, or destroy.

Even though the Fleet had traveled all over the known universe, it had never encountered another civilization with an *anacapa* drive. They had encountered other marvelous technology, but never anything as sophisticated and freeing as the *anacapa*.

Without the *anacapa*, the Fleet could never have continued on its extensive mission. Without the *anacapa*, the Fleet would never have left its own small sector of space around Earth.

The *anacapa* had enabled the Fleet to travel great distances, carrying its own brand of justice and its own kind of integrity to worlds far and wide.

Had the *anacapa* drive here in Sector Base V malfunctioned, forcing everyone to leave? He'd heard of malfunctioning *anacapa* drives before. They were one of the most dangerous parts of the Fleet. A ship with a malfunctioning drive sometimes had to be destroyed to protect the Fleet and anything around it.

But that made no sense either. Because the *anacapa* drive inside all the sector bases was tied to working equipment. Not just working equipment, but equipment that had been turned on and used manually by a human being within the past twenty-four hours.

It was a failsafe, designed by some far-seeing engineer—or, as Coop's father would have said, designed by a professional worrier, someone who tried to see all the problems and plan for them.

The failsafe had been designed to prevent exactly this kind of problem: a ship, arriving in an empty base, could get trapped. If the *anacapa* didn't work, and the corridors leading to the surface had collapsed, then the ship— and more important, its crew—wouldn't be able to escape above ground.

The human failsafe was necessary because no one knew—even now, after generations of using the drives—how long an *anacapa* could survive without maintenance. There were some in the Fleet who believed that an *anacapa* drive would remain functional long after the human race had disappeared from the universe.

The human race hadn't disappeared. The *anacapa* drive still worked. But something had happened in the repair area. Something bad.

"Should we go out there, see what went wrong?" Perkins asked.

No one answered her. She specialized in communication. She spoke fifteen languages fluently, another forty haphazardly, and had a gift for picking up new languages all the time. She wasn't as good as Coop's former wife, Mae, the *Ivoire*'s senor linguist. But Mae had come back from her experience with the Quurzod damaged. As she healed, she worked on the communications systems, not on the bridge.

"We can't go out there yet," Coop said. "We need to know what we're facing."

"You think the base was attacked?" Dix asked.

"Possible," Coop said. He didn't want to reveal his suspicions any more than that. He wanted the bridge crew to explore all options. "Let's figure out what's going on here before we make any moves."

"Sir?" Yash sounded strange.

He glanced at her.

She was pointing at an area on the wall screen. A woman walked toward the ship's exterior. The woman was thin. She wore a form-fitting environmental suit of a type Coop had never seen before. She had cylinders attached to the belt on her hip and what looked like a knife hilt.

He could only get a glimpse of her angular face through her helmet.

As he watched, she reached out and put her gloved hand on the *Ivoire*'s side.

"Is she the one who attacked us?" Perkins asked.

"We don't know if the base was attacked," Coop said.

"But it's been abandoned," Perkins said.

"There could be a variety of reasons for that." This time, Dix answered her. But he didn't elaborate and neither did Coop.

But Perkins wasn't dumb. Just inexperienced. "So is that woman part of a repair crew?"

"I don't think so," Yash said. "I don't recognize her suit."

"It could be special hazmat suits from Venice City itself," Anita said.

Perkins's eyes opened wider. "Hazmat? So it's toxic out there?"

Coop shrugged. "We don't know anything yet. All we know is that we're here, nothing is as it was when we left, and a woman is in the repair room. We don't even know if it's a woman we've met before. I can't see her face clearly, can you?"

"No," Dix said.

"But she's human, right?" Perkins asked.

"What else would she be?" Yash asked with a touch of impatience. The

Fleet, in all its travels, had never discovered an alien race, not as the Fleet defined it, anyway, which was a nonstandard, unexpected life-form of equal intelligence to humans.

"I don't know," Perkins said. "That woman looks weird."

Perkins's voice held an edge of panic. She'd felt responsible for the Quurzod disaster, even though the fault didn't lie with the linguists. She had held up well during the fifteen days in that unrecognizable area of space, but she must have been clinging to the thought that everything would be fine when they reached Sector Base V.

And now everything wasn't fine. It was enough to break a more experienced officer.

"When was the last time you slept, Kjersti?" Coop asked.

She looked at him sideways, understanding in her eyes. She knew that he had caught the beginnings of panic in her voice, knew that he was about to send her to her quarters.

"I'm fine," she said.

"Go rest," he said.

"Sir—"

"Kjersti," he said. "Go rest."

She straightened, recognizing the order. "Whom should I send to replace me?"

"No one," he said. "Not just yet. I'll send for you if we need anything."

She nodded, thanked him, and left the bridge.

The others watched, knowing they were as tired, as worried, and maybe even as panicked. They just had more experience and knew how to push the emotions away.

"Are we getting any readings on the environment out there?" Coop asked. "Any idea at all why that woman is in an environmental suit?"

"Everything reads normal," Yash said.

"But that stuff floating around her," Anita said. "What's that?"

Coop didn't see floating material. The entire repair room looked dim to him. Clearly Anita saw something. But she was closer to the wall screen.

"Maybe that's the hazardous material," Dix said.

"We don't know if it's hazardous out there," Coop said. "Perhaps the suit is just an excess of caution."

"Why would she be cautious about a base underneath a mountain?" Dix asked.

"Tunnel collapse?" Anita said.

"Sometimes planets themselves create a hazardous environment. When they built Sector Base S, they encountered a series of methane pockets," Yash said.

Everyone looked at her.

She shrugged.

"We had to study base building in training," she said. "Sector Base S is a cautionary tale. We actually learned how to build without exposing anyone to underground surprises."

"They weren't building anything here," Coop said.

"But a groundquake, a volcanic eruption, an explosion on the surface might hurt the integrity underground and cause something like Sector Base S encountered," Yash said.

"Wouldn't methane show up in the readings?" Anita asked.

"I'm not trusting anything we're getting right now," Yash said. "Some of the damage the *Ivoire* suffered is pretty subtle. We've only been focused on the major stuff. Once we look at everything, we might discover that some of the things we think are minor are more serious than we initially thought."

Coop had a hunch all of the damage on the *Ivoire* was major. But he had been operating from that principle from the beginning. He had been relieved when the trip through foldspace to here hadn't completely destroyed the *Ivoire*.

"Any way to hail that woman?" Dix asked.

Coop had just let his linguist go. He wasn't going to try to contact strangers without a linguist on deck.

"See what readings you can get off the base's equipment," he said to Yash.

"I'll do what I can," she said. "A lot of the equipment is still inactive."

"Inactive?" Coop said, startled. "Shouldn't it be dormant?"

That was the customary thing to do in leaving a base. If the area was safe enough to leave the *anacapa* drive functional, then the equipment around it needed to function as well. It had to remain dormant so that the touch of a human being could bring the equipment up on a moment's notice.

"Yes, it should be dormant," Yash said. "But these things were shut off."

"And the *anacapa* remained functional?"

She opened her hands in a how-should-I-know gesture. "Right now, nothing's working like it should."

"Is that because of a malfunction in the *Ivoire*?"

"Honestly, Coop," she said, dispensing with the "sir" now that Perkins was gone, "I have no idea. I won't know until I get out there and investigate."

He looked at the wall screen. "None of us is going out there until we know who these people are and what the hell's going on."

"How do you propose we find that out, then?" Dix asked.

"We be patient," Coop said.

"There could be an immediate threat," Dix said.

"There could be," Coop said. "But right now, we're getting no indication of that."

"Except an empty base, a stranger in the repair room, and malfunctioning equipment," Dix said.

"We waited fifteen days to get here," Coop said, "with a crippled ship and no answers to our distress calls. We were patient. We got here."

"Where things aren't good," Dix said.

"They're better than they were," Coop said. "We're not in an unidentified part of space. In that room, there are things that will help us repair this ship. If we're patient, we'll be able to fix the *Ivoire* and catch the Fleet."

"If that woman doesn't attack us," Anita said.

Coop gave her a sideways look. She wasn't speaking out of panic. She was just throwing out a possibility.

"One woman? Who happens to be carrying a knife? What do you think she'll do, Anita, stab the *Ivoire* to death?"

He hadn't meant to be that sarcastic. He was tired, too. And a bit worried about what he was seeing here. But no longer worried that the five hundred people in his charge would die on the ship in foldspace.

But whether or not they would die under Venice City was another matter. He was going to take this slowly, no matter what his crew wanted.

"How are our weapons systems?" he asked Yash. He hadn't had cause to ask since they activated the *anacapa* to get away from the Quurzod. Nothing had approached them for fifteen days.

"We've repaired some of them," Yash said, "but nothing we can fire down here."

"Why not?" Coop asked.

"Because the walls are made of nanobits just like the hull of the *Ivoire*," she said. The Fleet's technology was nanobased, with the help of the *anacapa* drive. The drive powered the technological change on a planet, essentially powering the nanobits that sculpted the interiors of mountains into the best bases he'd ever found in the known universe. "The shots will bounce off. They'll ricochet until the energy is spent."

"Damaging nothing," Coop said.

"Except the equipment," Yash said, "and anyone who happens to be in the repair room."

"Exactly," he said.

"But these weapons weren't meant to be fired in atmosphere," she said. "If there's a methane leak, for example, then we might have another kind of explosion."

"Or an *anacapa* malfunction," Dix said.

"The weapons won't cause an *anacapa* malfunction," Yash said.

"I know," Dix said. "I meant if their *anacapa* has malfunctioned . . ."

"It hasn't," Coop said. "It got us here."

Yash gave him a sideways look. He knew that look. It was one that cautioned him to silence. The two of them had served together since they were cadets, and they had bolstered each other from the beginning.

"You disagree," he said to her.

"Even a malfunctioning *anacapa* could have had enough energy to get us here," she said.

"Great," he said. "So we're back to square one. We won't know anything until we get out there and take some readings. And we're not going to do that as long as those outsiders are here."

He walked over to that part of the wall screen and peered at the woman. She was still touching the *Ivoire*'s exterior, as if she could gather information about the ship through the palm of her glove.

For all he knew, she could.

Her face was barely visible inside the helmet. He couldn't really make out her features, but he thought she looked intrigued. Like she hadn't expected the *Ivoire*. Maybe she hadn't. Maybe she knew the Fleet was long gone.

She tilted her head. It felt like she could see him.

But he knew that wasn't true. She couldn't see him at all. She probably didn't even know he was there.

"What's she doing?" Anita asked.

Coop shook his head. He had a theory—he always had theories, and he'd learned it was never wise to share them, at least not when he led a mission. Always better to gather information.

Behind her, he saw movement. Four others, huddled near the exterior door, nearly lost in the gloom.

Only it wasn't really gloom. The woman was teaching him that. Particles floated in the air around her. They were coating the exterior of the ship, which was probably why the base looked so damn dark.

Apparently he was finally able to see the stuff that Anita had been referring to.

"There's some kind of substance on the exterior of the ship," he said. "Look at her hand. It's clearer than everything else."

Her gloved hand. She had placed her palm flat against the ship. The glove was white, so tight that he could see the ridges in her palm, the bend of her fingers.

She knew nothing about the vessel. None of the outsiders did. From the way they huddled, they seemed frightened by it.

Of course, he was guessing. But they were human, and their body language wasn't aggressive. It was protective.

"Do you have a visual of our arrival?" he asked Dix.

"I'm sure we do," Dix said.

"Let's see it. Center screen."

Dix floated his fingers over his console. It took a moment, but the screen in the center of the bridge went dark, replaced by the shimmer created by the *anacapa* whenever a ship was about to arrive at its destination.

The shimmer looked silver, then slowly resolved into an image of the repair area's interior. The equipment, looking just as odd, the screens over the command consoles, showing what the ship was seeing just like they'd been programmed to do. Redundant imagery at the moment, but useful most of the time. The repair crew could look and see what a ship saw as it traveled to the base.

Sometimes they could even figure out where the damage was because of something coming through the feed.

So the screens were working, which he hadn't noticed after they arrived. Then he looked at the floor itself. It had yellow lines, outlining the landing area, and DANGER! written all across the face, so that no one would accidentally step on the pad.

Sometimes the repair crew didn't know when a ship was going to arrive. A vessel's *anacapa* drive could shut off and the vessel would appear on the landing platform, not realizing that the ship had just appeared where a human being had been standing.

Someone had been standing there in the feed. Someone wearing an environmental suit similar to the woman's.

Similar, but not the same.

So this wasn't a military team, then. Private? They didn't have matching suits.

The person—a man, Coop guessed just from his general shape—whirled as if in response to someone calling his name. The man hesitated for just a moment—and then he sprinted off the platform, diving toward the main door just as the ship settled.

Coop could barely make out the five people huddled against the door. All of their helmeted faces were turned toward the ship, but none of the people moved.

While Coop had been relieved, while he was trying to figure out where he was and what had happened, they had been trying to figure out what they were seeing.

Eventually, they determined that it was safe enough to approach the ship.

"Thanks," Coop said to Dix. "That answered a lot of questions."

And created a whole hell of a lot more.

SIXTEEN

"Boss?"

I'm standing beside the Dignity Vessel, my glove still pressed against it, staring at the hull before me as if I can see through it.

"Boss?" Kersting sounds nervous. "Shouldn't we get out of here?"

I don't move. I want to explore every centimeter of this vessel. "What are you afraid of, Rollo?"

"What if there are, you know, creatures in there?" He offers that last as if he believes it and is afraid we won't.

"Creatures?" DeVries's voice has a smile in it. "*Creatures?*"

"You know." Kersting sounds terrified now. Terrified and embarrassed.

"There's probably a better chance that we'll find bodies rather than creatures," I say. Or worse. An entire contingent of legendary heroes from the famous Fleet.

I shiver, just a little. Not from fear, but from anticipation.

"Bodies? How would they get here?" Kersting asks.

"We triggered something," Rea says.

"So?" Kersting asks.

I glance over my shoulder. The four of them are huddled near the door, as if the ship terrifies all of them, even DeVries, who sounded so mocking a moment ago.

"So the ship could be automatic," Rea says. "This place is."

"You're not going to go in there, are you, Boss?" asks Kersting. I can't tell if he wants me to stay out so we can leave quicker, or if he's afraid of what I'll unleash.

"Not yet," I say. "We need to figure out what this is, when it is, and what is inside."

"We only have ninety minutes left on this dive," Seager says.

Ah, ever practical. I start to say *So?* then stop myself just before the word emerges.

So . . . the rules are mine, and if I'm going to maintain any authority over this crew, I need to follow my own damn rules.

"Yes, we do," I say reluctantly. "We're not going in today."

"What if it's not here tomorrow?" Rea asks.

I nearly take a step backward. I hadn't thought of that, either. I'm so used to historical wrecks that something just as intriguing, but new, challenges my assumptions. This ship *arrived*, which means it can leave any time it wants to.

"Then we need to get as many readings off of it now as we can," I say.

"Are we staying longer?" Rea asks. He wants to as well. I can hear it in his voice.

Stay, and explore, and get tired, and then confront danger. It's a recipe for disaster, and I've had enough disasters in my career, disasters focused on the unknown.

"No," I say. "We leave in less than ninety minutes. But we'll come back after ten hours. If the ship isn't here, we'll leave again, but if it is, then we'll start our explorations."

"Explorations?" Seager asks.

She sounds even more nervous than Kersting. The real thing—a real ship, something dangerous, more dangerous than a tunnel under a mountain in an old city.

Finally they are being faced with the realities of their unique abilities. And at least two of them don't like it.

I can replace them with the other two, who are still standing in the corridor, unaware of what's happening behind this door. Maybe they'll do better.

"We're going to run this like a regular dive," I say. "We'll map before we go any farther."

"Map?" Kersting says. "Have you looked at how big that thing is?"

"It's no bigger than the Dignity Vessels we have back home," DeVries says with even more impatience.

"It seems bigger," Seager mutters.

"It does," I say. "I think that's the effect of the closed space, but let's make sure. The Room of Lost Souls changed sizes. The Dignity Vessels may have come in different models. After all, the exterior on this one looks different from any we've discovered."

I look at them. They haven't moved away from that door. It's as if the door is a lifeline to them, a lifeline to a world of theory and supposition, a world they're used to.

This is the future, and it terrifies them.

It thrills me.

I beckon them. "We need readings, and we're running out of time."

DeVries sighs audibly, but comes toward me, followed by Rea. Kersting hesitates for a moment, then comes as well. Seager brings up the rear, looking not at the ship, but at the space above it.

"How did that ship get in here?" she asks.

"Good question," I say. "I have a hunch we'll have a lot more questions than answers, at least for a while."

"You're comfortable with that?" she asks.

"Boss thrives on it," DeVries says, as if we're old friends. Or maybe he just understands me.

I do thrive on questions. I have enjoyed being on Vaycehn more than I thought simply because there are questions here, historical questions as well as scientific ones. This cavernous room excited me, and I was willing to spend weeks exploring it.

But this ship excites me more.

A living Dignity Vessel. An *active* Dignity Vessel.

Think of all we can learn.

SEVENTEEN

I hate working in atmosphere. I want to float around the ship, investigate all four sides of it, all at the same time.

The shape is the same as all the other Dignity Vessels we've found. It's rather birdlike, with a narrow front and a wide middle, but from where we stand, that wide middle is massive. Beyond it, the ship tapers a bit, but I know that from experience, not from investigating this ship.

The height impresses me the most. Maybe that's why I want to float to the top, so that I can feel as if I've conquered this thing. Right now, it looms over me.

We're not even going to be able to walk around it. We only have sixty minutes left. I've barely made it a few meters. I take readings, I record, I look.

The hull has damage. A lot of damage, in fact. Something has scored the side right near the place where, on the first Dignity Vessel I'd ever found, a hole punched its way toward the bridge.

I remember because that hole was my first warning about stealth tech. My team sent a probe into that hole—following procedure, just like I'm insisting here—and the probe got stuck.

If my team had tried to enter the Dignity Vessel through that hole, they would have gotten stuck in malfunctioning stealth tech. As it was, one of them did get caught in a stealth-tech field inside that bridge, and he died.

He mummified in a matter of hours. I used to think that was the first time I'd seen anything like it, but of course it wasn't.

The first time I had seen it, I had been four years old, trapped in the Room of Lost Souls with my mother.

My mother, who didn't have the genetic marker.

My mother, who died, just like any other unprotected person in stealth tech. She aged rapidly, entering a time field that sped up her future, but left mine alone.

Left me alone.

My father pulled me out. My father, whom I later realized had sent my mother into that field to test her. To test me.

The man was, even then, working to figure out stealth tech.

He became the lead imperial expert on stealth tech. He had managed to use me at the Room of Lost Souls to get his position with the Empire, and in doing so, he killed a friend of mine, just like he killed my mother.

My team—everyone in the company, really—believes that I'm funding stealth-tech research as a vendetta against my father. It doesn't matter that he probably died in an explosion. They think I'm always going to act on some kind of revenge cycle, determined to destroy anything that old man might have created.

I don't think my stealth-tech research is a vendetta. I think it's the only way to maintain the balance of power in the sector.

I have tried, over the years, not to think about what would happen once we understood stealth tech.

Now I'm faced with a working Dignity Vessel, which has arrived inside a cavern with a stealth-tech field, and I know I'm near a breakthrough. I may actually be looking at working stealth tech.

I have to keep this quiet, and I have to understand it.

I might even have to control it.

Somehow.

The scoring near that part of the ship disturbs me. Does that mean the stealth tech in this ship has gone awry as well?

I wish I could climb to the top of this part of the ship. Up there is a hatch—or there should be one—a hatch that will lead me through a shaft that will take me down to a maze of corridors. At the end of those corridors will be the bridge, and inside the bridge, I might actually find functioning stealth-tech controls.

"Boss?" Kersting again. He's probably going to nag about leaving. "I think I've found a door."

I turn, take a step back, and look at his position. He's near the wide part of the ship, inside an area just under one of the curves.

None of the other Dignity Vessels we've found has a door there.

I think.

There are still parts to those ships that we don't understand. And on most of them, entire sections of the ships are missing.

All four of us join Kersting. He has indeed found a door. It's barely out-lined against the blackness. In fact, Kersting found it not by looking, but by running his glove along the surface. The glove found a minor anomaly, something barely visible to the naked eye.

I run my hand over that area as well. My glove tells me that there is a minute crack, one that goes deep.

"I ran my hand all the way around the bottom," Kersting says. "I can't reach the top. But it seems to be a door."

I can't reach the top either. Neither can any of the rest of us. But it does seem to be door-shaped. It's large—twice as large as it needs to be to let in passengers.

It intrigues me. Have we missed this on the other ships?

"Did you find a latch?" I ask Kersting.

"No," he says. "But to be fair, I haven't touched the middle part, just that outline. And not the top either."

I want in. We all want in. But we can't hurry this, no matter how much I want to.

"I guess we start mapping here." I'm smiling as I say it. A Dignity Vessel and a door.

At the moment, the future of stealth tech doesn't matter.

At the moment, all that matters is the mystery before me—and the answers it may provide.

EIGHTEEN

*T*he woman stood outside the *Ivoire* for a very long time. The particles swirled around her, but she ignored them as if she expected them, or perhaps she was used to them. Coop watched her as she touched the side of his ship, as she beckoned the others to join her.

One of them, a different man than the one who had nearly been crushed by the *Ivoire*, found the ship's main exterior door. The outsiders gathered around it, clearly discussing what to do next.

Coop let them. They couldn't get in, not without codes and approvals. Or very powerful weapons.

And none of the five seemed to have weapons, aside from the woman's knife.

"Can you get any readings on the atmosphere inside the repair room?" he asked Yash.

"From what I can tell," she said, "the air seems fine. It seems to be recycling from the outside, just like it was designed to do. But I don't trust the reading."

"Because of the environmental suits," he said.

She shook her head. "Because of the particles. Those things are large, and if they get into lungs, they might do some damage, depending on what they are."

"Are the particles coming in from outside?" Coop asked.

"Doesn't seem that way." Dix was bent over his console. He'd been replaying the entry imagery—Coop had seen some of it as he had walked past Dix's station. "We're coated with those particles and we didn't bring them with us. So they're inside the base."

"We need to get that stuff off the ship," Yash said. "We don't know what it is and whether or not it's doing additional damage."

"We can't do anything as long as those people are so close," Coop said. He didn't want to accidentally kill the outsiders.

"How do we move them?" Dix asked.

"We don't," Coop said. "They're wearing environmental suits. That gives them some kind of time limit. Their oxygen won't last forever."

"What if they're just using some kind of filtration system?" Anita asked.

"Not likely," Yash said. "The woman has cylinders on her hips. Those looked like extra oxygen to me."

"You're guessing," Anita said.

"It's an educated guess," Yash snapped.

Coop glared at both of them. Nerves were getting frayed. He was going to have to relieve this crew relatively soon, even if they didn't know exactly what was going on.

"What kind of readings are you getting from the particles?" he asked Yash.

"Nothing definitive," she said. "But I'm not sure how well the ship's exterior sensors are working."

"Test the exterior sensors on the woman's glove," he said. "Tell me what it's made of."

Yash nodded. Coop moved closer to the woman's image, as close as he could get without pressing his nose against the wall.

"I don't recognize the material," Yash said, "although that's not unusual. It's composed of . . ."

She listed a series of ingredients, talked about how they combined into some kind of microfiber that had incredible tensile strength, and went on at great detail about how effective such material would be in an environmental suit.

Coop paid only the smallest amount of attention, enough to absorb the important information but lose all of the details. The upshot, as he understood it, was simple. The environmental suit, while thin, would work in space and be quite effective on short trips. But the suits on the *Ivoire* were vastly superior.

Yash concluded with, "If that suit's indicative of this culture, then these people are technologically inferior to us."

Which meant that they were far behind developmentally—at least, that would be how the Fleet's playbook called it. Coop didn't always agree with that. In some senses, the Fleet was far behind everyone else. The Fleet was operating on technology built by generations many years in the past. Yes, the engineers knew how to maintain the technology and how to replicate it, but they hadn't really developed anything new.

At least, not on their own.

They had developed additions to the Fleet based on technology they'd discovered as they'd traveled through the stars.

"You can tell all that about the suit," he said to Yash, "but you can't tell me anything about the particles."

"I can't tell you why those people are afraid of them," Yash said. "They seem like flakes off the equipment in the repair room or maybe some nanobits floating free."

"What would cause nanobits to float free?" Anita asked.

"Serious damage to the base," Dix said.

"Or some kind of decay," Yash said. "Something that made the bits' bonding fail."

"Some kind of microscopic weapon?" Coop asked.

"I don't know," Yash said. "I'm going to have to test with actual particles."

"So we're going to need some samples," Coop said. "Since these folks don't believe that the particles will hurt their environmental suits, we can assume our vastly superior suits will do just fine out there."

"You don't want to use one of the small probes, then?" Dix asked. Clearly that was what he had expected, probably what he would have ordered if he had been left in charge.

"I want a quick grab," Coop said, "maybe an airlock test for particulate toxicity, and then I want to explore that room."

More important, he wanted to check the equipment, see the records, figure out what the hell happened here.

"So what are we going to do?" Anita asked. "Are we going to go out there and introduce ourselves to these people?"

Coop shook his head. "They probably don't even know we're here—"

"Don't know we're here?" Anita said. "C'mon, Coop. That woman's been exploring the surface of the ship. She clearly knows we're here."

"She knows the *ship* is here," Coop said. "She doesn't know that we're in it."

"She'd think this thing is automated?" Anita asked.

"Why not?" Coop asked. "The base looks abandoned. That group of five people probably activated the beacon that brought us here. Face it, Anita, if we were all dead, the ship would have come without our guidance. It's designed that way. We turn on the beacon and the *anacapa*s does the rest."

It was another aspect of the failsafe mechanism. If the crew was in any way incapacitated, the ship would come here and, if they were lucky, someone would be here to help.

"You're making a lot of assumptions," Dix said.

"I certainly am," Coop said. "That's why I want some certainty. The sooner we can get out of here and explore that repair room, the happier I'll be."

"But you don't want to meet those people," Perkins said.

"We're going to wait until they leave," Coop said.

"And if another crew comes in after them?" Dix asked.

"We'll analyze the situation then," Coop said. "We have no other choice."

NINETEEN

We map. It seems to take forever. I've never mapped in gravity before.

The Six have cursory training in mapping. I've taken them on exploratory dives, and I've tested each in the ruined Dignity Vessels that we own. But to my knowledge, none of the Six have done real mapping—important mapping—aside from the work they've done in the caverns.

And, honestly, that work is simple compared with this.

We need to know each centimeter of the ship. We look for scoring marks, for damage, for design features and design flaws.

We are all working near the ship's door—all of us except Seager. I've placed her near the door to the room itself. We need to map this room as well, so that we understand all that's inside it.

I feel both overwhelmed and giddy. The gids haven't gone away at all. I'm thrilled by this whole discovery, but the discovery is terrifying in its own way.

I want to get as much information off the ship as I possibly can. Rea's observation that the ship might leave has frightened me. I will spend the rest of my life cursing my own caution if the ship disappears because I didn't investigate it while I could.

If I were younger, I would find a way into the ship. If I were younger, I'd stay in this room until I was too exhausted to leave. If I were younger, I'd find out everything I could before the ship disappeared.

But I'm both older and wiser. Sadly wiser. I've lost friends and colleagues because of mistakes I've made.

And I've learned that I regret the deaths more than the missed opportunities. Opportunities find ways of repeating. Human lives are finite and precious.

I learned that lesson the hard way.

I can't figure out what this ship is made of. I use the cameras on my suit to take images, and I use the chips in my gloves to take readings. I move slowly and wish I could vault upward so that when I finish a section, I'm really and truly done with it.

Right now, I can only map the parts of the ship I can reach. I'm working from eye-level downward, and I wonder what I'm missing. For all I know the latch to the door could be just above me. Or someone might have written the Old Earth Standard word for "danger" across the top.

We'll have to bring in ladders or something to stand on so that we can explore the upper part of this ship.

It seems to hum beneath my fingers, as if it's alive. I'm not sure if that's my gids or my imagination or the ship itself. I'm already imagining that it's the ship, that the ship is operating, even in this enclosed environment.

Of course I have no way to prove that.

A hand touches my arm. I nearly jump. Instead, I turn. It's DeVries.

"Time's up," he says.

I want to finish this small area. There's a dark score near the edge of it, and that's the perfect marker. I'll know where I ended up when I come back in a few hours.

If the ship is still here.

"I'm going to finish this section," I say.

"Boss, we don't have time," he says.

I sigh. "It'll just take a moment."

He tugs at me gently. "Listen," he says. "The worst thing we can do is take too much time and force Mikk to come in after us."

I almost say he wouldn't, but I don't know that. Mikk volunteered once to go into the Room of Lost Souls, even when he knew what it could do to him.

I curse softly and let DeVries lead me away.

The others follow. We meet Seager at the door. She taps a fist nervously against the side of her suit. She wants out; I want to stay in.

DeVries opens the door.

I take one last look at the ship. It gleams in the weird light. It looks like a predator, trapped in a room, and yet I think it oddly beautiful.

It might be gone when I return.

I pray that it'll remain.

I want to say good-bye to it, but I don't.

Instead, I let DeVries push me from the room into the darkened corridor as Rea pulls the door closed behind me.

TWENTY

It took another hour for the outsiders to leave. Coop watched them, both fascinated and tense. Everyone on the bridge remained silent, as if the people outside the *Ivoire* could hear them breathe.

Of course, no one could hear anything. Even though he had opened channels so the sound of the exterior came into the bridge, all he heard was the rustle of the environmental suits the five outsiders wore. They clearly had an internal comm system, one he couldn't seem to tap into.

Four of the outsiders spent some time crowded around the *Ivoire*'s main exterior door, probably discussing how to open it. The woman walked around part of the ship, touching it and peering closely at any change in the hull. The ship was much too large for her to go all the way around.

She was clearly examining it. She kept touching it. Yash believed she was running some kind of diagnostic.

Yash ran a diagnostic on all of them as well, but couldn't gather any more information than she had received from the initial impression she had gotten from the glove.

Coop had explored all kinds of unfamiliar environments in the past, but he had never observed anyone else exploring, and he had never before been the subject of that exploration. If strangers came aboard the *Ivoire*, they had already gone through diplomatic channels through another part of the Fleet. The *Ivoire* was not the flagship of the Fleet. Nor was it designated a first-contact vessel.

Coop had heard of these kinds of explorations, usually by natives of a newly discovered planet, but one that didn't have the technological advancement that allowed the Fleet to contact them. He had never been privy to one before.

Finally, one of the outsiders broke away from the group and loped toward the woman. She shook her head, as if participating in a conversation, and then the other person—one of the men—finally reached her side. He took her arm, gently but firmly.

She shook him off and moved away.

He took her arm again, and this time, she sighed visibly and walked with him around the side of the ship.

They joined the others, and together the group left through the door that led to the corridor.

"Maybe we should lock it." Dix's voice sounded unnaturally loud in the silence of the bridge.

"No," Coop said. "They'd notice that. It would make them more curious."

"I don't know how we can make them more curious," Yash said.

Coop didn't entirely agree with her assessment. If the outsiders were truly curious, they'd try to enter the ship. They would have stayed longer.

Instead, they had left, probably when their environmental suits noted that they were low on oxygen, just like he had predicted.

If that was the case, then the outsiders would be back. He only had a short window of time—and he wasn't sure how short.

"Send that tester through the airlock," he said.

Yash nodded. She had chosen a team of scientists to capture the particles, but the scientists would be monitored by the engineering staff—by Yash, really.

None of the bridge crew had gone down to the main exterior doors. Coop wanted the crew to remain on the bridge in case something went wrong.

He even insisted that a junior member of the science team take the particle sample.

Only two people, wearing their own environmental suits, would be in the airlock. They would take the particulate matter using some method that he didn't entirely understand, and then they would bring it back inside.

Coop wanted them to open the exterior door, scoop up some particles, close the doors, and get the hell out of the airlock.

And that was all.

Even though Dix initially protested. He had felt they should take advantage of the outsiders' absence to explore the room.

Coop had vetoed that. To begin with, exploring the room was the wrong phrase. It was a cavern, impossible to explore all at once. Besides, they'd all been in that area a dozen times before. They needed information, and they were going to collect it slowly.

Coop wondered how long those suits needed to be replenished. He also wondered if the team's leader was reckless. If the leader was, the same team would be back within the hour. If the leader wasn't, either a new team would enter soon, or the other team would wait some designated amount of time, maybe a full day, before returning.

Coop was going to try to get as much done as possible in the time that he had.

He didn't monitor the airlock experiment. He had Yash do that from the bridge.

It only took a few minutes. Some of the particles got into the airlock itself, and Coop asked that they be captured instead of expelled.

"We got everything," Yash said. "It looks like it's safe to go out there."

"Do the extensive tests," Coop said. He wanted to go out there as much as the others, but he had learned about caution the hard way. It was always better to take precautions.

"I'd like to go monitor the experiments," Yash said.

"No," Coop said. "I need you here."

"What for?" she asked. "Standing around waiting?"

He shook his head. "I was thinking we could scrub the particles off the ship's exterior now that the outsiders are gone. You think it's safe to do that?"

Yash shrugged. "The preliminary tests came back that the substance is harmless. Essentially, the particles are the same material as the walls, so far as we can tell. I think it's a bit of a gamble to scrub the ship, but not a major one."

"Scrub it," Coop said.

Yash entered the commands. At least that part of the ship was working. It scaled the particulate matter off its hull in a matter of seconds. More particles floated through the air, but the image on the screens was clearer than it had been just a moment ago.

The repair area was still dim. The lights had faded from their normal brightness to something that looked weak and grayish. Maybe that had something to do with particulate cover on the lights themselves. Coop couldn't know that without a clearer view.

As the particulate matter settled down, he noted that the equipment closest to the exits appeared to be running. He could see lights and some of the screens above the control panels. But as he looked farther into the distance, farther away from the main door, he couldn't see anything. The depths of the repair room seemed particularly dark.

"I still can't get the systems to talk to each other, Coop," Yash said. "I don't think the problem is on our end. I seem to be making an exterior request, but nothing is coming back at us."

He nodded, then folded his hands behind his back.

He was going to have no choice, then.

Someone was going to have to venture into that room.

TWENTY-ONE

"**B**oss? Come in. Boss?"

The moment we step outside the door, I hear Fahd Al-Nasir in my comm links. His voice is tense and strangled, as if he's holding back an even greater emotion.

"Boss? Orlando? Elaine? Anyone?" That's Nyssa Quinte. There's no strangulation in her voice. Just full-on panic. "Someone?"

"I'm here," I say, and I actually hear a sigh of relief, even though I can't tell whose it is.

The corridor seems the same. I can't tell what's different. There are no particles floating here. The lights are as dim as they were when we went in.

"Boss, we need to get the hell out of here," Al-Nasir says. "Right now."

"What happened?" DeVries asks.

"We're not sure," Quinte says, "but it's bad. It's really bad."

We sprint to the junction. I'm in the lead, my heart pounding. I almost pull off my helmet to get fresher air, then change my mind. I have no idea what "bad" is.

Quinte and Al-Nasir stand exactly where we left them, at the junction between corridors that lead to the room. Everything looks the same, except the two of them.

They're shaking, and Quinte's face is red inside her helmet.

"What happened?" I ask.

She points down the other corridor, the one that leads to Mikk and Roderick, waiting for us. It's dark down there, which strikes me as unusual.

"Were we inside longer than planned?" Rea asks. We all know that time fields around stealth tech can get screwed up.

"No," Al-Nasir says. "Go look."

The other three have caught up with us. The seven of us crowd the corridor. Seager hangs back, along with Kersting. They're past their limits; they don't want anything to do with another disaster.

I walk purposely down that corridor. And as I get closer, I see why it's dark.

Chunks of the black material, bolstered by rock, have fallen down at the very place that we believe divides the stealth-tech field from the normal area.

"Good God," I say. "Did you see this happen?"

I move closer as I walk. The closer I get, the more I realize that one of the walls has lost its integrity. In addition to the larger chunks, smaller rock and debris litter the floor.

"It got dark," Quinte says. "I walked up to see what happened and found that."

"It got dark all at once?" I ask.

"Yes," she says. She sounds less panicked now, as if she was more afraid of my absence than she was of the events before us.

"So this happened quickly," I say.

"We think so," Al-Nasir says. "But we don't know. We were more concerned with you."

"We weren't sure if we were in the only intact corridor."

Behind me, Kersting curses.

"Are we trapped?" Seager asks.

"Not at the moment," I say. "But we'll have to proceed with caution."

I stop at the dividing line. Inside the stealth-tech area, the wall remains intact. Outside looks like a disaster area.

I take a deep breath and step across that invisible line, careful to avoid big chunks of rock. I find areas on the floor to put my feet. It's probably not safe to stand here, but I do.

Instead of a fractured wall, the smooth blackness covers everything, as if nothing happened. I look at the ceiling. It too is intact. The lighting is gone on that side, however.

"Where did this debris come from?" I ask.

"The walls," Quinte says.

"But there's no damage," DeVries says.

"There was," Quinte says. "The black stuff is already covering it over."

"Impressive," Rea says.

I'm thinking the same thing. The guards had described this phenomenon, but to see it is another matter entirely. The black stuff seems almost magical.

I peer ahead. The corridor is filled with rock and debris. None of it shuts off the corridor, at least as far as I can see, although some of it comes close.

My mouth suddenly goes dry. We're outside the stealth tech. If this collapse happened throughout the corridors, then anyone in the caves could have been hit.

Could have died.

"Mikk?" I say into the comm. "Roderick? Come in, please."

I get no response. I look at the others.

"Have you tried them?" I ask Quinte.

She shakes her head. "We were afraid to leave the stealth-tech area."

I almost snap at her, and then I realize that their decision was the smart one. They're inexperienced. I urge caution on my inexperienced divers. Mikk, Roderick, and I would have gone into the danger area as soon as we realized the other area was safe, but the Six didn't know that.

They have no idea how to behave in a true emergency.

And, frankly, neither do I—not in an underground emergency, at any rate.

We can't just go back and find another way out. This is the only way out. We're a long way underground, and there's no blasting our way out of it.

I step back into the stealth-tech area.

"Have you been observing this corridor?" I ask.

Al-Nasir nods. "We've been going back and forth. One of us would stay at the junction and the other would investigate the debris. We'd go in fifteen-minute intervals."

In spite of myself, I smile. They did listen, after all. Their training has paid off. One of them would go forward, like a scout, then return. They'd wait for us, then the other would go out.

"Good job," I say. "That's exactly how you should have done it. Now, has there been any change since you discovered the problem?"

I've learned with tourist dives that any time you encounter something unexpected, you use the mildest word you can. While I'm thinking the debris is a possible disaster, I'm not going to let the Six know that. "Problem" is as advanced as I go.

"No," Quinte says. "It looks the same."

"How long ago did this happen?" I ask, even though I think I know the answer.

"About two hours ago," Quinte says, her voice trembling.

"When the ship arrived," Seager says to me.

"Ship?" Al-Nasir asks.

"We'll explain in a few minutes," I say.

I bite my lower lip, then stop myself. We're here because of the death holes, which we believe to be out-of-control stealth tech. The idea that the ship's arrival had caused a new death hole had fleetingly crossed my mind, but I had quickly forgotten it in the excitement of the ship itself. Besides, I figured the death hole would be on some other part of the mountain, not causing a disturbance in the corridor.

Although there's no death hole above that spot in the corridor.

"Have we heard anything about death holes getting filled in once they're formed?" I ask DeVries.

"No," he says. "From everything we know, they stay open."

"That's when the black stuff appears," Rea says unnecessarily. I remember that as well.

"If the ship caused it," Kersting says, "you'd think the damage would be worse here."

"What's this ship?" Quinte says to me.

"In a minute," I say. "There was no damage here at all?"

"No," Al-Nasir says. "Nothing."

"Did you feel the ground shift or shake?" I ask.

"No," Al-Nasir says.

"Hear anything funny or loud?" I ask.

"We couldn't even hear you until you came out of that door," Quinte says, as if it's my fault. "We've been trying to reach you since this thing happened."

I nod. "Seager, tell them what happened inside the room. We need all of us working from the same information."

I don't listen as she explains the ship's arrival, Rea's near-death experience, and the strangeness of the room. Instead, I step into the nonstealth part of the corridor again.

DeVries comes with me.

"You don't think we time-shifted, do you?" he asks. "I mean, what if the stealth field from the ship was so powerful that it reacted like a bubble, changing the way we experience time?"

"If that were the case," I say, "then the debris wouldn't be here. The passage of time doesn't do this."

At least I think that's true. I know so little about ground and gravity and the way that things work on a planet.

"Fahd," I say to Al-Nasir. "You're sure the black stuff reappeared on the wall while we were in the room."

"Convinced," he says. "We did what you said to do. We've recorded everything."

I smile despite the difficulty of the situation. "Well, that will help."

"Lapsed time was the same, then?" Rea asks from behind me.

"We don't know," Al-Nasir says. "We stayed inside the stealth-tech field. It seemed like time was passing at the same rate both inside and outside, but how can we tell?"

I increase the power of my comm link. "Mikk? Roderick? Are you out there?"

"If time passed differently, they could be long gone," Rea says.

"In the Room of Lost Souls," Al-Nasir says, "time sped up inside the stealth field. We should only have been gone for minutes."

"That's true," I say, "but this might be different. The ship itself might have caused our timeline to slow down. We don't know if the time changes are different in different environments."

"We can't blame it all on time," Kersting says. "In the previous explorations, those of us with the marker haven't moved on different timelines. When we work in a stealth field, time remains the same for us as it does for people outside the field."

"It only speeds up or slows down if you don't have the marker," Quinte says, with a bit of relief.

But I don't feel relief. Because they're right. And if the ship didn't change our time field, then the silence at the other end of the comm link has another explanation, one I like a lot less.

"You think the tunnel collapse is so severe that the rock is interfering with our communication?" Al-Nasir says.

I almost shake my head, but catch myself. I'm not going to let them know what's really worrying me. If the walls collapsed all the way along, then Mikk and Roderick aren't answering us because they can't.

Because they're buried under layers of rock.

TWENTY-TWO

An hour passed. The outsiders did not return to the room.

Coop paced the bridge, checking on his team's work. Dix bent over his console running multiple scans of everything he could think of. He was comparing the readings he had taken of Sector Base V a month before and the readings he was getting now. Occasionally he'd run a hand over his narrow face, a nervous habit he didn't realize he had.

Coop didn't like Dix's nervous tic any more than he liked the images he kept staring at through the open screens. The particles had settled, but enough of them still remained in the air to remind him of dark snow.

Yash ran the data she had received from the outsider woman's glove. Time and time again, Yash got the same result: the glove was not as developed as anything on the *Ivoire*. The technology of the outsiders was, she said, not as sophisticated as the technology of the Fleet.

Which didn't make sense to Coop. The Fleet had colonized Venice City. If the *Ivoire* had gone backward in time, the sector base wouldn't even have been here. There would have been no signal to respond to.

Going forward in time would have resulted in a more advanced technology. So far as he knew, cultures grew in technological prowess. They didn't revert.

The only conclusion he could make, and it was a just hypothesis at the moment, was that something had happened to Venice City. It had gotten conquered, maybe destroyed, maybe abandoned. Then, years later, an outside culture discovered it, one unconnected to the Fleet.

Which explained the backward technology and the clear lack of knowledge the outsiders had about the sector base.

They had seemed terrified by the ship, which no descendants of the Fleet would have been. Of course, any descendants of the Fleet would have understood that the base was designed to keep the ships running, and would have expected an occasional ship to drop in, seemingly out of nowhere.

Anita was sitting on the raised seat in front of her console. She rested her chin on one closed fist as she went through the navigational data, making sure they had arrived at the same place they had left from.

Her eyes looked sunken into her face.

Coop had already sent one member of the bridge crew away because of exhaustion. He needed to send this group away as well. They'd been working for twenty-four hours straight.

They were his best team, but that meant they were the best of the best. The other teams were equally good, just not as experienced.

He needed clear thinking—not just from them, but from himself as well.

He sank into his own chair and contacted his second officer, Lynda Rooney. "Bring your team to the bridge for a briefing," he said.

"Yes, sir." She sounded crisp and formal through the communications system.

Of course she did. He never gave orders like that. Usually he told her what time her crew needed to relieve his. This time, he had put her off, telling her to keep her crew rested.

Secretly, he had hoped they would come on once he solved everything, and have their usual day.

But, he suspected, usual days were a thing of the past.

"We haven't finished digesting all of this information," Dix said as soon as Lynda signed off.

"I know," Coop said. "But staying here won't help."

"I'd like to stay until we know what's going on," Yash said.

Even Anita was sitting up. "I'm glad they're coming," she said. "We're going to need fresh eyes on this. It'll help us figure out what's going on."

"We're going to stand down for a few hours," Coop said.

"Forgive me, sir," Dix said, "but I'd like to stay. We have a mystery here—"

"And we're not going to solve it immediately," Coop said.

"What happens when the outsiders return?" Yash asked.

"We'll observe them," Coop said.

"Or the second team will," Anita said, and she didn't sound worried about that, not the way Yash and Dix did.

"Or the second team will," Coop agreed. "We are going to treat this place as if we don't know it and it's potentially hostile. We're going to follow first-contact procedures."

"But we do know this place," Yash said.

"Do we?" Coop asked. "It doesn't look familiar."

"Our people built it," Dix said.

"They did," Coop said. "But where are they? What's happened to them? We don't know any of that, and we can't make assumptions, no matter how tempting it is."

Assumptions had gotten the entire Fleet in trouble on Ukhanda. He suppressed a sigh. The Fleet's diplomats had completely misunderstood the situation between the Xenth and the Quurzod. He had only just figured it out, but he figured it out in foldspace.

He couldn't go back to Ukhanda and let the Fleet know about their mistake.

At least not yet.

Not that he could do anything about it here. The best thing he could do here was proceed with caution, finish the repairs of the *Ivoire*, and head back to the Fleet, letting them know exactly what had gone wrong when his linguistic and diplomatic team embedded with the Quurzod.

"You think this is a long-term mission, don't you?" Anita asked him.

He looked at her. She sat up straight, one hand on her console as if she were bracing herself for his news.

"I think we have to operate as if it is," he said. "Unless you people think there's a reason for haste . . . ?"

Dix glanced at his console as if the information were written there. Yash sighed.

"We're stuck here until repairs are done," she said. "So whether we handle this like a first-contact situation or not, it won't make any difference as to timing. I don't think we'll have repairs done in less than two weeks with help. And since the base seems devoid of crew, I don't think we're going to get that help. So double the time."

"In other words," Coop said. "We can go on regular rotations, and get the proper amount of sleep."

None of the crew looked relieved by this. But Dix nodded, as if he understood.

Coop wished he did. But he had a hunch understanding would be a long time coming.

And he had to accept that.

TWENTY-THREE

"**O**kay," I say. "We're going to get out of here very carefully."

We're standing behind the stealth field, where everything is normal. If you can call being many meters underground in corridors lined with a strange black substance normal. Ahead of us lay the corridor we had come through to get to the room, only now that corridor is littered with debris.

Debris that Quinte and Al-Nasir tell me has come from the walls, but the walls themselves now look the same as the walls inside the stealth field. If I hadn't seen it without the debris a few hours before, I never would have believed that the debris had fallen off the walls.

I cross the invisible line, and then I stop and crouch, examining the rocks. They're jagged, the breaks obvious and, to my untrained eye, fresh.

I carefully pick one up. It's heavy. It also has no black material on any parts of its exterior. Some of that might be because it had broken away from an area behind the black material.

But I look at the other rocks littering the floor, and I see no black material on them either.

I want to know why. I'm back in diving mode. In diving mode I learn everything I can about everything I see. I absorb information. I question everything.

But I also know I can't get immediate answers. I collect information like some people collect toys.

I can't slow us down too much, however. I don't know what caused this debris field, even though I have a hunch, and because I don't know, I need to get my team out of here. We have no food and not enough supplies. We can't get trapped down here. For once, I didn't prepare for an emergency, and it is all my fault.

I'm inexperienced underground, and even though the archeologists had talked about how dangerous their work could be, I hadn't really taken them seriously.

Just like Mikk.

My heart twists at the thought of him. Have I killed another of my valued team members?

I make myself take a deep breath, then I turn to the team.

"Anyone have experience with this kind of thing?" I ask.

None of them move. It's as if movement would commit them to something difficult, something they're not prepared for.

"We figured you'd know how to get us out," Al-Nasir says, and this time his voice is the one that quavers.

"I have ideas," I say. "I'm just used to disastrous wrecks and debris in space, not debris on the ground."

And then, because they still haven't moved, and because they expect me to be upbeat and to get them out and to let them know they'll survive, I add, "This is a lot safer than it is in zero gravity. There we'd have to watch for floating debris. Here we just have to be careful about what's below us."

"Unless whatever caused this happens again," Quinte says.

"I think it was the ship," Rea says, his voice soft.

"We don't know that," Kersting says.

"We don't know anything except how to get out of here," I say. "And we're going to do that very carefully."

I wait until they're all looking at me—or until it seems like they're all looking at me. I can't see behind all of the faceplates, but their heads are turned toward me.

"Here's what we're going to do," I say. "I'm going to go first. Orlando, you're going to be last. The rest of you, I don't care what order you're in, but I do want you all to record our trip. We'll get different information because we'll be focusing on different things, and that'll be useful once we get out."

"If we get out," Seager mutters.

I turn to her. I wish I can see her face through the helmet, but I can't. I want to make eye contact.

Actually, I want to shake her, but I know that's not productive at all.

"We are going to get out," I say. "I've been in much worse situations *by myself* with no backup at all. We'll be fine if you listen to me and do exactly what I tell you."

"Okay," she says, but doesn't sound like she agrees.

"All right," I say, as if she is enthusiastic. "You will step where I step. You will touch what I touch. We're going to assume those rock piles are unstable. We're not going to disturb them. We're not going to step on them unless we can't get by any other way. We're not going to touch the debris on the floor. Is that clear?"

"You think the stuff on the floor could harm us?" Kersting asks.

"If we step on it wrong, yes, I do," I say. "I don't want broken legs or twisted ankles. I don't want any of us to bring rock piles down on us. We're going to proceed slowly. No crowding, no pushing, no panicking. If you feel yourself panicking, you will take a deep breath, silently count to ten, and release it. You will do that five times before you speak again. Is that clear?"

"And what if one of us sees something wrong?" Rea asks.

At least he's not asking out of fear. He's asking because he knows that despite our best intentions, someone might dislodge something and we'd lose half the group to a rock fall.

"Speak up immediately and calmly," I say. "Calmly is as important as quickly. Got that?"

They nod.

"Okay. If you see a problem beginning or if you're having trouble, say 'Boss, stop please.' I will stop immediately."

I pause until they nod again.

"All right then," I say, realizing I'm repeating that phrase "all right" as if I'm trying to reassure myself.

Maybe I am. I want to shut off the gravity. I want to float around the debris. I want to travel closer to the ceiling of the corridor because the debris piles are bigger at ground level. If we were able to travel along the ceiling, we'd be able to get out a lot quicker—and with almost no trouble at all, at least as far as I can see down this corridor.

"Orlando," I say to Rea, "you and I will have our suit lights on. The rest of you will not. Orlando, you'll train yours upward. Mine will focus downward for obvious reasons. If any of you lose sight of me or need to slow down, ask me to stop. We stay in communication at all times."

On a beginner's dive that has gone wrong, this is where I'd extend a tether. We'd clip to it and travel slowly, one hand over the other, until we reach our destination.

But a tether won't work here. In fact, a tether would be counterproductive.

So much of my training is counterproductive.

I take a deep breath.

"Ready?" I say, more to myself than to them. "Here we go."

TWENTY-FOUR

Coop sat in the conference room with Lynda Rooney. Lynda was a big-boned woman, raised planetside like Yash, but with more experience on a bridge than Coop had. A screw-up early in Lynda's career had derailed her climb upward for nearly ten years, but she was back on track, and now, more than ever, he was glad she was on the *Ivoire*, glad she was going to take command.

Much as he respected Dix, much as Dix deserved first officer status, when it came to running the bridge in his absence, Coop secretly preferred Lynda.

She sat across from him. The huge table, designed to handle twenty or more, seemed even larger than usual. He opened the wall screens here, too, so that he could monitor the exterior.

So far, the outsiders had not returned. That relieved him somewhat. He knew now that they didn't have extra teams, at least not extra teams on the ready. He suspected—he hoped—he would have time to work whenever the outsiders were not around.

He had briefed Lynda on everything that had happened since the *Ivoire* landed. Dix was briefing her bridge crew. Normally Coop would have briefed everyone together, but he needed to talk to someone who was fresh, someone rested, someone who was thinking clearly.

"I'm sending my team to get eight hours of sleep," he said. "I don't think we'll be effective if we stay on the bridge much longer, at least in this situation."

In a fight, in something harrowing, with the adrenaline flowing, he had no trouble keeping the bridge crew on for thirty-six hours straight as he staggered the sleep schedules. But he felt that inappropriate here.

Lynda did not say anything, but he hadn't asked her to. Not yet. She watched him, her face impassive, as she waited to find out what he really needed.

"I'm hesitant to do anything that might alert the outsiders to our presence," he said. He'd already explained to her that he believed the outsiders did not know whether or not the ship was manned. "I want to study them more. I also want to know what those particles are. We have a lot of data to sift through."

"Not to mention the ongoing repairs," she said softly.

He rubbed a hand over his face. He was tired. He was not as sharp as usual. "We definitely need the repairs," he said. "We might need to get out of here quickly."

"So I'm to keep my crew sifting through the information, facilitating repairs, and monitoring the sector base."

"Yes," he said, glad that his implied instructions were clear. "I also want you to continue trying to hail someone on the surface. See if you can contact the Fleet as well. Maybe someone is closer than we think."

Her expression wavered just a little. She didn't believe anyone was nearby. But she was a good officer. She said simply, "Yes, sir."

"Finally," he said, "the minute the outsiders return, you summon me."

"Even if it's only twenty minutes from now?" she asked. "Because we can monitor them just fine."

"I know that," he said. "That's why I don't want you to alert my team. But I want to know what these outsiders are up to, and until I have them figured out, I want to be on the bridge when they're in the room."

"Yes, sir," she said.

He was silent for a minute, gathering his own thoughts. He had called her in here to discuss possible scenarios, but now that she sat across from him, her hand resting lightly on the table, he worried that he would sound overly dramatic.

He sighed.

"I'm not sure what's going on here," he said. "But between us, I think something terrible happened to Venice City."

"I'm inclined to agree, sir." She sounded almost relieved that he had said that.

"We might have to leave immediately," he said. "So repairs are the top priority, especially to the *anacapa* drive."

"Yes, sir."

"Secondarily, I need you to get a team making sure our weapons system is fully functional."

"Sir?" She looked surprised at that. "We can't use most of our weapons down here."

"I know that," he said a little more sharply than he needed to. "But we might not want to be cautious, if you understand my meaning."

"You think we might have to blast our way out?" she asked.

He shrugged. "I want to be prepared for all contingencies. We need to figure out which weapons would be best to carve a hole to the surface if that's what we need."

"Yes, sir," she said.

"I don't want the bridge crew to overhear that instruction," he said. "Just like I don't want them focusing on the *anacapa* drive. We have engineers. Let them work."

"On that and the particles?" she asked.

"Yes," he said. "Plus we need the best assessment your team can put together as to what has happened here. We need to do whatever we can from inside the ship. I don't want anyone leaving the ship unless I order it. Is that clear?"

"Yes, sir," she said.

"When I leave here, I'm going to make a shipwide announcement, saying we've clearly arrived at an abandoned sector base, and no one should expect to leave the ship until it's cleared with me. If there are any problems, the crew should report them to the bridge immediately."

"Are you going to elaborate on what you mean by 'problems'?" she asked.

"No," he said. "Because I'm not sure what I mean by 'problems.' We're in a new situation, Lynda, something that's not in the guidelines. I told the bridge crew we're going to proceed as if this is a first-contact situation, but that's not entirely accurate. This situation is fluid and unsettling, and might be a lot worse than a hostile first contact."

"Worse how, sir?" She asked that with no trepidation. In fact she leaned forward slightly as if this was the piece of information she'd been waiting for.

"There is the possibility that we're not at Sector Base V," he said. "Just some place that resembles it. Our navigation equipment might be very far off. We could be in an ancient base. The *anacapa* was damaged worse than I initially thought. It could have sent us through a different kind of fold. We've heard speculation about the problems with foldspace all our lives. We might be in one of those situations."

She nodded, then swallowed visibly. "I've been thinking that since we got stuck, sir."

"We're going to take this one shift at a time, one problem at a time," he said. "It's our job to make sure the crew remains upbeat and working toward our future. But it's also our job to keep the promises to a minimum. I don't want us to reassure them that we'll rejoin the Fleet. I don't want to hear discussion of friends and family on other ships. If someone tries to talk about that, I want the conversation redirected or truncated as quickly and efficiently as possible."

"Won't that make people suspicious, sir?" Lynda asked.

He shook his head. "They're already suspicious, just like you were. They know something is very wrong here. We're going to prepare them by degrees for the worst-case scenario. If by some chance we get reunited with the Fleet and not much time has passed, then the crew will appreciate our caution. If we don't, then they'll have acclimatized more or less to the new reality."

Her finger tapped the table, for the first time revealing her nervousness.

"What do you think that worst-case scenario is, sir?" she asked.

"I don't know," he said quietly. "I honestly don't know."

TWENTY-FIVE

*P*icking our way through the rock-strewn corridor is easier than I expected. Some parts of the corridor have very little debris, just a bit of gravel, none of it black. The walls are pure smooth black as if nothing has changed. The ceiling is dark. The lights, however, are dim if they work at all.

I have to move slower than I want to. My heart pounds. I am having trouble regulating my breathing.

Because I thought of all the dangers that can occur down here, I'm now focused on them. I worry that the ceiling will cave in, the walls will crumble, big chunks of blackness will fall on us. I want to find out if Mikk and Roderick are still alive. I'm terrified that the opening of the cave is blocked.

For the first time in years, I'm afraid I'm going to die.

I am not monitoring the Six as well as I should. I should keep an ear tuned to their breathing. But I don't. I try not to hesitate, try not to show the fear that I'm feeling.

The rocks look eerie in the light from our suits. I have my lights on bright, casting a clear white light ahead of us, catching the rocks in shadow.

Rea's light from his suit, bringing up the rear, augments my lights. I can see the shadows of the Six elongated around me, as if they're right next to me. I use those to track their progress.

Often I stop, particularly after I've executed a difficult walking pattern. I watch them pick their way over the debris, turning their heads so that they can watch their hands or looking down to keep track of where they place their feet.

The Six are following my instructions. They're trying to walk in my footsteps.

I round a corner, and pause. Rocks litter the corridor in piles taller than I am. My light barely seems to penetrate the opening on the left side of the corridor.

A tight squeeze.

Something I've been afraid of.

I make my way there, careful to keep my boots away from the larger rocks in the center of the floor. I reach the huge pile, and hear a sound beyond it.

Voices.

In my ear?

"Mikk?" I say.

"Boss?" I hear relief in his voice, but it can't match the relief I feel.

He's alive.

"Is Roderick with you?" I ask.

"He's helping me," Mikk says. "Don't move. We'll get you out as quickly as we can."

Don't move?

"We've been moving," I say. "We just got here."

"All of you?" he asks. "You're all right, then?"

I don't want to explain what happened over the comm link. "We're fine," I say. "It's not so bad here."

"The rock fall blocked the corridor," Mikk says. "We've been trying to clear it, but the stack is pretty precarious. Don't touch anything. You might bring the whole thing down on us."

The others have joined me. They're pressing closer than I like, as if they want to see through the opening, just like I do.

"We'll wait," I say as much to the Six as to Mikk and Roderick. I can see their movement through the opening on the left side. The poor men—they're lifting rocks and moving them aside.

Have they been doing that since the rockslides happened?

I stand near that left side so they can see me. The rock fall is deeper than I thought. It is at least six meters wide. The fact that I can see through it is a testament to how hard they've worked.

"We should help," Kersting says, surprising me.

"No," I say softly. "They asked us not to. And this thing is pretty big."

We watch as they work. Our side is relatively clear. The block is on their side of the corridor. That's why my light had trouble penetrating the crack. I keep the light shining on their work area.

We take the time to rest.

And we wait.

TWENTY-SIX

It takes Mikk and Roderick nearly an hour to move enough rock for us to squeeze through. We have to slide past jagged edges that can destroy our environmental suits.

I'm thin. I have no trouble getting past. But I worry about DeVries and Kersting. They're big men—DeVries is tall, and despite the exercise he's getting, Kersting is still too wide.

I get through, sliding my back against the black wall, worrying that I'll dislodge something else or that the groundquake will happen again and I'll get buried under tons of rock. I continue to regulate my breathing, but it does little good.

I'm as nervous as a new diver on a training run. It's a good thing I don't have to rely on my oxygen canisters. I'd use them up in record time.

Finally, I squeeze out and there are Mikk and Roderick, their environmental suits on the floor, their shirts off, their bodies covered in sweat and black dust.

They look better than they ever have. I want to hug them, but it would be awkward with me in my suit and them without theirs.

"Boss?" Mikk asks.

I nod, and then he does hug me, wrapping his powerful arms around me and pulling me close.

Clearly he has no qualms about having my suit rub up against his bare skin.

I step back and Roderick grins. He doesn't hug me—people usually don't hug me at all—and I smile at him.

Then I realize he can't see me through my faceplate.

"The air's okay here?" I ask.

"It's fine."

"The corridor's open the rest of the way?"

Roderick shrugs. "We were more worried about you. We didn't hear. We thought you might be dead."

I thought they might be dead, too, but I don't say that. "We didn't know there was a groundquake."

"How could you not know?" Mikk asks. "That was the scariest experience of my life."

"The ground didn't shake," Roderick says. "It felt like it was coming apart."

I hear DeVries's voice, but I can't quite make out what he's saying.

"Let's help them out," I say. "Then we can debrief you."

We turn toward the opening and pull the Six out. Or rather, Mikk does, one by one. I step away from the rock pile and pull off my helmet. It's warmer without the helmet, but I feel free. And I feel like I can breathe normally for the first time since I saw the debris.

I look at the walls here. They are as unblemished as the walls inside the corridor.

Roderick watches me. "It grew back," he says.

He's not needed to help the Six out. Mikk just takes their hand, gives them a bit of encouragement, and then has them step out. Carefully he guides them to one side before reaching for the next.

They seem as relieved as I am. All of them see that my helmet is off and remove theirs as soon as they can.

"It was weird," Roderick says. "It started as soon as the ground stopped moving. The rocks were falling all around us. They kept tumbling, but Mikk pointed to the wall. The black was filling in the ruined areas, and then it smoothed right out."

"You didn't get hit or anything?" I ask.

"We covered our heads and crouched—or I did. Mikk stood in the middle and looked up, figuring he could run to avoid it all. But it missed us, mostly. Some smaller rocks hit my back and shoulders, but didn't do any damage. I don't know if they hit Mikk."

I can imagine him, standing in the center of the corridor defiantly, as if challenging the falling rock to hit him.

"We really thought you were dead," Roderick says softly.

"I'm sorry," I say. "We didn't feel anything. But when we got out . . ."

I let my voice trail off. It would do no good to let them know how frightened I was. "Well, we're not out yet, are we?"

"No one has come down for us?" DeVries asks. He has joined our conversation. His face is shiny with sweat. I can't tell if that's from the exertion or the warmer temperature in the corridor without our suits on.

"No," Roderick says.

"That's not a good sign," DeVries says.

"It's not?" Roderick asks.

"Think about it," DeVries says. "What would you do if you had a team underground and the ground shifted?"

"I'd try to get to them," Roderick says slowly.

DeVries nods. "No one is here yet."

"Does that mean we're trapped?" Quinte asks from behind me.

"There's no way to know," I say.

"What else could prevent them from coming?" DeVries asks.

I look at him, surprised. He's usually so level-headed. He sounds level-headed, even now. But he's not thinking clearly.

"We've had damage down here," I say. "We have no idea what's happened on the surface."

The others have joined us.

"What do you mean?" Kersting asks.

"We only know a few facts," I say.

Rea starts, "The ship, the—"

"Ship?" Mikk asks.

"In a minute," I say, just like I had to when we met up with Quinte and Al-Nasir. "What we know about Vaycehn is that it's plagued occasionally by death holes. We have no idea what happens underground when a new death hole appears."

Mikk breathes out a curse.

"You think there could be a new death hole on the surface?" Roderick asks.

"I think anything's possible," I say. "And there's no sense in worrying about what could be. We have to concern ourselves with what is."

They're all looking at me. Quinte and Seager look frightened. Even DeVries seems uneasy.

"And the only way to know what is," I say, "is to carefully make our way out of here."

"I don't like being underground," Roderick says softly, speaking to me.

"I'm not fond of it myself," I say. "But this is where we've chosen to work. Let's just be smarter about it the next time we come down here."

If there is a next time.

If we get out at all.

TWENTY-SEVEN

We walk.

We walk through the darkened corridors, stepping over fallen rock, dealing with dust that remains even though the walls are still covered with black. The air is humid and a little too warm for my taste, although I know it is cooler than the air on the surface.

Sometimes I think I should put my environmental suit back on. But I don't. Instead, I tell Mikk and Roderick about the ship.

"I'm amazed you left the room at all," Mikk says, but his eyes twinkle. He knows that I'm a slave to the schedule, but he also knows how tempted I can be by the unknown.

"We had no idea that anything had changed outside," I say. "We thought we'd take a break, sleep, eat, and come back to work."

Now I'm not sure when we'll be back. I'm not sure what we'll find when we get out.

If we get out.

I don't say those things, but I know the others are thinking them. We all know they're implied.

Finally we reach the end of the main corridor, where we left one of the hovercarts. This area is dark, and my heart starts pounding as we get close. Something is wrong. I can sense it, but I'm not sure what I'm sensing.

We round the corner—and stop.

I can't see the hovercart. There's a pile of rock where we left it, a pile that reaches to the ceiling and stretches as far as the eye can see.

DeVries curses. Quinte makes a small sound of dismay. I glance at Mikk.

"Roderick," I say, happy to have experienced people with me now, "you stay with the group. Mikk and I are going to see how far this goes."

Roderick nods. No one complains. Mikk and I walk forward, and as we do, he says softly, "We've been working with these rock piles. They're incredibly unstable. We have to be very careful."

"Do you think it would be better if you and Roderick investigate?" I ask.

"No," he says. "But you and the group will have to listen to me if we need to move rock. And you're going to let me go first here."

I almost protest until I realize he's right. He's got a few hours' more experience with this stuff than I do, and that's a few hours more than any of us have.

He slides into an opening along the left side—they all seem to have openings along the left side; I wonder if that means anything—and then beckons me forward.

The enclosure is tight, almost tighter than the one we came through earlier, but it's shorter. Mikk is standing in an open area. Another rock fall lies in front of him, and its haphazard pattern is what gave the illusion of an unbroken rock fall from farther back in the corridor.

The back of the hovercart is here, bent forward from the weight of the rock on its front. The back end is unbroken, not even marred by dents or dust. The bench seats, however, are full of rock.

"Where are the guides, you think?" I ask.

Mikk shrugs. He knows as well as I do that they usually don't wait near the hovercart. They often return to the surface while we work.

The guides might be under the rubble. They might be just fine up above. We might not know until we get out of here.

If the guards are under that rubble, they're dead.

We don't say anything more. We walk across the unbroken part of the corridor to the next rock fall. There I peer through the opening, which is, again, on the left side.

Through it, I can see natural light. The cave opening, up above. Several meters above, meters we've traveled only by hovercart so far.

"We can get to the opening," I say, "and there's daylight."

"That's one step," Mikk says.

We both know the next step will be even more difficult. Without the hovercart, getting to the surface will be incredibly hard.

We don't say anything, though. Instead, we return to the group.

Mikk is going to lead them through the two rock falls. This time, I'm going to bring up the rear.

It takes another hour to get us through this new series of fallen rocks. I don't watch the group make its cautious way through the pile.

Instead, I investigate the hovercart.

The force of the rocks has crushed the front half. The back is mostly intact. The middle is damaged, but not as badly as I would have expected.

Even though I touch the rocks and the ground near the cart with my bare fingers, I feel nothing liquid. No blood. I don't smell anything rank either, and death without environmental suits would have a smell. When they die, people's bladders void. Their bowels let go.

And in this warmth, the blood itself would have an odor.

It does not.

I am more relieved than I want to say.

I'm the last through the second rock fall, which is remarkably stable. I reach my group in the daylight-filled corridor. The Six sit, sharing a bottle of water. Mikk and Roderick are investigating the opening.

The opening differs from the openings you normally find going into ships. It doesn't come down in a straight vertical. It has a slope. The upper part of the opening is steep, but almost immediately widens into the cavern. The walls themselves go upward at an angle.

However, that angle gets sharper and sharper the closer to the top one gets.

There's a built-in ladder. I've noticed it every time we come down. It's precarious, and even more so now. The ground could shake again, and we'd be stuck. Whoever is on the ladder might get shaken off, might fall, might be crushed.

Of course, the group waiting below might get crushed too.

I saunter over to the Six as if I don't have a care in the world. I glance up, see no obvious debris on the edge of the cave opening above, and see no visible cracks in the wall.

"I'll climb it," I say.

"Boss," Roderick says. "We need you. If something happens . . ."

He doesn't finish the sentence.

"If something happens, I'm in as much danger down here as I will be on that ladder," I say. It's not entirely true; being shaken off the ladder might make me fall, and the fall could kill me.

"I'm not sure I can climb that," Kersting says.

"You don't have to," I say. "That's why I'm going up. We're either going to figure out if there's another way to lift you guys out or we're going to pull you up with some kind of rope. I won't know until I get up there."

"Boss, this isn't like pulling someone out of a wrecked ship," Roderick says. "We—"

"I know," I say. "Gravity isn't our friend. But I need you and Mikk down here to help the others. You're the strongest, most athletic members of this team. You can boost them if need be."

Roderick and Mikk can also tie rope properly, attach cable well, and can handle most emergencies. And, most important, Roderick knows how to pilot.

"So, I'm the logical one to climb." I sound braver than I feel. I've never climbed something like this in full gravity, but I have climbed, and I'm in good shape as well.

Before I can change my mind, I stand beside the ladder.

"I'm assuming you've tried to communicate," I say to Mikk.

He taps the communicator in his ear. "Nothing," he says. "I shouted too."

I heard him do that.

"No one has responded," Mikk says.

I nod. Those guides have never struck me as particularly trustworthy.

"All right, then," I say, and grab the rung directly in front of me before I can change my mind.

I'm not wearing gloves. I'm surprised at the coolness of the black surface. The rung is carved into the wall, not sticking out of the wall. I expected the rung to be smooth as glass. Instead, it's wavy, with a bit of roughness, something that will hold a boot.

And there's an actual hand-sized hole in the back of the rung, something I can easily grip.

I'm going to be free-climbing, but I'll be free-climbing with handholds and a relatively safe place to put my feet.

"Don't look down," Roderick says to me. He's speaking very softly.

He's right; I know that. I also know that if he had not reminded me, I would have looked down at some point.

It's not the same to look below you when you're working in zero gravity. First of all, what's below you might be above you if everything spins or shifts. But, second, if you lose your grip, you float.

I will not float here.

My heart is pounding.

I take a deep breath—and climb.

TWENTY-EIGHT

Hand up. Foot up. Followed by opposite hand. Then opposite foot. I concentrate on each movement, marveling at how well constructed the ladder is. The handholds fit my fingers. The rough surface keeps my boots steady.

The early part of the climb is easy. It's almost like walking. The slope is gentle, the ladder more of a guide than a necessity.

But a third of the way up, the wall's angle gets steep. Suddenly, I'm climbing, hand over hand, foot on one rung at a time, with nothing to support me except my grip and my caution.

I feel awkward, my torso hanging out in the air. I also feel heavy. I can feel the weight of my body with each movement.

My arms are tiring first. Apparently, I lack upper-body strength, something I didn't know. But my legs are getting tired as well. And I'm getting thirsty, which means I'm getting dehydrated. I have a slight headache between my eyes, caused by the growing dry heat.

Sweat drips off my nose and chin.

As long as I sweat, I'm all right.

I should have left the damn environmental suit on, though. I hadn't thought that through.

I really hadn't thought any of this underground stuff through, not until now.

When I'm halfway up, I hear sounds. I'm not sure what they are—some kind of rustling, or maybe even conversation. It's not what I expect in any way, but I haven't really listened before. The hovercart moved so quickly as it went into the caves that I couldn't notice details like sound and distance.

"Hello the top!" I yell as I pause, hanging there.

I don't like hanging. It feels precarious. It also makes me want to look down.

"Boss?" I hear a relieved female voice.

Then Ilona leans over the edge, her black hair surrounding her face. She's not supposed to be here. She's supposed to be collating the research and doing some work with the City of Vaycehn.

"That's me," I say.

"God," she says, and stops so quickly that I hear the rest although she doesn't speak it. *We thought you were dead.*

Yeah, well. We could have been.

"They wouldn't let us go down there. They say it's not safe," she says.

"They're right. It's not safe," I say. "There's fallen rock everywhere."

"Let me get you help," she says, and backs away before I can tell her not to. I don't want a rope or a guiding hand or some equipment sent down here. I want to keep climbing, one hand over the other, moving slowly, until I reach the top.

I think—just for a moment—of climbing faster. But that way lies error, and error can cause death.

I resume my pace—right hand up, followed by right foot. Then left hand up, followed by left foot. I climb another three meters before she reappears.

"Are you the only survivor?" she asks, and in spite of my best intentions, I shudder.

"The Six are fine. So are Mikk and Roderick," I say. "If anyone else was below, we haven't seen them."

Which is a polite way for me to tell her that any guides who were waiting by the hovercart have either fled or been crushed.

"Are the others climbing behind you?" she asks.

"No," I say. "I'm coming up, then we're going to figure out how to get them. I'm not sure the Six can climb this."

I barely can, although I don't admit that to her. I'm not sure I like admitting that to myself.

I continue to climb. I count to keep my pace steady. I make sure I breathe. I try not to notice as I'm getting light-headed with heat and the increasing light.

I can't get careless now, so close to the top.

"Are you up there by yourself?" I ask as I get closer.

"God, no," she says.

"Are there guides?"

"Yes," she says. "No medical personnel, though. They had to leave."

I don't want to know why.

"Get someone who can help me over the edge," I say. "I'll need water and food. In fact, we're going to need to send water and food down. Can you do that?"

"Easily," she says, and disappears again.

The medical personnel have left, even though we might need medical attention. Something has gone wrong elsewhere, or maybe even nearby.

As I reach the top, two of the guides lean over the edge.

I stifle a gasp. I'm afraid they'll knock me loose.

"Don't touch me," I say. "Help when I tell you."

Still they put their hands near me, so they can grab me if they need to. I'm alarmed at their closeness, but I'm comforted by it, too. I'm not alone here.

I was afraid I'd have to get over that edge on my own.

My head pops over the top.

Rubble everywhere, and another hovercart on its side. I see dust, rising in the distance, and hear faint voices from far away. The skyline looks different, but I'm not sure how.

I don't care how, not at the moment.

"Okay," I say. "Help me up."

They grab my armpits and pull me over that edge. I scramble several meters away before stopping. I don't want to fall back into that damn hole.

Ilona gives me a bottle of water. McAllister Bridge hands me some of that amazing applelike fruit that I enjoy. I'm surprised he's there. I look around, realize that everyone is here—everyone I brought with me, my entire team.

It's unbelievably hot, and I'm incredibly tired. But we're nowhere near done.

"Get food down to the others," I say to Ilona.

"Already doing that, Boss," she says.

I nod. I'm a bit dizzy, and there are black spots in front of my eyes. I will myself not to faint. I grab that water and pour it over my head, cooling myself down. Bridge hands me another bottle of water without saying a word.

I wipe the water off my face. My hand comes away black. I must be filthy.

"All right," I say. "Now how the hell are we getting the rest of the team up here?"

TWENTY-NINE

Coop managed four hours of sleep before his active brain woke him up. He went to the captain's mess, had a huge breakfast, and then headed to the communications array.

Shipboard communications ran through the bridge, but the bulk of the equipment was in the engineering area. Engineering covered the largest part of the ship. Located in the very center of the ship as a precaution, engineering was usually one of the most stable parts of the *Ivoire*.

Although the engineering section hadn't been stable since the Quurzod attack. Their quick, sharp one-man ships had gotten too close to the *Ivoire*, and their weaponry, while lacking power, had a directional focus that went into one part of a key system and moved through that system, effectively destroying it.

The engineers were rebuilding certain parts of the ship from scratch, including much of the *Ivoire*'s weaponry. The *anacapa*, the most protected part of the ship, had been damaged, but not destroyed.

The communications array, however, suffered the most damage. Coop needed his best engineers on the weaponry and damage to the *anacapa*, so he pulled some of the linguists to work on the communications array.

Linguists got engineering training on the communications array so that they could tweak it to meet the needs of some unknown language. Most of the linguists had no knack for engineering or repair, but one of them had an intuitive understanding of the array that bordered on genius.

Mae, his chief linguist. Also his ex-wife.

She stood near the door, a repair pad in hand, studying the schematics before her. The communications array filled the entire room and looked like many of the ship's important systems—tiny panels with flips and lights that provided a redundant entry to the touch screens on each panel's front.

An efficient communications array would be small enough to fit on the bridge. But the Fleet had more redundant systems than any other group of ships Coop had encountered. Because the ships of the Fleet were designed to operate on their own for years without going to a sector base, having redundant systems made sense. One part of the system might go down, but other parts would still function.

Every system on the ship had that kind of backup except, of course, the *anacapa*.

He stood in the doorway and watched the team of five work on the array. Mae didn't realize he was there. She seemed focused on the flat screen in her hand.

She was a beautiful woman, even with her red hair pulled severely back away from her face, a face that actually had some frown lines now. The lines gave her character, although he would never tell her that.

"Mae?" he said softly.

She jumped. She had been on Ukhanda for several months before the disaster. Her team had died at the hands of the Quurzod, and she had barely survived. It had taken her some time to heal once she returned to the *Ivoire*. Coop had pushed her into the repair work quicker than her doctors wanted, but he knew she had to keep busy.

And she couldn't be busy with language. She felt that she had screwed up linguistically with the Quurzod, and she had lost her confidence. He wanted to ease her back to work. He figured fixing the array would do it.

"Hey, Captain," she said with a bit of a smile, the smile she always used when she called him by his title and not his name. "I thought you'd be on the bridge, worrying about this strange place we find ourselves in."

Two of her team members peeked out from behind the array. She waved them back to work. The other two didn't even look up at Coop. They knew their priority was getting the array in top condition.

"So you've looked outside," he said to Mae.

"I think everyone on the ship has," she said. "We're relieved to be out of foldspace. Some people don't care that things are strange here. They're just happy to be *somewhere*."

He didn't correct her. They had been somewhere when they were in foldspace. He just didn't know exactly where.

"Repairs are slow, but happening," she said, anticipating his question. "But of course, you know that from the daily reports."

He nodded. She knew that he wasn't here for the update.

"When we came here," he said, "we came because they received our distress signal, right?"

She looked at him sideways. One of the benefits of closeness was that he understood the look without words. She wasn't going to talk in front of her team.

He pivoted and went into the corridor. She followed. They moved away from the door.

"We sent distress signals on all channels the entire time we were in fold-space," she said. "The base did receive our signal, but that's where the information gets fuzzy."

"Fuzzy?" he asked. She chose that word deliberately. Mae spoke twenty-five languages fluently, but her best language was Standard. She believed in precision on all things. So when she said "fuzzy," she meant "fuzzy."

"It blurs together," she said, "and the condition of our array does not allow me to figure out exactly what happened."

"What's your best guess?" he asked.

Her lips thinned. Mae did not like guessing.

"I need a theory," he said.

"From what I can tell, this sector base was offline for a long time." She held up her hand. "And before you quiz me, I can't tell how long."

He nodded. He didn't expect her to know when his bridge team hadn't been able to figure it out, either.

"The strangers in the base probably touched the consoles, activating them."

He nodded. His team had already figured that out.

"The activation," she said, "includes a scan of outlying systems, looking for missed communications."

"That's when the base heard our distress signal?"

"Probably," she said. "Then the automatic retrieval system activated, using their *anacapa* to power ours. At least, that's what engineering tells me."

"That's the theory at the moment," he said. "What's the problem?"

She took a deep breath, as if she were uncertain. He was still not used to an uncertain Mae. He kept forgetting how fragile she was.

"I'm not sure they received our distress signal at all," she said. "I can't find notice of an acknowledgment, a receipt, or even that mingling within our systems."

"Then how did they find us?" he asked.

She bit her lower lip. "I think this place sent out a signal when it activated, but it wasn't a communications signal. It was their activation beam, the *anacapa*, pulling in anything within range."

He frowned. "The system's not built for that, Mae."

"I know," she said. "But the first communication—if you want to call it that—that registered on our system was their *anacapa*."

He thought for a moment. Mae was thorough. He knew what procedures she would have run, but it was his duty to ask about them anyway.

"You don't think the damage to our systems prevented us from storing the communication?" he asked.

"I'm hoping that's the case," she said in a voice that told him she didn't believe it. She thought that the communication hadn't happened.

"But?" he asked.

She took a deep breath. "Ever since we arrived, we've been trying to communicate with the sector base. I've redoubled the efforts since it became clear that we wouldn't go out into the base for a while."

"And?" he asked.

"And we can't do it. We can't reach those consoles out there, even though we're only a few yards away. Either whatever's broken on our side interferes with communicating with them, or something's wrong on their side."

"Or both," he said.

"Or both," she agreed.

"You've looked at the scans of the consoles," he said.

She nodded. "They're in rough shape, Coop. I've seen it before."

"You have?" he asked.

"In our training. We had to take some ancient equipment and cobble it into an existing system. The ancient stuff had been in good repair. It was just old. The readings you got off the systems out there, they look a lot like the readings we got from the ancient equipment."

"I assume you double-checked those readings," he said.

"No," she said. "I don't have raw data. It was a school project."

Meaning it was more than a decade ago, and she'd jettisoned the information, if she ever had it.

"Ancient," he said, thinking of her precision with words. "Not old?"

"Not old," she said softly. "Time ravaged."

"Could other things cause that?" he asked.

She shrugged. "You need to ask a real scientist or a very experienced engineer. My specialties are communications systems of all types, and I remember that one. I could be wrong. I probably am—at least about this."

"I trust you, Mae," he said.

She looked down. "Maybe you shouldn't."

He wanted to put an arm around her, pull her close. But he didn't. She was going to have to recover her confidence on her own.

"I'd like you to take some of the team off the general repairs. I want them to focus on communicating with the section base. If you have to cobble something together, then do so."

She raised her head slowly. The frown still marred her forehead. "Do you think we won't be able to go out there and do some work in the base?"

"I don't know when the first team will leave the ship," he said. "I want to be prepared for everything. The more work we can do from in here, the happier I am."

She took a deep breath. "All right," she said. "I'll make sure we figure out how to talk to the sector base."

"And it can talk back," he said.

"Oh, it'll talk back," she said. "I'm just not sure we're going to like what it has to say."

THIRTY

They bring in a vehicle like I've never seen before. The Vaycehnese have special equipment for dealing with tunnel collapses and cave-ins and people trapped below ground.

The guides couldn't request it until they knew we were alive—a stupid rule, I think. But Bridge explains it to me.

The entire city's in chaos at the moment. A death hole has opened in a far section of Vaycehn, a section that has never seen death holes before. This death hole is huge, and it has swallowed an entire block. The rescue efforts are concentrated there; the bulk of the equipment is there.

The rest of the equipment is reserved for just this kind of emergency, but it gets prioritized. The equipment goes where human life is threatened first—where the Vaycehnese know that human life is threatened—and then it goes to the other areas.

We weren't a priority because they hadn't heard from us.

No one had until I started climbing out of that damn hole. The angle of that opening made voices from below impossible to hear. And there were no guides with us. Apparently, they had been waiting on the surface until an hour or so before we were scheduled to leave. Then they returned below.

So when the groundquake hit, our guides were above ground and nowhere near the opening. Ilona has no idea if they even tried to find us. She doubts it, but she's checking into it.

Of course, they admit nothing.

They did send a message for assistance, but got none because they had no idea if we survived. Then they contacted Ilona and asked her if she wanted them to wait. They were itching to help with the rescue efforts elsewhere.

She gave them what for. But before they even contacted her, the guides with medical training left so that they could help at the death hole.

Apparently, that's procedure in Vaycehn. Whenever a death hole opens, the most experienced emergency personnel and people with medical training flock to that site and help as quickly as they can.

It's a coordinated effort—"a beauty to behold," Bridge said to me with more admiration than I wanted to hear. Tourists and outsiders were left to their own devices, while the locals helped each other.

I was trembling with fury by the time I figured that out.

Or maybe just exhaustion.

The minute Ilona heard my voice, she ordered the guards to get the rescue equipment. They were already on it. Once they knew the outsiders were in trouble, they didn't want to seem callous. But it still took some time for the Bug, as they call the rescue vehicle, to get to our location.

The Bug is amazing. It is tall—three times the height of an average human—but relatively thin. Its center is a pod with clear openings all around. The operator is completely visible.

Its sleekness reminds me of a single ship—at least in the pod part. But the sleekness ends with the pod. The rest of the Bug is all mechanical legs, with many joints, "like spider legs," Bridge says, marveling again.

I take his word for it. I've never seen a spider.

The pod has legs on all sides. I count twenty, but I'm not certain because of the way they bend and hang and change. The Bug smells hot, and it groans as it moves, as if each bend in the legs needs lubrication.

One of the operators—a man whose name I didn't catch—tells me that sound is normal. It enables people inside caves and near the Bug to know when the Bug is coming. The sound also informs people to stay out of the way.

It walks across the surface to get here, picking its way over the rubble with a delicacy that belies its size. As it comes, I talk to the guides. Or rather, Bridge does and I listen. The guides still have trouble seeing a woman as the leader of our small group—although they seem to be afraid of Ilona now.

I wonder what she has threatened them with.

The guides say that the Bug fits only four people, including the operator. I have left eight below.

"All right," I say after it becomes clear that the Bug will have to make three trips below just to get my people out. "Kersting, Quinte, and Seager come out first. Roderick and Mikk come up last. You got that?"

I say this last to the operator. He shakes his head—our names are difficult for him.

Ilona sighs with exasperation and writes everything down on one of the passes we were given long ago. "You give that to them," she says to the operator.

He looks at Bridge, as if Bridge would contradict her.

Bridge takes the paper and hands it to the operator. "You must give that to them," he says, as if Ilona hasn't spoken.

She makes a sputtering noise. I put my hand on her arm. She glances at me, then rolls her eyes.

I hope no one else saw that. Right now, we need the Vaycehnese and their expertise.

The operator nods and gets into the Bug. He looks like an organic part of the machine, sitting in the very center, his hands on controls that look like miniature versions of the legs.

It's rare that I see a vehicle I cannot drive, but the Bug is one. I have no idea how he controls the legs, given that they each have such individual movement. He walks it over to the opening that I scrambled out of not long ago.

Then the Bug spreads its legs over the opening, using ten of them to surround the oval. The pod centers, then sinks inside. Other legs move inside with the pod, gripping the walls—or so one of the guides tells Bridge—while the ten legs remain on top for what seems like a very long time.

One by one, the legs disappear. I hurry toward the edge, but someone grabs my arm.

It's one of the guides. He frowns at me. "You cannot go there."

"I want to watch," I say.

"It will take no time. You could get hurt."

I shake him off and hurry to the edge. I can see the ends of three legs, disappearing along the slope.

If the Bug is already hard to see, then it's near the bottom. The guide is right. I could get hurt if I remain here. I hurry back to my people.

My heart is pounding. My fatigue is in the background, a steady thrum, but it has receded. The water and that little bit of food have helped.

Maybe I'm acclimatizing to the heat.

Or maybe I'm just ignoring it all because of the emergency.

Less than five minutes later, the Bug returns to the surface, coming up the way it went down. Leg after leg pops out of the hole, gripping the edge. Then the pod comes up, followed by the other legs.

This time, the Bug does not disengage itself from the opening. Instead, it leans the pod over one side and touches the pod to the ground. A door opens, and Seager steps out. She looks bewildered. She puts a hand over her face, shielding her eyes from the bright light. She is covered in blackness.

She stumbles as she steps away from the pod. Ilona heads over with water and food as Quinte comes out, then Kersting, who raises both of his arms over his head in triumph.

The Bug doesn't wait. As the three of them step away from the pod, the door closes.

Then the Bug centers itself over the hole again, and repeats the entire procedure.

I let out a small sigh of relief. My people are going to get out.

I'm not going to lose any team members today.

And considering how careless I've been with this underground work, that's damn close to miraculous.

THIRTY-ONE

We travel back to the hotel in one of the undamaged hovercarts. I finally understand the practicality of these vehicles. Their relative thinness allows them to go around debris fields—and there are several debris fields throughout this part of Vaycehn. The hovercart's pilot is very conscious of his passengers, never tilting the vehicle far enough to make us uncomfortable, but he still manages to maneuver around some dangerous areas.

Besides the pilot, there are only three of us in this vehicle. Bridge, Ilona, and I remained behind after the rest of the team went back to the hotel. Everyone got out of the cavern, but looking ragged. Even Mikk and Roderick, so seemingly indestructible below, looked almost ruined by the experience.

The tension, the heat, the physical labor had exhausted them like it exhausted me.

But my work wasn't done. I needed to let the guides know we were heading back into the cavern as soon as we could.

Of course, they didn't want us to. It quickly became clear that we would need permission from the city again, and I couldn't tell them why. I hadn't told Bridge or Ilona, either, when they started the negotiations with the guides. I didn't want the news of the ship to leak to the Vaycehnese.

Bridge managed to convince the Bug operator that clearing the debris and inspecting the caverns for more damage was a priority. He did that not with authority and argument but with money.

This trip is going to cost us a lot more than expected. But it'll be worthwhile—if the ship remains long enough for us to investigate it.

The guides don't want us to go below for more than two weeks. That's how long groundquakes continue after the first large one. But Bridge managed to get the guides to admit that such aftershocks only happened after a pure groundquake—one that occurred without an accompanying death hole.

The death hole quakes were usually one-time things.

Usually.

I know it will take a lot of argument and probably a handful of bribes to get us below. Bridge and Ilona are going to handle that, and I have told them to use their discretion.

We need to go below again, and the Vaycehnese shouldn't stop us.

However, a repeat of today's underground disaster could.

I'm not sure how many of the Six will be willing to go below again, and I'm not sure how to convince them.

I'm going to need to talk to the geologists and archeologists, and I've told Ilona I'll need some Vaycehnese expert, someone who'll help us prepare for disasters underground. At least, prepare better than we have been.

As we head back to the hotel, the damage from the quake becomes clear. Roads have collapsed. Some buildings have lost entire sides, while others remain standing undamaged.

The cloud of dust in the distance is, according to the hovercart's pilot, from the death hole itself. It blew outward, sending debris a kilometer into the air. Some of that debris will float around for days.

I want someone from our team to figure out exactly where that death hole is in relationship to the underground room we've found. I want to know when the death hole appeared and whether or not it really was tied to the ship. I want a lot of things, and I'm too tired to ask for them.

We'll need to have a meeting when we get back—I have to brief our people—but I'm not sure a meeting will be the most productive thing to do first.

First, we'll need sleep.

My brain is mush. I'm so tired I'm shaking. I realize now how close we came to a complete disaster.

And yet, part of me doesn't mind.

An intact *working* Dignity Vessel arrived in front of us. *Intact. Working.* It seems like a dream now, and I'm worried that when we get back the ship will be gone again.

We have readings from it, though. Readings and recordings, and I actually touched it.

I touched it. A living, breathing part of history. I'm still amazed.

The hovercart stops outside the hotel. We climb out—or rather, Bridge and Ilona climb out. I try, stagger, and nearly fall. Bridge catches me. His gaze meets mine.

He looks terrified.

"Are you sure you're all right?" he asks me softly.

"Nothing sleep won't cure," I say.

But sleep is still a long way off. Ilona talks to the hovercart pilot, probably telling him when to return, something I would normally do. But I'm barely able to walk.

Bridge puts his arm around me, supporting me. Usually I hate to be helped, but his arm is comforting. I need the assistance.

We walk through the main doors into controlled chaos. The furniture has moved. Some of the potted plants that had been on the counters were gone, bits of dirt still littering the floor.

People are standing in front of the desk, the line five deep, the hotel employees looking frazzled. Many of the people at the desk are trying to check out. Others stand near the chairs, looking up.

I glance up too. Nothing has fallen, nothing looks different, but I'm not sure of that.

The elevators are blocked off, as are the mechanical stairways. We have to climb to the top floor.

The muscles in my legs scream with pain. They barely function. Twice my legs wobble so badly that Bridge has to keep me from falling.

Halfway up the stairs, Bridge asks, "What really happened down there, Boss?"

"Gravity," I snarl. I'm beginning to hate gravity.

By the time we reach the top floor, I have decided that I'm not *beginning* to hate gravity. I do hate gravity. I hate it with every fiber of my exhausted being.

Bridge leads me to the door of the suite. "Maybe we should wait a few hours before we meet."

Sensible, of course. But the team needs to know what they're dealing with. Or do they?

If they don't know, they won't let anything slip to the authorities in Vaycehn.

"Tell Ilona to figure out how to get us down there again as soon as possible," I say.

Bridge is frowning at me. I want him to be taking notes. I want him to be nodding and agreeing. I don't want him to look so disapproving.

"We'll also need some training on surviving groundquakes, and we'll need better guides, some that will be able to help us get out should another groundquake occur."

"Boss, I don't think that's reasonable—"

"It is," I say.

"You're tired."

I pull away from him and draw up to my full height. He's treating me like a child. Like a stupid child who doesn't know her own limits.

"We made the discovery of a lifetime down there, McAllister," I say. "We have to get back to it and quickly."

"If it was there before, I'm sure it will be there later," he says in that same damn patronizing tone. I'm grateful for that tone when he uses it with the Vaycehnese. I hate it when he uses it on me.

"It wasn't there before," I say, "and it might be gone in a few days."

His frown grows. I get the sense that he doesn't believe me at all. Damn the exhaustion.

"I need rest," I say. "We all need food. Then we need to meet and look over everything the team brought back. We'll need a plan. But first, you and Ilona need to get us back to that room."

"When it's safe," Bridge says.

"As soon as possible," I say. "If you can't follow that instruction, then find me someone who can."

He holds up his hands. "All right."

He waits as I unlock the door. I step inside the room. It's cool and dry, the air on me like a caress.

"You're not going to tell me what you found," he says.

"No," I say. "It's better that you don't know when you talk to the Vaycehnese."

"It's that big?" he asks.

"Bigger," I say. "Much, much bigger."

THIRTY-TWO

Coop kept Lynda's team on the bridge for a ten-hour shift while his team rested. His entire team was up and ready for duty within eight hours, but he ordered them to take some downtime. Dix went back to his cabin to get more sleep. Yash decided to have a proper breakfast, something she hadn't done in weeks. Both Anita and Perkins went to the gym for some much-needed exercise.

He probably should have relaxed as well, but he wasn't able to. His mind worked too hard. He felt like they were still in the middle of an emergency, which they were and they weren't. Nothing actively threatened them—no attacks, no problems from the interior, no failures on board ship—but they still didn't know where they were or what they were facing.

He let Lynda run the bridge while he inspected various systems. He spoke with the engineers repairing the *anacapa*. The damage there was extensive, and they couldn't wait to get into the sector base to use backup equipment to make sure everything was running.

He didn't tell the engineers that he wasn't sure if the equipment was even in the base any longer, let alone whether or not it would be in any condition to use.

The other repairs were going slowly, but the mood on the ship had measurably improved. His crew usually didn't like leaving the *Ivoire*, but this time, everyone he spoke to questioned when they would be able to disembark.

Being in foldspace, not knowing how long they were going to be there, or when (if) they would ever be able to leave the ship again had had an impact on everyone. They all wanted to leave the *Ivoire* for a short period of time, not because they wanted to visit the sector base or Venice City, but because they wanted to exercise their freedoms.

He understood that. If he were a more impulsive man, he would have left the ship already, inspecting the sector base and trying to figure out what had gone wrong.

But being impulsive was the worst thing he could do there. He had a hunch that his presence—the crew's presence, five hundred strong—was an advantage he could keep from the outsiders. They had no idea how many people were on the *Ivoire*, whether or not there was *anyone* on the *Ivoire* at all, let alone the people who belonged on the ship.

He was going to maintain that advantage for a while longer, until he had a sense of the outsiders.

He stopped in the science labs last, just before he returned to the bridge. The science labs were a warren that ran along the belly of the ship. Each lab had protective walls so thick that nothing could get through. Each lab also had the capability of running its own environment separate from the ship, which enabled the scientists to run the occasionally risky experiment without endangering everyone else on board.

Coop inspected the labs twice a year, but otherwise he rarely went deep within them. He usually left the management of the labs to his chief science officer, Layla Lalliki.

Lalliki was a tall, thin woman with large dark eyes and dark hair cut so short that Coop could never figure out what color it was. Her skin was pasty, and her gaze always seemed distant, as if she was never really looking at anything in front of her, always seeing something in her imagination instead.

Still, she was a superb officer, and despite her occasional vagueness with nonscientists, she was very good at handling her staff. The scientists were a temperamental lot, and many of them were annoyed at serving on the *Ivoire* instead of the *Pasteur*, the Fleet's premier science vessel.

Fifty percent of the Fleet's best scientists scattered among the regular vessels, like the *Ivoire*. The rest went to the *Pasteur* and engaged in cutting-edge research—or so he was told.

He never really paid much attention. He was just happy to have excellent minds on board his ship. The brightest minds were spread among the various ships for just the reason he was encountering here—sometimes the Fleet's ships got cut off from each other. If all of the best scientific minds had congregated on the *Pasteur*, it would have done him no good.

He had brilliance here, and he knew he could rely on it.

Mostly the science team worked on their various projects, even while the ship was in a state of emergency. Not all of the geneticists, for example, needed to focus on foldspace or the current location of the *Ivoire*. They kept to their work and seemed content with it.

But several members of the science staff had been pulled to work on the sector base issue, as well as on those particles.

Lalliki managed all of it.

She met him outside the labs at his request.

She looked tired, the shadows under her dark eyes deep. He wondered if he looked as exhausted as well, then decided not to think about it.

"Lynda tells me that you think those particles are unbonded nanobits," he said.

"We have no idea," Lalliki said, sounding annoyed. "We have unbonded nanobits that we pulled from the airlock, but we have no idea if they're ours. We discovered that the Quurzod weaponry had loosened some of the nanobits on the exterior after we entered foldspace. For all we know, they could have floated inside when we were doing the grab from outside the ship."

He usually liked her caution, but on this day, he wanted some certainty.

"Those nanobits couldn't be the particles we're seeing, then?" he asked.

"Oh, they could be," she said. "Or that could be something else. It's just not safe to say."

He suppressed a sigh, then nodded. Normally, at this point, he would have asked about some of the other ongoing work, but he simply didn't have the energy or the interest.

Instead, he said, "As soon as I decide that we can enter the sector base, I'm going to need three of your people to investigate what's going on. In addition to good minds and great researchers, I'll need people who are good in an emergency. There's the possibility that we could get surprised once we enter the base, and I want to make sure the scientists can respond with force if need be."

Lalliki gave him a sideways look. "You think that these outsiders you've been monitoring could be hostile."

"There's that possibility," he said.

"We could lose people, then," she said.

"There's that possibility, too." He kept his voice soft. He understood her dilemma. Unlike other sections of the ship where the crew had redundancies, the science labs had individuals who specialized, and people who supervised them. Those who supervised often had better minds than those running the experiments.

A loss in the science labs meant the loss remained until the ship hooked back up with the Fleet. Even then, there was no guarantee. The loss of one particular scientific researcher might mean that research halted for good.

"I'll have names for you when you're ready," she said.

She didn't complain. She didn't argue. She knew how important this was. He appreciated that. He occasionally got arguments about his assignments from the medical staff. But Lalliki was much more professional than that.

He also knew she would struggle with the decision as she tried to figure out who would do a good job, who was good enough to back up the advance team, and who, at the same time, was expendable.

"Thanks, Layla," he said. "I'm hoping this is going to be an easy one."

She let out a small snorting laugh, the sound she made when someone said something too good to be true.

"It hasn't been easy so far," she said. "I don't know why things should change now."

Because I want them to, he almost said, but didn't. He knew that what he wanted and what was going to happen were probably two different things.

But he wanted to hold onto the illusion of control a little longer.

Even though he had a hunch it was an illusion they could ill afford.

THIRTY-THREE

Five hours later, I'm at the head of the conference table in the big meeting room in my suite. The entire team has gathered. It's a repeat of our first night—sort of. We're all ragged.

I've had four hours of sleep that, while not refreshing, at least took the edge off of my exhaustion. Except in my muscles. I tried to get out of bed, and I could barely move. My upper thighs had seized up, my knees ached, and I couldn't lift my arms over my head.

My second shower since I returned from that cavern helped, but didn't make it completely better. I got some movement back. Now, at least, I can walk around the suite without groaning like a sick person.

In the past, I've gotten exhausted diving into wrecks, but my muscles have never seized up. Some of the team tells me this is normal for people who exercise in gravity. If so, I don't see the point. As great as our discovery is, I am really beginning to wish it had happened somewhere in space, without all the hazards of sore muscles, groundquakes, and falling rock.

The hotel staff is surly. While they've put out a spread for us, they act as if we're being inconsiderate. Maybe we are, eating well while the city's in crisis, expecting service in the middle of an emergency.

But the staff hasn't gone home, nor is anyone from that staff out working with the emergency crews. Some of my people volunteered to do so. Bridge told me that as we tried to set up this meeting. I was worried that some of my team wouldn't be available, but they all are.

The City of Vaycehn refused all outside help, even though a few of my people had expertise in ground emergencies. The Vaycehnese don't want outsiders to see the damage that groundquakes can cause. They don't want us to know what really happens when death holes appear.

In fact, they initially asked us to leave Vaycehn altogether.

Apparently Ilona fought that battle while she was trying to get us out of the cavern. Of course, then she was arguing that she had no idea what had happened to us and that if we were missing, then of course our people had to stay.

I have no idea how her most recent discussion has gone.

I stand while I wait for the last of my people to filter into the room. I have my back to the conference table. I've already eaten—in fact, I've eaten enough to sustain me for the rest of my life. I was starved when the hotel staff brought in the food. I ate more than I've ever eaten in one sitting. I think some of that is a reaction to being alive, and some of it comes from the extreme exertion.

That's one of the reasons I don't want to sit down. If I do, I'm afraid I'll have trouble standing up again.

The other reason is spread out before me.

Every night, I've looked at the City of Vaycehn through these windows, sprawled across the hills and mountainsides. I've become familiar with the buildings, the skyline, the way the lights flicker.

Tonight the lights are in different places. The lights move, and they don't flicker. They're dimmer than they've been, because the air is still filled with dust.

In fact, a dust cloud still hovers over the edge of the city where the death hole blew an opening in the ground and swallowed an entire neighborhood.

One of the hotel's waiters told me that they believe fifty are dead. "But," he said, "in cases like this, the numbers always climb."

The number of wounded is staggering—in the hundreds, maybe a thousand or more. For a city that is prepared for groundquakes, these numbers surprise me.

The staffer told me that the death rate used to be a lot higher than it is now. Then the others shushed him and got him out of the room.

I thought of those numbers. I'm still thinking about them.

When I take tourists on dives, they complain about the danger. They hate the lack of gravity. They hate carrying their own environment.

I love it. I love the solitude, the self-sufficiency. Yes, I might die out there. But in some ways, the possible deaths in space seem merciful compared to the ones that happened here today. Crushed by rock. Suffocating beneath a building. Melted or evaporated or something equally horrible by the explosion of the death hole itself.

I shudder, then sigh.

I want out of here. I hate being on the ground.

At the same time, I want to stay forever—or at least until we can take the Dignity Vessel with us.

"Everyone's here, Boss," Ilona says.

I turn. Everyone is here, and they're not in their usual positions. Ilona sits near my right hand. Bridge sits to my left. The Six sit near each other, and look so exhausted that I'm afraid they'll pass out before the food reaches them.

Some of the archeologists look tired, too. Mikk has deep circles under his eyes. Roderick lifts his water glass slowly. His arms must hurt like mine do.

Only a handful of people seem all right. Tamaz seems relieved that he hadn't accompanied us below. I'm relieved, too. While he's an excellent diver and pilot, he wouldn't have been able to lift the rocks the way Roderick and Mikk did.

The scientists look all right as well, if a bit worried. Some of them volunteered to help with the rescue efforts—one of them even has medical training I did not know about—and they were very angry at the rebuff.

I look at them all. They each have food in front of them. Some have water. The hotel brought alcohol, but I made them take it back. I need everyone thinking as clearly as possible tonight.

I put my hands on the back of my chair.

"All right," I say. "I'm sorry I was so mysterious with some of you earlier, but I wanted everyone to hear this story all at once. We found a Dignity Vessel today. Or rather, it found us."

I then tell the story of the Dignity Vessel's arrival. Everyone looks riveted, even those who have heard it before. The Six watch me as if the entire event is news to them as well.

Maybe they feel like I do—what happened with the Dignity Vessel seems like a very long time ago. The adventure of leaving the cavern somehow overtook the miracle and made us feel like we've gone through something horrible.

I pause and take a sip of water before I discuss what's been bothering me since we got out; the fact that we didn't feel the groundquake at all. But Lentz, the scientist who had the university ties that initially got us so much information, takes my momentary silence as an opening for conversation.

"I timed it," he says.

"Timed what?" Ilona asks, with a sideways look at me. The sideways look is permission to have the conversation even though she has a hunch I'm not done.

I don't let my expression give permission one way or the other. I take another sip of my water and look at Lentz.

"The groundquake," he says. "About how long into your dive do you estimate the ship arrived?"

He's already figured out what we suspected: the ship itself caused the death hole.

DeVries glances at me. I don't answer. DeVries was monitoring the time more than I was. He tells Lentz to the minute when the ship arrived.

"It corresponds," Lentz says. "I have a hunch that's the exact moment."

"And we know the death hole caused the groundquake and not the other way around?" Lucretia Stone asks. After our initial wrangling over control, she's been quite easy to work with. Of course, she's been focusing on the archeology, while I've been worried about the stealth-tech areas and the room.

In fact, I've somewhat lost track of the archeology, not that the ground has interested me much anyway.

"We don't know anything," Ilona says quickly, apparently afraid there will be some kind of verbal tussle.

"We don't even know how the ship got down there," DeVries says. "One minute the pad was empty; the next it had a ship on it."

"Was it there all along?" Bernadette Ivy asks. She has been the most annoying member of our team. She continues to scrub her hands raw. If I could, I would replace her. But I can't do anything about her.

"No, it wasn't there all along," I say, setting down my cup of water. "I told you. Rea was standing on that pad seconds before the ship arrived."

She flushes. "I mean, we know stealth tech opens other dimensions. Was the ship on the pad in the other dimension?"

We don't know that stealth tech opens other dimensions. I am about to say that when DeVries speaks up.

"The ship was cold," he says. "Extremely cold. It came from space. Somewhere."

"And magically appeared." Gregory, one of the other scientists, taps a finger against his chin as he considers this. "There are no holes in the ceiling, nothing opened up?"

"No, nothing opened up," Kersting says. He sounds as annoyed as I felt a moment ago. But Gregory's question is a good one. If the mountain had an opening that allowed ships to come in, then it would have been reasonable to assume that the opening activated, causing the death hole.

"I didn't look up," I say. "Did anyone else?"

"I did," Kersting says, still sounding annoyed. "That was my first thought. Maybe the ship came in from somewhere. But it didn't."

"He's right," Seager says. "One moment the pad was empty. The next, we had a ship. It just . . . materialized, for lack of a better word."

"And you felt no energy release?" Gregory asks.

I shrug, trying to remember. I was more focused on the ship itself than any feeling of power in the room.

"If that ship wasn't there, and then it was, there was some kind of displacement," Lentz says. "Even if it was just air molecules moving around."

Normally I find speculation fascinating, but not today. It's a sign of my continued exhaustion.

"I haven't finished," I say.

They all look at me. Ilona puts up a hand just slightly, as if she's afraid someone will interrupt me. I wonder if I look volatile or intolerant or if everyone just knows to avoid me when I'm tired.

"We had no sense at all of the groundquake," I say. "We were surprised by it."

"'Surprised' is an understatement," Kersting says, then looks at me hesitantly, as if he knows he shouldn't have spoken.

"We didn't feel anything, not even when that ship appeared," Rea says. "The floor in that room didn't vibrate at all. Nothing fell. We had no idea anything happened until we got to the edge of the stealth tech."

"Then it looked like someone had set off a bomb in the corridor," Seager says.

I don't mind their input. It reinforces what I had to say.

"You didn't feel that groundquake?" Stone asks. "You're kidding, right? It should have been more intense underground."

"We felt nothing," I say.

"But we did," Roderick says. "That was the scariest five minutes of my entire life."

"They were just outside the stealth tech," I say.

"We saw it," Quinte says. "But we were inside the stealth tech too. We watched the rocks fall outside the tech, and didn't feel a thing. It was surreal."

"The rocks fell silently, too," Al-Nasir says. "We didn't hear anything."

"It sounded like we were under attack," Mikk says. "With everything falling? It was thunderous."

We stare at each other. No one says anything for a few minutes.

We've always known that stealth tech creates its own environment, and that only some of us can survive in that environment. But we assumed—or at least, I assumed—that there was no difference between a stealth-tech area and a non-stealth-tech area for those of us with the marker.

If there was noise outside the stealth-tech area, I thought anyone with the marker inside the stealth tech could hear that noise. I figured that the marker simply leveled out the stealth-tech environment.

But I'm no scientist, and I hadn't thought it through. If people without the marker die inside stealth tech because time speeds up for them, then the environment is different. And stealth tech is supposed to be a kind of cloak for Dignity Vessels.

Only "cloak" isn't right, because if it were a cloak, then that ship should have been on that pad the whole time.

Instead, the ship came in from somewhere else.

I put a hand to my forehead, sigh, and finally slip into my chair.

"You know," I say after a moment, "I thought the day that we found a working Dignity Vessel was the day all of our questions would be answered. I never expected it to create more questions."

"Tougher questions," Bridge says.

"Fascinating questions," Lentz says.

"Deadly questions," Ivy says, and looks pointedly out the window.

"Well," I say. "We have a lot of work to do. We have to review all the material that my team brought out of that room. We have to investigate that death hole, somehow. And we have to keep the Vaycehnese from finding out about that vessel."

"They have to let us stay in Vaycehn first," Ilona says.

"Are they kicking us out?" I ask.

"If there are more groundquakes or death holes, yes," she says. "I'm not sure I can do anything about it."

"Then maybe we'd better tell them we know what's causing the death holes," Stone says.

"We don't know," I say hastily. "And until we do, we can't make that promise."

"But we can tell them we have an inkling," she says.

I shake my head. "We can't talk to anyone outside this room about that Dignity Vessel or the stealth tech. We know less now than we did a few hours ago. And my greatest fear is that by the time we get back down there, that Dignity Vessel will be gone."

"You're in no shape to go back down there," Bridge says to me. Then he looks at the Six. "None of you are."

"We're the only ones who can do it," Kersting says, surprising me. I would have thought he would never want to go down there again.

"I think it's pretty important that we keep going," Quinte says, also surprising me. "People are dying up here, and I think Lentz is right. I think it's not a coincidence that the ship returned at the same time the death hole formed. I think we might actually be able to help Vaycehn solve a centuries-old problem."

I look at all of them. They seem like they have more energy than they had at the start of this meeting.

"You always preach caution, Boss," Tamaz says. "We can't dive tired. You all are exhausted."

"We are," I say. "And this whole incident has shown me how ill prepared we are to deal with land problems. I need a lot from you in the next few hours. I need someone to coordinate efforts on the ground here, so that we're better prepared for our underground adventures. I need permission from Vaycehn to stay. I need everyone to review the information we brought to the surface. And I need the Six to rest before we go back down."

"When will we go back?" DeVries asks.

I shrug. "The Vaycehnese have to clear those corridors first. Any ideas on that?"

I direct that last to Ilona, but Bridge is the one who answers.

"I didn't go through the city," he says. "That Bug driver will be working on his own to clear the debris."

"That's why he took the money," I say.

Bridge smiles. "Yep. He's not going to share it with anyone."

"Is that safe for him?" Mikk asks.

"I get the sense he's done work off the books before," Bridge says.

"I hope so," Mikk says. "Because it's a mess down there."

Ivy stands and looks out that window. "It's a mess everywhere," she says.

Except in that room. With the Dignity Vessel.

And I can't wait to return.

THIRTY-FOUR

At the end of Coop's thirty-six-hour cutoff, the outsiders had not returned.

He sat in the captain's chair, hand on his chin, elbow resting on the chair's solid arm, as he stared through the screens to the sector base. Most of the particles had settled, although they still coated everything.

The room was empty and mostly dark.

It looked abandoned. He felt abandoned, which surprised him. He had expected the outsiders to return. The fact that they hadn't seemed quite odd to him.

If he had been a betting man—and he wasn't—he would have laid money on their return within eight hours or, on the outside, ten. What he understood of the body language of their leader (if, indeed, she was their leader), was that she was intrigued by the ship, by the room, by everything.

Maybe the rest of the team had to drag her out because their time underground was limited. Maybe they had left the entire region.

Or maybe a commander outside the sector base had ordered them to proceed with more caution.

His mistake, Mae would tell him if he gave her the chance, was that he expected other cultures to behave like his. For all he knew, they operated on a weekly cycle instead of an hourly one. Maybe they were more cautious than he was. Or maybe their goal hadn't been exploration at all. Maybe they had some other goal for the sector base, and the arrival of the ship had ruined that goal.

Coop needed to send in his team. He had waited long enough.

Dix had spent the last hour looking pointedly over his shoulder at Coop and then staring at the screens. Coop hadn't moved; he'd been studying those screens for at least two hours now. And he'd noted how many times his quite superior bridge crew had given him surreptitious looks.

Maybe the sector base itself could help with the decisions Coop needed to make. The repair room might have sophisticated ways to track the Fleet.

The Fleet always traveled on the same trajectory. The problem was that the Fleet's mission determined its timetable. The Fleet's mission, which it had adhered to without fail since it left Earth, was to support the underdog, fight the right battles, help individuals, nations, and entire regions of space become self-sufficient, able to protect their own peoples without hurting others.

The mission was vague, and sometimes the Fleet ended up on a side it didn't want to be on, but mostly it had worked. And when the Fleet felt the peoples, the nations, the regions of space were stable, it moved on, secure in the knowledge that it had done its job well.

Sometimes, to do that job well, the Fleet had to stay longer than expected. Sometimes on a random stop for supplies, the Fleet would encounter a group that needed their help. Sometimes, no one they met needed help, not for years.

So the Fleet's location along its chosen route would be a suggestion, a hope, rather than an actual schedule. And the stragglers could catch up, because the *anacapa* worked by folding space and could, with the right calculations, fold the *Ivoire* within a few years (and a few light-years) from the Fleet itself.

If the *anacapa* worked. If the *Ivoire* retained enough power to travel that far. If they didn't get attacked by those outsiders.

If, if, if.

Coop stood up. He couldn't think about that yet. He needed to focus on now, which meant repairing the *Ivoire* and figuring out exactly what had happened here. Then he would worry about catching up to the Fleet.

"I guess we send in our exploratory team," he said to the entire crew.

"Why are you hesitant?" Dix asked.

"I keep expecting the outsiders to return," Coop said.

"If they do, our people can take care of them," Perkins said.

Coop resisted the urge to shake his head. Sometimes Perkins's inexperience grated on him.

"We don't want our people to take care of them," Anita said, using a tone that was a bit too patronizing. "We want to stay out of their way for a while, figure out what they're up to."

"We could talk to them and figure that out," Perkins said, and Coop finally understood what was behind her seemingly naïve comments. She wanted to work too, just like everyone else. Only she had no work to do, not yet. Her job in first contact was to figure out the language and start the communication.

"We might not ever talk to them, Perkins," Coop said gently. "They may never know that we exist."

She sighed, but didn't respond to that.

"I'll summon the exploratory team to the conference room so you can brief them," Dix said.

"I asked Layla to pick the scientists for the team," Coop said. "Make sure I get their background information before that briefing. I want to know strengths and weaknesses."

"Already have them on file," Dix said. "I've had it for hours."

Coop bit back a defensive response. He knew the bridge crew thought they should have gone into the sector base much earlier. The fact that the outsiders hadn't returned made the bridge crew feel their point of view was the correct one.

But he knew that waiting had been right. He wished that the outsiders had returned so that he would know what they were doing.

Instead, he would have to warn the exploratory team to monitor the door, so that they could sprint for the ship if the outsiders returned.

He wanted the first contact on his terms, if there was going to be a first contact at all.

THIRTY-FIVE

*E*arly the next morning, I head back to the caves. I take Bridge with me. Bridge has been the one talking with the Bug driver. I figure Bridge can continue talking with him. These Vaycehnese and their unwillingness to deal with women have driven me crazy so far, and I don't want to fight that today.

I've sent Ilona to work with the Vaycehnese government to get us back into those caves as quickly as possible. She's also supposed to argue for letting our experienced team members help with the groundquake/death hole emergency. But I have another reason for getting them involved. I need the scientists and archeologists to see that death hole up close.

I'm not that interested in the death hole. I want to get below, figure out what's going on with the ship, figure out if the ship is still there. And I have a hunch that if I don't push the Bug operator, he'll take all of our money while he's taking his own sweet time.

More than one person has expressed concern that we're keeping the Bug away from rescue work. They tell me he needs to be at the death hole and the groundquake destruction. I've had to remind each and every person who mentions this that we might hold the solution, not just to this groundquake and death hole, but to all of the death holes in the future.

We might be able to stop them.

Future thinking is not something my group is good at. Some think very well about the past, others think quite well about the small things that make up our universe, but very few of them have training in thinking about what lies ahead.

I have that training, but it's hard-won. It comes from diving, where each handhold might cause a possible disaster. It comes from planning trips to far-away areas of space, where I'm often on my own. And lately, it has come from fighting the Enterran Empire, who would love to know about this discovery, deep underground here on Wyr.

I have more than one reason to keep this discovery silent as long as possible. I want to figure out how to get that ship out of here, so that we can study it.

If we can't get the ship out of here, I want to claim it somehow, so that the Empire can't. I'm not sure how to do that; this is Enterran space, after all. We're in their territory, whether we like it or not.

I only got five hours of sleep even though I was exhausted, mostly because I've been worried about this aspect of our discovery. As excited as I am, I'm afraid we may have given the Empire exactly what it needs: a working stealth-tech model, so that they can build their own stealth-tech ships.

My only hope is to work quickly, and my only hope of working quickly comes from getting this damn Bug operator to clear the caves.

The morning dawned clear and hot. I am beginning to understand that there are degrees of hot, that what I thought was hot when we first arrived wasn't hot at all by Vaycehn's standards. This morning, before the sun is even all the way up, is hotter than any day we've experienced so far.

Bridge and I have arrived at the same time that the Bug driver has. I hadn't seen him put the Bug away the night before. We left before he did. This morning, it arrives with him, a big clunky machine that walks uneasily across the rubble-strewn landscape.

The pod sinks down a few meters from the hole. Then the driver gets out. He's a burly man, younger than I would have thought, with muscles like Mikk's, although only on his arms. His brown hair is cropped short. He wears a shirt with no sleeves, and very short pants, revealing hairy legs. His feet are encased in sandals.

He walks over to Bridge, gesturing as he does so.

Even though I'm several meters away, I can tell that the operator is unhappy. He thought he'd be here alone this morning.

And that's a good sign. It meant he was going to honor his commitment to us, rather than take our money and go on to another job.

Bridge talks to him, and nods toward me. The man looks over Bridge's shoulder and shakes his head slightly.

Bridge already told me what he was going to do. He was going to play to their prejudices, say how difficult it is to work for a woman. He was going to complain that I want to go back down, even though he has tried to talk me out of it. He told me this before we came, and spoke hesitantly, as if he expected me to disapprove.

To his surprise, I didn't disapprove. I am for anything that gets us back to that ship quickly.

Both men are laughing now, and I'm sure it's at my expense. My cheeks warm, even though this was planned. I clutch my bottle of water and wander toward the men, taking my time.

First I look at the opening to the cave. It's so much bigger than it seems when you take a hovercart through it. Or when you climb out of it while completely exhausted. Big enough to swallow a small building.

I resist the urge to groan. My legs are even sorer this morning than they were last night. I had no idea that was possible. I feel ancient and injured, even though I know I'm not.

I'm glad I've given the Six the day off, as well as Mikk and Roderick. They're right; I should have taken it too.

But I won't move much once I'm in the Bug.

"Boss!"

I look over at Bridge. He's gesturing to me. I smile as if I don't know what he's been up to and walk carefully over to them. I'm not going to let anyone know how very sore I am.

"This is Paplas," Bridge says, indicating the driver, who watches me closely. "He owns and operates the Reclaimer."

The way Bridge says the machine's name is also a direction; we're not to call the machine a Bug in front of Paplas.

I nod. Paplas's gray eyes watch me, then he nods back.

"He's going to let us go with him," Bridge says, "but we have to follow his rules."

"We do not come up until I say." Paplas speaks Standard with that lovely lilt all of the Vaycehnese have. "I stay there, with my lunch, until I am done for the day. I do not work extra hours. It taxes the Reclaimer."

He's making sure I know that he won't bend for me, or for Bridge for that matter.

"All right," I say.

"If you are ill, if there is a problem, you tell me now," Paplas says. "I will not come back except for an emergency."

"I understand," I say.

"You will sit behind me," he says. "You will ask no questions."

I open my mouth, then close it as Bridge gives me a sideways look. He has permission to ask questions. I do not. In other words, I'm to sit there quietly and watch while the men take care of business.

I hope Bridge will ask the questions we need. If not, I hope he'll confer with me, maybe quietly, so that he can ask the questions I think of. We might need answers later.

I am worried about a repeat of yesterday's events. I hope Bridge will discuss that with him as well.

"I understand that, too," I say.

Paplas nods and walks away from me. He's heading back to the Bug. We follow.

Up close the pod looks huge. It is both wider and taller than it looks when it's in motion. The gigantic legs bend and tower above us. Their sides have movable blades that dig into mountainsides. There are several other pieces of equipment attached to the legs that look movable as well. I can't tell what those pieces are for.

The bottom of the legs themselves—the feet, for lack of a better word—are bendable. They seem to have a way to adhere to a surface.

Suddenly, my technical interest is piqued, and I wish I can talk to Paplas, one pilot to another. But I cannot.

Bridge sees me looking at the legs, but doesn't understand that I have questions.

The questions aren't important yet. They can wait. I have a hunch we'll be back tomorrow, and if we are, then Bridge can ask about the working mechanism of the legs and feet.

Paplas stands near the door of the Bug. It's clear, like the rest of the pod. Inside there are two seats up front, and a bench seat in the back. The ceiling is high.

What surprises me is that the equipment, and the seats, are in the exact middle of the pod. Like a single ship, then, the pod is designed to work in any direction.

I didn't expect to see something like that on land.

"You will strap in," Paplas says. "You will not touch the restraints except when we have to leave."

He points out a service area in the very back, which has a bathroom and a place to store our gear. Nothing will remain loose in the pod itself.

He explains why, but he doesn't need to—at least for me. I understand. The pod will rotate 360 degrees at various times during the day. Anything loose will fall on us.

The pod doesn't have artificial gravity.

"You will sit there," he says to me as he points to the part of the bench farthest from him. "Go."

I don't need to be told twice. I climb up the tiny set of stairs, then boost myself up to the seat. As I clamber over to it, I glance behind me. Paplas looks amused.

I seem to have passed the first test.

I figure out the various straps and restrainers while Bridge climbs in beside me. As Paplas gets in, I look at the controls. Dozens of them, all of them marked in Vaycehnese. The handles look well used, and the lettering has come off of many of the labels.

This machine is older than she looks, well loved and well maintained.

That makes me feel better—or at least it does until he starts her up. The pod jerks as he puts it into some kind of gear.

Then we rise.

None of the movements are smooth. I have a good sense of direction. I also do well under g-forces and in strange positions. But Bridge looks a bit ill. I hope he can survive something that will whip him around like a ball on a string.

But I don't warn him. I've been told to remain silent, and I do. I do, however, see a small group of sick bags tucked behind the pilot's seat. I point them out to Bridge.

His eyes narrow—*I don't need that*, he seems to say—but as I look away, I note him checking their position.

It will be a long day. But, I hope, it will be a profitable one.

We need to get back to work.

I am more worried about that ship than I can say.

THIRTY-SIX

*T*he Fleet had two theories of leadership. The first theory espoused that the leaders had the most expertise and therefore were the least expendable; the second theory claimed that the leaders had the most expertise and therefore had to be first on the ground, to make sure everything was fine.

Coop's training made him a believer in the first theory. He knew that others could run the *Ivoire*, but few could do it as well as he could. Leading a vessel in the Fleet was a specialized skill, just like being a top-notch linguist was a specialized skill.

Still, he wished he espoused the second theory on this day. He wanted to go into that base. He wanted to be the one to touch the equipment, to assign the person to the door, to see the *Ivoire* from the outside, so that he could view for himself the kind of damage she had sustained.

But he wasn't going to do that. He was going to follow his own policies, just like he demanded his own people do.

Still, he held a longer-than-usual briefing with the exploratory team, some of whom he didn't recall seeing before, even though he met everyone when they first came on board to serve on the *Ivoire*.

This team had some highly qualified junior officers, scientists chosen by Layla, engineers chosen by Yash, and one superb team leader whom Coop wished he could promote.

The team leader, Joanna Rossetti, was thin and small, wiry and tough, more suited to space than to land-based missions. She could fit anywhere, get into any small area, and often did. She had spent half her life training in zero-g, something a lot in the Fleet never did, and so was adept at all kinds of space missions, from those in zero gravity to those in low gravity. Her small size made heavy gravity possible as well; she didn't feel as crushed by it as someone who weighed more.

She was also a thinker. She solved problems as fast as Coop did, faster than most of the people on his excellent bridge crew.

That was one of the many things he liked about her.

Coop let her choose the two officers who would go along with her. He figured she needed people she could trust. He hadn't been surprised when she chose Adam Shärf. Coop had been watching Shärf as well. Shärf was young, agile, and intelligent. He had a spotless record and was known for stopping fights instead of starting them.

Her choice of Salvador Ahidjo did surprise Coop. As far as Coop knew—and he tried to keep track of all of his officers—Ahidjo had done nothing to distinguish himself throughout his career. Ahidjo was older than Coop and had remained at the same rank for nearly two decades. His work was fine but never outstanding. There was never any reason to promote or demote him. He was simply a solid member of the core who did his job rather quietly and never rose to anyone's attention.

Except, apparently, Rossetti's.

But the scientists and engineers were the key to this mission. At his request, Yash picked the best engineers who had once worked at a sector base or alongside sector base technicians. Yash had protested; a lot of these engineers were key to the ship's repairs as well. But Coop wanted expertise and familiarity with the equipment.

Just like he wanted creative thinkers among the scientists.

During the briefing, he resisted the urge to quiz the scientists he didn't remember and the engineers he wasn't that familiar with. Instead, he forced himself to trust his officers.

Just like he was doing now, as Rossetti and her team stepped out of the airlock and into the sector base itself.

He monitored it all from his position on the bridge. The bridge team watched as well, their bodies tense. They wanted to go into that base as much as he did, and they understood why he wasn't letting them.

Rossetti's tiny form looked even smaller as she climbed down the ladder from the exterior door and stepped onto the floor. Particles rose around her, thick and heavy, more of them than Coop had seen before. Some of them came from his cleaning of the ship, but the rest had to be coming from somewhere else.

The particles floated around her like snow. She captured some of them in her glove and closed her fist, clearly doing a small test of her own.

Coop didn't say anything. He watched, the wall screens on full, which made him feel as if only a thin membrane separated him from the repair room outside the ship. As he watched his team step onto the repair room floor, he felt as if he could take one step through the membrane and join them.

After all, he knew what it felt like to be in that room.

The last time he had been there, only a month before, the room had been slightly cold. The equipment functioned better in chilly conditions, so the staff kept the room cooler than the interior of most ships. And, one of the staff explained to him, the newly arrived ship always chilled the air as well. It still carried some of the cold from space, and that brought down the ambient temperature all by itself.

The air also had a metallic tang. The local staff claimed they couldn't smell it, but he could. Every section base he'd ever been to had a version of that smell. Sometimes the smell was tinged with sulfur, thanks to underground springs nearby, and sometimes it was laced with a chalky smell, one that came from the inside of the mountain itself.

Every place was different. He knew if he had to, he could identify the section bases he'd been to by smell alone.

Although the team he'd just sent into the repair room wasn't feeling cold or smelling a metallic tang. They were snug in their environmental suits, suits made of material so strong that the knife the outsider woman had worn wouldn't penetrate them.

The air filters were built into the suits themselves. The suits looked thin, but they weren't. They had three layers. The exterior was made of that impermeable material. The middle layer carried the oxygen stores, so that the suit's wearer didn't need oxygen canisters like the outsiders had. The interior layer measured and controlled body temperature, as well as maintaining every other part of the environment that gave the suits their name.

These suits didn't even have separate helmets. Instead, they had full-face hoods with clear material that ran from the ears to the eyes, wide enough not to impede the wearer's vision, but much more protective than a glass or plastic plate over the face.

The only problem with that part of the suit design was that Coop had to intuit mood. He couldn't see expression, except through the eyes themselves.

Not that it mattered in this instance. In this instance, he had told the team to communicate everything, so that he, Yash, and Dix could track what they were doing.

Through a special earpiece, Dix monitored the scientists on one channel. Yash monitored the engineers on another. Coop monitored the leaders on a third. The team spoke among themselves on a fourth channel, using it only when necessary, so that they didn't clutter up each other's hearing with needless chatter.

There wasn't much chatter on Coop's channel while the team waited on the floor for everyone to emerge from the airlock. He watched them in relative silence. Rossetti updated him with names as each person joined the group.

Once the team was assembled, she gave them instructions. They divided into three groups, each composed of an engineer, a scientist, and an officer. The engineer and the scientist had been assigned to a section of equipment. The officer guarded them and provided advice.

Because this was a first-contact team, it also had two guards, whom Rossetti sent to the outside door. They stood just behind it, using sensors to monitor the exterior as best they could. Coop hoped that they'd know well in advance if the outsiders were returning.

Rossetti's team stayed closest to the ship. Coop had determined that. He wanted her near that door in case the outsiders returned. He also figured the active equipment up front would have the most information, so he made certain that his best team was on that section, instead of the farthest back.

Ahidjo's team took the middle section. Shärf's team took a far section. They only covered about an eighth of the repair room. More equipment faded into the dark. Coop would save that for later missions, if he needed them.

Of course, Rossetti's team reached their equipment first. They split, the engineer looking at the actual workings, the scientist taking the readings. Rossetti hung back, looking around as if she expected something bad to happen.

"Sir?"

Coop started. Rossetti's voice had come along a fifth channel, one that went directly into his earpiece. It sounded like she was standing beside him.

He had to change frequencies on the small mike he had placed in his front teeth. "What?" he subvocalized, so that he didn't disturb Dix or Yash.

"Something's odd here," Rossetti said.

He wanted to say, *No kidding,* but he knew better than to waste precious time talking. He simply waited for her to continue.

She did. "You've known me for some time. I'm not superstitious, but something feels wrong here. I can't quite figure out how to describe it."

"Try," he said.

She nodded once. Her head bob made more particles swirl around her. It looked like his team was in a particle storm.

Ahidjo's team had just reached the second section of equipment. The engineer touched the edge of the console, and lights flickered on.

Coop smiled. He had expected that. It confirmed what he had thought earlier; the outsiders had turned the equipment on when they started exploring the room.

On the third channel, he said, "Ahidjo, Shärf. Make sure your teams shut down that equipment before you leave today."

"Yes, sir," they said in unison.

Rossetti turned her head toward them, observing their progress for a moment. Then she continued on the fifth channel.

"If I had entered this place without knowing what it was," she said, her tone measured as if she was choosing each word carefully, "I would think that it had been abandoned long ago."

"Why?" he asked.

She shook her head, but he didn't think that was her entire response. It looked more like an involuntary movement, an I-don't-know kind of reaction.

After that, she paused for a very long time.

"I can't give you a definitive answer to that, sir," she said. "It's just an impression."

Then she fell silent. Coop didn't expect her to say more. His people were used to quantifying things. The fact that she couldn't figure out a reason for her feeling probably bothered her more than it bothered him.

It had taken a bit of courage for Rossetti to tell him about that sense of abandonment. Yet she felt it important.

She wasn't sensing lingering violence, the way he had upon entering an area after a battle; she was sensing emptiness.

Coop didn't like emptiness. He would have preferred the lingering violence. It suited his training so much better.

The third team reached their piece of equipment. The lights came on, but they looked very far away and faded. The particle storm made them hard to see.

Maybe the particle storm gave Rossetti that feeling; maybe it was something else. When the others returned, he would ask them if they had felt something similar.

At the moment, however, they worked, updating him periodically, not saying exactly what they found—that was for the return briefing—but letting him know that the work was proceeding, that no one had entered the room (even though he could see that), that the equipment seemed to be working fine.

So far, no one had found any communications problems in the sector base's equipment, which meant that the *Ivoire's* communications array had been damaged, just like Yash suspected. The engineers on his ship had even more work to do than they all initially suspected.

The time passed quickly. Yash and Dix monitored their frequencies as well as did some work on their own consoles. But Coop just studied the repair room, unable to shake what Rossetti had said.

He had experienced that feeling of long-abandonment in a place recently vacated just once in his career. He'd been twenty-five. He was at Sector Base T, and he accompanied a senior officer as they did a final inspection of a decommissioned ship.

The ship, the *Défi*, had been badly damaged in an attack. Rather than repair it, the staff at Sector Base T would use it and another badly damaged ship to build an entirely new ship.

The *Défi* had been Coop's home during the last of his education. A lot of cadets went there for officer training. The ship had had a lively, active student community, as well as the usual crew complement and domestic side. He had loved that place.

But it had seemed entirely different on that final walk-through, as if someone had taken the heart out of the ship. Which, apparently, they had. Without the human population, the *Défi* had become just another junked ship, ready to be torn down into its various parts.

That ship still haunted his dreams. Sometimes, old friends long gone would run down its corridors, laughing as they coaxed him into the Grog, the cadet bar. He didn't drink much—never had, really—so his presence in the Grog was always an event.

He would wake up feeling sad for something he had lost.

Maybe that was what Rossetti was feeling. She had been here just a month ago as well. He had no idea what kind of experiences she had had during their layover. Maybe those were coloring her reaction now.

But that wasn't something he could discuss with her on Channel Five or on Channel Three. He would wait until she returned.

At four hours and thirty minutes, he reminded his team that they had to shut down before they returned. He also wanted additional cameras (if there were any) disabled. He wanted the interior to look as much like it had when the others left as his team could make it.

They began their shutdown procedures. In the distance, he saw the lights of the far sector shut off. At least that was working. Then middle section went off. If the team returned quickly enough, maybe the particles would have stopped swirling.

He stood near the wall again, hands clasped behind him. His heartbeat had risen just slightly. He wanted the team to move quicker, although he didn't say anything.

He wanted them out before the outsiders returned.

At the end of their fifth hour, the exploratory team was all inside the airlock. The lights on the far panels had gone out, and the teams had reported that they had altered the feeds on all the cameras they could find.

The particle storm settled.

Just like Coop, the base seemed to be waiting for the outsiders to return.

THIRTY-SEVEN

*O*nce the Bug stops walking, its movements become smooth. Paplas positions it over the cave opening. For one heady moment, I can see down the hillside into Vaycehn itself.

Dust still rises from the new death hole, but the dust is now just a blight on the landscape, not the overwhelming part of it. A fire burns a few kilometers from the death hole, the result—one of the hotel staff told me that morning—of damage from the groundquake.

Apparently groundquakes don't just cause things to collapse, they cause systems to fail. The collapse might ignite a fire or start a flood of water in addition to the damage from the collapse itself.

As Bridge and I look at the city, Paplas adjusts the controls. His hands fly across his control panel, stopping occasionally to grab a lever and pull it. It's almost as if Paplas himself has dozens of arms just like the Bug does.

Finally he stops moving for a brief moment. He turns his head slightly, looks at Bridge, and says, "Now we descend."

The Bug's pod floats downward, almost like a ship. In fact, I would think of it as a ship except that it is not moving on its own propulsion, but being levered down by the legs. Some remain on the surface as the pod eases into the darkness. Others float past us as they make their way down, anchoring those bendable feet on the side of the cave itself.

It's not quite right to say that the walls have closed in. We just feel closed in because the big black legs take up so much space inside the hole.

I'm also not in control—of the mission, of the Bug itself, of Paplas. So I sit, with my hands clasped, letting someone else do work I would rather do.

I glance at Bridge. His expression is hard, as if he's willing himself to remain calm.

Paplas is grinning, his hands moving delicately over the controls.

It takes less than three minutes to descend to the cave floor, the same distance it took me half my life to climb up. No wonder I had no sense of how deep we were before. The equipment the Vaycehnese use is so quick and sophisticated that it makes long distances seem short.

The legs work their way down and settle around us. Paplas turns to Bridge.

"Now for the fun," Paplas says.

Bridge frowns at him, not understanding. I do. Working equipment in a particular setting, even if the setting is ruined and dangerous, can be a great deal of fun.

With a jerk of the pod, Paplas moves the Bug forward. I can't tell if that jerk comes from a part that needs repair or a flaw in the design. As the Bug flattens itself out to move into the corridor, Bridge says to Paplas, sounding a bit nervous, "I guess you assessed the damage yesterday, huh?"

"Assessed?" Paplas says, not looking back.

"You know," Bridge says, and he *does* sound nervous. "Figured out how bad the damage is, how much work you'll have, how long it will take?"

I suppress a smile. Bridge has worked with me long enough to learn my work habits. He's come to expect them from everyone who does work in places that Bridge sees as alien.

"Why would I do that?" Paplas asks.

Bridge looks at me, panic clear on his face. I smile and shrug, expecting this. Paplas has a system. He's clearly done this before. To him, this is a clean-up task, not an exotic adventure.

I glance at the control panel. On it, Paplas has a map of the corridors, some areas shaded dark. A small red beacon shows where we are.

It takes just a moment to get to the first rock fall. The Bug stops. Paplas grabs something from under his seat, then turns to us.

He's holding ear protectors.

"I almost forgot," he says. "Put these on."

I take mine. They're a bit greasy, either from being under the seat so long or from the previous user. I wipe the part that will go against my ears, then put on the ear protectors. Instantly, all ambient noise vanishes.

Bridge deliberately widens his eyes as he looks at me, an expression that means *You've got to be kidding.* Fortunately, he doesn't say that to Paplas.

Instead he wipes off the ear parts and stick them on, then glances at me.

Paplas has put on his own ear protectors. He doesn't look at us as he moves one of the legs forward.

It feels odd to see the leg move and not hear the attendant sound, almost like we are in space. I'm suddenly more comfortable.

Bridge is not. He squirms in his seat.

I smile reassuringly at him.

The leg jams against a head-sized rock. Instead of picking it up, as I expect, the leg starts vibrating.

It takes a moment, without the sound, to realize what the leg is doing. It's pulverizing the rock.

I frown. I thought we were going to lift the rock out of the cave, carrying it in those legs just like Mikk and Roderick had done as they worked to get us out of one of the corridors.

Instead, Paplas is destroying the rock.

I want to ask what's going to happen to the dust, but I can't. Even if he let me talk, he wouldn't be able to hear my question.

Instead, I sit forward on my seat so that I can see better. Half the legs have moved to the front of the pod and started pulverizing.

I know now why we needed the ear protectors.

The Bug vibrates a little. I want to know why the sound won't cause the rock walls around us to vibrate and collapse. I want to know if Paplas has done this before (although it seems pretty clear that he has).

Bridge clutches the edge of his seat. I lean as far forward as I possibly can without attracting Paplas's attention.

The rocks gripped in the legs grow smaller. Dust forms, and so far, none of my questions have been answered.

THIRTY-EIGHT

*C*oop paced as he waited for the team to arrive in the briefing room. He, Yash, and Dix had places at the head of the table. Lynda's crew now had control of the bridge, and the rest of Coop's team had gone to dinner or to their evening recreation.

Anita and Perkins had both protested; they wanted to be part of the meeting. But Coop wanted the briefing to remain as private as possible. After his conversation with Rossetti while she was in the base, he was worried about the information the exploratory team would bring back.

The exploratory team arrived in the briefing room with their handhelds. They all had wet hair and loose-fitting clothes, having cleaned up after their mission. The white environmental suits looked gray upon their return, and they'd peeled them off in the airlock, but some of the particles still stuck to their clothing, which was why Coop had approved real-water showers as well as the standard sonic shower. He also made them change in the decontamination area just in case.

The scientists and engineers moved toward the back of the room. The commanders clustered near Coop, Yash, and Dix. Rossetti had turned on the wall screens when she came in. She had plans for this briefing, then, which was one of the things Coop liked about her.

She thought ahead.

Currently, the screens had no images, just an occasional multicolored line through the center to show that the screens were drawing power.

Coop closed the briefing room door, then took his seat at the head of the table. "What've you got?" he asked Rossetti.

She was the only one of the group who didn't look tired. She sat, spine straight, her small hands flat on the tabletop.

"First," she said, "we don't need the suits. Every test we did says the atmosphere inside that room is fine."

"And the particles?" Dix asked.

"Harmless," she said. "They've been through more testing than we usually do on anything. They seem to be unbonded nanobits, and we've all worked around unbonded nanobits before."

They had. The bits occasionally got into the lungs, but could be removed with little effort. Many of the Fleet's crew members had no reaction to nanobits at all, and could, in fact, absorb them. It was, one of the medics once told Coop, a genetically desired trait that seemed to have developed in the Fleet's population over time.

Rossetti glanced at the others from her team, then said, "It would be easier to work in the repair room without the environmental suits."

Her team had clearly asked her to say that. She hadn't done any hands-on work, so this wasn't coming from her experience.

"So noted," Coop said. He would make no promises without consulting with his best people. "What else do you have for me?"

Rossetti took a deep breath, then pressed her hands against the tabletop. He finally understood why she sat that way; it was a calming gesture, one she clearly needed.

"Do you recall what I told you, sir, when I was on the repair room floor?"

"Yes," he said, and didn't elaborate. He hadn't mentioned it to his team, but he would tell them if they needed to know.

"Apparently, I was right. The sector base had been long abandoned, sir. The mandatory shutdown sequence began one hundred years after we left." She spoke flatly, as if the news hadn't bothered her at all. But her splayed hands belied that.

"One hundred years?" Dix's voice rose slightly. He looked surprised.

But Yash didn't. Her features remained impassive.

Coop's heart was pounding. "We left a month ago."

"Yes, sir," Rossetti said. "But the elapsed time in the station is at least two hundred years, maybe longer."

She hadn't insulted his intelligence by explaining how such a thing could happen. They all knew. It was one of the risks of the *anacapa* drive.

"You're certain of this?" Coop looked at the scientists and engineers. What he had initially taken for exhaustion was defeat. And fear.

If their calculations were right, they were at least two hundred years in their own future, in an empty sector base, with a damaged ship.

They saw only catastrophe.

Coop didn't. If he could repair the *Ivoire*, he could send her through fold-space to the place where the Fleet might be. His calculations (and theirs) could be as much as fifty years off, but that wouldn't matter. The Fleet followed a set trajectory. Only battles and meetings with other cultures changed the timeline. Coop's team could guess the farthest that the Fleet would get on that trajectory, and go there. If the Fleet had already arrived, they could continue until they caught it (which wouldn't take long). If the Fleet hadn't arrived yet (which was more likely), they could wait for it to catch them.

The older members of the crew might never see the Fleet again, but the younger members would.

"Two hundred years is manageable," Yash said softly, clearly mistaking his silence for shock.

"I know," he said, just as softly, silencing her.

He folded his own hands on the tabletop. He was strangely calm. Now that he knew what was happening, he would probably remain calm until they had a firm plan.

"What kind of evidence do you have?" he asked Rossetti.

She turned to one of the engineers, the only one who Coop had ever interacted with, an older man by the name of José Cabral.

"The equipment itself gives us the timeline," Cabral said. "The sector base closed one hundred years after we left. A rudimentary staff remained, those who didn't want to travel with the Fleet to Sector Base Y, which was where this group would be posted. This staff continued to live on the surface, charged with maintaining the equipment at low power levels for the next fifty years."

Coop nodded. This was standard procedure.

Dix shifted in his chair. The news clearly made him nervous.

"After fifty years without human contact," Cabral said, "the equipment went dormant. Everything shut down except the touch command."

Touch command. Meaning that the systems would only reactivate if the equipment got touched by human hands. Coop would have to confirm that with Yash, but he didn't think that some kind of falling debris would activate the system. Just contact from a member of the Fleet. At least, that was what he had been told.

"How long has this base been dormant?" Coop asked.

"Impossible to tell, sir," Cabral said. "When the system goes dormant, even its internal clock mechanism ceases. Only the *anacapa* drive continues to function, at a very low level, of course, and then only because it is safer to keep the drive running than it is to shut it down."

Coop nodded. He had been told that as well.

"If I may, sir." One of the scientists, a middle-aged woman, spoke up. She was thin, with harsh lines around her mouth and eyes. Coop had to struggle to recall her name, which he had only heard in the context of this mission. "The evidence points toward the machinery being off for a very long time."

One of the other scientists held up his hand, as if to stop her, but she caught his hand in her own and brought it down.

"What evidence?" Coop asked.

"The particles, sir," she said. "Nanobits are durable. They don't lose their bonding except in a few instances. Most nanobits lose their bonding through a particular kind of weapon fire, which we see no evidence of here. It could also be caused by a chemical reaction, which we also have no evidence of. In fact, if the chemical reaction had occurred, the room itself would be toxic."

"And the other instance?" Coop asked.

"Time," she said. "Specifically, five hundred to a thousand years, sir."

"We don't have proof of that," said the scientist whose hand she still held. "We just have supposition."

"And past experience," she said. "We've encountered this before, and by we, I mean the Fleet. Never have the nanobits lost their bonding in less than five hundred years."

Coop's stomach flipped. He had to work to keep his hands relaxed, so that his knuckles wouldn't show white.

"We'll have to test to be certain," said one of the other scientists. He wasn't looking at Coop, but at Dix. Dix, who sat rigidly next to Coop. Dix, who, rumor had it, had fallen in love with one of the chefs on the *Geneva*.

The *Geneva*, which was traveling with the Fleet.

If the Fleet was five hundred years distant from them, in no way could Coop plot the Fleet's course. There were too many variables. Two hundred years was at the very edge of possible.

Five hundred years meant that the *Ivoire* might never rejoin the Fleet.

Coop wouldn't let himself think of that. He didn't have proof.

"The equipment itself isn't damaged," Rossetti said, trying to take control of the briefing back from her scientist. "It's just old."

Coop nodded.

"We should be able to use information in the database to help us fix the *Ivoire*," she said.

He nodded again. He wasn't thinking about that quite as much. He knew his engineers could fix the *Ivoire*. She had extensive damage, but none of it was catastrophic.

He was more concerned about their current situation.

"The outsiders," he said, and paused. Everyone looked at him. They clearly hadn't expected him to mention the outsiders at this point. "You told me their suits looked underdeveloped."

He said this last to Yash.

She nodded. "Ours are technically superior, if that glove is any indication."

"Oxygen cylinders, knives, inferior suits," he said. "Their society didn't develop from ours, then."

"Probably not," Yash said.

"So the settlement on the surface is gone," he said.

She shrugged. "We don't know that."

He nodded again. Two hundred years was a long time. They were going to need to know about the history of Sector Base V as well as Venice City, what they had missed, and what they faced.

"I assume that the shutdown was a standard shutdown," he said to Rossetti.

By that, he meant that the sector base was shut down because the Fleet had moved on, not because of some problem on the planet itself.

Rossetti had to look at her team.

José Cabral nodded. "Yes, sir," he said, answering for the team. "The shutdown was ordered by the Fleet and completed according to procedure. Staff remained behind. At that time, Venice City was a thriving community, and many people did not want to leave."

"No indications that anything went wrong on the surface?" Coop asked.

"None," Cabral said.

Coop nodded. "Clearly, we're going to need more information. We need to know how much time has lapsed. We're going to have to try to figure that out. I assume there are tests you can use on the equipment which will tell us how long it has been unused?"

He directed this last at the scientists.

"Yes and no, sir," the woman said. "We will know within a few decades how long the equipment's been sitting there. But we might not learn exactly. It depends on the conditions underground. Without an accurate history, we won't be able to be precise."

"Doesn't the equipment record conditions in the room around it?" Coop directed this last at Cabral.

Cabral looked at the other engineers. They silently conferred.

"I know for a fact that we'll have a record of the first one hundred and fifty years, sir," Cabral said. "After that . . ."

He let his voice trail off as he looked at the other engineers again. None of them spoke.

They didn't know for certain.

"We can date the parts, do experiments to track decay," one of the scientists said, sounding a little more excited than Coop expected.

"But we'll just be guessing," another scientist said.

"We'll be accurate within a fifty- to hundred-year range," said the woman.

"I think closer to two hundred years," said the scientist whose hand she held.

"Clearly, we don't know, sir," Rossetti said, more to stop the argument among her people than anything.

"Can we map the corridors from the repair room? Get a sense of the surface?" Coop asked.

"It'll take time," one of the engineers said. "The equipment will need a little repair."

"I think we can map the corridors, sir," the woman said.

"That's a start." Coop stood. He paced for a moment, thinking this through. Then he paused and glanced at Yash.

"Let me see the schematics of the base from our files," he said.

She pressed a button, and the base's plans appeared on the screens. A warren of tunnels and corridors and exits onto the surface.

On another screen, she put up a map of Venice City, without him having to request it.

He studied the maps. Cities weren't like ships. Cities changed over time.

Sometimes cities built over their past. Sometimes they retained their historic buildings.

But every city he had ever visited, whether established by the Fleet or not, had historians and libraries and methods of keeping track of its own past.

"We're going to need to go up there," he said, more to himself than to everyone else.

"And how are we going to explain our presence?" Dix asked, his voice wobbling.

Coop turned and looked at him. Dix was gray. He looked ill.

For the first time since Coop met him, Dix actually seemed terrified.

"I mean, if they're sending outsiders down here, and the outsiders seem surprised at the room itself, and they wear environmental suits that they don't need—"

"We don't know if they don't need them," Yash said. "They might."

"You think they have different physiology?" Dix asked.

Yash shrugged. "I don't know. People get used to different things. Maybe other parts of the sector base are toxic. We don't know anything."

Dix's mouth thinned. He didn't like what she was saying.

"That's a side track," Coop said to Dix. "You were making a point."

Dix nodded. "Let's assume that on the surface, they don't know this base exists. Then we pop out of the ground. How do we explain that?"

"Isn't that the least of our worries?" Rossetti asked. "After all, we don't even know if the map is accurate, if the corridors have fallen in, and if the exits still exist."

"We don't know if Venice City still exists," the woman scientist said.

Coop shuddered at that thought. Maybe the old-timers had been right. Maybe they should have been careful about how they named their city. They had named it Venice City because the Earth city had been built on canals. But it had eventually disappeared under the water.

What if this Venice had disappeared as well?

"The history still might be there," Coop said. "It might help us refine the timeline, if nothing else."

"We're going to be here for a long time, aren't we, sir?" That was Shärf, who hadn't spoken up at all until now.

Coop looked at him. Unlike Dix, Shärf didn't seem panicked. In fact, it seemed to Coop like Shärf had asked the question not for himself, but for the other people in the room, as if he was trying to prepare them for the inevitable.

"There's that possibility," Coop said. "But we knew that before we landed. Even if the sector base were here and running the way it had been a month ago, we still would have been here a long time. We sustained a lot of damage. We need to do the repairs. We have the time to figure this out."

As he said the sentence, he felt the irony of the word "time." They had a long adventure ahead of them, whether they were two hundred years behind the Fleet or five hundred years.

The emergency that he'd been feeling since the attack of the Quurzod more than two weeks ago had coalesced into something else. A situation, a crisis. But a slow-moving one.

One that would take patience and effort and a lot of hard work to resolve.

He would have preferred a fight to the death.

But he didn't have that. Instead, he had to rely on his specialists.

He stood behind his chair and gripped its back. Then he looked at everyone, taking the time to meet everyone's eyes before he spoke.

He wasn't quite sure what he would say. He knew he had to reassure them. He also knew that he needed to set up a plan so that they could all move forward.

He couldn't make that plan with a committee. He had to figure it out on his own.

He nodded at them, silently acknowledging what they all knew. Things had changed, and it would take a little while to get used to that change.

"Thank you all for the work," he said. "You'll have new orders tomorrow. We're going to figure out exactly when we are. But know this: we'll be all right."

He sounded confident even though he didn't feel confident. He felt as if someone had shut off the ship's gravity and he was floating, unfettered, in a world he thought he knew.

The others, though, seemed calmer. Maybe it was the shared knowledge. Maybe it was the fact that they were not in charge of it; he was, and as their commander, he was the one who needed to solve the problem.

But he knew, as a commander—as a human being—that some problems had no easy solution.

And this problem was one of those.

THIRTY-NINE

*T*he rock pile grows smaller, and as it does, I realize something.

The dust pile is growing smaller as well.

The floor has absorbed the dust.

Now my questions become urgent. I want to ask Paplas how this functions. I want to know the answer immediately. It's one of the stranger things I've seen—and I've seen a lot of strange things.

But I cannot ask, and Bridge looks too frightened and too confused to know that these questions might be important. I can't even tap Bridge, like I had planned, and whisper a question to him. With his left hand, he clutches his ear protector as if he wants to pull it off. His other hand squeezes his knee.

Paplas grins as he moves forward. He loves this job, working alone, underground, using his gigantic machine to crush rock.

I can empathize. I love working alone as well, and I'd probably be just as annoying with strangers in my ship as he has been with us.

It's a way of maintaining distance.

I grip the seat in front of me with one hand, wishing I could move up front. I want to watch the procedure. I want to see what the equipment's control panel says, even though I really don't understand Vaycehnese.

I'm fascinated and a bit worried about the vibration and the rock walls, although it seems to make no difference to Paplas at all.

It takes less than an hour to work our way to the crushed hovercart. All that rock, gone. The Bug slows as it reaches the back end of the hovercart, and those big legs move almost daintily across its back.

They take rocks and move them a few meters away, then pulverize them. It takes me a moment to realize that Paplas is trying to protect the hovercart.

Does he think there are bodies inside?

I want to tell him that there aren't, but I don't. His admonition against me was strong enough that I don't want to put my presence here in jeopardy.

Instead, I watch the deliberate movements he uses to get each rock out of the cart itself. Within fifteen minutes, the back end is clear. Then the front, with the controls.

Oddly, the seats are relatively undamaged. The benefit of a cart, I guess. It just filled with rock. I can't see well enough to know if the floor of the cart is all right, but it just might be.

The Bug carefully lifts the rocks off the front end. Each rock seems larger than the last.

I finally understand why the cart is bent at an upward angle. The rocks almost flattened the very front part of the hovercart. Had anyone been standing there, they would have been crushed.

I shudder. My people faced this, without me. We were somehow protected in that room.

I would rather die in the vastness of space, slowly freezing to death, unable to breathe as my environmental suit shuts down (or gets breached) than I would being crushed by a load of rocks in an underground cave.

No wonder some of my people looked at me with great hesitation when I said we needed to get back down here quickly. They have vivid imaginations. They know that they could die like this, that the ground around us is horribly unstable, and that it's worse inside these caves.

They know it and they don't want to come back down.

Is it fair to ask my team to come with me?

I'm not sure on that.

Fortunately I have some time to think about it. Although I have less time than I originally thought.

Paplas finishes digging out the corridors with surprising speed. When he's done, he says nothing to us. He does pull off his ear protectors. Then he rapidly rotates the pod 120 degrees, so that we're now facing the way that we came into the corridor.

Then he marches the Bug forward, as if we're late to an appointment.

Bridge clutches his ear protectors, uncertain whether or not to remove them. I pull mine off.

Suddenly, noise fills the little pod. The grinding gears, the thudding from the massive feet, a humming sound, probably caused by our proximity to the stealth tech—something I had forgotten to warn Paplas about.

My heart rate surges, and for a moment, I feel guilty. I have been so absorbed in the process that I have forgotten the real danger.

But Paplas has that map, and the area just beyond that last rock fall is marked in black. I finally realize what the map is. It is a map of the areas inside the caves where people have died mysteriously.

Bridge leans forward. "Can we take off our ear protectors?" he says, just a little too loudly.

"Why not?" Paplas says, as if the very question is ridiculous.

Bridge whips his off and juts them forward, as if he expects Paplas to take them from him.

"Hang onto them," Paplas says, his hands busy with the controls. The Bug hasn't moved this fast since we got below ground. In fact, I didn't know it could move this fast.

Bridge hangs the ear protectors over his right knee. Then he rubs his ears with the flat of his hands, an expression of distaste on his face. I understand what he's done; my ears feel a bit slimy as well. But I'll wait to wash them when we get back to the hotel.

Apparently Bridge can't wait.

I lean into him and say as softly as I can, "Ask what happens to the pulverized rock."

Paplas tilts his head. He's heard me. But stubborn creature that he is, he doesn't answer me. He waits until Bridge repeats the question.

"The dust vanishes," Paplas says. "The rocks would eventually vanish too if we just left them there. The piles were probably smaller this morning than they were last night."

Now Bridge is interested. He has forgotten the slimy feeling of his ears. The fingers of his right hand close around the ear protectors—probably unconsciously—as he leans forward just a bit.

"How does that work?" he asks.

"No one knows," Paplas says. "It is as mysterious as the black walls. Many of our scientists believe that the pulverized rock becomes fuel for the black coating, but they do not know where the coating comes from, or where the rock gets stored since it is rarely used immediately."

"So rock falls always go away?" Bridge asks.

"If we wait long enough," Paplas says. "The corridors are always open."

Bridge and I exchange glances.

"So you just developed this machine to hurry the process along?" Bridge asks.

"We developed the machine for above ground," Paplas says. "And to rescue people trapped below mountains of rubble. Sometimes you cannot wait."

There's a bit of judgment in his tone, as if we should have thought of that. I remember his caution on the hovercart. I wonder if anyone told him it was there. If not, he was probably angry when he came upon it, thinking that there might be dead people inside, people he could have saved.

I keep my word, however. I remain silent.

"Have you ever wondered what created these caves?" Bridge asks. "Have you ever wondered what keeps them running?"

"No," Paplas says so quickly and so curtly that it's clear he's lying. "I have never thought of it at all."

FORTY

We return to the hotel, hot, tired, and a little confused. My mind is full of shattered rocks, open corridors, and floors that absorb one material, but not others.

Bridge doesn't say much, either, except to rub his ears. He veers off the moment we get inside the cool lobby and heads to his room, determined to shower. He's mentioned that intent twice now, and I have no doubt he's thought of it even more.

I stop at the desk and set up a catered dinner spread for the evening. Then I leave a message for the rest of my team, just to make sure they know the time as well as the place.

I still have my lunch. We never had time to eat it, not that it's much past lunchtime anyway. I carry it upstairs to my room, where I sink into the privacy, and my own exhaustion.

I'm not used to being glassy-eyed, to have something as simple as sitting and watching tire me out. Usually I can go for days while others cannot. But my muscles ache, my eyes are tired, and I'm ragged from the heat.

The meal doesn't refresh me, so I lie down on the bed—and immediately slip into sleep.

I dream . . .

I'm back at the Room of Lost Souls. It's vast and empty, an abandoned space station or something, left by the ancients or a community unknown. I am aware enough in this dream to know this is not the Room of Lost Souls of my childhood, nor is it the recurring nightmare I've had all my life.

In that nightmare, I am still a child. I accompany my mother, holding her hand, as we go into the room. We see lights, hear music, and—

I wrench my mind from that. I am standing in one of my skips, my hands clasped behind my back. My team refuses to let me pilot the skip, refuses to let me dive the Room, because they know my emotional history with it.

My father is with us, and curiously, he is in the skip. He shouldn't be. I have banned him from the missions.

I turn to him and see him as I last saw him, standing before a bottle of working stealth tech, a bottle he has created. He is conquering the technology, and he has done so by betraying me.

He has twice sent me into the Room, twice testing to see if I have the genetic marker that allows me to survive in stealth tech. If I do not have it, I will die as hideously as my mother, thinking I am alone, abandoned, as time leaches the oxygen from my environmental suit, as I struggle against a door I cannot open to get back to a world I can no longer reenter. I will die by degrees, but to those with the marker and those not inside stealth tech, it will seem as if I died in a moment. All that time passes for me, and none for them, and I cannot save myself.

I look at this man, this man who should have loved and protected me from the start, and I go to him, my fists clenched. I am not sure now who I am—the child he sent into that Room? The adult woman he tried to send in again?

"You wouldn't have died," he says. "You've done much more dangerous things on your own."

He's holding that bottle of stealth tech. It pulses in his hand.

I want to snatch it from him.

"Do you know what the difference is?" I ask. "The difference with those dangerous things?"

My father shakes his head. He actually looks interested.

"The difference is that I chose to take those risks," I say. "I didn't choose this one."

He opens his hands as if he's going to hug me. The bottle of stealth tech is gone.

"You said someone is going to die on this mission." He speaks softly, reminding me. "I heard you. You said it more than once."

My breath catches. My heart pounds. My fists are so tightly clenched that my hands hurt.

"I always tell my teams that," I say. "It makes them vigilant."

"But this time you believed it," my father says.

"Yes," I say. "Because someone always dies."

I sit up. My heart is still pounding. I can barely breathe. My fists are clenched.

But I'm in a bed in a hotel in Vaycehn, after having gone into a group of caves in which none of my team has died.

No one died. Not here.

Not yet.

I rub a hand over my face, then get out of bed. My legs are so sore that it feels as if they creak when they move. I wouldn't be surprised if I heard that same grinding noise I heard from the Bug every time I move a limb.

I stagger to the bathroom before getting sick.

I haven't told this team that someone could die. I haven't said a word, like I usually do on diving missions. I have believed what other people told me. I believed that being on the ground was safe.

And I am wrong.

My God. Sometimes you become your parents without even realizing you've made the transition.

I get up, splash cold water on my face, and turn on the shower.

Tonight's meeting is going to be different than I planned.

Tonight's meeting might change everything.

FORTY-ONE

Coop stood in the center of the captain's suite, hands clasped behind his back, studying the walls. He had the screens on. He was staring at images of foldspace.

The captains' suites in all of the Fleet vessels were located in the same place and had the same basic structure. Five rooms, including private galley. The suite also had a full kitchen plus dining area that had doors that closed it off from the rest of the suite. The head chef used the full kitchen to prepare meals for the captain's private guests whenever he chose to have a dinner party. He didn't do that often, so that part of the suite rarely got used.

He'd learned to cook while in school and usually made his own meals in the private galley. One of those meals cooled on the table behind him. He didn't feel like eating, but he knew he had to just so that he could keep up his strength.

The living area smelled of roast beef. The beef was not really beef; it was something that the chef had found on Ukhanda that approximated beef, but cooked properly, it tasted of beef, something Coop usually loved.

He had made a meal that he usually couldn't ignore, and here he was ignoring it.

That showed, even to him, the level of his distress.

He sighed and made himself turn his back on the wall screens, if only for a moment. He was as shaken as his crew at this news—which, he had admonished them, they couldn't tell anyone else. Not yet.

Five hundred years in his own future, a thousand.

He sat at the table and listened to the chair squeak beneath him. He picked up his fork and stared at the beef. Potatoes—real potatoes, grown in the hydroponic garden on board the ship, along with three varieties of lettuce for his salad, and the carrots he had cooked with the roast. A small bowl of strawberry compote waited for him to finish the main course.

He twirled the fork. He had no appetite. This had happened to him before, when he knew he had to divorce Mae. As his mind had accepted the new reality, his stomach twisted in knots and refused sustenance, as well as sleep.

He'd been finishing his captain's training at the time. His instructors figured out what was wrong and forced him to eat.

A captain of a flagship vessel in the Fleet couldn't afford human weakness. He couldn't afford to lose his appetite. He couldn't afford to lose sleep.

He couldn't afford to collapse.

Coop ate a bite of the beef. The gravy coating it had the proper amount of richness, just a hint of exotic spice from a community that the *Ivoire* had visited during the first year of his command.

The memory made him smile for just a moment, until another thought collided with it.

That community was gone. Changed. Different. Even if he went back (and he wouldn't have; the Fleet never went back), he wouldn't find the couple who had taught him how to grow that spice and helped him transplant the tiny seedlings into a pot to take with him to the hydroponic garden where, it turned out, the botanists had already taken some of the same plants.

He chewed, swallowed. Took another bite. Tried to swallow past the knot in his throat.

Nothing in those images of foldspace told him how the *Ivoire* had gotten here. For two weeks, he had looked at the unfamiliar stars, the strange ridges of light, the area of space that had defied matching a star map, and he had figured out nothing then.

He figured out nothing now.

Coop took another bite: potatoes this time. Carrots, roasted. Beef again. Chew. Swallow. Try not to think about the lump in the throat.

After a century or two of separation, he wouldn't be able to use the math to catch the Fleet. He would have to use investigation, cunning, and research.

He and his team would have to estimate where the Fleet might have been, then use the *anacapa* to get there. And that first trip with the *anacapa* drive, after this one, would be scary enough. If they overshot, if they miscalculated, they would have to work their way backward.

And how would they know if they miscalculated?

They would have to ask. They would have to research. They would have to look on the nearby planets themselves, going into various communities. The ship would become one gigantic investigative team that searched for word of the Fleet.

Once they found word of it, they'd move forward on the trajectory, stopping often, asking again, searching for word of the Fleet, looking at timelines, listening to memories, figuring out when (if) his people had passed through.

He might spend the rest of his life searching for the Fleet.

He set the fork down and rubbed his eyes, then blinked just for a moment. Made himself swallow, breathe. He had to stay calm, not just for himself, but for his entire ship.

He stood and walked back to the screens. With one quick verbal command, he changed the image from foldspace to the abandoned sector base.

It was still empty. The equipment still looked abandoned. The occasional unbonded nanobit floated by.

In his lifetime six ships had disappeared from the Fleet, maybe forever.

In his father's lifetime, ten.

In his grandfather's, none at all.

It simply depended on events, on the uses of the *anacapa*.

Although in his grandfather's lifetime, six ships had been destroyed by one form of disaster or another without once using the *anacapa*. Enemy fire, malfunctioning equipment. Coop's grandfather spent half of his life going back and forth between sector bases as the Fleet got repaired and upgraded for the hundredth, maybe thousandth time in its existence.

From some people's perspective, from the perspective of Dix's chef, for example, the *Ivoire* would be lost. If, indeed, the information that Coop had was correct. He would rejoin the Fleet and there would be new commanders, new crews, new everything.

Except a new mission.

He sighed and stared at the empty base before him. The lighting was dim. The emptiness continued into the darkness as far as the eye could see.

When he had last left here, he'd had an imagined future, one that consisted of some kind of variation of the life he'd led, going from place to place with the Fleet, remaining in his place within the generations, with the people he knew.

An imagined future that he didn't know—and they didn't know—was completely wrong. Because no matter what happened now, his future was not as he had planned it.

Unless he became very, very lucky, he would never again see anyone he knew, except for the crew of this ship. Everyone else would be gone by the time he caught the Fleet. If he never caught the Fleet—if his son or his son's sons caught the Fleet (if he had children at all, now)—then he would spend his life chasing what amounted to a phantom.

A phantom Fleet of ghost ships, once filled with his friends and colleagues. And cousins and aunts and uncles.

He brought his head down. No wonder he was shaken. No wonder he had trouble putting this aside.

Many of the people he knew were effectively dead to him. The life he had was gone.

His imagined future could never, ever happen.

He was now the top of the heap. His people would listen to him and would have no other authority to appeal to. He was not only the oldest person in his family; he was the only person in his family.

And he had to be strong.

He had to figure out a way to keep his people together, keep them from falling apart.

He had to manage them and his own mind.

His own heart.

He turned away from the screens, turning them off. He returned to his plate. The gravy had congealed just a bit, but no matter.

Maybe once the *Ivoire* was repaired and had left this place, he could take a few days, talk to one of the counselors, let himself feel the crisis.

He had no time to do that now.

But he would continue to eat dinner alone, so no one knew how very hard this all was.

Especially on him.

FORTY-TWO

"**I** think I've been unfair to you."

I am standing before my entire team. They sit at the large table in my suite, a spread of food before them. The room smells faintly of coffee, exotic spices, and baked bread.

Everyone is staring at me, and they all look startled. Apparently, I don't use the word "unfair" very often—especially in connection with my own actions.

"I didn't listen to you," I say, looking at my archeologists. Lucretia Stone's lips purse. "When you discussed groundquakes, I had no idea how serious they were. I didn't really believe you when you said that working underground can be dangerous."

Stone opens her mouth, apparently thinking I have given her permission to speak. I haven't, so I hold up one hand to silence her.

"I have learned this in a way I didn't want to," I say. "I know that Vaycehn is dealing with devastation right now, and there's no guarantee something similar won't happen again tomorrow."

"Well, I really think we're right about the death hole," the scientist Lentz says.

I raise a finger at him, silencing him, and give him a bit of a smile. At least, I think it's a smile. It doesn't quite feel like one.

"You'll have your opportunity," I say. "But you have to let me finish. All of you."

Mikk is watching me as if I have lost my mind. The chair he sits on, four down from mine, looks tiny against his muscular bulk. Ilona sits next to him, her hand over her mouth as if she's watching a disaster. Maybe she is.

I rest my own hands on the back of my chair and try not to clutch the fabric.

"Because I was unaware of the severity of the dangers here," I say, "I didn't give you my speech. All of you have heard it. Some of you know it by heart."

Tamaz frowns. Roderick bites his lower lip. They know what's coming. They seem surprised by it, however.

"What we're doing here is extremely dangerous," I say. "And we could die."

Bridge folds his hands on top of the table.

"The risk is particularly bad for the Six."

I look at them. Kersting has the only glass of beer among my entire group, and he has just set it down. Seager is biting her right thumbnail—chewing on it, really, as if it were a bit of gristle. DeVries has unconsciously mimicked Bridge's position—hands folded on top of the table. Al-Nasir's hands are under the table, but he can't hide the fact that he's shaking, just a little. Quinte is slowly peeling one of those applelike fruits, not meeting my gaze at all.

And Rea, Rea's back has straightened, his eyes brightened, as if adding a bit of death to the trip has made it all the more adventurous for him.

"I don't see how the risk can be bad for you Six," Gregory, one of the scientists says before I can stop him. "You guys were the only ones not affected by the groundquake."

"We could have been trapped in that room with no way out," I say. "Rocks blocking the door, the corridors filled. We'd have been stranded."

I don't go on to say that they all could have died, and no one would have known we were there. Bridge starts to speak—and I know what he's going to say as soon as he starts, that he's going to mention the way that the rock clears itself, something I haven't told them yet—but I don't want him to bring this up.

"Please," I say, "let me finish before we discuss the rest of this."

I pause now, almost daring them to interrupt me.

"I came here reluctantly." I nod at Ilona, acknowledging that she was right. "I didn't prepare the way I normally do. I thought we'd come in, look around, realize this isn't the place for us, and leave. Instead, we've found absolute treasure. We've found a working Dignity Vessel."

Everyone smiles at that. Just for a moment and the smiles fade.

My fingers squeeze the chair's back. "But this is my obsession, not yours. You all work for me, and our job is dangerous. We all know that sometimes things go wrong, and someone dies."

Mikk looks down. He's gone through this before. So has Roderick, who looks away, and Tamaz, who studies his water glass as if it has writing on it.

"The problem is," I say, "I have just realized that this mission is so dangerous that many of us could die, and some of us might die trying to rescue others. I can't, in good conscience, let you go back into those caves without telling you this. And I can't, in good conscience, let you continue your work without giving you the option to walk away."

They are all looking at me again, my long-term team, with great surprise.

"I won't be upset," I say. "You can stay in the hotel if you like, continue to draw your paychecks, have these meetings with us and offer your expertise, or you can return to the *Business* and wait for us there. I'm going to return to that Dignity Vessel, and I hope enough of you stay to help me with that. But I understand if you don't."

No one speaks. For a moment, I wonder if I've been clear.

Then Bernadette Ivy says, "I don't want to go back into those caves."

"Me, either," says Gregory.

Ilona has taken out a pad and starts tapping in names. Thank goodness, because I hadn't thought to do that.

"Oh, for God's sake," Bridge says. "This is just getting interesting. Why quit now?"

"I don't mind the danger," Mikk says.

"I wish I could see that ship." Roderick sounds plaintive. He keeps thinking that we see marvelous things inside stealth tech, and until that ship arrived, we never had.

"I'd love to see it too," Ilona says softly. "I have always imagined what the Dignity Vessels looked like new."

I'm watching my team with a bit of surprise. Some of them share my obsession, something I hadn't realized.

Several people haven't spoken up at all, as if they're thinking about this. I look at the Six. They're the ones who matter. I want them to accompany me into that room. We'll get so much done if there are seven of us.

If I'm alone, this might take months. Years.

I'm a pilot. I know science. I know history. But I'm not a scientist, nor am I an engineer. I'll be guessing at so many things if I go in alone.

I don't want to guess. I want to know.

Rea looks at the other members of the Six. They don't meet his gaze. He shrugs and grins at me.

"I'm fascinated," he says. "I can't wait to go back."

Kersting picks up his beer. "Never say that Rollo Kersting isn't up for an adventure."

"An adventure that might kill you?" Seager asks.

"Life kills you," Kersting says. "It's just a question of how you'll go out. Imagine if I go out trying to start up a Dignity Vessel."

"What if you go out crushed under tons of rock?" Al-Nasir asks.

"Hell, the way I eat," Kersting says, "I might have a massive heart attack in my sleep. I'd rather have a romantic death, even if it involves rocks and a groundquake."

"You're unrealistic," Bernadette Ivy says. "If you get crushed by rock, it won't be a quick death. You'll suffocate, most likely, from collapsed lungs and broken ribs. It'll be agonizing. Or it might take a few days, because no one can find you."

Ilona looks at me, as if she expects me to stop this part of the conversation. But I'm not going to. They have to be able to imagine the risks now, when I'm giving them the chance to quit.

Because the one thing I haven't told them is that this is a one-time offer.

"You're extremely dramatic, you know that?" Kersting glares at Ivy. "I'm saying the risk is worth it to me. I've been dragooned into working in stealth tech by Boss's dad, and he was one big ass who never told me the risks. I've been part of this group for a long time now, and we're finally getting to the good stuff. I have a weird genetic ability, and it lets me see things that—no offense, Bernadette—you might never have the chance to see. So I'm going to quit right now? You have to be joking. Of course I'm not going to quit."

"Me either," Quinte says, surprising me. She had been so afraid when the groundquake quit. She'd been terrified on most of the journeys we've taken together.

But she hasn't quit, either. She hasn't walked away.

"Really, Nyssa?" Al-Nasir turns slightly in his chair so he can see her better. His voice wobbles.

"Really," she says. Then she looks at me. "I know I'm not the best person you have. I'm probably the worst. I don't think well in a crisis. But it seems to me that unless another groundquake happens, and it somehow affects that room, we're moving into a research phase of this operation, and I like research. I grew up on stories of the fleet of Dignity Vessels, and I've always wondered what they were like. I used to think they were so romantic, showing up places, rescuing people, moving on. I thought they were fiction. And now to discover that they're not . . ."

She shakes her head, then shrugs and grins.

"I love the idea of them," she says, "and to think I might have a small part in understanding them makes me happier than you could ever know."

Al-Nasir bites his lower lip. Then he stops and rubs his hand over his mouth, as if he's suddenly aware of what he's doing.

"I'm inclined to stay above ground," he says to me, as if we're alone in the room. "I won't lie. I was terrified down there. But I'm also terrified of not going down. I walked to some of the groundquake rubble with Lucretia this afternoon, and I could just as easily have died in this hotel or on the street."

"Maybe more easily," Lucretia Stone says. "They're not as quake-proof here as they say they are."

"I never dreamed I'd be doing any of this," Al-Nasir says, as if Stone hasn't spoken. "So I have no romantic illusions about Dignity Vessels. I've seen people die in stealth-tech experiments, and I've seen what the Empire can do, and what's really scary is if we don't do this job fast, they might hear about this ship, and then they'll have it."

He takes a deep breath, stopping himself.

"I guess," he says more slowly, sounding a bit surprised. "I guess I'm convincing myself to continue."

"You're convincing me, too," Seager says.

"And me," DeVries says. I look at him, eyebrows raised. I thought he'd come with us. He seemed so coolheaded when we were in the room. I hadn't realized that he was disturbed as well.

"So all six of you are coming back?" I ask, and I let my surprise into my voice.

Kersting looks around, then grins at me. "Guess so."

No one denies it. They all stare at me.

"I don't want you changing your minds once we go below ground," I say. "Tonight's the night for decisions. After that, we're not going to discuss death or risks or possible trouble unless we need to do so to avoid it."

Al-Nasir glances at everyone else. Kersting is nodding. Rea is smiling. Seager makes little fists and raises them, in a let's-do-this gesture. DeVries nods once. And Quinte puts her hand on Al-Nasir's shoulder.

"We're coming," she says.

"Fahd," I say to Al-Nasir. "Don't let them pressure you. Are you going to join us?"

His mouth thins. He takes another deep breath, as if that's the only way he can calm himself.

"I'd be stupid not to," he says.

"We're all staying," Mikk says.

"Bernadette, Gregory," I say. "Are you willing to stay in Vaycehn and help us?"

Bernadette shakes her head. "I think you guys can send me the information on the *Business* and I can work there."

"You'll be working alone," Gregory says. "I don't like it here, but I'd rather be here than orbiting Wyr for six months while everyone else gets all the glory."

"Fahd is right," Stone says. "Every place is a risk. And now that you're willing to listen to us, Boss, we'll be able to mitigate some of it."

Her tone makes me bristle, but I don't show it. She's right. I was wrong to ignore the warnings of the archeologists. I'm going to listen. We're going to plan this properly.

We're going to do this next stage right.

FORTY-THREE

We go back to the room in the same configuration we used two days ago. Mikk and Roderick wait as close to the stealth-tech field as they can. A hovercart sits near them in case we need it quickly. Four guides bring us down, and they have a hovercart too.

This time, however, they have orders to remain below ground, and Bridge has volunteered to stay above ground to make sure they follow those orders.

The only other change is one that the Six have asked for: all of them get to go into the room at the same time.

"After all," Quinte says, "no one can get into the stealth-tech field unless they have a marker, so I don't think there's a reason to guard the door from the outside."

"And rocks can't fall inside a stealth field," Al-Nasir says, even though we've discussed this. We don't know if that's true or not. Still, he's got a point. If a disaster happens inside the room, it won't matter if we have someone outside or not.

I personally think they don't want to repeat the experience of waiting in those corridors with nothing to do. They're not trained divers like Mikk and Roderick. Al-Nasir and Quinte are not used to waiting long periods of time.

I see no harm in letting them accompany us into the room.

So I let them.

We go in as silently as we can. I go first, which is risky, because I have no idea if we're alone. I'm worried that we'll encounter someone—or lots of someones, someones who think we're invading their private area, someones who are used to this place when we are not.

I've been thinking about it all night, and I have found myself wondering if this isn't normal for Dignity Vessels. Maybe they have bases like this all over the known universe, dark except when a Dignity Vessel needs repair.

I keep remembering those laser score marks on the side of the ship, and I wonder if it was damaged in some kind of fight, and if so, if this is where it is supposed to go for repairs.

Of course, I also wonder if it is a dead ship whose arrival was somehow triggered by us. I spent half the night on that, pacing and worrying that I want to believe this scenario, because that means I can figure out how to open the ship, then go inside and investigate it.

The second scenario also means the Dignity Vessel is mine—or can be mine, if the Vaycehnese government never finds out about it, and we can somehow figure out how to get the ship out of this enclosed underground room.

One problem at a time, though.

We stand at the door. My heart is pounding. I can tell from the readings on the Six's environmental suits that their hearts are racing as well. They're trying to control their breathing, but they're as nervous as I am, maybe more so. Their palms are sweating, and their suits are trying to cool them down.

I'm not that nervous. But I'm excited.

I can hear Squishy's voice warning against the gids, and for once, I care. I want to survive this trip into the room, and the next, and the next. I want to enjoy every minute of this discovery.

And I want the discovery to be there.

That's what really has my heart racing: I'm afraid the Dignity Vessel is gone.

I put my hand on the door itself, ready to push. First, though, I turn to the Six.

"Be prepared for anything," I say, and then I try the door.

It opens easily. It's not locked or barricaded.

I step into the room, and the particles swirl around me. I can't help myself—I immediately look at that landing pad.

The Dignity Vessel is still there.

I let out a small breath. Relief.

I step all the way inside, cautiously. I look around.

To my quick gaze, nothing looks different. The Dignity Vessel sits on the pad, the screens above the equipment show the inside of the room and nothing else, and the rest of the equipment looks like it has been off for a very long time.

Now mingled with the relief is just a bit of disappointment. I half hoped someone would be exploring or using the room. I was ready to have a difficult conversation with one of the people who had arrived on the Dignity Vessel.

But if no one has emerged in forty-eight hours, then I'm more inclined to think the ship is empty, drawn by something we did, some button we pressed, something we activated.

After all, we have found seven half-ruined Dignity Vessels throughout the sector. We have no idea if anything is wrong with this one. For all we know, the interior may be partially destroyed, the controls gone, some part of the vessel that we can't yet see open to space.

DeVries stops beside me. Rea walks just a little ahead, as if he can't believe that the Vessel is still there. I can feel Quinte behind me, and I know without looking that Al-Nasir is behind her. Seager is on my other side. The only person I seem to have lost track of is Kersting.

I turn slightly. He has wandered in the opposite direction from me, head tilted back, looking up at the Dignity Vessel.

I sense the awe in his movements, and I smile.

I feel it, too.

"It's still here," I say, stating the obvious. But someone has to. I have to let the relief I'm feeling become part of the group's emotion.

"I didn't think it would be," Rea says.

"Me, either," Seager says.

We all stop. We have an agreed-upon plan for this trip, one of two that we made. We agreed that if the Dignity Vessel was here we would proceed with caution. DeVries, Rea, and I would search for a way into the vessel. Kersting and Seager would go to the first section of equipment and take readings off of it, recording as much as they could so that our linguists and scientists can figure out what's going on here. Most of what we got the last time was distorted by our own movements.

Quinte and Al-Nasir will explore the area near the door, to make sure that there are no hidden ways to lock us in or activate something that we don't want to activate.

Their instructions specifically warn them not to touch anything.

They were both happy with both parts of the instruction: the fact that they'd be looking and not touching, and the fact that they would be closest to the door in case something went wrong.

I get the area near the door. DeVries goes toward the back where the ship's wings stretch out. Rea is going to walk beneath the curved front of the ship—or what I think of as the front—and see if there is a hatch anywhere. On half of the Dignity Vessels we've found—or I should say, on the half we've found with an intact front—we've found hatches.

That was one of my first clues that not all Dignity Vessels are exactly alike. They were altered, either by time or convention or need or all three.

We move cautiously, as if we are diving. That was my instruction up top, and I plan to live up to it down here, despite my own excitement. We're also running on a time limit: six hours, which might feel extra long, considering how much oxygen we're using.

We're all nervous and excited. The causes may be different—I think Al-Nasir is frightened enough for all of us—but the result is the same.

If we were actually in space, I'd worry about our oxygen use rate. I'm less worried about it here.

We're taking more readings from the air and the particles. We can breathe here if we need to. It's not the oxygen that's the problem; it's those particles. And with the groundquake, the rescue, and all of the things that followed, our own team of scientists hasn't had a chance to adequately test anything we brought back from our last trip.

We're proceeding exactly the same way in this one as we did the last time, because we have no new information.

I move slowly across the floor, stopping after each step and looking around, just like I would on a dive. The others do as well. It looks like we're doing a particularly well-timed ballet, but we need to be cautious.

Part of me feels as if something has changed here, but I have no idea what that would be. And I can't really trust my feelings at the moment. They might be based on excitement or expectations or sheer nerves, nerves I'm not entirely admitting.

Still, I have a sense that we're being watched.

I force myself to concentrate on the ship as I walk toward it. The laser sears are as I remember them; the door is in the same place, and it is closed.

But there is a difference.

A vast difference.

One that makes my breath catch.

The exterior of the ship is different. The color is richer. The score marks look deeper, more damaging. The outline of the door is clearer.

And the ship itself glistens as if it's waiting for us.

As if it's waiting for me.

FORTY-FOUR

"**T**hey're back." Anita Tren sounded excited. She blew up the real-time image of the exterior of the *Ivoire* without Coop's permission. Suddenly all of the screens on the bridge were filled with images of the abandoned sector base.

Coop shifted in his command chair, turning toward the full wall screen on the left side of the bridge. That screen showed the door leading into the sector base.

The door was easing open.

He almost corrected Anita, but didn't. His breath had caught, and he felt just a little redeemed. He had thought the outsiders would return.

And now they had.

This time there were seven, not five.

"Compare, would you?" he said to Dix. "I want to know if any of those people are the same ones who were here forty-eight hours ago."

Dix didn't answer. He had been unusually quiet since getting the news about the sector base. He seemed shrunken in on himself, exhausted, as if he couldn't sleep.

Coop had seen him like this before, and he knew that Dix, despite his emotional upset, would get the job done.

Coop's eyes already told him that the person who had come in the door first was the woman he had noticed earlier. The woman who had put her glove against the ship, as if it were a miracle, something she had never, ever expected.

He couldn't tell, however, if the others were people who had come in before.

"Shouldn't we go talk to them?" Perkins asked.

She stood near the screens, her hands clasped behind her back, unknowingly mimicking the posture that Coop had every single time he stared at the same images in the captain's suite.

Only he was trying to quell his own emotions, to keep his mind even, focused, and calm.

Perkins, so far as he could tell, was excited. She wanted to throw herself into the work.

"Not yet," Coop said to Perkins. "We don't want to startle them."

She turned and gave him a winning smile. "C'mon, Captain," she said in a wheedling tone. "They know we're here. How else would the ship have come in?"

"The *anacapa*," Dix said, his tone as dismal as his posture. "Working automatically."

Perkins frowned at him. "They're outsiders. How would they know that?"

"How do they know anything?" Yash asked. She was going over the data in front of her as well. "They're explorers in this place. That's clear from the way they move. We have no idea how they manage or what they do."

"Which is why we're not going through that door until we're ready," Coop said. "We don't want to surprise them. For all we know, they've never seen a spaceship before."

"I'd wager you're right," Yash said. "I can't imagine how those environmental suits would survive in space. They probably have just started developing their own space program. And those suits aren't going to take them very far."

"That we can tell," Perkins said. "Cultures always mix old and new. Sometimes people wear things that are ceremonial."

"With *equipment*?" Yash said. "I don't think so."

Coop smiled. Yash wouldn't. She always wanted the latest, best, most improved. That was one of the reasons he had hired her in the first place, because she tinkered and improved everything around her.

The seven outsiders clustered in a group, and the woman gestured. He was right; she was the one in charge.

"Five are the same, two new, just like it looks," Dix said without inflection.

"Do you think they're always going to be coming in forty-eight-hour intervals?" Anita asked.

"Doubtful," Coop said. "If I had to guess—and it would just be a guess—the two new are arbiters of some kind, or people with a particular expertise."

Perkins shifted, as if she couldn't contain the energy she felt. "I could go ask."

"And get attacked?" Yash asked. "They're wearing knives."

"Knives, I know," Perkins said. "How old-fashioned is that?"

"Actually," Dix said, "only one of them is wearing a knife, and it seems more like an all-purpose tool than a weapon."

"The woman in charge," Coop said.

Dix nodded. "She's also carrying something that looks like a laser pistol. Her hand hovered near it as she came in the door. She was expecting an attack."

"Or worrying about one," Coop said more to himself than the others.

"They shouldn't see anything different," Yash said. "We made sure of that."

"I think we should go out there," Perkins said. "If they're already expecting us—"

"To attack them," Coop said. "They thought we might attack them. Coming out the door is not the best idea at the moment."

Although he wanted to go out there himself, quiz them, and figure out if all of the readings his team had taken were right. He wanted to find out what was going on, what had happened to Venice City, if there were still members of the Fleet (or descendents of it) on Wyr.

Perkins sighed, but said no more. She understood she'd been overruled.

The outsiders split into three teams, two people staying by the door, two going to the equipment, and three coming to the ship itself.

"I hope they don't touch anything they shouldn't," Anita said.

"They can't tamper with much," Yash said. "Most of the equipment is in shut-down mode."

"Who knows what time has done to corrode it?" Dix said, without looking up.

"I guess we'll find out," Coop said, as he settled in to watch.

FORTY-FIVE

The hours pass quickly and we haven't found anything. Or at least, we haven't found anything we understand.

We've gotten lots of information, recorded many things, explored many parts of the room and a little bit of the exterior of the ship. We even found a name and a vessel number on the Dignity Vessel. I can't read the name because it's in Old Earth Standard—or at least, I think that might be standard. It's an ancient Earth language, anyway, and my Old Earth Standard is mostly limited to helpful words like "danger" and "keep out."

I've given up on the door. I found the latch quickly enough—it is exactly where latches always are on Dignity Vessel doors—but I can't open it. I've pressed it, moved it, changed it, and it still won't budge. Either the door is locked from the inside—which is something I've never seen in a Dignity Vessel—or it keeps relatching every time I think I've opened it.

Al-Nasir and Quinte have found some overrides for the door leading to the corridor. They've also found a way to turn on the interior lights—all without touching a thing.

The interior lights came on after Quinte ran her hand over a part of the wall nearest the door.

We all blinked in the brightness and then got back to work. Or at least, I did. DeVries and Rea and Al-Nasir and Quinte all stared as if they hadn't seen the place before.

And when I finally gave up on the latch, I stared, too.

It's not exactly what I thought it was. When the room had been shrouded in darkness, it had the feeling of a place that went on forever, of a room that led to other rooms, which led to even more rooms, which then became a compound.

Now that the lights are on full, I realize that the room is really one gigantic repair shop. There are several platforms marked "danger" in Old Earth Standard, and unlike the one I'm standing on, those are all empty. There are other equipment consoles built into the walls around each platform, and those consoles show nothing on their screens.

I wonder idly what would happen if we touch them. Would we get another Dignity Vessel?

I'd try, except that I want to find out more about this Dignity Vessel first, and then there's the problem of the death hole.

This morning before we left, Gregory informed me that the new death hole—the one we think the Dignity Vessel caused (and by extension, we probably caused)—is the largest in Vaycehn's recorded history.

I don't want to do that again. I didn't want to do it before.

So I've warned my people away from the other consoles, at least for the time being. Not that they were hurrying over there. We're swamped with the consoles we have.

I'm proud of Kersting and Seager. They're going over the consoles we have touched millimeter by millimeter, making sure they miss nothing. I can hear their conversation in my comm—*"You take that." "Got it." "I'm finishing this." "Good."*—and it feels like an accompaniment to the constant strumming of stealth tech.

I wish my equipment measured the sound of stealth tech, because it seems to me that the sound has changed since the last time we were here. It was louder just before the ship came in, and slightly different once the ship arrived. Now the sound has less treble and more bass. Even the treble has a bit of vibrato in it that wasn't there before.

It's distracting, and the conversation between Kersting and Seager takes my mind off of it.

I moved away from the door two hours ago and walked under the ship, looking for the hatches that I know are there. I found one, welded closed (or, at least, it looked like it was welded), and another that's barely within my reach.

As I stand on tiptoe to inspect the top part of the hatch, I brace one hand against the ship itself. I run my hand across the top of the hatch and feel nothing. The hatch should have a latch in the very center, if it follows the same design as the other Dignity Vessels I've encountered, but I save the center for last.

I'm not used to standing on my toes for prolonged periods of time and, if truth be told, my legs are still incredibly sore. So I drop down to the flat of my feet and look at the rest of the room.

I'm tempted to go down there and see if there are ladders or stepping stools or even chairs, something that will allow me to stand above that hatch opening.

But I can't touch anything down there, not yet, and I'm not going to. Every time I think of walking outside of this small area, I force myself to remember that death hole.

The far end of the room curves. There isn't a platform that I can see, but there are even more consoles and, it looks like, places to hang smaller pieces of equipment. I have a hunch there are doors down there that lead to storage or maybe a place to stay.

I can't imagine employees coming down here through those corridors every day, not unless there were hovercarts back when this place was in full use.

Something else for my historians to research. But after my encounter with Paplas yesterday, I'm beginning to understand the difficulty.

Either the Vaycehnese don't want to discuss these caves, the black stuff on the walls, and their technology with outsiders, or the Vaycehnese really don't know where a lot of the things they live with come from. I'm betting it's a combination of both.

I rise to my toes again and run my hand along the edge of the hatch, finding little, not even particles, which surprises me. I haven't found any on the ship, when it was coated two days ago. That very detail unnerves me.

When we started, I asked Kersting and Seager if there were particles still on the equipment. Kersting said no, but Seager said there were still some on the underside of the consoles.

Almost as if someone had wiped them off.

I move my hand from the edge of the hatch toward the middle when DeVries says, "Boss."

His inflection is so flat that I know he's not telling me he found something. He's reminding me our time is up.

I look at my suit's internal clock. We have a minute to spare. He's probably been waiting for me to notice.

I suppress a sigh. We're going to be here a long time.

"All right, gang," I say. "Let's go."

No one complains. No one even gives their work a second glance. We head toward the door. We're still tired and nervous from our last trip down here.

And this trip was a victory the moment we opened that door to the room and saw the Dignity Vessel.

It's still here, and someday I'm going to get into it.

Someday, I'm going to make it work.

FORTY-SIX

Before the outsiders left, Coop prepped his team to go into the sector base. But he warned Rossetti to prepare for one more addition to the team: him.

He wasn't going to sit in the command chair any longer.

After Coop had spoken to Rossetti, Dix had given him a baleful glance, but hadn't said a word. Instead, Yash had spoken up.

"You said this is a first contact." She turned to him, arms crossed.

"It is," Coop said.

"Then the captain doesn't go near the site until we understand the nature of those outsiders." She sounded fierce.

"The captain won't go near the outsiders," Coop said, although he wanted to. He wanted to more than he would ever admit to anyone. "They won't be back for hours, if not days."

"You hope," Yash said. "You have no idea if they had to leave the site to get those extra two people."

"I know that they limit their time in the base to six hours. They've done it twice, and I think that's a pattern. So we'll honor the pattern," Coop said.

"And if you run into them?" Yash asked.

Coop shrugged. "I'll say hello."

She shook her head in exasperation. "We can't afford to lose you right now."

He raised his eyebrows and then smiled. "You can afford to lose me at other times?"

"You know what I mean," she snapped.

And the truth of it was, he did. He did know what she meant. When a captain died within the Fleet, the Fleet command appointed a new captain. Sometimes that captain came from within the ship's ranks, and sometimes the captain came from another ship. The captain wasn't always promoted. Sometimes the captain was moved laterally because he or she had skills that particular ship needed.

No one on the *Ivoire* had lost a captain in the middle of a command—or at least, a command like this one, where there was no Fleet backup at all.

"I'll be fine," Coop said, and he firmly believed he would be.

If he didn't believe it, he wouldn't be suiting up with Rossetti's team. They agreed to wear the environmental suits without the face protection, not because they needed their own environment, but just in case the outsiders returned.

The environmental suit would provide protection against attacks from various kinds of weaponry, including that large knife the woman carried.

Coop's hands shook as he detached the hood from the collar of his suit. He wasn't nervous about going in; he was excited.

Finally, after two-plus weeks of ordering everyone else to take action, he was taking action, too. Real, physical action.

Lynda replaced him as acting captain. If she ordered him back inside the ship, he would have to listen. He didn't mind. He saw envy in her eyes when she reported to the bridge.

She knew how he felt about moving around; he had a hunch they all did.

He was the last one into the airlock, and he went by himself. He was last as a concession to Yash, who demanded that he protect himself at all costs.

He listened to the airlock door latch behind him. The required seconds between the latching of the interior door and the opening of the exterior door felt like hours to him.

He would have to pace himself. He wanted to run through the entire base, checking on everything and maybe catching a ride to the surface.

He wasn't going to, of course. He knew better. But the impulse was strong.

As he stepped out the exterior door, down the small steps that extended whenever the door opened, he glanced at the base's main door. He wanted the outsiders to come back. He wanted them back the moment the ship's exterior door closed.

Then he would go talk to that woman, knife be damned.

But no one came in. Just Rossetti's teams, moving to their assigned places.

Rossetti herself walked across the sector base floor and turned on the interior lights, lights the outsiders had thoughtfully turned off before they left.

In addition to gathering information, Coop had instructed everyone to leave the equipment running. He also instructed them to leave a couple small things—a partially eaten apple and a mug of coffee.

He wanted to let the outsiders know that people were inside the *Ivoire*. Subtle was the best way to do so.

He stepped into the base proper. It smelled different. It had the same somewhat sulfuric odor that Sector Base V had always had, but it also had a musty smell of decay. The scent, old and dry, not mildewy like he would have expected from Venice City's hot climate, made the hair rise on the back of his neck.

The conversations from the other team members echoed in the emptiness. The base felt bigger than it actually was. Bigger and lonelier.

The last time the *Ivoire* had been here, there had been two other ships in the bays.

He walked under the *Ivoire*, deliberately tracing the outsider woman's steps. She had known where the hatches would be—or at least it seemed that way. She had also released the latch on the door four separate times.

Fortunately, Dix had programmed the doors to guard, so no one could get in without using a weapon.

But the woman's ability to release that latch caught Coop's eye. He hadn't mentioned it to the bridge crew—he would later, during a briefing— any more than he had commented on her ability to find the hatches.

He was convinced she had touched a Fleet vessel before. Her actions belied his earlier supposition that the outsiders had never seen a spaceship before.

They had—or, at least, she had—and they had seen a ship from the Fleet. They had been close enough to it to know where the lower hatches were.

He checked the sides, saw no knife marks, nothing except a glove print near the hatch's release on the far side.

He smiled. Maybe that meant she spoke Standard. Maybe he would have someone to talk with, after all, someone to tell him the history he had missed, the things he needed to know.

He hoped so.

But he wouldn't count on it. He needed to find out information on his own.

He walked to the far end of the sector base, crossing landing pad after landing pad, trying not to think of the openness and the emptiness.

As he walked, lights came on just ahead of him, revealing consoles covered in unbonded nanobits and even more, sending up a dust cloud along the floor. He coughed once, thought of returning for his hood, then changed his mind.

Instead, he headed to the personnel quarters, storage, and the emergency lift.

It took him nearly fifteen minutes to reach the far side of the bay. When he did, he pulled off his glove and put his hand against the door leading into the personnel quarters.

For a moment, the door stayed dark, and he wondered if the recognition lock had broken. Then lights came on, revolving slowly around his hand.

A creaky voice, sounding just a bit warped, said, "Jonathan Cooper, captain of the *Ivoire*. Recognition queried, but granted."

He nodded. He had expected *queried but granted* status, although he had hoped for just a simple *recognition granted*. *Queried but granted* meant that he didn't belong in this place; he was an anomaly. But the system had to recognize anomalies, since the *anacapa* sometimes created them.

So long ago—from his perspective, decades (maybe centuries) before he was born—someone had invented the *queried but granted* status. What it usually meant was that someone else, a living person, would double-check the credentials later, and then update the system.

He doubted that would happen here.

Not that it mattered at the moment.

What mattered now was that the door slid open and the interior lights went on.

A waft of dusty, stale air greeted Coop. He didn't even have to go inside. Normally quarters on a sector base were for guest workers or people who hadn't yet been cleared to join the community up top. The quarters were state-of-the-art, built for comfort and relaxation.

Every other sector base quarters he had visited smelled of food and cleaned air. A month before, this one had, too. But it didn't now. It had no furniture. Only a slightly dusty floor, and doors that opened into the room, revealing more empty quarters beyond.

He had hoped to find furniture, a functioning kitchen, maybe even a caretaker hiding from the ship. Not more emptiness.

Although the emptiness didn't surprise him. It made sense, given the information his crew had already gathered.

He stepped back, let the door slide closed, and then put his hand on the door to the supply area. He had a hunch he would find the same thing, and he did, except it looked like the tool safe remained. That part of the supplies closet was supposed to exist as long as the base did, in case someone needed handheld tools in order to repair something.

Like a ship.

He opened the safe long enough to see that, yes indeed, there were tools inside. Whether they were the proper tools or the best tools or the most useful tools, he would let Yash decide.

He closed the safe, then backed out of the supply area.

Finally, he walked to the emergency lift and pressed his hand against the door, waiting for it to identify him.

It did, with the same *queried but granted* notification the other doors had given him. The door slid back and revealed something he didn't want to see.

The lift was gone, filled in with dirt and debris, trapped on the lower level by a wall built of clear nanobits.

Exactly as the handbook said that any emergency lift should be decommissioned. When a base was deemed no longer useful, the lift to the surface was shut down, so that a gaping hole would not exist beneath the ground, something that could cave in once the passage of years let everyone forget exactly where the emergency lift opened onto the surface.

"Dammit," he said softly. Of course it wouldn't be that easy.

Nothing had been that easy on this trip. And nothing would be.

Not for a while, at least.

Maybe not for years.

FORTY-SEVEN

We huddle outside the door to the Dignity Vessel room, all seven of us. The moment feels momentous. We've tested and retested all of our findings about the particles. They're large and could be harmful if swallowed, but they have no effect on the skin—at least short-term. They don't hurt us in any known way.

The air inside the room is a bit stale, but otherwise fine, and the temperature is just a little cooler than the caves themselves.

In other words, we don't need the environmental suits.

However, I'm going to wear mine, all except the helmet, which I have attached to my belt. Lentz's university professor friend has surreptitiously given us two dozen face masks, the kind that the Vaycehnese wear when they go deep in the caves.

The Vaycehnese have encountered the floating particles as well, and have found that some people suffer no ill effects from them whatsoever, while others end up with lung problems for years. The masks have a thin weave that prevents the particles from being inhaled. The masks go over the mouth and nose, and their bright whiteness looks a bit odd against the skin.

At our meeting last night, Lentz laughed when I mentioned that. He reminded me that the mask will probably get caked with particles in a matter of minutes, taking it from white to gray to black.

Some of the others—Quinte and Seager, in particular—have decided to wear the helmets, although I made them bring masks as well. We're carrying quite a few things, actually. A small ladder, a pouch of tools, and my own personal pair of grippers so that I can climb the side of the ship and see what's above us.

We're stopped outside, however, because Al-Nasir is dithering. He holds his mask in one hand. In the other he clings to his helmet. He hates being confined, but the room still makes him nervous.

We're all a bit more nervous than we've been, although the smoothness of yesterday's mission has gone a long way toward calming us down.

I pluck the mask out of Al-Nasir's hand. "Put it on. You'll feel better."

He takes it from me, stares at it, then puts it in the pouch along his waistband. Then he takes his helmet and attaches it to the rest of the suit.

I suppress a smile. I knew if I made the choice for him, he would know what he really wanted.

I put my hand on the door. "Same order as yesterday," I say. Which means me first.

I pull the door open, and freeze.

The lights are on. We figured out how to shut them down just before we left yesterday. They were off. I'm as sure of that as I am of my own name.

"Okay," I say softly, the mask moving gently against my lips and nose as I speak. "We could have a problem. Rea, DeVries, I need you with me. The rest of you can wait here if you want."

I don't wait for an answer. I pull my laser pistol and go in, heart pounding.

Someone has been here. The lights are on, the equipment is on all the way around the room, the various screens showing parts of space both familiar and unfamiliar.

One screen shows my science station back home. The station is empty, but through the glass viewing area on the far side of that room, I can see one of my scientists, taking readings.

I step all the way inside. Rea and DeVries follow me, laser pistols out. The two men are flanking me, as I taught them when they first came into the group, back at their very first tourist dive.

The other four come in as well, proper position, half a step behind each other, as if we're a trained military unit. Without my telling them to, Quinte and Al-Nasir remain by the door, and they keep it open, making it easier for us to escape if we have to.

I glance at Rea and DeVries, then nod. We pointedly do not look at the screens, and we carefully examine the room from our stopped position.

I see no one, not out here, not with us.

But I have a hunch I'm not supposed to see anyone.

This is a message.

Someone is on board that Dignity Vessel—and they want me to know it.

FORTY-EIGHT

Coop stood as the door to the repair room opened. Everyone on the bridge turned toward the screens. Even Dix looked up, and Dix hadn't looked at much of anything in days.

The outsider woman stopped when she saw the lights. They glistened off her hair, a chestnut brown that surprised Coop. She wasn't wearing a helmet, but she was wearing a mask of some kind over her mouth and nose. The particles worried her.

For some reason, that reassured him. These people weren't that different after all.

As she looked at the lights, she drew her weapon—not that silly knife, which he couldn't even see. From this distance, the weapon looked like some kind of laser pistol, but bulkier than he expected.

"Zoom in on that weapon," Coop said to Anita. "See if we can figure out exactly what it is and does."

"I don't blame her for drawing it," Perkins said. "She doesn't know—"

"I don't blame her either, Lieutenant," Coop said. "Let's just watch and figure out what they're going to do."

"Can't I suit up?" Perkins asked.

He glanced at her. She had turned toward him, her back straight, her eyes glistening. She wanted to go into the repair room.

And she was right; she was the one who should go out there. He had said first-contact situation, which meant the linguists were in the main team, and Mae, his best linguist, wasn't on rotation.

"Yes," he said to Perkins. "I want you in your dress uniform."

"Sir?" She sounded surprised.

"And no weapons," he said.

"But they have them," she said.

"And I would too in this circumstance, if I were them. But we have the upper hand here. So let's use it." He turned his attention back to the screen.

All seven had come into the repair room, and they were using a flanking maneuver he hadn't seen since military training. Half of the woman's team wore the same kind of mask she did. The rest still had on their helmets, which had to limit visibility.

They all carried those laser pistols, and the hands of at least three of the seven shook as they clutched the grip.

Great. Amateurs. Frightened amateurs.

This could get dangerous.

He almost rescinded the order to Perkins, thinking he didn't want his people in the middle of a group of scared amateurs. Then he changed his mind. The amateurs would be scared no matter what, and then, if his people didn't appear, they'd get emboldened.

He needed to retain this upper hand.

"Dix," Coop said, "I need Rossetti up here now."

"Yes, sir," Dix said.

"You're sending them out immediately?" Yash asked.

Perkins shot her an almost angry glance, then hurried off the bridge, as if her absence would prevent him from changing his mind.

"No," Coop said. "I'm going to give the outsiders an hour. They need to regroup, think a bit, calm down. We surprised them. The last thing we should do is surprise them again."

"I think you should observe more," Yash said.

"Duly noted," Coop said, closing debate. "What are those weapons, Anita?"

"Laser pistols," she said. "They have the right power signature, but they're pretty unwieldy. I wouldn't want to fire one."

"I assume they'll do a lot of damage if they hit someone?" he asked.

"Can't tell without actually test-firing one. But that's a safe assumption."

He watched the outsiders, slowly exploring the room, clearly responding to commands. The woman kept glancing at one of the screens; it seemed to make her nervous.

They all made Coop nervous. The screens were all tied to ships within the sector, and showed what the ships saw. But, logically, there shouldn't be any ships in the sector. They should have left decades ago with the Fleet.

The visual that disturbed him the most was the one the woman kept glancing at—three screens down, it looked as if he were looking at some kind of station, one he didn't recognize.

Questions, questions, and more questions.

He hoped that once his people talked to the outsiders, he would finally start getting answers.

FORTY-NINE

I know we're being watched. I can feel it, even if I can't see it. I've had the feeling from the beginning that we weren't alone, and now I have confirmation of it.

Yet there's no one visible in this gigantic room.

"Did we interrupt them?" Seager asks, her voice shaking. "Are they hiding from us?"

"Have you looked at that ship?" Quinte says. "Do you know how many people can be in that thing?"

The best guess of our own tech people is that the average Dignity Vessel held at least one hundred people, and possibly as many as a thousand. It depended on how many were needed to run the various ship's systems, and how many people got crammed into the various rooms.

I have always doubted the thousand number. The rooms on the partially intact Dignity Vessels we found looked more like suites or apartments than single bunks. But who knew how these ships were used.

And really, we don't know what they were used for.

What they *are* used for.

I look up at the side, exactly where the cockpit is on every single Dignity Vessel I've encountered. I stand in front of it for a long time, just to make sure that they're all watching me.

And then I slowly, carefully, ostentatiously, holster my laser pistol.

"Boss! Don't!" Rea says. "We have no idea if they're hostile!"

"If they're hostile, they would have lain in wait for us," I say. "They observed us the last two times we were here. This time, they would have sent out a small crew, and blasted us away."

At least that is what I would have done. If I felt threatened by people coming near my ship, and I thought those people were dangerous, I'd attack first and ask questions later.

I extend my hands, showing that they're empty.

Come and see me, I'm trying to say. *We're harmless. Let's talk.*

But the door remains closed.

"Put your weapons away," I say to my team.

"I don't want to," Rea says.

"I don't think it's wise," Kersting says.

"Can't some of us keep them?" Seager asks.

That seems the most sensible. A few weapons, but not a bunch. The problem is that I doubt anyone except me and Rea have experience with weapons, and I'm not really sure about Rea.

I'm more worried about an accidental discharge than I am about the people on that Dignity Vessel.

"How about this?" I say, willing to compromise with my team. "Seager, Quinte, Kersting, lower your weapons. Point them at the floor. If something goes wrong, raise them and use them. But wait until my signal."

"What if something happens to you?" Quinte asks.

"I think that would substitute for a signal, don't you?" I can't help the sarcasm. I miss my real team. I miss Mikk's quick thinking and Roderick's impulsive piloting skills. I miss Tamaz's muscle. I miss their loyalty and their ability to anticipate what I'm about to do.

"The rest of you," I say, after I manage to regain control of my voice again, "holster your weapons."

I turn toward them. Rea clutches his like a lifeline.

"*Now*," I say, wondering how I'll enforce this if they don't listen.

But they do. Rea makes a show of holstering his. DeVries puts his away as if the grip has already burned him. Al-Nasir carefully holsters his as if he thinks it'll go off if he hits it wrong.

I sigh. I'm stuck in the strangest, possibly the most dangerous, experience I've had since some of us went after the Empire's guards, and this time, I have a bunch of tourists who can't think clearly if their life depended on it.

And of course, their lives do depend on it.

As does mine.

"Now what?" Rea asks.

"Now," I say, "we wait."

FIFTY

"**M**y God," Dix said. "They're putting their weapons away."

Coop looked up from his consultation with Rossetti. She was in full dress uniform as well, just like he had requested, but she would be putting an environmental-suit over it for added protection. The dress uniform was for her and not the outsiders. It was to remind her—and her entire team—that they were in a diplomatic situation, not a military one.

Apparently the outsiders thought they weren't in a military situation, either —or at least the woman did. She held her hands out, showing that they were empty.

That fabric mask she wore over her mouth and nose moved slightly—she was talking to her people. Three of them had holstered their weapons, and the other three had turned the muzzles downward, although the heavyset man would probably shoot his own foot if the weapon discharged.

Amateurs.

That detail still disturbed Coop.

Still, he couldn't prevent a small smile. He and the woman were communicating already.

She wanted him to know that her people were not a threat. She wanted a dialogue. But she also wanted him to know that she would shoot if shot at.

"Get out there," he said to Rossetti.

"I had told my team we had another half an hour," she said.

"I don't care," he said. "They're ready for us now. Get out there as quickly as you can."

"Yes, sir." She nodded and left the bridge.

"This isn't some kind of ploy, is it?" Yash asked, looking at the outsiders.

"What kind of ploy would that be?" Coop asked. "We're the ones who notified them we were here. They didn't seem too concerned about us before today."

"They didn't know we were here before today," Yash said.

"We'll be careful," Coop said.

"I hope so," Yash said. "I really do."

FIFTY-ONE

*T*he ship's door opens. It rises upward, and a small staircase eases out, sliding its way to the floor. I've seen the doors open like that on Dignity Vessels we've found, but I've never seen the staircase. It makes my breath catch again. The magic and mystery of the Dignity Vessels. I'm so overwhelmed, I have to remind myself to remain calm.

A woman emerges. She holds herself rigidly. She's wearing an environmental suit without a helmet, but an environmental suit unlike any I've ever seen. It's more like a membrane than a suit, and beneath it, I can see a black uniform—or what I'm imagining to be a black uniform.

Her gaze meets mine, and she holds it as she comes down those stairs. She's already figured out that I'm in charge, and she's coming directly for me.

"Boss," Rea says, sounding nervous.

I signal him to remain quiet with my right hand. In fact, I hope my entire team got that signal. I want to be the one doing the talking here. I should have told them that.

Behind the woman comes an entire group of people. Men, women of varying heights and appearances. Some are spacer thin, but some aren't. Some look like they were raised in real gravity.

I wonder how that's possible, given what I've heard about Dignity Vessels. Then I have to remind myself: everything I've heard might be wrong.

The group lines up in front of us, two deep, with the woman who came first only a few meters from me. She's taller, and looks stronger. She's also younger. Her eyes are dark brown, her chin raised slightly.

Her posture is military.

Finally, a woman emerges not wearing an environmental suit. She's wearing a black uniform with gold decorations down the sleeves and along the shoulders. Her hair is red, her skin unlined, her bones large and strong from being raised in gravity.

The door closes behind her. She's the one who walks up to me.

She nods and says something completely incomprehensible.

I've done this a few times before, usually on a space station, usually in a bar where someone else can identify the language and save me from myself.

But I'm here alone with my team, and all of my people who can understand various languages don't have the damn genetic marker.

"I'm the boss of this crew," I say. "We're explorers. We didn't expect to find your ship. Is this your base?"

The woman tilts her head slightly, and I can tell from the expression in her eyes that she doesn't understand me any more than I understand her.

She nods at me, holds up a hand as if to say, *Let's try this again,* then taps herself. She makes four distinct sounds.

Then she points to me.

I don't say anything, not yet.

She repeats the gesture and the sounds.

Her name and/or her rank. Her identification, at any rate.

I tap myself. "Boss."

She repeats that. Then taps herself a third time, and repeats the four sounds.

I say them. She smiles. Communication of a sort.

She glances at the rest of my team, then says something very slowly. I don't understand a word of it, but I make sure I'm recording it all. Maybe someone back at the hotel will understand.

I shrug, and feel someone near my side.

Al-Nasir has joined us. I glance at his hands, worried about his laser pistol. It remains in its holster.

"I think I understand them, Boss," he says.

How can he, when I don't?

"You've got to be kidding," I say.

He shakes his head. "I had fifteen years of linguistics in school," he says. "We went backward, looking at the way Standard evolved. I think she's speaking a variation of it."

"Give it a shot," I say.

She's watching us closely, as if she's trying to understand.

He nods at her, then extends his hand toward her and repeats those four syllables.

She nods.

Then he taps himself and says, "Fahd Al-Nasir."

She repeats his name. Then she says very clearly, "Boss," and I jump.

"Yes," I say.

She looks at me sharply. She seems to understand *yes.*

"Yes?" she repeats, but her emphasis is odd.

"Yes," I say.

"Good," Al-Nasir says, but he says it oddly, almost unrecognizably. "You speak Standard."

His inflection is weird.

She frowns at him and says something in return.

"Yes," he says.

"You'll have to translate for me," I say.

"I think she said, *You're speaking Standard?*"

"You think?" I ask.

"I think," he says, looking at me.

She's watching closely.

Al-Nasir taps himself again. "I am Fahd Al-Nasir." Then he puts his hand on my arm. "And she is my boss."

The woman's eyes light up. "Boss," she says just as clearly. "Title?"

At least, I think that's what she says. Al-Nasir seems to understand it that way, too.

"Yes," he says, and gives me a sideways glance. He's not going to explain that it's also what everyone calls me. Probably too confusing anyway.

He looks at her, then at the ship. "Are you the boss?"

"No," she says.

Even I understand that. So there's someone else in charge.

"May we speak to your boss?" Al-Nasir asks.

She says something in response. Al-Nasir repeats the question. She slows down what she says. At least, I think it's the same thing she said. I don't have a facility with language. Clearly, Al-Nasir does.

He repeats the question a third time, and this time she says, simply, "No."

My heart sinks. "Do they want us to leave?" I ask.

"I don't know," he says testily. "I can barely understand her as it is."

"Try this," I say. "Tell her we're recording the conversation. Tell her that we'll find someone to translate her message if she just repeats it a few times."

"Oh, yeah," he says, "with my magical ability to speak a variation of Standard I've never heard before."

She's looking at us.

I sigh. I hold up my hands and say, "We would like to figure out a way to communicate. Does anyone on your ship speak Standard?"

She answers me. Al-Nasir says softly, "She says she is speaking Standard."

"Let me try again," I say to her, ignoring Al-Nasir. "Does anyone on the ship speak the version of Standard that I know?"

"No," she says. I swear she's understanding more and more as the conversation goes on.

"We would like to have some kind of dialogue. Is there a way we can do that?" I ask.

"Yes," she says. Then she says something else rapidly. I don't understand any of it. Al-Nasir doesn't seem to, either.

She reaches into her pocket and pulls out a small device. It looks official. I watch as she clicks it on and off. My heart soars for a moment.

She's recording us, too. She'll work on our language, just like we'll work on hers.

She puts the device back in her pocket. Then she reaches toward me, slowly, and carefully takes my hand. On my arm is my wrist guide. She taps it, and says one word slowly.

Al-Nasir repeats it. It sounds almost familiar.

She smiles at him. Her smile is lovely. "Yes," she says.

"Yes," he says, and they nod at each other.

Then she looks at her team, says something in a different tone, and they file back up those stairs into the ship, leaving us standing outside. As the last woman goes inside, the stairs disappear.

"What was that?" I ask Al-Nasir.

"I think she wants us back tomorrow at the same time."

"You think?" I ask.

"You saw her," he snaps. "What do you think?"

I smile at him. I'm suddenly giddy. We just met people from a Dignity Vessel. In uniform. And they seem official.

It's like a dream.

"What do I think?" I say, grinning like an idiot, glad no one can see it under the mask. "I hope to hell you're right."

FIFTY-TWO

Coop wanted to run to the airlock and find out exactly what had happened, but he knew better. He waited on the bridge and watched the outsiders.

The woman gazed wistfully at the *Ivoire*'s door. Then she nodded to her people. She put a hand on the arm of the man who had done much of the speaking and talked to him for a moment.

The three who had their pistols out holstered them. And then the group headed to the door.

The woman looked at the consoles, stopped, and held up a hand. She stared at the far console again, the one showing that space station. Coop frowned. She knew something about that, or it disturbed her in some way. Coop couldn't tell which it was, and he wasn't going to know, not for a while.

The others looked at her; she tilted her head slightly, as if she were saying something self-deprecating, and then they left the repair room.

He wondered if he would have stayed. Would he have investigated those consoles as the woman was clearly tempted to do? Or would he leave, worried about what the people on the ship were thinking?

He didn't know, partly because he didn't know what their mission was. If the outsiders hadn't known what the room was, or what the ship was, they might have stayed. Or maybe not. Maybe they were worried about a greater force, the clear military bent of the people on the ship.

"Captain?" Perkins spoke from behind him. "Do you want me to brief the entire bridge crew?"

Coop turned. A few nanobits glistened in her hair. A few more rested on her sleeves and shoulders.

"Just me," he said, and led her into the conference room. He kept the screens off. He pulled out a chair for her, so that she would be comfortable as they spoke, but she didn't sit down.

Instead, she paced, filled with an energy he hadn't seen in her before.

He didn't sit, either.

"I captured a lot of their speech patterns," she said. "They spoke to each other quite a bit, and I captured that, which is good."

Coop had forgotten this about her. Perkins never gave a report in a linear manner.

"They don't speak Standard, then," he said.

She paused and looked at him. Then she gave him a rueful smile. "Oh, yeah. Sorry. You weren't listening in. I'm not sure what they speak. It sounded familiar when the woman started talking to us, but I couldn't understand her. I thought at first that she was speaking Standard, but pronouncing it differently, so differently that I had trouble processing it. Then I realized that the words sounded familiar but weren't familiar."

"Which means what?" Coop asked.

"Which means they might be speaking a mangled form of Standard or some kind of pidgin language. It might also be a related language with similar sounds. I already have the computer working on it, and I expect to have results before our next meeting with them, which I'm hoping will be tomorrow."

"Did you set that up with them?"

She shrugged. "As best I could. They seemed pretty startled by us. They seemed even more shocked that we had trouble communicating."

He wasn't surprised. He had encountered many different languages on his travels, some of which were so different that it took months to get as far as Perkins had gotten today. Basic introductions were difficult, and from what he saw, she had gotten through those.

"Did you understand anything they said?" he asked.

"I think so, but I'm not sure."

Coop frowned. She had never given him that response before. "What do you mean?"

"It's that soundlike thing I mentioned," Perkins said. "I gave the woman my name. The woman did the same thing, but I think she gave me her rank."

"Which is?"

"She's their leader."

"That's clear," Coop said.

"But I'm not sure that's what she said," Perkins said. "I thought we were doing pretty well. I said my name, she responded with her title, and then I asked her where we were. The man stepped forward and introduced himself."

"I noticed that," Coop said.

"His name sounded very different. She spoke a one-syllable word, short and curt. His name was smooth, filled with 'ah' sounds that blended into one another. I couldn't tell how many syllables he used, and I'm not sure, when I repeated it back, whether or not I said it right."

She clasped her hands behind her back and walked alongside the table, talking to herself as much as to him.

"Names are tricky," she said. "Because they work off several traditions. Names often have a family history and go through time, all the way back to the beginning of the family. If you do a family tree, you might find that name runs through hundreds of generations. If, of course, you can trace the family back that far."

"You think that's the case with his name?" Coop wasn't sure how she got that from the short conversation.

"I don't know," she said. "Names are the trickiest part of language because names aren't fixed. You're the captain. You're Captain Cooper. You're Jonathon Cooper. And you're Coop. You might also be Captain Coop Cooper—"

"I get your point," he said dryly.

"And Coop is a word. Captain is a title, a name, and a rank. Jonathon is one of the oldest names we have, going all the way back to Earth, and Earth documents centuries before space flight use that name."

"I see," he said, trying to move her along. "How is this tied to the woman?"

"I think the man introduced himself. And then, I think he said 'she's our leader.' But he might also have just given me her name. I don't know. What I understood is this. Imagine if you were her. You tapped herself, and said 'Captain.' I repeated it, not quite understanding, and gave my name. Then the man came over and introduced himself, followed by, 'And he's our captain.' Or he might have said, 'and he's captain,' and that was a name, not a title."

"All right." Coop reached out to put a hand on her shoulder, to calm the pacing. It didn't work. She didn't look up. "I want you to consult with Mae."

"I plan to," Perkins said. "I'm going to get as much help on this as possible because so far as I can tell, time is of the essence, right?"

He looked at her, feeling the irony.

"Yes," he said. And considering that she knew that, considering how the meeting went, he asked, "Why did you leave after less than half an hour?"

First contacts could go as long as six hours, if the linguists and diplomats felt they were making progress.

Perkins looked at him, a frown creasing her brow. "The name thing. I got so confused that I wasn't sure what I was doing. If I was truly misunderstanding everything, then I was just making the situation worse."

He had never heard her say anything like that before. Perkins had been his most fearless linguist, one Mae worried about because she was afraid that Perkins might inject a misunderstanding into a conversation, due to arrogance.

"You're thinking of the Quurzod, aren't you?" he asked.

"If someone like Mae can make a mistake that big, one that would lead to them firing on us, imagine what I can do here."

Coop shook his head. "What happened with the Quurzod was much more complicated than translations gone wrong. When we get back to the Fleet, I'm going to talk with the command center. I think the Xenth set us up. I think the error occurred long before Mae and her team embedded themselves in that Quurzod village."

"But you don't know, do you, sir?" Perkins said, suddenly sounding formal.

"I know enough to know that the problem was not with the linguists," he said. "The problem was with the diplomats. We're not even to that stage here. I need you to talk with the outsiders. I need you to figure out who the outsiders are."

"So we can get back to the Fleet," Perkins said.

"So that we can try," he said.

He sighed for a moment, thinking of all the difficulties he had left behind. If he never returned to the Fleet, they would move on, and the problems with the Quurzod would evolve into a full-scale war, one he could actually prevent. Tiny details, important details.

He felt a sudden urgency, and then tamped it down. He couldn't focus on that. He had to think of his own crew, his own timeline, his own future.

"When do you think I can talk to them?" he asked.

Perkins looked at him, surprise all over her face. He had never before asked to speak to a first contact before the language issues were sorted out.

But this wasn't about the language. It wasn't even, really, about a proper first contact. If things worked out right, he would never see these people again.

"Sir," she said, speaking slowly, as if to keep her surprise under control, "this could take weeks."

"Not if the language is related."

She bit her lip and tilted her head in an acknowledgment that could mean yes or could mean no.

Finally she said with a firmness she had never used before, "I said I'm guessing."

He felt a touch of color warm his cheeks. He had vowed he wasn't going to let the crew know about his impatience, and then he had revealed it to Perkins. "The sooner we can question them about substantive things, the better off we are."

"I know, sir," she said, "but it's better to understand them than to guess, don't you think?"

He nodded, reluctantly. He wanted that conversation, and he wanted it soon. Just like he wanted the ship repaired. Just like he wanted to know when they were.

"Good work," he said to Perkins. "Let me know when you have enough of the language to act as a translator."

"I will, sir," she said.

I hope it's soon, he almost said, but didn't. *I really, really hope it's soon.*

FIFTY-THREE

We don't have linguists; we have historians and archeologists, and they have studied languages only so that they can understand the things that they find. I want a linguist, because my historians and archeologists disagree about what they've heard.

We're sitting in the large room of my suite, which I'm beginning to hate. I had hoped we'd meet the crew of the Dignity Vessel, we'd talk, and we'd all learn something. I'd dreamed that I would be able to convince them to come back to the Nine Planets with us and see the other Dignity Vessels, help us figure out how to use them, and warn the Dignity Vessel crew about the Empire.

Of course, I knew that such a scenario was hopelessly naïve, which is why I haven't admitted it to anyone. But dreams can be such powerful things.

I was excited while we were in that large room, but I'm a bit wary now. Wary and exhausted. It's clear to me that we have a lot of work ahead, and that work involves painstaking effort on both sides.

It also involves remaining on Vaycehn for several weeks, if not several months.

I have ordered Ilona to look at renting a house or an office for us, to cut down on expenses. She's doubtful this can happen, simply because the Vaycehnese do not want us to have free rein in their city. No one from our team can get near the death hole site even now, and someone has been following a few of the historians.

We have to watch our step, and we have to be cautious about where and when we discuss the Dignity Vessel. We keep scanning our rooms to make sure no one is recording us here or watching us without our permission.

So far, we have found nothing, and for that, I am profoundly grateful.

I am not, however, grateful for the discussion we're having over dinner.

The historians, archeologists, and scientists have listened to the recording I brought back of our first meeting. We all agree that the Dignity Vessel's crew speaks a familiar-sounding language, and everyone has complimented Al-Nasir on his quick thinking below.

But no one knows, exactly, what to do about this language issue. Our scientists want to augment a language program that the Empire uses for strange dialects throughout the sector. Our archeologists want a written version of everything the Dignity Vessel crew says.

Only the historians seem comfortable with the spoken language.

"I'm guessing," Dana Carmak says as she takes a slice of orange cake from the center of the table, "but I think that they're speaking a language older than Old Earth Standard."

She seems excited by this. Her color is up, making her seem abnormally red. Her strawberry curls tumble around her face, longer than they were when we got here, which tells me just how much time we've spent on Wyr already.

"How can you know that?" Lucretia Stone asks with more than a little condescension in her voice. "We haven't seen the language."

"We see it all the time," Dana says. "The Dignity Vessels back home have it."

I'm pleased that she calls our base home. My group has coalesced around that place and wants to return, which is a good thing. Some of my team is still uncomfortable with me, and with the mission. My speech a few days ago didn't calm everyone. In fact, it made some of the team nervous.

"We have seen Old Earth Standard," Stone says.

"There are some differences, which we attributed to the way the words were written in the Dignity Vessel," Carmak says. "But I think now that they're actually part of the evolution of the language."

"Do we know the evolution of the language?" Mikk sounds a bit skeptical, although not as contemptuous as Stone. I realize that he's actually interested, and trying to mask that interest like he always does, pretending to be the muscle instead of one of the brains.

"We know a lot," Carmak says. "We know that Earth developed a language for diplomacy, but that language was not the main language spoken on the planet. Several other languages thrived there—how many we don't know."

She looks at Mikk as if to stave off that question.

"We know that the diplomatic language became the language of space, and eventually, that language became known as Standard. Standard has both evolved and codified. There are a thousand known dialects, some of which are simply older versions of Standard spoken in older parts of the known universe. I suspect if we had a way to get close to Earth we'd find people who could speak easily with the crew of this Dignity Vessel."

"Supposition is not science," Stone says.

"I'm not striving for science," Carmak says. "I'm striving for understanding. The language is close enough that you, Fahd, were able to communicate with that woman."

"I think I was communicating," Al-Nasir says. "It felt that way at the time, but I do not know for certain. I worry about that."

"We do the best we can," I say, not really caring how the language evolved. "What I want to know is whether or not we can talk to these people."

"Eventually," Carmak says.

"How about soon?" I ask. "We don't want them to leave before we talk to them about their ship."

And stealth tech, and the room, and the death holes. I have so many questions. The problem is that even if we do have a grasp of the language, it's the common parts of the language we share. The technical parts—how the machines work, what the black coating is—we might not be able to communicate about for a very long time.

"If you don't mind," Carmak says, "I'd like to work with Fahd. He's got a facility for this language, and he might move quicker than everyone else."

Meaning me.

"Simultaneous translation is not easy," I say.

"We might be able to develop a program for that," Bridge says. He's been looking at the language, too. "That'll take a few weeks at best, but it might help."

"All right," I say. "Fahd, when you're not with us in that room, you'll go with Dana, and the two of you will do your best to understand the language."

"What about the rest of us?" Stone says. "We have language training."

"It's the spoken language I care about, Lucretia," I say. "You can continue to work on the written language. If nothing else, we'll write them notes. But it would be better if we can actually talk to them."

She purses her lips, but it's clear she understands me.

"Were you able to understand what they said today?" I ask Carmak.

"I think Fahd is right," Carmak says. "They want to meet tomorrow."

"Any reason they broke off the discussion today?" I ask. I've been thinking about it, and I haven't come up with a reason.

"It sounded to me like they were confused," Carmak says. "They kept asking your name."

I feel my cheeks heat. "We didn't use my name."

"That's the point, and the problem. If they know the word 'Boss,' then they're not sure if the questions were asked and answered right. I think it's probably best if Fahd is going to deal with them on a personal level. Unless you're willing to use your real name . . ."

Carmak let her voice fade down, but I can hear the question in it. I don't tell people my name, not because I've disavowed it, but because it doesn't have much meaning for me. My parents gave me that name. More specifically, my father gave it to me. Before, I only told a select group of people my name. Now, I don't bother.

"All right," I say. "I'll do my best not to confuse things."

"I think you should keep getting information from all the equipment," Stone says to me.

"I think you're right," I say. "Let's hope they don't take offense at that."

"You'll still bring your weapons in, right?" Bernadette Ivy asks. She opted not to return to the *Business* when no one else decided to go, but she still approaches everything around here with something akin to terror.

"We will," I say, "but I don't think the laser pistols will mean much. We saw a lot of people this afternoon, and to my eye, they all looked military. Which means that there are a lot more people on board that ship. We were outnumbered today in that room. We might be outnumbered in actuality by hundreds."

Everyone stares at me, looking appalled. The Six, in particular, have stricken looks on their faces.

"What if they decide to take us hostage?" Quinte asks.

"We can't come in and rescue you," Roderick says. He looks worried.

"If they take us, they take us," I say. I have to be honest about this. "We don't have the numbers to fight back. The rest of you will have to monitor us. If we don't come out of that room within the scheduled time, then you wait a few days. If you still haven't heard from us, then you follow the emergency evacuation plan."

Stone and Mikk look at each other. If something happens to me, there will be a little battle for control of this group.

The rest of the group looks alarmed. I'm going to quell this current panic now.

"I don't think we have a lot to worry about on that front," I say. "They could have taken us any time in the previous two missions. Instead, they came out and tried to initiate a dialogue. They're as curious about us as we are about them."

"I doubt that," Kersting says softly.

"If they're anything like the Dignity Vessels of legend," I say, "they get to know people before they make decisions about them. They're trying to get to know us now. We're not going to make any threatening moves. I suspect we'll be fine."

No one speaks for a moment. Then DeVries looks at me.

"Don't you think something is off here?" he asks softly.

"What do you mean?" I ask.

"I mean, we've always heard about a fleet, but we've only found individual ships, and they've been old and ruined. Now we have an intact one. Do we even know this is the original crew? Or maybe these people are another group who have hijacked that ship, and don't know how to work it."

A chill runs down my back. I've been so excited to see a working Dignity Vessel that such a thought has never crossed my mind. And I'm usually enough of a pessimist to see problems like that.

"It's a possibility," I say. "But they can clearly operate in a stealth-tech field. So they have the genetic marker, at the very least."

"Which means what, exactly?" Mikk asks. "Maybe they're like your father, ruthless in picking their crew members, letting the ones without the marker die."

"Maybe," I say, "but I keep coming back to their military precision. Thieves usually don't have that."

"Neither do wreck divers," says Tamaz with a grin.

He doesn't know how accurate he is. I felt like a bumbling fool when I saw the care the ship's crew used as they came down the stairs.

"We'll figure this all out," I say. "It'll just take time."

"'Time,'" DeVries repeats, as if he didn't want to hear that.

"Let's just hope," I say, trying to keep the group calm, "that the crew of that vessel is as patient as we are."

"Who says we're patient?" Kersting asks, and everyone laughs.

I laugh, too, but I really don't find the comment funny. I'm not feeling patient. I'm not feeling patient at all.

CITY OF RUINS

FIFTY-FOUR

*I*t took Perkins nearly two weeks to figure out the outsiders' language with any kind of precision. During that time, the engineers repaired the *anacapa* and most of the weapons systems. Other repairs remained, but none to the major systems. Coop sifted through much of the information pulled from the repair room's equipment, but he didn't come up with any more information than his team was finding.

He repeatedly had communications contact Venice City, but didn't get any response. He mapped the underground caverns around the repair room a second time. The entire complex was much bigger than it had been the month before.

And as the remaining sensors came back online, he had his team see what they could find on the surface.

There was a city in the narrow valley, just like there had been for decades. But the city was no longer in the same place. Instead, it was scattered along the mountainside, far away from the city center that Coop had visited several times.

All of these pieces of information didn't add up to anything coherent, not yet, which made talking to the outsiders all the more imperative.

The number of outsiders never changed, and although Perkins asked the woman what their group was called, she never got an answer she understood.

Perkins was understanding more and more, however, partly because of the outsiders themselves. After a few days, the man showed an increasing ability to speak Perkins's language. It took Perkins another day or two to understand him because the man mangled every single word he tried to say. It was almost as if he was familiar with the language in its written form, but hadn't ever spoken it.

At least, that was Perkins's hypothesis. Coop wasn't so certain. If the outsiders could read Standard, then how come they hadn't heeded the warnings written all over the floor in the repair room? How come they seemed surprised when the ship nearly crushed one of them?

Still, Coop wasn't the linguist, and he had to rely on Perkins's expertise to figure out what was going on. In less than two weeks, Perkins decided that the language the outsiders spoke was a form of Standard, but so changed by time and distance, as well as influence from other cultures, as to be practically unrecognizable.

The fact that the man could speak her language, though, didn't bode well, as she told Coop in one of their briefings.

"Sir, I think all of this means that we speak an old and possibly forgotten form of their language. One that is no longer active, but lives only in archives."

He felt a chill run through him. "How long does it take for a language to change like that?"

She shrugged. "There are instances of that happening within a few hundred years of no contact."

"But?" he asked.

"But generally, it happens over many centuries. Five, six, seven hundred years or more."

He stared at her. It was within the realm of possibility. They had gotten the ship to talk with the equipment in the repair room, but hadn't gleaned any more information about the time factor. Some of the scientific tests had come back that the equipment itself had aged several hundred years, but, as the scientists said, some of that could have been due to the proximity of a working (and possibly malfunctioning) *anacapa* drive.

"They can't be from the future of Venice City," he said. "Their suits aren't as evolved as ours."

She shrugged. "They're from our future somewhere. Somewhere they acquired our language. Then they lost touch with us, and the language changed, as languages do."

"It's time for me to talk to them," he said. "Can you clearly translate for us?"

"If we do it in the *Ivoire*," she said. "I need the computer and our linguistic team to back me up."

He thought about that for a moment. He had always envisioned the meeting to take place inside the repair room. He hadn't wanted the outsiders in his ship.

But he understood Perkins's point. And he needed the information now more than he needed to protect the ship's secrets.

Not that it had a lot of secrets from the outsiders. They had access to similar equipment in the repair room, and they clearly hadn't understood that.

"All right," Coop said. "Set up an appointment."

"Yes, sir," Perkins said.

"And I don't want her whole team in here. Bring her and the man who speaks the language into the briefing room. You and I will talk to them."

"All right, sir," Perkins said, and looked relieved. Everyone on the *Ivoire* was nervous. Everyone wanted answers because, as Dix told Coop, they were making up worst-case scenarios the longer this went on.

Coop had been making up a few on his own.

Initially those scenarios had involved being stranded in Sector Base V forever, but now that the *Ivoire* was getting repaired, he knew that wouldn't happen. Now he just had to figure out where he would take his crew, and when.

And for that, he needed to talk to the outsiders.

FIFTY-FIVE

We have been struggling against the language barrier for more than two weeks. Every day seems the same; we go below, go into the room, and separate. Al-Nasir walks to a small table that the Dignity Vessel crew set up on the second day, sits down, and talks to their lieutenant, doing his best to understand her while she does her best to understand him.

The rest of us scatter and look at the equipment. Only now, we each have someone from the Dignity Vessel shadowing us. They watch what we do, not that we're doing much. We're afraid to touch the consoles. We still don't understand them.

I've been going to the console that sits below the image of our science station. I think I've got some of these images figured out. The consoles are tied to particular Dignity Vessels, and the vessel that my people are currently working on is intact enough to send this image to the room.

However, the ship isn't working well enough to appear in the room itself. Or maybe I need to pull a lever or press a screen, which I have not done.

I have spent a lot of time near that console, taking images back to our scientists and engineers on the surface. My people there are working as hard as we are below. They're trying to decipher the secrets of the language and the secrets of the room, trying to figure out the parts of the conversations that Al-Nasir is having with the lieutenant that he can't entirely understand. It's slow going, but Carmak and Stone both assure me he's picking up the language quickly.

I have walked the length and breadth of the room, startled at its size. The minders have opened the doors in the back for me, and I am stunned by their emptiness. A gigantic room with shelves and storage. Suites of rooms behind another door that might have been quarters or a living space for the ship's crews. And a door that opens onto what seems like nothing, but looked, after closer investigation, like a blocked tunnel.

I am intrigued and frustrated. I want to learn more, but everything I see raises more questions.

My team on the surface feels the same way. They have finally been allowed to visit the death hole. Stone has asked for permission to explore it, but so far the Vaycehnese government has refused her. She has walked around the edges, which, she tells me, have been smoothed by the same blackness we see below.

The guides have been asking questions about our work, wanting to know what we're doing so deep in the corridors. I simply say, "Exploring," and don't explain any more.

Ilona has asked for an extended stay, saying that we've discovered a few things that might prevent death holes. She has told the Vaycehnese government that the death holes and the dangerous parts of the caves might be caused by the same thing. She has also told them we are searching for a solution to their problems.

So far, they haven't asked much, but that worries me. I hate having governments watch everything we do.

I am standing in front of what I now think of as my console, staring at the screen, when a hand touches my shoulder.

I turn, already protesting that I haven't touched anything.

Al-Nasir is behind me.

"They have a request," he says. "And I think you need to deal with it."

I don't even try to hide my surprise. I haven't talked with their lieutenant since the first day. I follow Al-Nasir across the floor, heading toward that little table.

Someone has brought out a third chair.

The lieutenant stands when she sees me. She's no longer wearing that black uniform, which I gather was something official. She wears a white shirt and black pants, along with a loose jacket that has writing on it that I can't read. I suspect this is a more informal uniform, but I don't really know.

She's also younger than I would expect. I've only watched from a distance, since there is no way I can oversee this language transfer.

She smiles at me, and beckons toward the chair.

I put my hand on the side, then wait. She understands. We sit together.

Al-Nasir sits as well.

I wait for her to speak.

She says, "Boss—?" then looks at Al-Nasir for confirmation.

He nods.

She says in good, if accented, Standard, "My captain would like to meet you."

"Okay," I say.

"He would like it one leader to another," she says.

"Okay," I say, not quite sure what she wants.

"He would like you and Fahd to come on board . . ." and then she says a word I do not understand. "The meeting would be private."

"On board the ship?" I ask.

She nods.

"I haven't figured out that word yet," Al-Nasir says to me softly, even though we both know the lieutenant can hear. "I think it's the name of the ship."

My heart is pounding. I would love to go on board that ship. "My team will come with me, of course."

She shakes her head. We're communicating a lot better than I would have expected two weeks ago.

"My captain would like you and Fahd only," the lieutenant says. At least I think she said Al-Nasir's first name. She mangled it terribly.

"That's not our custom," I say. "I go with my team."

She looks at Al-Nasir. I can't tell if she wants him to convince me otherwise or if she doesn't understand me.

"Boss wants all of us to go with her," he says to the lieutenant.

"I understood that," she says without frustration, even though I can see it in her eyes. "I do not know the word 'custom.'"

"Now you see what we've been doing?" Al-Nasir says to me. "It seems fine, and then we hit a word that we can't translate."

"I have no idea how we'll have a meeting, then," I say.

She looks at me. She understood that.

"I am a—" And then she says another word I do not know. "I learn—" Again, a mystery word. "—and I am good at it. But I cannot learn—" A third unknown word. "It is too much to learn in a short period of time. So, we have a—" I'm getting really frustrated with this. I'm suddenly quite happy that Al-Nasir has taken point on it. "—and it can figure out—" I glance at Al-Nasir. He's staring at her as if he's getting some of this. "—faster than I can."

"I'm sorry," I say, letting my frustration show. "I didn't understand that at all."

"I think she said they have a computer program that will help us communicate," Al-Nasir says.

She looks at him, then at me.

"Maybe we should wait until we understand each other better," I say. Much as I want to get inside that ship, I don't want to do it on their terms. I want my team to come with me. I want us to be safe.

She sighs and looks at her hands. Then she glances at the ship, then she looks at me and leans forward just a bit.

"We have waiting too long," she says, and the grammatical mistake makes me relax a little. She's not scary brilliant, just good with languages, like Al-Nasir. Unlike me.

"We need to know things," she says, "and we cannot get that—" Another word, but this time I can guess. "Information," "knowledge," whatever those things are that she needed to know. "—from our—" And as she says that last word she looks at the consoles.

"You need information?" I ask, looking back and forth between her and Al-Nasir, to make sure we both understand correctly. "From us?"

She nods.

"And you need it now," I say.

She nods again.

"Why not two weeks ago?" I ask.

"We cannot understand enough then," she says. "This is the first time we can talk clearly. With you and my captain. And the help of the—"

This time I recognize the word she used. She used it before.

"That computer program or computer or whatever," Al-Nasir says.

"You're sure of the translation?" I ask.

He shrugs. "I'm not sure of anything, Boss."

"Can you bring the—" I try to say the word she used, mangle it, wave my hand, and then look at Al-Nasir. He says it, and I continue. "Can you bring it out here?"

"No," she says. "A small—" And she mimes handheld while she says another word. "—is not good enough yet."

She's convincing me. Or maybe I'm easy to convince. I really want to go in there.

"Why only two of us?" I ask.

Al-Nasir starts to rephrase the question, but she waves him off.

"We are a—" Another of those unknown words.

Al-Nasir fills in. "Military, I think."

"—ship," she says. "We do not let most people inside her. Only leaders."

A military vessel that only allows people inside who are military or heads of state. My stomach twists. Apparently I was wrong about the origin of the ship after all.

"I thought you were a Dignity Vessel," I say.

She starts and repeats, "Dignity Vessel?"

"Part of the Fleet?"

She relaxes a bit. "We are part of the Fleet."

"And the Fleet is military?" I ask.

Al-Nasir says the word she used, but I don't wait for her answer.

"What government do you represent?" I am suddenly worried. Are they a part of the Empire now? Has the Empire acquired enough Dignity Vessels that they are actually using them?

"Government?" she asks slowly. She bites her lip. She's not sure she understands me. "We are govern us. We belong to no other country. We are the country."

"The Fleet governs itself?" I ask.

She nods.

"The military serves only the Fleet?" I ask.

She nods again.

"Who runs the Fleet?" I ask, trying to get to it a third way.

"The Fleet has a ship of leaders," she says. "Ours is not that ship."

I let out a small breath. I hope I'm understanding her right.

"No one hurts us," I say. "We leave when we want to."

"Yes," she says. "Tomorrow, then?"

I can tell she has said that phrase countless times to Al-Nasir.

"Yes," I say, and clasp my hands together so that they don't shake.

Tomorrow I will go inside my first working Dignity Vessel. Tomorrow I may get some answers of my own.

FIFTY-SIX

Coop was nervous. He hadn't expected to be. He barely slept, thinking about the upcoming meeting.

So much could go wrong.

He was trusting, when he wasn't sure he should.

According to first-contact protocols, if he were actually following them, he was making a large mistake. He should know who the people he was talking to were, how they fit into their society, and what their society was.

All he knew about them was that there were seven of them, their spokesman had said yes when Perkins asked him if they were explorers, and they seemed to be technologically behind.

But he knew nothing for certain, and that fed his nerves.

Although that wasn't the only cause. He worried about what the woman might tell him.

He spent the morning overseeing the preparation for the meeting. He used the formal briefing room, one usually reserved for heads of state. This briefing room had state-of-the-art screens and sideboards for meals should a meeting go late. The crew kept the table that dominated the room polished so that the fake wood shone. The chairs surrounding the table had padding and could actually be adjusted for the sitter's comfort.

Coop hated this room—he wasn't a formal man—but he was taking no chances here.

The communications team, led by Mae, had set up the translation programs, with a receptor near each seat. Even if someone spoke softly, something would pick up the sound and translate it. Mae's team would monitor the entire conversation in real time in the communication's array.

Perkins would be in the briefing room itself to facilitate the translations. She would have a chip in her ear so that she could hear any corrections or alterations Mae made to the translations, although Mae had already told Coop she wouldn't actively participate in the conversation.

Perkins seemed as nervous as Coop. She double-, triple-, and quadruple-checked the systems, then went early to the airlock just in case their guests arrived early.

He had his personal chef make some pastries and lay out various snacks. He set out bottles of wine he had picked up at Starbase Kappa. He also had flavored waters cooling on a sideboard, and various hot liquids on the other side of the room.

He wore his dress uniform. He posted two guards inside the room as a show of force, and had several others standing by. But he still planned to meet the woman and Al-Nasir with only Perkins at his side.

He adjusted everything as he waited, the bottles of wine, the dishes, even the chairs. He had the screens on so that he could monitor the repair room. He would watch the woman make her way to the briefing room, as if her movements might give him a clue to her personality.

It unnerved him that he knew nothing about her. He wasn't even certain of her name. Perkins called her cagey, as if she thought about every statement, and he got the sense that Perkins didn't much like her.

Her team seemed to respect her, though, and it didn't seem to be a respect based on fear.

He had to trust that as well.

He knew her voice better than anything else. He had listened to her conversation with Perkins in the communications array with the linguists. The conversation showed confusion, but it also showed thought.

And it had caught everyone's attention when the woman used the phrase "Dignity Vessel."

Dignity Vessel was the original name of the ships in the Fleet. The name came from the Fleet's original mission, to bring peace and dignity throughout the known universe.

The Fleet never did bring peace. They focused more on justice. And they did try to restore dignity where there was none.

But they didn't call themselves Dignity Vessels, although the words were still part of the ships' identification numbers. That these people knew what Dignity Vessels were gave Coop hope that less time had passed than he feared.

A movement caught his eye.

The outsiders had entered the repair room, all seven of them, none of them in environmental suits. The woman looked different. She wore something flowing, a dresslike top over a pair of tight-fitting pants. Her shoes remained practical, however.

Her companion, Al-Nasir, wore a white shirt and black pants, almost looking like a member of Coop's crew in casual dress. Everyone else on her team dressed as they had before, as if they expected to work.

The five who would stay in the repair room wore their masks. The woman and Al-Nasir did not.

Coop watched them, no longer pacing.

The other problem he had with this meeting was one of intent. He knew what he needed from her. He needed to know who she was, and who her people were. But that was secondary to the history lesson she could give him.

He had never gone into a meeting like this needing something. Usually he'd been the mediator or the person who could grant someone else's wishes.

This time, the woman had that control.

She could leave at any moment, and take her answers with her.

And he had no idea how—or even if—he could stop her.

FIFTY-SEVEN

I feel like an idiot. Ilona and the historians convinced me to dress as if I were meeting with the head of the Vaycehnese government, which I have. I brought one very dressy outfit (which, honestly, is all I own), for just that sort of meeting, and now I'm wearing it in the room I should be exploring.

I miss my environmental suit. I feel more like myself when I wear that.

I'm not carrying my laser pistol, although we discussed it. I don't want to go into this meeting armed. Al-Nasir and I are already outnumbered just by the lieutenant and her people. If there are more—and there is at least one, this mysterious captain—then we're seriously outnumbered.

A laser pistol won't save me.

I am, however, carrying Karl's knife. It's strapped around my waist. I doubt they'll let me bring it inside the ship, but I'm going to try. I'm going to tell them it's ceremonial, which it is. I keep the knife close, for sentimental reasons and as a reminder that things can go wrong.

We're inside the room. The others are going to wait. Seager and Quinte will guard the door. They're to leave as quickly as they can if it looks like things have gone badly. Rea, DeVries, and Kersting will continue our not-so-great investigation of the room. I'm sure they'll attract minders, and that's all right.

Al-Nasir stands beside me. He keeps rubbing the palms of his hands together. He's afraid he'll screw up the translations. I figure if the conversation doesn't seem to be going well, I'm going to leave. The Dignity Vessel people can try to stop me if they want to. But I've asked for respect, and I'm going to continue to demand it.

I wish we had a translation program, too, but my people couldn't put one together yet. I'm rather astonished that the Dignity Vessel people have. Stone believes—and I actually agree—that this is a sign of a full complement of crew on the ship itself. If five people work on something, they, by definition, work slower than fifty. A group doesn't have downtime. They can work more efficiently.

The ship's door opens as we approach. The staircase lowers, and then two men in those black uniforms emerge. They walk to the base of the stairs and move to the side. Either they're going to guard the ship or they're going to escort us.

They each extend a hand. The person on the right extends his right hand and the person on the left extends his left. It's choreographed, formal, and immediately sets a tone.

Ilona was right to make me dress up—much as I hate it.

"You ready?" I ask Al-Nasir.

He nods, then takes a deep breath and squares his shoulders. We head into the ship, me first.

We'd argued about that. Everyone wanted me to go second, as if that makes a difference. If something goes wrong, I'm going to be in the same amount of trouble whether I hit the danger first or I hit it second.

Besides, my going first shows leadership, and that's what I need to do here.

As I put my foot on the first stair, my heart rate increases. I am going inside a working Dignity Vessel.

The first time I went inside one, I had to lower myself through a hatch, with all of my suit lights on. I felt like a tourist then, nervous on her first dive, and Squishy warned me that I'd get the gids.

She was right.

If I were wearing a suit, I'd have the gids now.

I step inside the door into the airlock. It's familiar and unfamiliar. We have this part of the ship on two different Dignity Vessels, but neither of those vessels work. Here there are lights in places I don't expect them, circular lights on either side that are clearly assessing me and the kind of threat I pose.

Al-Nasir comes up beside me, and as he does, the door closes. The lights grow brighter.

The interior door opens, revealing a bright corridor and the lieutenant, standing just inside it. She's wearing her black uniform, her hands clasped behind her back.

She's nervous, too.

With the lights on and the environmental system working, the corridor seems bigger than it actually is. This one now holds me, Al-Nasir, the lieutenant, and two guards.

"Welcome," she says, speaking a Standard so clear that it startles me.

"Thank you," I say.

She smiles. "Please come with me."

She's practiced this part. That's all right. I've practiced a few phrases too. I hope I can pull it off.

We walk too quickly through the corridor. I want to go slowly, like we would if we were diving.

I want to mark each intersection, take note of every turn. I want to examine doorways and the ceiling, and figure out exactly what the glowing panels are.

Our feet tap against the floor. The sound seems odd, dampened somehow, not at all what I'm used to when I go into one of the Dignity Vessels.

We go up two levels. I make a map in my head, compare it to what I know. We're heading toward the cockpit, but I have a hunch we're not going there. We're going to one of two large rooms that I believe to be conference rooms. One is just off the cockpit, and I can't imagine a captain bringing strangers there.

The other is one level down, and several meters away. That's the one I would use, and as we turn right, that's the one we're headed to.

I don't say anything. I'm too busy looking at things—the black walls, just like the walls in the caves; the writing that is missing in my Dignity Vessels; and the cleanliness that comes from constant maintenance.

None of the ships we've found have these smooth black walls. I suspect that beneath them is the gray metal we're used to, with the rivets and the welded parts. This blackness is something new, or it's something that doesn't last when a ship loses power for centuries.

We reach the door to the conference room. The door is closed. There are no guards outside it.

The lieutenant stops and looks at me.

"The captain wants to have only four of us inside," she says slowly.

"All right," I say.

Then she swings the door open and waits until we go in.

I step in first.

The room is nothing like I imagined it to be. Only the dimensions remain the same as the rooms I've seen in the other two Dignity Vessels.

This room has a table down the center, so well polished that I can see my own reflection. A dozen chairs are bolted to the floor, and there are actual sideboards. The walls show an unfamiliar skyscape, but that's no painting. It's a recorded image being shown on the screens that encase us.

A man stands at the head of the table. He's surprisingly tall and broad shouldered, with dark hair that touches his collar. His eyes are blue, his features sharp.

He doesn't have the thinness of someone raised in space. He's muscular with strong bones, certainly not something I would have expected, even though the lieutenant doesn't look space-raised either.

He bows slightly to me. "Welcome," he says in Standard, mangling the word so badly that I almost don't recognize it.

"Thank you," I say in his language. I'm probably mangling that phrase as badly as he mangled "Welcome," but I don't mind. The phrase brings a smile to his face, one that softens his features.

He greets Al-Nasir personally, and Al-Nasir answers. Then the captain offers us refreshments from the sideboard. There are baked goods I do not recognize, carafes of something that looks like wine, and a variety of fruits and cold vegetables.

He lets one of his hands linger near a carafe. I nod. He picks up a glass, pours an amber liquid for me, another for Al-Nasir, and hands them to us. Then he pours two more, one for himself and one for the lieutenant.

Apparently the polite customs are the same in both of our cultures.

He indicates the chairs near the table. The lieutenant sits, then looks pointedly at Al-Nasir. He sits near her.

The captain stands near the head of the table. He says very slowly, "My name is Jonathon Cooper. I am captain of this ship. People call me Coop."

His nickname. "Coop," I say, careful to pronounce it the same way. "People call me Boss."

He pulls out his chair and sits. I sit at the same time, taking the chair to his right.

"Boss," he says as he sits. "Lieutenant—" And then he says that word I can't quite understand, clearly her name. "—is not sure Boss is your name or your title."

"Both," I say.

He doesn't understand that, but she does. She repeats it to him.

He replies in his own language and looks at me. I don't understand a word, but she is able to translate.

"They call you by your title?"

"I prefer it," I say.

The conversation is slow as the translations go back and forth, but it feels right, as if he and I are actually talking. I glance at Al-Nasir. He nods. He's understanding us both so far.

The captain says through the lieutenant's translation, "Surely you understand my position. As commander of this ship, I cannot call someone else Boss."

I shrug. I expected this. "Then call me what you will."

His lips twist into a slight smile, and the game is on. He now knows I'm only going to tell him what I want to tell him and nothing more.

"Fahd Al-Nasir will do his best to translate for me," I say.

No one has said anything about my knife, which surprises me.

"I have a team of linguists monitoring the conversation," the captain says. "They might be able to assist if we need it."

"A team of linguists," I say. "I am impressed. How large is your crew?"

"Five hundred strong," he says.

Five hundred. The number staggers me.

"We guessed perhaps a hundred," I say.

"You've never encountered one of our ships before?" he asks.

I'm going to be as honest as I can with him, unless I believe some of the information is not to our advantage. "Not a working vessel," I say.

He frowns. That answer clearly disturbs him. "How many of our ships have you encountered that don't work?"

"Five," I say.

"Five," he repeats, then holds out his open hand. "Five?"

"Yes," I say.

"Do they have any crew?" he asks.

I study him for a moment. He expects Dignity Vessels to have a crew. I expect them to be abandoned and ruined. Something is quite off here.

"No," I say. "They have all been abandoned."

The lieutenant touches her ear. She repeats my word again. Clearly the linguists are working on it.

"They're empty," I say to him. "The ones I find are derelicts."

The lieutenant looks at me, her face a little slack, not from the linguists nattering in her ear, but from my words.

"Empty," she repeats. "Destroyed?"

"A couple of them," I say. "I don't know if they were ruined by time or by some kind of battle."

"You found them all in the same area of space?" she asks, her Standard fluid.

"No," I say.

She looks away from me, blinks hard, and frowns. The captain says her name sharply. She nods but doesn't look at him. Then she swallows visibly.

My words have disturbed her.

The captain asks her something in their language. Al-Nasir answers, slowly, trying to translate my words.

The lieutenant raises her hand, as if asking for a moment. Her palm is shaking.

She then turns to the captain and speaks rapidly. Al-Nasir leans forward as if he's trying to understand.

The captain's frown deepens, and he looks at me. He says something to the lieutenant, clearly meaning for her to translate.

"How long abandoned?" she asks.

"We don't know exactly," I say.

She repeats this. The captain speaks. She translates: "You have a guess."

I shrug a shoulder. This seems momentous to them.

"Please," he says to me in Standard. "Please."

That moves me more than I expect. Beneath this show of diplomatic courtesy, beneath the rigid military behavior, beneath the patience of the past two weeks lives panic.

I have just tapped into it.

And I think I'm about to make it worse.

"My guess is based on what little we know about Dignity Vessels," I say. "We believe they're legend. Myth."

The lieutenant translates. The captain looks surprised. He narrows his eyes and looks at me. Then he nods, asking me to continue.

Maybe the mood in the room is catching, because I'm suddenly nervous. "The ships we've found are at least five thousand years old."

The lieutenant doesn't translate. She tilts her head and looks at me as if I'm crazy. I feel crazy.

"I know it sounds impossible," I say. "We have no evidence that the Dignity Vessels could travel more than fifty light-years from Earth. But clearly you're here, and they got here, and something enabled you to get here. But we've done studies on all of the ships we've found—not just us, but the Empire, too, and we know those ships are at least five thousand years old, maybe older."

She still doesn't translate. Her mouth is open slightly.

The captain says her name. She doesn't respond. He says her name again, then touches her shoulder. He says something else.

Al-Nasir leans into me. "He's asking her if she needs to leave, if they need to bring in someone else."

She's shaking her head. She rubs a hand over her mouth, squares her shoulders just like Al-Nasir did before we got on the ship, and then she speaks for several minutes to the captain.

He repeats a phrase a couple times. I don't need Al-Nasir to tell me that the captain is asking about my numbers, about that five thousand years.

He turns to me, his lips thin, his eyes steely. He's not angry. He's not upset like the lieutenant is. But he's disturbed and trying to hide it.

He asks something with a great deal of intensity, the words sharp and hard.

"How long has this base been empty?" the lieutenant asks slowly, as if she's afraid of my answer.

"I don't know," I say.

"What do they say in—?" and then she uses a phrase I've never heard. Before I can ask her to clarify, Al-Nasir says, "Vaycehn. She's asking about Vaycehn."

"What do they say about the base in Vaycehn?" I ask. "They have no idea it's here."

The captain speaks without her. "You know."

I understand him. He's not commenting. He's asking. How did I know the base was here?

I try to think of a way to answer him, one that will be understandable without a lot of explaining in languages neither of us completely understand.

"We didn't know," I say. "This place surprised us."

That much is true. I brace myself for the next question, trying to figure out how to explain energy signatures and death holes and all of those problems in a way that the lieutenant and those unseen linguists could understand.

The captain asks his question, and the lieutenant translates.

"How long has—Vaa-zen—been here?" she asks, mispronouncing Vaycehn.

"Here?" I ask. "On Wyr? This planet?"

She nods.

"It's the oldest city in the sector," I say, stalling because I know instinctively that he's not going to like the answer. "Vaycehn has been here more than five thousand years."

FIFTY-EIGHT

Five thousand years. The woman who wouldn't tell him her real name kept saying five thousand years.

The woman watched him, concern on her face. Coop had a hunch she understood more than she was saying. Al-Nasir had his hands clasped, his forehead creased with worry.

And Perkins fidgeted beneath the table, having as much difficulty as Coop, but in a different area. She believed the number.

He did not.

Five thousand years just wasn't possible. At least that was what his logical brain told him.

But his subconscious kept whispering that five thousand years was possible. The *anacapa* could have malfunctioned badly. No one knew exactly where it would take people when it did malfunction. That was the danger of the Fleet vessels.

Coop shook his head slightly, banishing that thought which snuck into his mind. He wasn't going to deal with that, not now.

He had another problem to deal with first.

"She keeps saying the same phrase over and over," he said to Perkins. "You're translating that as five thousand years. Are you sure you're right?"

She looked at him. The terror in her eyes was answer enough. But she said through her comm link, "Please check that phrase through the system again."

Coop had already told the linguists this conversation would have to remain secret. But he wasn't sure about something this big. It would be hard for anyone to keep it secret.

If the translation was right.

"It's a fairly simple phrase," the lieutenant said. "And their word for 'thousand' is remarkably similar to our word."

"You told me that similar words could make people misunderstand languages. It's a common mistake, you said."

She nodded. "I'm not sure how to check this."

He knew how to check it. The woman and Al-Nasir were watching closely. Coop picked up a pad from the sideboard and typed in the number: 5,000.

Then he slid the pad to the woman. "Is this the number?"

She bit her lower lip, then looked up at him. He knew the answer before she spoke.

"Yes."

He ran a hand over his face. Five thousand years was impossible. Five thousand years *forward*. The Fleet might not exist anymore. She said it was a legend, that they had only found ships without their crew, long empty.

Not abandoned. Maybe no longer useful.

Maybe no longer in use at all.

He stood up, clasped his hands behind his back, not so much to prevent them from shaking—although he needed to do that as well—but to make sure he stayed calm.

Five thousand years.

He took a deep breath. He couldn't settle the conundrum of five thousand years right now. But he still had a few questions for the woman.

He turned. She was watching him, her body tense. She clearly wasn't afraid of him, but it was also clear that she wanted to be prepared for anything.

"Why were you here?" he asked. "What made you come to the sector base?"

Perkins had to translate. She seemed relieved to be talking again.

The woman said, "It's complicated. The short version is that we came because of the stealth technology."

"Are you sure you got that right?" he asked Perkins. "Did she say stealth technology?"

"Yes," Perkins said.

"Ask her to explain," he said.

The woman talked for a moment, waving her hands, indicating the ship itself. Coop silently cursed his lack of understanding. The language barrier was worse than he expected, but why wouldn't it be, with five thousand years between him and this woman? It was amazing they could talk at all.

"I think I have this right," Perkins said to him when the woman was finished. "The old Fleet ships that she has found give off an energy signature that they call stealth technology. They call it that because they believe it's a cloaking device that the Dignity Vessels have."

"The *anacapa*," he said softly.

Perkins nodded. "I think so. She says that it was unusual to find the signature underground, but they came down to investigate, and found the room."

"Does she live in Venice City?"

"No," Perkins said.

"So what brought her here?" Coop asked. "How did she even know the signature existed? And why now? If it's the *anacapa*, the signature has been here for five thousand years."

Perkins repeated the question. The woman looked nervous for a moment. She glanced at Al-Nasir as if silently asking him a question. He shrugged.

The woman was clearly deciding what to tell Coop, and she was making that decision on her own.

"What remains of the stealth technology is malfunctioning," she said so slowly that Perkins was able to simultaneously translate. "The malfunctions are not as big a problem in space because a person actually has to go into an empty Dignity Vessel to encounter it. But here, in Vaycehn, the stealth technology is causing something the locals call 'death holes.'"

"Death holes," Coop said to Perkins. "That's the phrase? You're certain?"

Perkins nodded, then asked the woman to clarify. This time, the woman spoke for a moment before Perkins translated.

"As best I can understand it," Perkins said, "something goes wrong, and a wave of energy explodes out of the base, blowing a hole in the surface. Then the nanobits coat that hole, and a new part of what she calls the caves are formed. The problem is that no one on the surface knows when or where a death hole will happen. Holes just open up and suck people and buildings into them."

"My God." Coop understood the phenomenon the woman described. It was the way the base got built. The base engineers would pick a spot, then start the nanoprocess on the surface, guiding it with their equipment and burrowing into the ground or a mountainside or wherever the base was supposed to go. Then the nanobits would coat the surface, so that nothing could leak or fall or create problems.

The system was supposed to remain self-repairing, even after the shutdown, so no one could get trapped in the base. But it wasn't supposed to malfunction. It wasn't supposed to do this.

"How long has this been going on?" he asked.

The woman shrugged. "Throughout Vaycehn's known history."

Someone shut down the base wrong, or something went awry and never got fixed. He should have been horrified—maybe he was, beneath it all, beneath the shock of five thousand years—but he was actually a bit relieved.

"We can fix this," he said to the woman.

"Good," she said, and he actually understood that word. Then she spoke a bit longer, and Perkins had to translate. "Do you mean you can stop the problems here on Vaycehn or can you help us with the malfunctioning Dignity Vessels as well?"

Dignity Vessel. That term still startled him. "One problem at a time. We can stop the death holes."

"Then you need to know something else," the woman said through Perkins. "The worst death hole in centuries happened when your ship appeared."

He frowned. That made things more complicated. The problem was tied to the *anacapa*, as he had thought initially.

"My engineers will need to see this, and all the records," he said. That would also get his people on the surface, gathering history so that they could figure out what exactly happened to Venice City.

"There's one more problem," she said. "The people of Vaycehn don't know that you're here."

Something in her voice made him stop. He looked at her, really looked at her. She was worried now, maybe even frightened.

"Why don't they know about us?" he asked.

She glanced at Al-Nasir. He was biting his lower lip so hard that it was starting to bleed. Something was going on here, something Coop didn't understand.

"We're a group of scientists, explorers, and academics," the woman said. "We're here to study the phenomenon. You were a surprise."

"Clearly," Coop said.

"Politically, this is all complicated," she said.

He shrugged. "Why should that matter to me?"

"It shouldn't, I guess," she said. "You can come and go as you please. But I would request that you don't leave until we figure out how to solve the death hole problem."

Coop nodded. "We will," he said. "It won't take much to fix it."

"Good." She sighed. "Otherwise, the minute you leave, more people will die up there."

"That seems to make it more imperative that they learn about us," he said. "They'll know that their long-standing problem will be solved."

"But it will create a new one," she said, "one that might cost infinitely more life."

He sat back down and waited for her to explain.

FIFTY-NINE

How do you explain five thousand years of history succinctly? How do you describe the sector as it is, without sounding overly dramatic? I glance at Al-Nasir, who looks terrified. My heart is pounding hard, my mouth dry. I somehow did not expect this to be an issue.

I didn't expect any of it, really. For some reason, I thought the Dignity Vessel was a modern ship, with modern experiences, part of the Fleet that continued on and had somehow got called back here.

I didn't expect the captain's shock at five thousand years. I expected him to be surprised by distance, yes, but not by time.

The captain sits across from me, his emotions now so deeply under control that his features are smooth. He watches me with those intense blue eyes. The lieutenant keeps glancing at him, as if she can't tell his mood either.

All my study of history has taught me that there's a right side to history and a wrong side. No matter where these people are from—somewhere far away, but part of our timeline, or somewhere from the dark and distant past, brought here through that malfunctioning stealth tech somehow, in a reverse of what happened to my mother and my teammates—these people are not part of our history. They don't understand the details, the agreements, the deaths, the dangers.

Those things don't really matter to them.

And I want this to matter.

"Can you translate what I have to say in parts?" I ask the lieutenant. "I don't want you to miss anything."

She nods.

I look at Al-Nasir. "I need you to help her as best you can," I say. "And help me."

He nods.

The captain looks at the lieutenant, and she translates what I've said. Then I take a deep breath and begin.

"Much of this sector is part of the Enterran Empire," I say. "Vaycehn is part of that Empire. My people are not."

I feel my stomach twist as I say this. We haven't told anyone on Wyr who we really are.

"We're part of the Nine Planets Alliance," I say. "The Nine Planets have an unstated truce with the Empire at the moment. Eventually, it will try to swallow us up."

I pause so she can translate. He doesn't move, and he keeps his gaze on me.

"The Empire is what the Empire is," I say. "I don't like it, but I don't aim to bring it down. I grew up in it. And, at the time, I didn't really notice parts of it. It's just big and wants to get bigger."

I glance at Al-Nasir. He shakes his head. It's impossible to say all of this without sounding ridiculous.

"It shouldn't get bigger," I say. "The bigger it gets, the more unwieldy it is, the less it knows what its governors and leaders in the various communities are doing. People become less important—"

I stop. I'm about to go into a rant about a subject the captain knows nothing about. He probably doesn't even care. He only wants to know how it would affect him.

That's what I would want to know.

That's what I used to want to know about the Empire, before I learned about stealth tech. I just operated small, stayed out of their way, and didn't let them notice me. I figured as long as they didn't notice me, I wouldn't matter.

I didn't realize that I had already lost my mother to their desire for stealth tech. I didn't realize that when I was as young as four, the Empire's reach completely altered my life.

I glance at the lieutenant, who is waiting for me to continue. I sigh, then shake my head slightly, mostly at myself.

"I can give you history lessons all that you want," I say in a less strident tone, "and you can figure out how you feel about the Empire and the Alliance, and all the politics in the middle of it, which probably will not matter to you at all. What matters to me is this."

I pause here so that she can translate. Also, I get to choose my words as I get deeper into the discussion.

"The Empire wants your stealth technology. They've been trying to re-create it in the lab for more than one hundred years. The Empire's scientists kept doing it wrong. They've lost, I don't know, dozens, hundreds, maybe thousands of researchers and scientists to these experiments. People die in rather hideous ways."

I don't tell him about Vallevu, settled by survivors who keep waiting for the scientists to return, or Squishy, who sees her work with us as a penance for all the people she inadvertently killed working for the Empire. I can't make it understandable.

"Years ago," I say, "I found a Dignity Vessel. It had malfunctioning stealth tech, and it killed some of my people."

I stop, unable to explain all the complicated emotions—my initial unwillingness to destroy history; the way that ship started everything, my entire current life, with all of its ups and downs.

"It's a long story, too," I say, "but eventually that ship got into the hands of the Empire, and they started using it in their stealth-tech experiments. They even re-created some parts of stealth tech through the ship, and through the Room of Lost Souls."

The lieutenant repeats the phrase, "Room of Lost Souls," asking me what that means.

I shrug. "I'm sorry. I think it's an old base. It has stealth tech too."

She nods, then translates for me.

The captain frowns at her, then shakes his head. They're not sure what I'm talking about.

"Okay," I say. "Here's the thing important to us. If the Empire gets stealth tech, they're unstoppable. They'll take over the rest of the sector and then move on to other areas. Right now, they're limited in their resources and through their own abilities. They can't fight every single enemy they encounter. Their ships are too vulnerable. Stealth tech will allow them to encircle a planet and launch an attack without anyone even knowing they've arrived."

The captain frowns as if he doesn't understand any of this. The lieutenant has been speaking slowly. So have I. I touch Al-Nasir's arm, then nod toward the lieutenant.

"Is the translation going right?" I ask softly.

"I think so," he says. "She seems to be doing okay. The Room of Lost Souls threw her."

"A lot of this is throwing me," the lieutenant says to me. "I'm doing what I can. We are still new at the language."

"Yes, we are," I say, then look at the captain again.

His gaze meets mine. I'm startled at the power in that gaze. I feel a slight flush build in my cheeks.

"Look," I say to him as clearly as I can. "If we discover how stealth tech works first, 'we' meaning my people, we'll be distributing it throughout the sector. That way the balance of power remains the same. The Empire doesn't have the ability to suddenly take over a planet or an area of the sector. We remain on equal terms."

"No," he says, even before the lieutenant finishes. He speaks quickly to her.

She shrugs, then looks at me.

My flush has grown deeper. "They'll try to take your ship," I say. "If they find this room, it's one more gigantic piece in the puzzle. They have good people working on this, and eventually they'll figure it out. The entire—"

He holds up a hand and stops me. "Let me speak to my people," he says, and walks out of the conference room.

SIXTY

*T*hey didn't understand the *anacapa* drive. At all.

Coop walked down the corridor, unable to stay in the room for another minute. The woman, clearly intelligent, was speaking to him as if the *anacapa* drive was a simple cloak, and it wasn't.

The Fleet used it to avoid fighting. From the perspective of the foe fighting the Fleet, the *anacapa* could be the best cloak ever. The ship would disappear, and never show up on scans.

But it was so much more than that, and so much more difficult. Traveling through foldspace was perilous, as he well knew.

And these people—if that woman was to be believed—were playing with the technology as if it were a simple cloak.

No wonder so many were dying.

The corridors were empty per his orders, except for the guards he had stationed near the doors. He walked all the way to the bridge, where Lynda was leading his team. Dix glared at him over the console. Anita straightened her shoulders, trying to look taller, which she often did when she was nervous.

Yash's level gaze met his.

"I need you to send your best people into the sector base," he said. "The *anacapa* is malfunctioning. It's occasionally sending out streams of energy that are so strong they're blowing through rock and opening holes on the surface. At least that's what the woman is telling me."

"It would explain the strange map we got of the facility once the sensors came back online," Yash said.

"That's what I thought," Coop said. "I want you to check on this, of course, but it would explain a lot. It would also explain how we got here, whenever here is."

Yash nodded. "A buildup of energy in the systems. I'll put someone right on it."

Coop nodded. "Dix, I'm going to need a team. At least a dozen soldiers, you, me, and Rossetti. I need them ready in half an hour."

"Are we in some kind of trouble, sir?" Dix asked, suddenly formal.

"I'm not sure," he said.

"The woman and her translator, are we holding them?" Dix asked.

Coop shook his head. "They're going to take us to the surface. They just don't know that yet."

"You want a landcar ready, sir?" Dix asked. "We're a long way underground, and the emergency lift doesn't work."

"I know," Coop said. "But if the *anacapa* is malfunctioning badly, I'm not sure what added energy from our landcar would do. I'd rather not risk that at the moment. We'll either use the woman's transportation or we'll walk."

"Getting out—"

"Will be hard, I know," Coop said. "We might have to come back for the car. But there are too many questions here, and I need them answered before we go any further."

"What's going on, sir?" Anita was having trouble remaining still. She wanted to be part of this as well.

"I'm not sure," Coop said. "I'm hoping this woman is lying to me. Because if she's not . . ."

He let his words trail off. He shook his head.

"If she's not?" Lynda asked. They all needed to know.

"We're in trouble," Coop said. "And the situation we landed in is a real mess. Maybe the worst we've ever encountered."

"Is it our business, sir?" Dix asked.

"I'm not sure yet," Coop said. "But I'm terrified that it might be."

"Terrified?" Anita asked, her voice trembling.

He looked at her. He realized he had never used that word, not once, in his entire command.

"Terrified," he confirmed. Then he nodded once and left the bridge.

SIXTY-ONE

I sit there, my mouth open. The captain has just left. I'm not even sure what he's understood, what he's really been told.

Al-Nasir is sitting stiffly beside me. The lieutenant gets up. She sweeps a hand toward the food. We haven't touched any of it.

I get up as well. I haven't left the table since we started this discussion.

"What was the last thing you told him?" I ask as I reach for a pastry. It looks fresh and home baked, and I even recognize the form. Some things do move from culture to culture. "Did you tell him that the Empire would try to take his ship?"

She smiles at me distractedly. She takes a pastry, too, then waves a plate at Al-Nasir. He shakes his head once.

She sets her plate in front of her place, as if we're at a formal dinner.

"No one can take this ship," she says.

I frown. "We've found a lot of damaged Dignity Vessels."

"You do not know if they were damaged by time or by someone else."

"You have weapons scoring on the side of your ship."

She blinks at me. For a moment, I think she's going to pretend she doesn't understand. Then I realize she's listening to a link in her ear. Someone has confirmed the translation for her.

She nods. "They did not take our ship, did they?"

I set my plate down, then walk back to my seat. But I don't sit. Instead, I take a sip of the wine. It's strong, too strong for a business meeting. I set the glass aside, then go back to the sideboard for some water.

I am moving because it keeps me calm. I want to try the door, to see if Al-Nasir and I are prisoners here, but I do not. I said some alarming things to their captain. Perhaps he is checking on them. Perhaps he is consulting with their people. Perhaps he is checking the translations. I don't know, but I'm going to give him a little time. Not a lot, but enough to give him the benefit of the doubt.

I hold up a pitcher, silently offering Al-Nasir some water. He nods. I pour him a glass as well, then give it to him. His hands are shaking.

"So what is going on here?" I ask the lieutenant.

"I'm not exactly sure," she says.

"And if you were sure," I say, "you wouldn't tell me, right?"

"I do not know," she says. "It would depend on my orders."

She's honest, at least.

I take a sip of my water, which has a filtered taste. I don't try the pastry, not yet. I did sound melodramatic, telling him about the Empire. He has no way to confirm what I've said, either. It would sound as strange to me as the stories I heard about the Colonnade Wars when I was searching for information about one of their generals, years ago. Something that didn't concern me, except in the way that it had just intersected with my life.

The door opens, and the captain comes back. His cheeks are flushed, his eyes radiant. He looks like a man who has come to some kind of decision.

I set the water glass down so that my hands don't shake. I want to be prepared for anything.

His gaze meets mine, and he speaks with more animation than I've seen from him. The lieutenant translates.

"I'm sending a team to fix what you call the death holes. It shouldn't take long. It's a relatively common malfunction that we usually have safeguards for. Clearly all of the safeguards have failed."

"Clearly," I mutter. A common malfunction that kills a lot of people.

"What I need from you," he says, "is guidance. I'm taking a team to the surface. I want you, Al-Nasir, the lieutenant, and I to accompany them. I need to see this Vaycehn myself."

My breath catches. In my shock, I note that he actually said "Vaycehn" and pronounced it correctly.

Al-Nasir speaks before I do. He's shaking his head as he does so, speaking in their language. I know what he's saying. I walk over to him and place my hand on his arm. The protest should come from me.

"Captain, if you go to the surface, you jeopardize my team, my work, and this room, as well as your ship."

"You have told me that they do not know we're down here," he says.

"And suddenly a military force climbs out of the hole?" My voice rises. "They'll know then."

I make myself take a deep breath as the lieutenant translates my words. Before she finishes, I add, much more calmly, "Al-Nasir and I will take you and the lieutenant to the surface. We'll leave two of our people here, and hope the guides don't notice the difference. We'll show you around, and you can see for yourself—"

The captain is shaking his head before the lieutenant even tries to translate. Either he understands what I'm saying or he knew I was going to protest and is prepared for it.

The lieutenant gamely tries to translate, but he talks over her.

"I am sorry," he says, and this time, it's Al-Nasir translating for me. "But I cannot rely just upon your word. I have problems of my own that the Fleet needs to know about. I need to know where and when I am. My ship is in no danger, and we will be fine."

I start to protest when the lieutenant's translation gets to "my ship is in no danger."

I say, "You have no idea what the Empire can do."

"If what you tell me is true," he says, "then we have nothing to worry about from your Empire. My ship can take care of itself."

I flush. What I'm telling him *is* true, and something I said made him leave. Not, then, that the Empire would try to take his ship. Something about stealth technology.

"What did I say earlier that caused this decision?" I ask.

He tilts his head slightly. I can see him thinking about how to answer me. He's weighing a few options. Then his mouth tightens and he nods, as if he's picked an option.

He says in Standard, his words so clear the translator is redundant. "Five thousand years."

There is an honesty to those words. I probably would have believed him even if I hadn't seen his reaction to that number earlier. In spite of myself, I understand. I remember finding the first Dignity Vessel, not believing that it was what my eyes and my computer told me. No Dignity Vessel could have been in our sector of space, and yet there it was.

This captain doesn't believe me in the same way I did not believe in that Dignity Vessel. He needs to know, and he will not stop until he gets answers.

Only he wants to do it right.

I understand that, too.

I also understand that I will not be able to change his mind.

I sigh.

"Give me five hours," I say. "I need to get my people off Wyr before you get to the surface."

"You have two," he says, through the translator. "And I would like you and Al-Nasir to stay as we prepare."

Even though the lieutenant couched that as a request, it is clearly not a request. We must stay. He doesn't trust us, yet he needs us. We're his guides to the surface.

"I will get you off planet if there is trouble," he says.

"In your damaged ship?" I ask.

"The damage is repaired," he says.

"There will be trouble," I say. "So let Al-Nasir leave, too."

"No, Boss," Al-Nasir says. "You need me."

"I can survive," I say.

"It's all right," Al-Nasir says, even though we both know it is not. I had thought so little of him, and here he is, trying to protect me. He shouldn't protect me. I need to take care of my people.

"Let me go to the room, at least, to get my people out of Vaycehn," I say. "It would be better if you give us more time."

"I am giving you as much time as I can," the captain says. "And even that is too much if you are untrustworthy."

I stare at him. I hate understanding this. I hate the realization that I would make the same requests.

"All right," I say because I have no real choice. "Two hours. And this better work."

SIXTY-TWO

I don't look at anyone as I leave that room. I know my way out of this ship. I've been inside several Dignity Vessels, and the structure of this one is no different from the others. I know my way to the door as if I had marked it in my diving suit.

The guards look alarmed, and I don't care. Nor do I care if anyone is following me. I expect Al-Nasir to keep up. I'm sure we're going to pick up other handlers along the way.

I reach the main door in only a few minutes. My hair flies around my face, and my breath is coming in rapid gasps. There are two female guards in front of the door, and a team of people talking to one side. They appear to be gathering equipment.

"Let me out," I say to the guard in Standard. I don't care that they can't speak my language. They should understand my tone.

They answer with a phrase that I now know means "What?" or its equivalent.

I slam my hand against the door. "Out," I say in what I think is Old Earth Standard.

The smaller guard looks at the other. She nods once and hits the release beside the door. It slides open, and I hurry into the airlock before the guards change their minds. I hear a commotion behind me, Al-Nasir yelling "Wait!" and against my better judgment, I do.

He's running, and he finally reaches me, sweat pouring off his face, his shirt drenched. He's not in the right kind of shape to keep up with me.

The door closes behind him, and the exterior door opens. I hurry down the steps.

The room is transformed. Dozens of people are inside, all wearing the black uniform of the Dignity Vessel. They're underneath consoles, around consoles, near the back walls. In the very middle, a crowd has gathered, and something has risen out of the floor. They seem to be taking it apart.

My team is separate from all of the action, watching but not touching.

Rea and DeVries are the deepest into the room, looking at that middle section as if they've never seen anything like it. Seager is near the door, and Quinte has moved toward the original console, the one that we had initially touched, her hands behind her back, staring at the blank screen.

All of the screens are off. In fact, it looks like the consoles are off as well. And the hum I've come to recognize as stealth tech is gone.

Kersting is the only member of my team who I don't see immediately, but when I shout "Hey!" he appears from beside the ship.

"I need my team now! Right now!" I yell as I get close to the main door. A few people stop work and look over their shoulders at me. None of the rest of the ship's people bother with me at all.

Seager looks alarmed, but doesn't move since we're coming to her. Quinte comes over, as does DeVries. Rea seems reluctant to leave the middle of the room.

"*Now!*" I yell again. I don't think I've ever sounded this shrill in my life.

"Hurry!" Al-Nasir adds.

We gather near the door. If I look anything like Al-Nasir, I look panicked. His hair falls all over his face, his clothes are sweat-stained, and his face is flushed.

I wait until everyone is within hearing distance.

"The captain of this ship is sending a team to the surface in two hours, and we can't stop them."

"Oh, my God," Quinte says.

"He can't," Kersting says at the same time.

"Doesn't he know—?" Seager starts.

"Yes, he knows," I snap. "He doesn't care. I've already argued with him. They're going. He gave us the gift of two hours. He could have gone right now."

Al-Nasir looks at me in surprise at my use of the word "gift." Apparently he thought I was angry about the two hours.

"I'm evoking our emergency procedures," I say. "You have to get out of here now, and after you get out of the stealth-tech field, you need to contact all of our people on the surface. Tell them to drop whatever they're doing, gather the equipment, and get the hell off Wyr. As soon as a group is assembled, take a ship and go to the *Business*. Make sure everyone is out of here. If you have to leave equipment behind, then do it. People are more important."

"What about you?" Rea asks.

"I'm staying," I say. "I'm going to escort them to the surface, and try to minimize this thing. After you've gotten out, send the hovercarts back down for us. We need to get to the surface, and I don't think they'll be using their own equipment to get us there. At least I hope not. So go, and don't assume you have more than the two hours he gave us."

"I'm staying, too," Al-Nasir says. "She needs a translator."

I shake my head but don't argue.

Kersting frowns. "What about you and Fahd? Will we ever see you again?"

"The captain assures us he can get us to the *Business*. Pull out of orbit and wait for us at the rendezvous spot. If we haven't arrived in three days, head home."

Rea is shaking his head. "But—"

"The captain's got a powerful ship, and he assures me they've fixed it. So I'm going to trust him. Think of it this way: I get to ride in a working Dignity Vessel."

They all smile at that.

"Now get the hell out of here," I say.

I actually give DeVries a little shove. Rea doesn't have to be told twice. He pulls open the door and hurries through it. Quinte and Seager take off at a run. Kersting gives me a haunted look, then jogs out.

"Go," I say to Al-Nasir.

"No," he says.

We stand at the door and watch them run until we can't see them anymore. I wish the captain had given us five hours. I wish he wasn't going to the surface at all.

I hope to hell the Vaycehnese government doesn't notice that we're leaving like scared rabbits.

I hope to hell no one says a word to the Empire.

But I have a hunch my hopes are just that: hopes, and nothing more.

SIXTY-THREE

Coop's land team was gathering near the doors, but Coop was still on the bridge, making final plans. He wished he hadn't given the woman two hours. He should have stuck with one hour, but he hadn't.

Still, she'd been incredibly panicked when she heard they only had two hours. She'd fairly flown off the ship, and her people had vanished instantly. She'd stayed, however. She didn't come back inside the ship, choosing to wait and watch one of the teams fix the *anacapa* inside the base itself.

Al-Nasir had stayed with her. Coop was a bit surprised at that. He had worried that all of her people would leave. The fact that they didn't led credence to her story—credence he wasn't sure he wanted.

Dix was already below, preparing. Lynda was in the captain's chair.

Coop signaled Yash. She had been monitoring the *anacapa* repairs from her station. She left it reluctantly.

"If this woman is right," he said without preamble, "we might have to leave here quickly. We're not going to be able to use the regular drive."

The regular drive worked like any other ship's drive. The *Ivoire* had left the sector base using the regular drive a little over a month before. The technicians inside the base had opened the base's roof, and the *Ivoire* had floated out.

Even if the roof opening was working—and there was no guarantee that it was—Coop didn't have a good map of Vaycehn. For all he knew, opening the roof would destroy entire neighborhoods and kill countless people.

"Given the problems with the base's *anacapa*," he said to Yash, "can we safely use ours?"

Yash frowned. "How soon?"

"Maybe later this afternoon," he said.

"If we manage to finish the repairs to the base's *anacapa*," she said. "If the problem is as simple as we both think—and so far, my team has no reason to doubt that—then we should be able to activate our *anacapa* without any risk to anyone."

"Not even us?" Coop asked softly. "We're not going to be sent through the wrong fold in space again?"

"I'm not sure we went through the wrong fold in space this time," Yash said. "But whatever malfunction brought us here shouldn't repeat. We fixed our *anacapa*. I think it was both *anacapa* drives, malfunctioning in tandem, that caused the bulk of the problem."

"You think or you hope?" Coop asked.

"I think," she said, but she sounded doubtful. "I can go out there and help with the repairs."

"Will it speed them along?" Coop asked.

She grinned like a kid who had gotten caught. Like everyone else, she wanted off the ship, even for a short time. "Probably not."

He smiled. "Then you know what I'm going to say. We need you here."

"We need you here, too," she said. "It's foolish for you to go to the surface. Dix and Rossetti can do just fine."

"I know," he said softly. "But I have to see this. I can't work off supposition any longer."

"You don't trust your team?"

"Of course I do," he said. "But if this woman is right . . ."

He let his voice trail off. He didn't want to give voice to his thoughts. If the woman was right, then his life would never be the same. None of their lives would. And he would have to lead his people through this without too many breakdowns, without too much despair.

He needed to know first, not last. He needed to be prepared.

"Just make sure everything is functioning," he said to Yash.

"It won't be," she said. "We still have a lot of work to do."

"But not on the *anacapa*," he said.

"Not on our *anacapa*, no," she said. "I hope we don't have a lot to do on the base's either. But some of the secondary systems on the *Ivoire* still need work."

"We can do that in space if we have to," Coop said. "We do need the weapons systems online, however."

She looked at him sharply. "You think we'll need weapons?"

"We might," he said. "I'm not sure what we're facing."

"Good God," she said.

"I want all of the weapons working," he said. "Even the minor ones. *Especially* the minor ones."

Her face had paled. "You think we might do some shooting down here."

"I doubt it," he said, "but I want to be prepared for all possibilities."

She put her hand on his arm. "Let the others go up there, Coop. It sounds more and more like this trip is completely inadvisable."

He studied her for a moment. She cared about him, yes, but also she cared about the ship. She knew that in a moment of crisis, the last thing the ship would need would be a new commander.

"The trip has been inadvisable," he said, "from the moment we listened to the Xenth about the Quurzod. We can't change that. We're here now, and I'm going to figure out what to do."

"Even if it makes things worse?" she asked.

"It can't make things worse," he said. "No matter what way this goes, we're only facing different degrees of the same problem."

She was silent for a moment. Then she nodded.

"I hope you're right," she said, and returned to her post.

SIXTY-FOUR

I fidget in the center of the room. The engineers from the ship are working on something I've never seen before. I've seen the shell, though. It looks like part of the stealth tech we've seen on the various Dignity Vessels.

The shell is contained inside a part of the floor that rose up when the engineers started their work. They're delving deep inside it, and of course, they're speaking in a language I don't understand.

Al-Nasir isn't listening. He's pacing. He keeps looking at the exterior door, his expression tight. I wonder if he's regretting his decision to come with me. He could be on one of our ships, heading to the *Nobody's Business* right now, and he knows it.

Safe, without any complications.

And God knows there are going to be complications.

At exactly two hours, the door to the ship opens. People step out, one at a time. They're all wearing the black uniforms that I'd seen, and they all have a weapons belt around their hips. Their laser pistols—if indeed that's what they have—are smaller than ours, but they look just as lethal.

Everyone is expressionless. Soldiers, heading into battle.

Three, six, nine, twelve. More than I ever expected. My heart twists. What have I done?

What have I agreed to?

I always try to stay away from the military, and now I'm marching with them into a city that has done nothing to me except make me follow a few rules.

The lieutenant comes next, followed by the captain. As he comes down the stairs, he scans the room until he sees me. Our gazes lock.

He nods.

He looks so official in his black uniform with its gold trim. None of the other uniforms have as much gold trim, so his must show his rank somehow. His shoulders are square, his jaw set. He looks like a captain of legend, which, I suppose, he is.

I'm doing nothing to hide my qualms. I'm staring at all of those soldiers with complete dismay. Men, women, all of them staring straight ahead, all of them in some form of position, awaiting command.

I hate this.

He stops in front of me and bows a little. He speaks slowly, but I still don't understand what he's saying.

The lieutenant reaches his side, but before she can translate, Al-Nasir says, "He's apologizing for inconveniencing us. He hopes that nothing will go wrong, and he'll do everything in his power to make sure we're all safe."

"I'm sure the soldiers will guarantee that," I mutter.

To my horror, the lieutenant translates my words.

The captain's mouth thins, but he's clearly not angry. "It's a first-contact team," he says through the lieutenant. "We bring a team like this whenever we're faced with people we've never interacted with before."

"And you come with them?" I ask. "Really? That's not wise."

"That's not procedure," he says. "But I have to see. . . ."

Her translation misses his wistful tone. He's worried that I'm right. I wonder what he'll do when he figures out that I am.

"Let's go, then," I say, and I lead. If I have to march with a group of soldiers, I'm not going to hide behind them.

"Please," the lieutenant says, "stay in the center with us."

"No," I say, and walk to the door. I pull it open and step into the corridor. It looks normal to me. I've been in and out of here so many times that I'm used to it.

But I wonder what he's seeing, what he's feeling. Is this corridor normal for him? Is it unusual? Is it what he expected?

No one talks as we walk. When we reach the demarcation line between the stealth-tech field and the rest of the caves, I half expect to see Mikk and Roderick waiting for us.

But of course they aren't. They've evacuated, just like everyone else.

For the first time, I realize just how alone Al-Nasir and I are. If something goes wrong, if the captain's military proves hostile, we're as good as dead.

I continue to walk and don't look around. The hovercarts aren't where we left them, but that's also as it should be. If the hovercarts are still below, they'll be just below the cave's entrance.

I should have asked for someone's weapon. I went into the Dignity Vessel unarmed, which means I'm unarmed now.

So is Al-Nasir. Everyone else has those laser pistols and a lot of determination.

My curiosity brought me here. From the moment I saw that first Dignity Vessel until the moment I walked on board the captain's ship, I've been curious about the ships and their crews. Now I know. The military forces of legend aren't romantic and sweet.

They're as tough and dangerous as any military force.

As the Empire's force.

And I'm leading them to the surface.

I only hope that my people have had enough time to get away.

SIXTY-FIVE

*T*he woman set the pace faster than Coop would have liked. Had he set the pace, he would have lingered and examined the walls, noting that the lights lining the edge of the ceiling were gray with unbonded nanobits. He would have asked someone, maybe Dix, how that was even possible. The nanobits were black; how had they turned gray?

But he didn't. He walked rapidly to keep up with her, just like the rest of his team did.

She didn't like the team. He could tell that from the start. She didn't greet them, didn't talk to them, didn't seem at all curious about them. That edge of panic she'd had since he had told her he was going to the surface remained.

The corridors looked familiar and unfamiliar. He'd been in a thousand corridors just like this, in various sector bases. The newer sector bases had smooth corridor walls like this, or the newer corridors had them, before someone went in and reprogrammed the nanobits to make some kind of art. The reprogrammings were limited in time, so that various artists had a chance to work. He never knew what he would see going through a corridor, from representational art to calligraphy to school projects by very young children.

What had been here when he left was long gone, no longer even remembered. If she was right.

They rounded a corner and the light changed. Natural light filtered in with the lighting created by nanobits. The team wasn't far from the opening.

They rounded one more corner, and there were four vehicles parked side by side.

His breath caught and he looked at the woman. She looked relieved to see them.

"Tell her to wait for us," he said to the lieutenant.

He studied the vehicles. Flat, open, with bench seats and controls that looked primitive. He walked to the nearest, ran his hand along the edge, and shook his head slightly.

What had happened here? He had left a thriving community filled with scientists, engineers, and intellectuals, a community that used the cutting edge of the Fleet's technology to build these caverns as well as the repair room, to keep the *anacapa* running and to create a city above.

He had returned to a place with technology that looked ancient and unwieldy, to people who did not speak his language and who thought energy spikes that blew holes in the ground were some kind natural phenomenon that they superstitiously called death holes.

"Coop?" Dix came up beside him. "She wants us to go up in these things?"

"I haven't asked," Coop said, "but since they're the only vehicles here, I'd think the answer is yes."

He walked around them and headed to the opening of the caves. The ladder remained, carved into the walls, just like he remembered. But the opening was twice as high as he remembered. That climb would tire all of them.

The woman spoke.

"She says you don't want to do that," the lieutenant said. "She did it a few weeks ago, and it exhausted her."

Coop turned and looked at the woman. She had her arms crossed. "Did these vehicles fail?"

"There was a groundquake when we arrived." The lieutenant didn't even translate his comment. She had known this. "It destroyed their vehicles. She's the one who climbed out for help."

Coop watched the woman as Al-Nasir translated for her. She climbed out for help, even though her people looked fit. She didn't command others to do the hard tasks. She did them herself.

She might not have a military force, but she acted like a leader.

He walked over to her, the lieutenant trailing him.

"Please," he said in her language. Then he had to use his. "Sit beside me as we go to the surface."

She didn't take her gaze off his face as Al-Nasir translated for her. "Why?" she asked.

He wasn't sure why. If he were to give a reason, he would say that he didn't want her to go first to warn people on the surface, but that wasn't the reason. Whether she was right about the five thousand years or not, something was very wrong at this place, and she had nothing to do with the wrongness.

He wanted her beside him because, even though they didn't speak the same language, they had the same attitude toward the people under their command. It was a small bond, but it was the only one he had at the moment, and he valued it.

He didn't say that. Instead, he said, "So you can explain what I'm seeing."

She sighed and looked at the vehicles. Then she said, "I'm driving."

"Perhaps she'd better show the rest of us how to drive these things," Dix said softly to Coop.

He nodded. "We're going to send a team up first," he said to the woman. "Would you show Rossetti how to pilot this?"

The woman beckoned Al-Nasir, then walked with Rossetti to the vehicle closest to the opening. Both women leaned over the controls. The woman spoke as her hands illustrated her instructions.

"I got it," Rossetti said to Coop. "It's pretty straightforward."

"You hope," he said.

"*You* hope," she said.

"Make sure there's no one waiting for us up there," he said. "If there is, and there are too many of them, come right back down."

"Got it," she said. She picked a team of three, and they climbed into the vehicle. Then she got in and started it. It immediately rose an inch above the ground. She did something that Coop couldn't see and it wobbled precariously, then righted itself and floated slowly upward.

"Teams of four," Coop said to the others. "Dix, you're in the next vehicle."

"Yes, sir," Dix said.

"Perkins, you're with me and our guests," Coop said.

She nodded.

Everyone else got into the various vehicles. Dix's vehicle slowly followed Rossetti's. Then the next vehicle.

The woman climbed into the last vehicle, her hands moving with an expertise that none of his people showed. He shouldn't have trusted her to do this, but he did. Even though he knew she could upend the entire vehicle and hurt both him and Perkins, or maybe even kill them.

Theirs was the only vehicle that floated up smoothly without a single wobble. The cave's opening narrowed toward the top, but there was still plenty of room to go out.

The other vehicles had landed around the opening. Several of his people had gathered around two other people, preventing them from moving, maybe even detaining them.

The ground didn't look the same; he remembered dozens of buildings here, vehicles, people. Now there was only one outbuilding, the opening, and a broad expanse of dirt.

"Can you ask her to take it high enough so that I can see the city?" Coop asked.

The lieutenant complied.

The woman let the vehicle rise even higher.

Along the mountainsides, he saw buildings, more than he could have imagined. The city had sprawled outward. He looked into the valley and saw some buildings, but not nearly as many as he expected.

But the ground itself was familiar. He knew the peaks on those mountains, recognized the orangish red color of the sky. The air smelled right—a mixture of dryness and something a little sweeter than any other place he had ever been.

His heart ached.

This was—or had been—Venice City. He was on Wyr. He recognized the mountains, the valley, this little bit of the planet itself.

But the city, the city was terrifyingly unfamiliar.

No city grew like that in a few years.

"What happened to the valley?" he asked through the lieutenant.

"Death holes," the woman said. "I'm told it wasn't safe to live in the old city any longer."

Death holes. For centuries. The *anacapa* had been malfunctioning for centuries.

He was shaking. This was what he wanted—some kind of confirmation that the Venice City of his memory had become something else.

Years had clearly passed, but he had no way to know if there were eight hundred years or five thousand.

Although no military force awaited them. And, he realized, the woman had no reason to lie.

"You want me to go higher?" she asked through the lieutenant.

"No," he said in her language. "Thank you."

She moved the vehicle toward a landing spot and slowly brought it down.

He glanced at his team. Rossetti was standing on the edge of the landing area, staring at the city beyond. Dix was beside her. Four of his men had detained two heavyset men who were dressed in brown uniforms.

"Those two men," Coop said to the woman, "are they yours?"

"No," she said with force. "They're our guides. The Vaycehnese government insists that they accompany us at all times."

"Locals," he said.

"Yes," she said. "They know the history of Vaycehn. You can probably ask them all the questions you want."

He studied them. They looked confused and terrified. They clearly hadn't expected a force to come out of the caves.

Talking to them would be easy. But he wasn't ready for easy.

Besides, they could lie to him.

He needed someone not connected to the woman and her friends.

"Later," he said. "Is the old city habitable?"

"Yes," the woman said.

"Then I'd like to get close. I'd like to see it."

She gave him a sideways look, filled with something—sadness? Compassion? He didn't know, and he wasn't going to analyze it.

"We can take the cart," she said, and without giving him a moment to answer, let it rise.

He felt dizzy for a half second as he realized what she could do. She could take him and Perkins into the city, without the rest of his team.

But she didn't. She hovered there while he instructed everyone except the four guarding the guides to get into their vehicles and follow her.

They did, and then she led the way, driving the vehicle above a mountain road as if she had done this every single day of her life.

SIXTY-SIX

As we rise out of the cave, I say to Al-Nasir, "See if you can reach anyone from our group."

I'm hoping he can't. Right now, they should be on our ships, heading toward the *Business*. Our communicators are for land only, and have limited range. We shouldn't be able to reach anyone if they're off-planet.

He nods. I glance over my shoulder at the captain and his lieutenant. The captain's expression is fixed, but he can't control the slight frown forming between his eyes. He recognizes Wyr.

I recognize the guides, surrounded by the captain's people, and I curse. The two men are our two most regular guides. They know all of us. They were probably wondering why most of the group left, and why they insisted on having four hovercarts waiting below ground. And I'll wager that none of my people took time to explain beyond "Boss wants it."

When the first hovercart rose out of the cave, those guides had to know why I wanted it. They were probably shocked at seeing a military group, but these two guides know their stuff. And as they tried to flee, I'm sure they contacted someone. Police, the guide office, the regular government—I have no idea.

But someone in authority on Vaycehn now knows that we've brought military to the edge of the city, somehow.

The captain really isn't noticing any of this. He's asking me questions about the city, about death holes. I'm keeping my eye on Al-Nasir, whose gaze is focused far off.

So far, so good. I can tell just by his expression that he hasn't contacted anyone.

I'm not sure what we're going to do next. That's the captain's decision, although at some point I have to tell him that the city government knows about us. I'm hoping he'll just look around and then go back below ground.

I try to lead him in that direction when I ask him if he wants to go higher.

Of course, he doesn't. He wants to get as close to the old city as he can.

I'm going to stay in control of this cart and keep the right height. If I see locals heading this way, I'm turning us around, no matter what the captain says.

We float several meters above the ground. The air is hot, particularly after a day spent inside the room. Some kind of insect buzzes to my right. The city sprawls below us and around us. It's familiar to me now, but to him, it must look like some crazy quilt made of the remnants of a place he once knew.

If it's that familiar at all.

"Where are you?" Al-Nasir says, putting a hand to his ear. I glance over at him.

His gaze meets mine. He looks terrified.

"Who are you talking to?" I ask.

"Mikk," he says.

I curse. Behind me, I can hear the lieutenant attempting to translate. I don't give a damn. Instead, I set the cart to hover right here, over just a road and bare patch of ground, and I tune in. I hear Mikk's voice saying, ". . . locked down. I'm not sure what we can do."

"Mikk," I say. "How many are with you?"

"Four," he says. "Boss, we're in deep trouble here. I can see the spaceport from here, and there are a lot of official vehicles. Several passed us as we came over the rise. We're trapped."

I curse. "Can you get out of the area?"

"I think so," Mikk says. "No one seems to have noticed us yet."

"Keep it that way. Come to the caves. I'll see what I can do. Let me know if there's trouble."

"Oh, there's trouble," Mikk says. "I'll let you know if it gets worse."

He signs off.

I whip the hovercart around and head back to the cave opening.

"What's going on?" the captain asks. The lieutenant translates, but it's not necessary. It's pretty clear what he asked even before he asked it.

"Just like I told you," I say. "We're in trouble now. The guides let the authorities know about your little invasion force and now the rest of my team can't get off-planet."

"They had two hours," the lieutenant says before she translates for the captain.

"Yes, they did," I snap. "And clearly that wasn't enough time."

"What will happen to them?" she asks.

"Arrest, a trial for treason within the Empire, probably. And then the

Empire will know about you, your ship, the underground room, and the fact that there are now what—five hundred?—people somewhere in the area who not only know how to operate stealth tech, but can repair and build it." I curse again.

She translates. We reach the top of the rise. Al-Nasir is holding onto the front of the cart for balance, which means my driving is a little shaky, not that I care.

We land near the other hovercarts.

I turn in my seat and lean toward the captain. To his credit, he doesn't lean back, and most people do when I get angry at them.

And he knows I'm angry.

"You can get out here," I say. "If you want to be suicidal enough to go into that city, be my guest. But you're going without me and Fahd. If you want to learn the history of the area without going in, talk to the damn guides. They're trained in Vaycehnese history. They'll be able to tell you more than I can."

The lieutenant simultaneously translates, but neither of them move to get out of the vehicle.

"Get out," I say.

"What are you going to do?" he asks through her.

"I have no idea," I say. "I'm hoping they make it up here. Then I'm going to see if we have enough time to get a skip down from the *Business*—that's my ship in orbit—to load up the group before the authorities get here. Otherwise, we're all in trouble. Unless you want to have an old-fashioned shoot-out like the Fleet of legend, protecting the underdog."

I say that sarcastically, but I'm half hoping he'll say yes. It's our only hope. We need their military might to protect my people long enough for one of my ships to get down here.

His frown grows. "Why can't they just come with us to the ship?"

I roll my eyes. These people really don't know the trouble they've caused, do they? And somehow I'm elected to tell them.

"Because it will kill them. They don't have the genetic marker. They can't go into a stealth-tech field without dying."

He stares at me as the lieutenant translates.

And then he smiles just a little and shakes his head.

"No," he says in my language. "No."

Then he talks rapidly, and I don't understand a word until the lieutenant translates.

"It's fine," she says for him. "Anyone can go in and out of what you call a stealth-tech field—"

"Not anymore," I say before she finishes her translation. "Something has gone horribly wrong."

"No," she says. "If what you say about stealth tech is true, then no one we meet in our travels could go in our ships or onto our bases. We could not interact with the populations we meet, and that's not true at all. What you call stealth tech is only deadly when it malfunctions. The genetic marker that you discovered only functions in that circumstance. It allows us to repair our own field—and to survive in it, should something go wrong."

I pause, struggling to understand. "You think my people will survive going into your ship?"

"We're fixing the . . . drive now," she says, using a word I don't know and don't understand. "Ours is repaired. You watched us work on the one in the room. As Captain Cooper said, it is an easy fix. It should be done when we get back."

"Should be," I say. "If not, five of my people will die."

He speaks. She translates: "They could die anyway. If the authorities shoot first trying to capture them. I take it you do not know what these Vaycehnese will do now that we're here."

"That's right," I say.

"Waiting for your skip, which might not make it to the planet, is not an option. We will help you."

"You will attack people you've just met?" I ask him.

His gaze meets mine. "We will rescue people who have done nothing more than help us."

I study him. He seems determined.

Either way, I risk losing five people. If we wait for the skip, all of us could end up in prison and tried for treason.

If we go with this captain, then five of my people could die.

I don't feel like I can make the decision for them, and yet I'm the only one who can make the decision.

Besides, the Vaycehnese might attack my skip. Maybe more than five people will die.

"I hope to God this works," I say to the captain.

"It will," he says. "Believe me. It will."

SIXTY-SEVEN

The captain climbs out of my cart, along with the lieutenant. As he does, he snaps his fingers and gives orders in a voice I never want to hear directed at me.

Suddenly six other people join us. The captain gives instructions, and Al-Nasir translates for me before the lieutenant can.

"He wants them in the other hovercarts," Al-Nasir says. "He says two people per cart, one driving and one with a weapon, would be best."

A weapon. I frown at the captain. I don't want to hurt anyone. I almost protest, but then I don't. It's better to be prepared. How many times have I told my people that?

"You get in another cart," I say to Al-Nasir.

"But you need me," he repeats.

"I can talk to Mikk just as easily as you can," I say. "If something happens to me, you can lead the others to our group. Get them off this damn planet, okay?"

He nods, then scrambles into a different cart. The captain watches, catches my gaze, and nods at me. He approves.

A woman gets in beside me. She's one of the people the captain has sent ahead. He clearly trusts her. She taps her chest. "Rossetti," she says.

"Boss," I say.

She nods, but doesn't repeat my name any more than I repeat hers. She pulls out that small laser pistol and holds it. I glance behind me. Two people per cart, just like the captain ordered—one in the driver's seat, the other holding a weapon just like she is.

Al-Nasir is driving, just like I am. I don't know if he's ever driven a cart. That should be interesting. But I am not going to watch.

I tap my ear. "Mikk, your position?"

He tells me. They've made it away from the spaceport. They're in a vehicle, but it's a land vehicle.

"We're coming for you," I say. "Take this route."

I'm going to get him as close to the cave opening as I can. With all of us on the move, we'll get him here quicker.

I glide down the mountainside, wishing for more power. These hovercarts aren't built for speed. They're built to carry cargo and people into different environments, not to go speeding down a mountain toward a spaceport.

But I open up as best I can, not caring if the others can keep up.

As I glide, I see the roads spread before me. The spaceport glows yellow in the distance, the fog lights giving the place an odd tinge even in the daylight.

Official vehicles, with Vaycehn's city insignia on the side, are speeding toward the spaceport from the city itself.

But Mikk is on one of the side roads, climbing up the mountain. The city officials don't believe my people would go back to the caves we fled. As far as they know, we're all trying to get off this godforsaken planet—which we are. We're just taking a different route than they expect.

I glance over my shoulder. To my surprise, Al-Nasir is the pilot who can keep up with me. The others wobble behind us, uncertain about the speed and the balance of the machine. Instead of clutching the weapon the way that Rossetti is, the other soldiers are clutching the side of the cart.

A cloud of dust heads toward us. Mikk isn't on the side roads. He's blazing his own trail.

Two official vehicles have made U-turns and headed on the side road he initially took.

We're running out of time.

I kick the cart into the highest gear. It dips, and for a moment, I think the power is going to fail. Then it recovers and we head toward that first cloud of dust.

It only takes a few minutes to reach it. I float above the vehicle, see that Roderick is driving, Mikk beside him. My two best people. What the hell are they still doing here?

Then I see their passengers: Lentz, Bridge, and Ivy. Of course, the ones who didn't quite understand the meaning of "emergency" and didn't get off-planet quickly enough.

Mikk and Roderick clearly tried to save them.

Dammit.

Roderick stops the vehicle, kicking up even more dust. It gets into my mouth and eyes, and as I cough, I hope to hell that the dust doesn't have any effect on the inner workings of the cart.

Al-Nasir arrives just as I lower the cart. He lowers his as well.

"Mikk, Roderick," I say, deciding not to greet the other three. "I want you two to pilot the other two carts. We're heading back to the caves."

"Have you called for a skip?" Mikk asked.

I shake my head. "We're going to try something else."

The third cart lands, then the fourth. One of the other pilots says something.

Al-Nasir translates: "The city vehicles are getting close."

"Tell them that Mikk and Roderick are piloting. Lentz, Bridge, you're with me. Ivy, you're with Mikk."

"Gee, thanks, Boss," Mikk says softly.

"Everyone else with Roderick and Fahd," I say.

Al-Nasir translates for them. My rearrangements still keep one person with a weapon in each vehicle.

Bridge climbs into my cart, Lentz right behind him. Ivy needs to be helped to Mikk's cart, not because she's injured, but because the stupid woman is frozen with terror.

The dust cloud is coming closer. We only have a few minutes.

Everyone rearranges.

"Let's get the hell out of here," I say, making the cart rise. This time, I wait to make sure the others can get off the ground, that the dust hasn't had an effect on their equipment.

Roderick takes off faster than I realized a cart can go, with Mikk on his heels. Al-Nasir and I will be bringing up the rear this time.

The city vehicle is so close I can hear the thud of its wheels on the ground. Rossetti has turned so that her weapon is pointed at the city vehicle.

Someone in the city vehicle shoots up at us. I hear the shot whiz by. Rossetti is about to answer with her own weapon when I touch her leg and shake my head. Not yet. If we can get out of this without anyone getting hurt, I'll be happy.

It doesn't surprise me that the Vaycehnese are shooting. They now see us as hostile, which makes getting off Wyr all the more dangerous.

"What the hell happened?" I snap as we head back up the mountainside. "When you got the evacuation order, you were supposed to drop everything and run."

"We did," Bridge said. "Bernadette and I were at the death hole. We couldn't get back in two hours."

"And you, Lentz?"

"I was talking to a friend about the problems here on Vaycehn," he says. "I couldn't bring my communicator into the meeting. I had no idea until Mikk found me."

"Risking his life," I say, and then bite back the rest. Recriminations won't help.

Mikk and Roderick are good. Their carts are much farther ahead of mine. I stay back just enough to give Al-Nasir cover. More and more city vehicles are coming in our direction.

A small army is heading up this mountainside, and we're only moments ahead of them.

"Fahd," I say into my communicator, "tell one of your people to let the captain know we're coming in hot."

"Okay," he replies.

Rossetti seems focused, as if nothing exists but those vehicles below us. She isn't shooting, but I'm not sure if the vehicles below have shown the same kind of restraint.

I'm pushing this hovercart as fast as I can make it go, but I'm beginning to doubt that "as fast as it can go" is going to be fast enough.

SIXTY-EIGHT

Coop could see the trouble building down the mountainside. Roads filled with official-looking vehicles. He knew that there would be a small army of people heading up to the cave opening before he officially found out the group was in trouble.

Immediately, he had Dix and Perkins stop interrogating the guides and move them to a rock formation some distance away. Then Coop got his team into position around some of the rises on the mountainside.

He gave the team a simple order: disable the ground vehicles, but not the people in them. He wanted everyone to get out of this with no injuries at best, minor bruises at worst.

The old-fashioned carts were coming in low, and not nearly fast enough. More and more vehicles were joining the chase up the side of the mountain, both on and off the roads.

A few people in those vehicles were standing and firing some kind of weapon at the carts. He couldn't tell if those were projectile weapons or not, only that the shots didn't seem to be causing any damage.

He sprawled next to his team, his own weapon out. Then he gave the order to fire.

First they shot up the ground ahead of the land vehicles, hoping that would stop them. But the damn things just bounced over the ruts. So he gave the order to shoot the vehicles themselves.

The carts got closer, and they were full.

That was the biggest problem he could foresee. Those carts were badly built, with technology so old—new? (the idea of that made his brain hurt)— that they might not be able to take the weight of the additional people they'd have to carry.

He hoped those things would get them back into the caves, at least. From there, some of his team could run if they had to.

He counted at least twenty vehicles. He shot two. Four others spun out and blocked the road. The others just went around.

The carts came in low. For a minute, he thought they would just go down into the caves, leaving his team to fend for itself. Instead, they touched down.

He signaled his team to shoot as they hurried toward the carts.

He and Dix came in last, disabling three more vehicles before running to the carts.

Two carts had already gone underground, with four of his people gone. Only he and Dix remained.

One of the carts had a driver he didn't recognize; the other was the woman they all called Boss.

Coop leapt into her cart, Dix into the other.

She waited for that cart to head into the caves before she followed.

Ground vehicles came up over the mountaintop. Coop and Rossetti shot at them, overturning one and knocking it into another. Three went around.

Coop cursed. He hoped to hell those ground vehicles couldn't go into the caves. If they could, someone was going to get killed.

And he was going to make sure that if anyone died, it wouldn't be someone on his team. Or Boss's team.

He was going to protect them at all costs.

SIXTY-NINE

They're shooting out of the back of my cart, and I can't even turn around to see how many people they're killing. Dammit, this is exactly what I didn't want. Now the Empire will really have reason to search for us.

If we get out of here at all.

The carts in front of me are wobbling and bucking with the extra weight. I'm not sure we'll make it all the way to the room. Not that I'm even sure my people will survive the stealth-tech field.

But one thing the captain was right about: there is no way we could have waited for a skip.

We're the last ones underground, where it's dimmer and blessedly cool. I hadn't realized how hot I was until I got out of that sun. Sweat is running off me and I'm a little light-headed.

We duck and weave into corridors. Ahead, I hear someone screaming.

No one has to tell me that it's Ivy.

"What the hell are we doing, Boss?" Bridge asks.

I can't glance back. Someone else is shouting ahead. The carts have stopped at what once was the entrance to the stealth-tech field.

I almost crash into them.

Ivy is wailing. Mikk's cart is blocking the way in. Al-Nasir is arguing with them. I stop behind them.

"You're going in," I say.

"We'll die," Mikk says.

"They've fixed the problem." I say. "You'll be fine."

Even though I don't know that. None of us know that.

"Go!" the captain says in my language, waving his hand beside me. "Go now!"

"Mikk," I say, "you'll have to trust me."

"I've seen what happens in those fields, Boss. I'm not going in."

"Then you're going to die out here," I say. "All of you. Trust me. We'll be fine."

"I trust you," Roderick says, and raises his cart over Mikk's, driving into the field area before anyone can stop him. He pauses just past the next bend in the corridor.

Death inside a stealth-tech field takes only a few minutes. Roderick sits there, his life the only one at risk, since he has only people from the ship in his vehicle. He grins and whoops.

"We're going to be fine!" he says.

"Unless they only managed to make the field recede," Bridge says beside me.

"If you stay here, you risk everything we've worked for," I say.

"I don't care," Ivy says from Mikk's cart. "Let me out! Let me out!"

"I'm fine!" Roderick yells from inside the field—or where the field would have been. "Come on!"

Ivy starts to climb out of her cart. One of the soldiers grabs her and she shakes him off, nearly upending the cart.

Mikk guns the cart, moving it toward Roderick's as if they're on a collision course. Ivy screams, and only the soldier keeps her from toppling out of the cart.

So far, so good. They're alive.

Al-Nasir follows, and I bring up the rear. I think I hear something behind us, although it's hard to tell with Ivy screaming the way she is.

It only takes a few minutes for the carts to go through the rest of the corridors. One of the soldiers gets out of Roderick's cart and pulls open the door. The carts can't go through it.

We stop all in a row.

Roderick peers inside the room.

"Oh, my God," he says. "It's a goddamn Dignity Vessel."

"No kidding," I say. "Get in there."

Ivy is still sobbing, but she's pliable now. The soldier drags her in. My group gets out. Once Ivy's in the room, I hear the sound of voices behind us.

The captain says something.

"He wants to know if they're going to follow us in here," Al-Nasir says.

"Tell him I have no idea. They have maps that show them where the stealth-tech fields are. I'm not sure if they'll cross those fields."

So the captain and four of his soldiers indicate that we should go into the room. They bring up the rear.

My people slow down, looking stunned at the room's size, and at the Dignity Vessel itself.

No one is in the room. Apparently the captain contacted his people. Something whistles in my ear. Both Al-Nasir and I have our hands to our ears, but no one else does.

"What's that sound?" I ask him.

"They tell me it's the ship powering up."

The captain and his team come in. They pull the door closed, then the captain waves his hand at the ship.

I catch his arm and point at the equipment. It's going to fall into the Empire's hands.

He nods and points his weapon at it, miming a shot. I'm not sure what he means, but I think I know. He's going to destroy the equipment.

I hope he's going to destroy it.

The stairs have come down, and the door into the ship is open. My people are scrambling inside, followed by the soldiers. Al-Nasir and the lieutenant go in. The captain and I are last.

He has his back against mine, his weapon pointed at the exterior door. He's pushing me inside and guarding me at the same time.

I stumble into the airlock.

He follows.

The door closes.

We're inside the Dignity Vessel, and it's about to leave.

SEVENTY

*T*he moment Coop got inside the ship, he started barking orders. First, destroy the equipment inside the room. Second, begin the *anacapa* sequence and get them the hell out of this room.

Dix was waiting for him, just inside the corridor. "Sensors show a lot of people inside the caves."

"I figured," Coop said. "You get anything from those guides?"

Dix was supposed to have been asking them about the history of Vaycehn. "We didn't have a lot of time."

The outsiders were milling around, looking at the inside of the ship as if they had never seen one before. All except the woman who had been screaming. She looked almost catatonic, her face blotchy and tear-streaked.

"I know that," Coop said. "Did they tell you anything?"

Dix gave him a baleful look. "They told me that Vaycehn was the oldest city in the known universe. They told me it was founded more than five thousand years ago."

Coop's knees nearly buckled. He had to will himself to remain upright.

The woman hadn't been lying, then. She had been telling the truth all along.

He turned toward her. She was standing just inside the door, watching her people, looking relieved. She had thought they were going to die, too.

She had taken a hell of a risk.

Slowly she looked over at him, and she said something.

"She wants to watch the ship leave," the lieutenant said. "She wants to be on the bridge."

He didn't give permission. He just looked at the woman, wondering what it took for her to trust him like she had.

"She also wants to know if you can do something to make sure the Vaycehnese won't be able to use the room."

"Tell her it's already under way," he said.

Then he extended his hand.

"Come," he said in her language.

She grinned. She was prettier than he realized. Her smile—a real smile—took all the edges out of her face.

She put her hand in his. "Thank you," she said in his language.

He brought her to his side, then let go of her hand and put his hand on her back for just a moment, indicating that she should come with him.

This wasn't first-contact procedure. It wasn't any kind of procedure. Outsiders, no matter who the hell they were, were never allowed on the bridge.

But who was going to punish him now? Who would take away his command? He was on his own out here, five thousand years into his own future, in a universe that had backward technology and ruins instead of cities.

He didn't pretend to understand it.

But he would have time to figure it out. More time than he probably wanted.

"Let's go," he said to her in his language, knowing she didn't understand the words but that she would understand the sentiment.

She nodded, and they hurried, all the way to the bridge.

SEVENTY-ONE

I know enough from any time period, any military vessel, any vessel at all, to know that I shouldn't be on this cockpit. I should be in some public area, away from the inner workings of a vessel I don't comprehend.

But the captain has brought me here as more than a courtesy. He knows he is giving me a gift.

I stand near the door and marvel. The first time I saw the cockpit of a Dignity Vessel, it was an image taken by my divers, grainy, filled with particles that I didn't entirely understand, the furniture and equipment piled against one wall, as if some field had pulled it all there.

Then I dived that ship, and tried to rescue one of my dead teammates, stuck in a stealth-tech field, his face mummified behind the cracked mask of his visor.

In a Dignity Vessel.

I had once tried to imagine what these places had been like in their day. This is their day. It's mine, too.

The equipment is bolted down, just like I knew it would be. And where there was a fist-sized hole in the Dignity Vessel I dove, there's some kind of control, something that I recognize only by its black casing. That's where part of the stealth tech is.

The walls in front of me—all of them—are screens.

There's a captain's chair in the middle, but the captain isn't sitting in it. He's standing beside me. The lieutenant is on the other side, and God bless her, she's translating.

Four other people are in the cockpit, including a woman who had been sitting in the captain's chair. She looks at me with great curiosity, but doesn't say anything. A small woman up front grins at me. I can't help but grin back.

The tall, thin man who had been with us on the surface has moved to the console nearest the black casing. He looks grim, miserable. He's the only one who doesn't look up as the captain speaks.

The screens in front of us show the room itself as if we can just reach out and touch it. The equipment looks fine.

The captain says something; the screens opaque, but not enough to completely block the whiteness that engulfs the entire room. When the whiteness fades, the image crisps up. But there is no more equipment. It's gone.

"What was that?" I ask the lieutenant.

"We got rid of anything your people can study," she says.

"They're not my people," I say, and then realize I sound churlish. "So thank you."

She nods and smiles.

The captain puts his hand on my shoulder. "Now," he says in his language, a word I'm beginning to recognize. Then he changes to my language. "We go."

My breath catches. I get to see the Dignity Vessel in action.

The screens blank out. The whistle fades, and I don't hear the thrum of stealth tech at all. The ship shifts slightly, as if we all collectively tripped over something and righted ourselves at the same time.

The screens turn back on, and I am staring down at Wyr. It's blue and brown and green, with the mountains rising through whitish clouds.

I'm very dizzy.

"What did you do?" I ask.

"That's our . . . drive," the lieutenant says, using that word I can never seem to catch. "You call it stealth technology, but it is so much more."

Clearly.

The captain's hand is warm on my shoulder. Companionable. It feels like he's holding me up. Maybe he is.

He says something to me, softly.

"He wants to know the coordinates of your ship," the lieutenant says. "So we can rendezvous."

I give her the coordinates. The sooner we're away from Wyr, the better we'll all be.

I look up at the captain. "Thank you for saving my people," I say.

"Thank you for saving mine," he says through the lieutenant. "We would not have escaped foldspace without you activating the repair room."

"Foldspace?" I ask.

He smiles. "I will explain if you let me. When we get away from your Empire. Can we return to your base?"

I smile at him. I was going to ask him to come with us, but he's already thought of it.

"I'd love to show you our base," I say.

He keeps his hand on my shoulder, and we stand inside the cockpit of his Dignity Vessel, watching on the screens as we move through space toward

Nobody's Business. As if this ship is conventional. As if we haven't already had a grand adventure.

As if standing with a man who was born five thousand years ago was the most natural thing in the universe.

Maybe it is.

There is so much that we don't understand about this universe. So many mysteries.

And I was right all those years ago, when I first saw the Dignity Vessel.

Mysteries are fascinating.

They lead us to places we would never expect to be, help us discover things we never even knew existed.

I lean into him just a little. A legend made real. A man, above all. On a ship that shouldn't exist. In a place we don't belong.

Heading home with us.

Heading home. With me.

AUTHOR'S NOTE

The stories about Boss and her companions first started as novellas in *Asimov's Science Fiction* magazine. The first two, "Diving into the Wreck," and "Room of Lost Souls," won the *Asimov's Reader's Choice Award*. "Diving" also won the UPC Award in Spain.

The stories so far in the Diving universe are:

- "Diving into the Wreck," first published in *Asimov's*, December 2005. Reprinted in *Recovering Apollo 8 And Other Stories*, Golden Gryphon Press, 2010.
- "The Room of Lost Souls," first published in *Asimov's*, April/May 2008. Electronic edition published by WMG Publishing, 2011.
- "The Spires of Denon," first published in *Asimov's*, April/May 2009. Electronic version published by WMG Publishing, 2010. Reprinted in *Five Short Novels* from Five Story Publishing, 2010.
- "Becoming One with the Ghosts," first published in *Asimov's*, October/November 2010.
- "Becalmed," first published in *Asimov's*, April/May 2011.

And of course, the novel that introduces Boss, *Diving Into the Wreck*, from Pyr, 2009.

Not all of the stories feature Boss. "Becalmed," for example, tells the story of Coop's ex-wife, Mae, and explains exactly what happened to provoke the Quurzod into a war.

Eventually all of the stories will be available electronically through WMG Publishing.

There will be other stories in the Diving universe. You can find more information about them on my website, www.kristinekathrynrusch.com or on the Diving website, www.divingintothewreck.com.

ABOUT THE AUTHOR

Kristine Kathryn Rusch is an award-winning, bestselling science fiction writer. Once upon a time, she edited the *Magazine of Fantasy & Science Fiction*, winning a Hugo Award for her work there. But she gave it all up to write fiction.

In addition to her stories in the Diving universe, Rusch has also created the international bestselling series The Retrieval Artist. The next book in that series, *Anniversary Day*, will appear in 2011. After nearly a decade wait, she is reviving her popular Fey fantasy series with a novel exploring the Place of Power, in 2012.

She is also a bestselling mystery writer under the name Kris Nelscott. And she's a popular paranormal romance writer as Kristine Grayson.

Over the next three years, WMG Publishing will put her entire backlist into print, including her award-winning short stories. Many are already available in electronic editions.

To find out more about her work, go to her website, www.kristine kathrynrusch.com.